HALFKINDS VOLUME 2: HORUS

By Andrew Vu

Copy Edit by Cyndy McClay

Recoil Books
ISBN-13: 978-0988520615
ISBN-10: 0988520613

2

HORUS

Table of Contents

Chapter 1 - Brock West

Elite

April 25, 3043 11:00 AM

"Welcome to the mission," a man says to me as I sit down on a padded chair. I'm in a large conference room in the Bay Area. It's chilly in here, but comfortable. The room is covered in a shade of dimmed lights, making the walls a hue of slate gray. There's a fancy-looking table in front of me that has a bunch of communication devices scattered about. Tablets, earpieces, video interfaces, the works. This isn't my kind of environment.

The man who talks to me is a portly fella. He's balding, has a mustache and a double chin. He wears a white shirt and messy looking pants. He's not the cleanest guy and has a disheveled quality about him. I've never met the man before, but I certainly know about him. He was demoted after he reported a mission was a success, only for that to be a lie. In truth, his team failed said mission and let a hostile escape.

He was the supervisor of that operation, and was supposed to give direction. But he let his commander do everything while he ate donuts and slacked around. He just gave his team a quick rundown and thought that they could do the rest. I read their profiles, they were a team that had never worked together. Me and my soldiers have been working together for years. I can't imagine a bunch of random commandos becoming a cohesive unit in a few hours.

When the team failed, the United Species Alliance had to blame someone, and this chubby man who stands in front of me fit the bill. He was an easy scapegoat, and it didn't help that he had the reputation of being a big sleazebag, some kind of wannabe poon hound who was as perverted as he was dishonest. Now he's stuck here being an usher for people who actually know what they're doing, people like me. What a loser, I can't believe I have to meet him before the operation. This is a waste of my time.

"Thanks," I say coldly. "What was your name again?"

"Leons," he says. "Don Leons."

"Right, Leons. The same one from Operation Halfkinds?"

He looks uncomfortable by my question. I see his brow furrow a little, and he runs his hands through his hair nervously.

"Um, yes," he says. "That one. So you're aware of what happened?"

"For the most part," I say. "Operation Halfkinds was a secret mission organized by our superiors in the United Species Alliance. It was spearheaded by the Human Council. The team they sent went to a small town near Las Vegas to exterminate the mission's namesake, eleven halfkinds. These beings were half-man, half-animal abominations. Both sides suffered casualties, but in the end the wolf agent Fenrir Snow was the lone survivor and reported that all of the halfkinds had been terminated. Or so it seemed."

"Yes, so it seemed," Leons says in a regretful tone.

"When the United Species Alliance Science Division came to investigate the fallout, they found the bodies of the reported halfkinds, but two were missing," I say. "The twins were nowhere to be found. The Science Division told you their findings, but you said

Snow reported their bodies had burned along with their house during the final phases of the mission. That was two and a half years ago. Then, a year later, the truth came out. After extensive analysis, Iris Lawton's remains were nowhere to be found in the ashes of the house. Someone had tampered with the USASD's report, and there's suspicion that that someone is you."

"That charge was never proven."

"But here you are, demoted."

He looks uncomfortable with my rundown. The embarrassment and bad memories are running through his mind. My tone is spiteful but with a hint of satisfaction. I love seeing the sleazeball squirm.

"No one has seen a trace of Iris Lawton since," I say. "And Fenrir Snow has gone missing since the news broke out a year and a half ago. Some say he assisted Iris in her escape, but those are rumors. Others think that he might have been murdered by members of the Brotherhood of Wolves for insubordination."

"It's good that you did your homework," Leons says sarcastically.

His tone annoys me. Who does this guy think he is?

"It's too bad you didn't. If you did a more thorough follow up, we might have realized that Iris Lawton was alive much sooner. We could've located her, but your slack for the job gave her enough time to escape. And then you tried to cover it up," I say.

"Accusations," he says dismissively.

"Yeah, whatever. Anyway, if it was up to me, I would've checked every nook and cranny to make sure she and her brother were dead. I'm a man of integrity, unlike you. I don't even know why they keep you around after what you did. But I guess they never proved anything, huh? Because if they did, you'd be in jail."

I stare darts straight at him and he glances away. Avoiding eye contact, he walks towards a tablet that is on the desk and throws it at me. I turn it on and see a holo image of Maya Lawton appear in the air.

"What can you tell me about her?" he says.

"She's Maya Lawton, the interspecies prostitute wonder," I say. "The first woman in the world to give birth to a family of halfkinds."

"What if I told you she wasn't the first woman to give birth to halfkinds, just the first to have a family of them," Leons says.

I've done my research, and I'm already two steps ahead of him.

"Ah, yes, you're referring to the prostitutes who were associated with HORUS," I say.

"Yes, HORUS," he repeats. "The Human Organization Reestablishing Untainted Society. The ones responsible for Maya Lawton and the other prostitutes' uterus implants, the same implants that allowed all those women to give birth to halfkinds."

He looks at me cautiously and sizes me up from head to toe.

"So you already know why you're here?" he asks.

I've been fully briefed by my superiors at headquarters out in Allied City prior to my arrival in the Bay Area. I don't need anymore information. My team and I could've headed straight to our mission without stopping by the office. I guess they want me to keep Leons on his toes. This is such a waste of my time, but I suppose orders are orders. What the Alliance wants, the Alliance gets.

"Yes," I say. "I've gotten all the intel."

"Then why are we meeting?" Leons asks me.

"You tell me. In my opinion, this meeting isn't helping me. I don't need a washed up desk jockey telling me what to do."

Annoyance and anger flush his face. My words have riled his senses. I no doubt pushed some buttons. He pauses and puts his hands on the table in front of him, leaning toward me.

"The Alliance told me to meet with you not to tell you new information, just to make sure you know it," he says holding back his rage. "It's standard protocol."

I flash a smug smile and stare right back at him. He's surprised by my brashness and reactively backs away.

"Of course it is," I say. "And it seems like you don't know much."

He looks befuddled and shakes his head to get his mind back on track.

"Um, yes," he says hastily. "So, um, what do you know about HORUS?"

I lean back in my chair and put one foot on the desk.

"HORUS was founded in 3002 by Lionel Changer, a brilliant yet mentally unstable geneticist," I say. "Lionel was a successful owner of a biotics, biological robotics, company, Implantus, which specialized in human, biomechanical implants for organ repairs. He went off the radar from the public eye around 2999, and a few years later he used his funds to secretly create his illegal organization, HORUS."

"Yes, he sold his company abruptly and disappeared from the general population. Most people think he's dead," Leons says.

"Let me finish."

Leons tightens his lips as I look at him.

"Go on," he says.

"Throughout his life, Changer was a noted human supremacist," I said. "He contributed several donations to big animal hate groups such as the Clan of Intelligence and the First Walker Society. Like all those loonies, he hated other animals. The fact that humans live in a world with them disgusts him. Implantus was always suspected of human-only hires and, although he was a private man, there were rumors that the mere suggestion of animal hires would cause him to go into a rage."

"Seems odd then that he would start an underground organization whose goals were to combine the genes of humans with their animal brothers," Leons says.

"It does," I say. "But, then again, Changer was an eccentric, even in the ranks of human supremacists. Unlike your average, uneducated, run of the mill hate harborer, Changer was a visionary. Mind you, he did create one of the more successful implant companies. Implantus was known for their state of the art tech when it came to replacing a human heart, arm, liver, or any other organ. He was also the driving force behind his company, developing most of the schematics that Implantus still manufactures today. In a sense, it's too bad he left Implantus more than forty years ago. Since then, the company has failed to make the breakthroughs for humans the way it used to. Without his brilliance, Implantus lost its edge."

"Why did he leave all of a sudden? And why did he start HORUS? Like I said, it seems odd that he would leave all that behind to start the animal, human freak show he's developed."

"I don't know and, quite frankly, I don't care. I have my mission and that's the only thing I came here for."

I take a tablet out from my pack and toss it to Leons. He turns it on and looks over the document that's been prepared for him.

"A gift from my superiors at the Alliance," I say. "It's a copy of the briefing I received concerning my task. They said to keep you in the loop, just in case. Don't know why you would need to know, though, you're only my contact out here. Not like you're supervising my mission or anything."

I look at the screen and he overviews the dossiers of various prostitutes.

"They were all part of his ring," I say to Leons as he reads the details.

"Ring?" he asks curiously. "You make it sound like he was a pimp."

"He kind of was one."

I take the tablet back from him and show him the image of a young woman.

"Allison Ton," I say. "She was rumored to be receiving credits from HORUS starting in 3015. It was during this time HORUS put several prostitutes under their payroll. In 3025, she died of synconium poisoning. Around the same time, several other prostitutes started showing up dead with the same stuff in their bodies. They all had uterus implants."

"HORUS had a whole stable of hookers they were doing these experiments on?" he asks.

"Affirmative," I say. "We suspect all these hookers had given birth to halfkinds at some point before they died. Some could have had one, some could have had ten, but it's hard to pinpoint exactly how many halfkinds HORUS conceived from the baby mill they were running with the prostitutes."

"Let me get this straight," Leons says skeptically. "You're saying that HORUS hired a bunch of prostitutes from the early 3000's to now and put these birthing implants in them to create, like, an army of halfkinds or something?"

"Perhaps not an army, but a sizable group."

"And the scientists couldn't figure out what the implants were for? I mean when I ran that first mission and the boys at the USASD found Maya, they were stumped. I thought from all the other similar cases, they would've been able to deduce something."

"Science is a hard thing to pinpoint, especially if you don't have all the pieces," I say bluntly. "They had never seen anything like it, nor had they seen anything so advanced. Changer must have had a personal hand in developing the tech. It wasn't until they found Maya Lawton's body and that frog son she had was when they could put the two and two together."

Leons still looks confused, as if the concept is so difficult to understand.

"When did all this start?" he asks me.

I scroll through the tablet and pop up a rendered hologram of a tall, red-headed woman.

"Isabella Starla was the first victim of synconium poisoning we found," I said. "At the time, the technology seemed to be prototypes, making it very volatile. At today's standards, the synconium in the implants would probably take fifteen to twenty years to poison their victim, but for her, it took less than two. She died in 3012."

"It took Changer and HORUS about ten years to develop the technology?" he asks.

"It seems so."

Leons scratches his head again.

"Maya Lawton's death was the key to finding all this information then?" he asks.

"Yes," I respond. "For years, our scientists were baffled at what they were looking at, but after her death, we were able to find out much more."

"Why's that? What makes her so special?"

"She was the only one who actually kept her kids."

Leons looks shocked. I'm not sure why he's so surprised.

"That mission you supervised, the one to kill the halfkinds, it was the first time we made contact with HORUS's creations," I say. "Her children were the only children raised outside of HORUS's facilities."

"So you're saying all those other prostitutes gave birth to a bunch of halfkinds and then dumped them off to HORUS's hands?" Leons asks.

"I wouldn't say dumped. More like sold. Remember these women were desperate for money. They needed a quick stash of credits, so they volunteered for this sideshow, got the implants, gave birth to monsters, left, and never turned back. But Maya Lawton was different, she had eleven of them and grew attached. After she had her youngest, the frog halfkind known as Leonard, she left HORUS and raised the kids on her own. Unlike those other whores, she actually loved them."

Leons lets out an exasperated breath.

"Wow," Leons says. "So all those other halfkinds that those women birthed are within HORUS's walls?"

"Yes," I say.

Leons looks at me curiously.

"How long have you been researching this case?" he asks me.

"I was assigned to it after you and Simon Trevor supposedly succeeded in your mission," I say. "After the first encounter with the halfkinds, the Alliance appointed me and my team of soldiers to find the root of this operation. And, of course, when it was discovered you failed, that pushed them to give full support to me. All the information I knew and presented to you about HORUS, the prostitutes, and halfkinds are the result of my investigation."

Leons smiles smugly.

"I guess I'm the reason you got to work on such a high level task," he says.

I smile smugly back at him.

"I suppose so," I say. "Your fumbling of the mission made the Alliance call a real group of professionals, not some mixed bag of unquote, elite soldiers. Even when you said the mission was accomplished, the Alliance was suspicious and called in the best to continue the job. Good thing they were right with their hunches."

"Will you lay off already!" he yells at me. "I did what I could, okay? I mean, Fenrir told me that Iris Lawton was dead, how was I supposed to know he was lying?"

"You could've followed up, maybe look for a body or some evidence to make sure he was truthful."

"Why wouldn't he be? I had no reason to be suspicious. If he said the halfkind was dead, then she's dead."

"That's what I'm talking about. If you had paid more attention, actually cared about your job, then you would've done everything to make sure it was over.

But you didn't. You slacked off and let him and his halfkind friend vanish into the shadows until it was too late. And when you found out the truth, you tried to hide it from our leaders. That's treason, my friend. You're lucky they had mercy on you."

He perspires from his forehead and wipes it off immediately.

"I did my best," he grumbles.

"Well," I say smirking, "your best is pretty shitty."

He's stuck on a response. I know he's thinking of what to say, but can't muster the strength to say it.

"I guess I can't blame you completely," I say. "Your whole team was rather incompetent. Trevor, Bradley, Freeley, Zuma, hell even Bornoa and Snow were all in over their heads."

"What are you talking about?" Leons says defensively. "They were the best of the best of their species."

I give off a light chuckle.

"Sure they were," I say snidely.

"You sure like to trounce on the dead," Leons says. "Have some respect. They were handpicked by the Alliance. They died in the service of their respective species. What gives you the right to bash them like that?"

"I read their profiles and the details behind their mission. And judging from how they did, I don't have to respect them. They died because they weren't equipped for the job."

Leons slams his fist on the table.

"How dare you!" he yells.

"How dare I?" I say amusingly. "Let's run through the facts, shall we? You had a blowhard gorilla whose only concern was to shoot big guns, a suck-up dog and his soft human commander, and an elephant that on paper was an all-star, but never said shit."

I take a brief moment to catch my breath, and continue.

"Then you have Fenrir Snow," I say. "He completed so many missions in his young life. But he was in a fragile state of mind, a wolf that had a nothing-left-to-live-for mentality. He wanted to die on the battlefield."

"Losing a loved one will do that to you," Leons says.

"I suppose so. Finally, you had a pig who was assigned by politics. Hell, judging from all their profiles, politics probably had to do with their selections. They weren't the best of the best, just a mediocre squad who knew the head honchos."

Leons looks dumbstruck, unsure how to react.

"Worst of all, aside from the dog and human, they never worked together," I say. "The mission was thrown together haphazardly and in a rush. I read Trevor didn't have any time to prepare, that he was given short notice, and was catapulted in with his team immediately. I've been preparing for months, no, years, on this raid. I can't imagine being thrust into the situation like he was. Lack of preparation isn't something you'll see from me. I've worked with the animals that I'm leading on several tours. I've been on countless missions with them, life and death struggles, and I've never questioned whether they have my back or not. This won't be like Operation Halfkinds, this will be a success."

"They… they were on the clock," he mutters solemnly. "We had to hurry if we wanted to get those halfkinds. Time wasn't a luxury we could afford."

"And how'd that turn out?" I ask. "One of them got away, and Fenrir Snow is nowhere to be found. Since you were the only person around who was involved with Operation Halfkinds, and you were supervising it, all the blame falls on you. Try to run away from your legacy as much as you want, but you should be grateful that you still have a job within the Alliance, even if you are just an admin to the real soldiers. If it was up to me, you would have never stepped in an Alliance building again."

The last remnants of his fiery temper have disappeared. The only thing that lies before me is a broken man.

"Let's talk about your mission," he says, changing the subject. "I know you've studied and analyzed every turn, but for my sake, can you fill me in on the details?"

"Sure," I say. "That's why I'm here, to assure you that I know my task, so you can relay my status to the big wigs upstairs."

"Yes," he says somberly.

"After years of investigation following the fallout from Operation Halfkinds, we've tracked every lead and clue to come to this moment, the raid on HORUS. We've been able to determine that their headquarters are on the outskirts of the city state, in the western mountainous areas outside of San Francisco. I will prepare my team of nine and raid the facility, taking out every human, animal, and other in my sight. It's going to be a complete annihilation. We're not chasing random halfkinds, we're wiping them out, finishing the job that Simon Trevor couldn't handle. The Alliance has approved every resource we might need. We'll initiate our strike on May 7."

I slide Leons a tablet with some images, holograms, and schematics. His eyes open wide and he stares at me.

"No expense, huh?" he says.

"Yeah," I say. "We're not going to be armed with puny energy pistols and spitfires. They gave us some real weapons to play with. Like I said, this is going to be an all-out assault. No halfkind or member of HORUS will leave the facility alive."

I can sense a certain amount of horror radiating from Leons. Per his job, he seemed to be aware of what my task would be, but the level of execution and lack of mercy disturb him. Or perhaps it's my steely determination. I admit what the Alliance has asked me to do is grim, but I've taken on worse missions. And I've never flinched while doing it.

Leons looks at me cautiously, scared to ask a question or respond.

"Good luck," he mumbles out anxiously.

I look him square in the eyes, piercing through his fragile psyche.

"I won't need it," I say.

Chapter 2 - Fenrir Snow

Pieces

May 2, 3043 1:05 PM

It's starting to warm up around here. We've been hit with a hard winter, but Iris and I were able to handle it. The cabin we've been living in is surprisingly durable and sustains heat well. She has less fur than me, so she needs to cozy up more than I do. I'm surprised that she's even able to withstand the brutal weather. Her human DNA doesn't really provide the traits to tolerate cold, but, then again, she's a halfkind, not a human. It's hard to determine what makes up her biology, since I'm not exactly a scientist.

I'm outside right now, on the prowl for some meat. My helmed weapon is equipped to kill. Even though hunting is becoming less and less popular amongst wolves, I take pleasure in the most primitive aspects of our nature. And I haven't been on a mission for almost three years, so this sport is one of the few things that helps me cling to my former job. Besides, deer is delicious, and if I can bring one home, I know Iris can do something amazing with it. For a halfkind, she sure does have a knack for adapting the recipes of different species. It's one of her many hidden talents.

The woods are thick and the green is bright. The winter snow has melted and created an enchanting landscape in this once frozen atmosphere. The sun trickles in through the canopy and I can feel the moisture of the afternoon dew on my paws. In the distance, I see the mountains melting away their snow caps. When I was in service with the Brotherhood, I rarely got to come out here for rest and relaxation. I didn't know I was missing out on so much. I was so focused on my duty that I couldn't enjoy the tranquility within the deep forest. It's too bad, but I'm glad I have the opportunity now.

I hear birds chirping in the background, the dumb kinds, not the smart ones like eagles. They know not to enter the Wolf's Den without permission, even the most remote areas of it. I won't have to worry about them spying on me. I have to worry about others.

It's been some time since the incident in Primm. An hour after Apollo had died and Iris embraced me, I got on my communicator and told Leons that the mission was over, the halfkinds were dead. Iris spent this time mourning her losses.

Leons asked where the bodies were and I realized if her body didn't show up, they would come looking for her. I had to make sure they thought she was terminated.

"They're burned up, along with the Lawton residence," I told him. "There was a massive standoff and our energy weapons tore through this dilapidated house like a piece of paper. Apollo, Iris, and Isaac all died in the fight. Since this place was so old, the energy emissions started a fire and the house is burning at a considerable pace. Soon, there will be nothing left but a pile of ashes."

Surprisingly, he believed my story and didn't follow up with anything else. He told me I did a good job, and that a deposit of credits for my work would be waiting for me when I returned to the Wolf's Den. That was the last time I spoke to him. I was suspicious at first about why he didn't ask me more. I thought maybe he was on to me and had some kind of ulterior motive.

But as I pondered it, I realized he was lazy and didn't care. Guess he was useful for something.

After I got off my communicator, I turned to Iris and told her, "We have to burn this place to the ground."

"But, what about Isaac?" she said hovering over her brother's body. "I want to bury him."

"The United Species Alliance will come to sweep things up. They'll be looking for you and your family members' bodies. When they don't find yours, they'll know you survived and their search will continue. They'll send team after team to track you down. It'll be relentless. I told Leons that you died, that you and your brother's bodies burned in a fire at this house. It's the only way that they'll think you're dead. I'm sorry, but if they don't find his body, they'll know I lied, and a new mission will begin."

"We have to burn him?! No!" she yelled.

"Iris, listen," I said. "You're the only one left. You have to live. Think about last night, about your brothers and sisters. The Alliance sent soldiers to kill all of you, they sent animals like me to hunt you down. Their orders were to show no mercy. If they have even the slightest hint that you're still alive, they'll stop at nothing to kill you."

She looked at her brother and back at me.

"Why should I listen to you?" she asked in a brave tone. "You were one of them."

"I was," I said solemnly. "But when I saw Apollo kill your brother, I saw the monster he became after losing someone. He was bound by rage and grief, and the only thing that occupied his mind was the mission. I looked into my own soul and saw a beast like him, a hollow mind enslaved by his orders, hoping they would find him some peace. I'm done being like that."

Her face softened, and she approached me cautiously.

"You lost someone, too?" she asked.

"My mate, five years ago," I say. "Has it been that long?"

"How did she die?"

"She got some kind of disease. They couldn't cure it."

"I'm, I'm sorry."

"Thank you."

I walked outside and looked at the sun, which had risen up into the sky.

"I've done a lot of things in the name of the Brotherhood to escape my grief," I said. "But I'm done doing it. The second you embraced me, I realized the old me is in here somewhere, the one who loved life instead of hating it. It was the first time I felt any peace in a long time. All those assignments from the Brotherhood sank my spirit deeper and deeper into a dark hole, but what I did this morning makes me feel like I can climb out of it. I want to thank you for this. I'm my own wolf now, and I will help you. At least I can start making amends for my past deeds. But in order for you to escape cleanly, we have to follow this plan. I'm terribly sorry, but there's no other choice."

She was ready to burst into tears, already reeling from the loss of all her family members. Now I was asking her to say goodbye to the house she grew up in. It was too much for her to handle.

But then she looked at me, with this odd stare. It wasn't one of fear, but awe, as if I mesmerized her. She didn't say anything or utter a peep. She just gazed at me and nodded her head. She understood what she had to do, and that nod was her way of telling me that she trusted me.

And I returned the look, nodding as well, telling her without saying a syllable that I would help her. Words can't explain the connection we made that day.

"Okay," she said. "Let's do it."

She looked over her brother's corpse and said, "I'm sorry."

She walked out of the house and I doused it with some flammables that I had on me. I fired one energy shot and 1523 Chakming Drive quickly became engulfed in fire.

"We have to hide until night," I said. "Then we can access the remnants of the Li station and make it to the Wolf's Den. We'll cover your face to make sure no one is suspicious of what you are. I know a place where you can hide there, if you don't mind living in a cabin for a while. But you'll be safe. Is that okay with you?"

She looked at me and then at the house that blazed in front of her.

"Yes," she said quietly. "Thank you."

"Don't worry about it. The Alliance will come by soon to check things out. Let's get a move on."

"Okay."

She never looked back. I was able to smuggle her safely out of Primm and set up her shelter in the barren, frozen landscape of the Wolf's Den. For almost three years she's been living in that cabin away from the persecution of the Alliance. No one knew of her existence there except me. I was able to cover whatever tracks that might lead curious minds to her. I made my accounts anonymous and deleted any records of our activity. I was relentless in my detail, to make sure not a single clue was left behind.

I also stopped taking missions for the Brotherhood. Operation Halfkinds was my last one, and I don't miss any of it. My colleagues thought I was taking a long vacation, and I slowly faded away from the tangled web of service. By the end of that first year, I had lost contact with almost everyone, including my family members.

I come from such a strong military background that everyone I know is knee deep in Brotherhood command. If I did talk to them, it would only be about this initiative or that initiative. And if they knew where Iris was, they wouldn't hesitate in turning her and their own brother in. They're indoctrinated. I'm tired of living that life, and I feel free now that I'm completely relieved from it.

I eventually discovered through the grapevine and the infospace that the Alliance had unraveled my deceit. Leons was demoted halfway to hell and is now stuck as some usher to the military superstars. And I'm sure I'm a wanted wolf. The Alliance and the Brotherhood have probably used all their contacts trying to find where I am. But when the news broke out, I was already well off the grid from modern society. If they do try to find me, they better send the best of the best, because it's going to be very hard.

At first, when Iris was out here alone, I would only visit once or twice a month. But with time off and not much to do, I became compelled to visit her more often. By the time the eighth month rolled around, I practically lived here. I had my own den area and she learned how to cook wolf style food, not like there was much to it. I'm not particular about my taste, as long as it's meaty. I already had all my things in the cabin. She was my roommate. Well, perhaps she's more than that. I don't think I'd be where I am today without her. I was broken before her, a bleak, angry mind who filled his void with countless, empty missions. I had no purpose but to serve, I felt no joy from anything I did. I was drifting away.

Iris brought me back to the right path. She was the light I sorely needed. For someone who has lost so much, she carries on with hope and optimism. She has a way about her that's pleasant despite her dreary circumstances. I know she feels gratitude for what I did for her that day, for saving her. I can tell in her actions. She cares for me, does small things like prepare meals, and fills my head with thoughts of a better future. Her compassionate nature has helped me look beyond my past and bandaged the mental scars that ravaged my psyche for years.

I can't pinpoint what it is about her that makes me feel so at ease. I guess she reminds me of my mate, of Eve. Both met me when I was in a joyless place in my life, tired and weary from serving the Brotherhood. I was battle-worn, my mind had seen things on the field that were hard to shake. Both Eve and Iris helped me release the anxieties that plagued my memories.

Like Iris, Eve had a gentle nature about her. I met her when I was young, and those days were the happiest in my life. Her love taught me that life beyond the mission was possible, that the greatest joy doesn't come from serving your fellow wolves. The greatest joy comes from the warmth that your mate brings you.

I loved Eve with everything I had. It was because she was so different. I was brooding, cold at times, yet she pierced through this facade with aggression. She spoke her mind, but did it in a way that wasn't invading. She made me want to open up to her. All my life, I had been taught that the duty is the most important thing. Your thoughts, your affections, they're all secondary. But after I met Eve, she was the primary. I had never known anyone who could care for me, I thought I had to earn it with valor. That wasn't necessary with Eve, she gave all she had and asked for nothing in return. To meet someone like that is once in a lifetime.

And then she died so abruptly. It happened in a matter of days, and on her deathbed I looked into her eyes and saw a terrible fear come across them. She was afraid to step into uncertainty. She didn't know what was waiting at the end and that petrified her. All I could do was stand there and watch her face it alone. I couldn't save her, even after she saved me. I wish I could've gone with her, so that she didn't have to go into the unknown by herself. But she did, and that lasting image of fear would haunt me forever. I'm a wolf who takes action, but I was helpless.

She was taken from me, and my anger and callousness returned. I hated the world for making me watch my mate die, for making me realize the only thing I had left was my responsibility to the armed forces. I used to think that the world was ruthless. Eve taught me different. But when she died, I thought that I was right all along. The world is that cruel.

I quickly reverted back to where I belonged, with the Brotherhood. They had known what happened, and. sadly, they seized the opportunity. They saw I was a wolf on a mission, ready to do anything to forget my pain. They sent me on assignment after assignment, and I was a machine that produced for them. I fulfilled every task I was sent on with fervor and tenacity. I didn't need the creds, I never did. I needed a way to forget the memory of her, because it haunted me everywhere I went.

They gave me the dirtiest, toughest, most morally questionable operations they could get their hands on. Need someone to wipeout a village of drug producers targeting wolves? There was a political enemy to the Brotherhood that needed to die? Those jobs are for me. I was the one they called when no one else wanted to get their paws dirty. Instructions were always to kill without prejudice. And I did so.

But with every task, every command, nothing helped me forget the pain I felt over Eve's loss. I was looking for something that would make me forget her memory, or maybe I was looking for an end to my suffering. I found neither.

When I took Operation Halfkinds, I approached it the same way, without prejudice. But as the mission progressed, and the line of morality was getting blurred, I wondered if all those assignments were worth it. They were for my Brotherhood, for the wolves, but as I thought about it, I realized the Brotherhood was wrong. It took that one job to make me understand that I was their puppet. All that garbage about duty and honor meant nothing because the Brotherhood had none. They manipulated me at my lowest point, taking advantage of my grief. They might as well have spat on Eve's grave.

The last straw came when Apollo was about to kill Iris. I looked in her eyes and I saw something that reminded me of Eve. The helpless expression of facing the darkness of death. I remembered how I couldn't do anything to save Eve, but I could do something to save

Iris. So I did. The second the shot rang out of my helmet, a small measure of peace had been restored. I was finally able to save someone from death instead of putting someone there.

And since then, she's helped me pick up the pieces day by day. I feel like parts of my soul have been restored over the past years, and I will be forever grateful for the second view she has given to me.

It's been an hour since I've been away from the cabin, and I haven't found any deer. It's not a big deal, we have plenty of meat in storage. Iris will be worried, I better head back. I run to the cabin within a few short minutes and bark out the unlock command. The front door slides open and there's Iris, putting the finishing touches on lunch.

"You're back," she says with a smirk on her face. "I was getting worried."

"Worried?" I say slightly astonished. "About me? What could possibly be out there that could give me trouble?"

"Oh, I don't know. Secret Brotherhood spies, Alliance soldiers, you know the usual suspects. Or there might be a dinosaur out there."

"I don't know about that last one. Seems pretty farfetched."

"So is my existence."

I let out a small laugh. Her humor is dry, but she has fun with it.

"In all seriousness, though," I say. "I couldn't find any deer out there today. Guess we'll have to rely on what I have saved up."

"No sweat," she says cheerfully. "Did you need me to order anything on the insta-item?"

"No, I think we're good for now."

We've been living off the mass of creds that I have saved from my service with the Brotherhood. They pay handsomely, one of the few perks they offered. There's also a lot to sustain us out in the woods. My survival training sure comes in handy during these strange times.

Iris also has stored a few creds herself selling knick knacks and crafts that she's made. She sells anonymously on the infospace retailers, and sends it with our insta-item. The infospace and insta-item have made living in the shadows pretty easy. I guess this is what Tiago Lawton must have imagined for himself. If Iris is able to sell items here and there, it's a small taste of the freedom her brothers and sisters had hoped to achieve. Her sales are mainly chump change, but we can use it to make sure we don't drain all our savings, and, more importantly, it keeps her occupied.

She's adapted to life in seclusion rather well. She did have years of training living underground.

"What's on the agenda today?" I ask her.

"Oh, I'm not sure," she says. "Maybe I'll clean up a bit, see what there is to watch on the streams."

"Do you want to join me on a hunt? We've gone over the basics, but you still have to learn more. Just in case."

I'm trying to get Iris to learn the same skills I've acquired over the many years. It'll help her in case something happens to me.

"Oh, you worry too much, Fenrir," she says. "We'll be fine."

Her comments are always relaxed and light-hearted. She brushes off my concerns with reassurance as she begins to set our lunch.

"Perhaps you don't worry enough," I say snarkily.

"Well I can join you," she says calmly. "But I really do want to clean up the place first. It's a bit of a mess."

I look around to see my gear strewn about and her cot messily undone. The floors are muddy, fur is everywhere, and there are some deer bones on the floor, all thanks to me. It's been two or so years, and I still act like I live alone.

"Sorry about that," I say embarrassed.

"About what?" she says confused.

"About that."

My eyes are homed right on the bone.

"Oh, I wasn't referring to that," she says. "I wanted to tidy up in general. I didn't even notice the deer bone."

"Thanks," I say. "Old habits, I guess."

"You can't change in a day."

She looks at me and smiles.

"C'mon," she says. "It's time for lunch."

She sits on the floor, legs folded, and sets our dishes there. There's a pile of seasoned meat for me, and a smaller pile of meat for her. She sticks with her cat roots, she's a true carnivore.

"Smells good," I say.

"Thanks," she responds. She seems delighted with my approval.

"What did you use to-"

Something catches my ear. It's a rustling sound ten or twenty meters outside. I look at the door, and it's still open.

"I hear something," I say.

Iris stands up slightly alerted. She looks outside, her eyes fixated on the open door.

"I don't see anything," she says.

"I don't smell anything, either," I say.

"Must be the wind or a small animal or something."

"Maybe."

I hear it again. This time it's a bit further away.

"I don't want to take a chance," I say. "Something is out there and I'm going to go for a quick look."

"Aww, c'mon," Iris pleads. "It's probably nothing. Besides, I don't see anything. No visions. Let's just eat."

"Sorry, Iris, no chances. But don't worry, it shouldn't take that long. I'll be back in no time."

"Okay."

I step outside, my ears are my guide. I turn back and look at Iris. She appears a little apprehensive and senses my concern, but she knows that I need to do what I need to do.

"Go on," she says. "I'll make sure your food stays warm."

I flash a nod and smile.

"Thanks, Iris," I say. "You're always thinking of me."

"I just want to make sure you're happy," she says.

"I am."

There was a time when that response was a lie. It's not anymore. I hear the rustling again and turn my body back to its path. If I'm lucky, we'll have another deer to add to the stash. If I'm not, then I'll do whatever is necessary to make sure Iris is safe.

Chapter 3 - Fang Snow

Bloodlines

May 2, 3043 12:01 PM

"He's back!" Raymus says over our communicators.

"Don't say it so loud, he might hear us," I admonish him.

When he returned from Operation Halfkinds, I was already able to sense something different about Fenrir. He wasn't his old self. He didn't have that shroud of gloom over his head. He seemed relaxed and relieved, as if a great burden had been lifted off his shoulders. It was weird, it wasn't him.

Fenrir kept his guard around us, but he was obedient and loyal. He was supposed to be dedicated to this family and what we stood for, to serve the Brotherhood through thick and thin. That reason was the only reason for our existence. We were taught this ever since we were young. And throughout most of our lives, Fenrir was the prime example of our cause, the oldest brother, the one who excelled at serving the Brotherhood.

But when he returned from his mission, all that changed. He vowed never again to take another assignment from the Brotherhood. All four of his siblings, Raymus, Patrice, Danzel, and I were rocked to our core. For years and years, even after Eve's death, he had taken any task the Brotherhood requested. He hit his objectives hard and furiously, and the Brotherhood was always pleased with his work. He was the shining example of what the Snow family had to offer. So when he told us that he was going to quit, my three brothers didn't know what to do. They were caught completely off guard by the news, and begged him to reconsider. But he made it clear to everyone that he was retired.

Unlike my brothers, I wasn't surprised. The other three are a lot younger than Fenrir and I, and my intuition told me that Fenrir never enjoyed what he did. I could tell from his attitude, that menacing, surly, sullen one, that he had no passion for the job. It was forced upon him, starting from the day he was born. He did things because he had to, not because he wanted to, and to an observant eye, this was obvious.

It's the key difference between he and I. I loved, love, my job, and wouldn't hesitate at anything the Brotherhood ask. I carry my missions with enthusiasm, because it's a privilege to serve them in such capacity. Few other wolves had the positions we had. Many dreamed of being close to the inner circle, and we were the Brotherhood's go-to force. Their honor is the most important thing to uphold.

Growing up, I took my education with excitement and pride. I wanted to show my family that I was the best that the Snows had to offer. Yet despite all my training, I didn't have the natural talent Fenrir had. It took me years to perfect my skills as a soldier; Fenrir was full-fledged within one. He could track better, shoot straighter, and run faster than I ever could. My brothers idolized him and wanted to be what he was, and I would have given anything to have what he had.

But Fenrir didn't see his raw talent as a blessing. It was a curse. What Raymus, Patrice, and Danzel failed to see was that while Fenrir had the gifts to be the best, he never had the heart. Even before Eve's death, I knew he hated being born a Snow. He would tell himself that he wanted to serve the Brotherhood, but it was a lie. He could care less about the family legacy.

The Snows come from a long line of military members. Our great-great-great, even greater-grandfather was part of the Brotherhood's first command, a member of their elite forces. In fact, if I remember correctly, he was one of the wolves fighting on the ground when the Ark Rebellion happened. After the battle was over and we got our share, the Brotherhood rewarded him handsomely. He eventually retired and had children. He trained them from the ground up so they could join the high ranks of military officials. And after they succeeded in their goals, they had children, and their children became elite soldiers, and their children after that, and after that, and after that, and so on.

Over the generations, our family has built an incredibly strong reputation as one of the top powerhouses within the Brotherhood's inner circle. We've always been the cream of the crop. My ancestors cemented their sturdy standing through the centuries, and the most important thing that my brothers and I were taught was to do whatever it takes to keep our heritage afloat. Above all else, the Snow family's primary objective is to make sure the Brotherhood is served. And not once have we failed them, not once. We pride ourselves on being the most dependable soldiers they can rely on.

That is until I found out why Fenrir acted so differently after Operation Halfkinds. He failed the mission, and to make matters worse, there were rumors that he aided one of them in their escape. If I said I wasn't completely floored when I heard the news, I'd be lying. I suspected that Fenrir disliked his lot in life, but I never thought he would do what he did. I couldn't see him as a traitor. He wouldn't turn his back on us.

I should've noticed the signs. Right after the mission was over, we saw him less and less. Mind you, we didn't see him that much before, but in the months following Operation Halfkinds, it was like he never existed. He didn't return our messages and we rarely saw him face to face. When we asked him where he was, he dodged the question or gave incomplete answers. As his behavior grew stranger and stranger, I tried to investigate. I dug into his records in an attempt to find where he had been spending creds and who he had sent communication to. But my search was fruitless, everything was wiped clean. He did his due diligence and made sure no one could track his activities. As suspicious as he was, I couldn't deduce why he was acting so bizarre.

Then I got the call from the Brotherhood elders. They asked me if I knew anything about Fenrir's involvement in Operation Halfkinds. I told them the same story he had told me, that all of them died and he was the lone survivor of the mission. But then they told me the United Species Alliance, specifically the Human Council, had reason to believe that Fenrir lied. They had USASD findings that proved the halfkind he supposedly killed actually lived. The facts piled up, the halfkind known as Iris Lawton was probably alive somewhere, and the only creature who could've helped her escape undetected was my brother, Fenrir Snow.

It was made official that Fenrir betrayed the trust of the United Species Alliance. His actions caused the Alliance to doubt the integrity of the Brotherhood. Naturally, this didn't go over well with them and, since Fenrir wasn't around to punish, the Brotherhood came down on the rest of the Snows hard. The family legacy went down the drain almost overnight. The Brotherhood excommunicated us, shunning us from future assignments and cut communication. Our careers, our reputation, our years of service meant nothing with a single order from the elders. The patriotic name our ancestors spent years cultivating vanished as fast as Fenrir did.

We relied on our military service almost as much as the Brotherhood did. Without it, we were stuck for jobs and lacked identity. No wolf within the Wolf's Den would hire us for government work. They wanted nothing to do with the Snows. They didn't even bother to hunt down Fenrir. With the mission over, the Alliance moved on, and the Brotherhood didn't want to waste their time on an outlaw wolf and a renegade science experiment. Apparently, the Brotherhood has more important things to do.

With few outs and shut door after shut door being slammed on our noses, we fell to the last resort, the one thing I thought I'd never do: mercenary work. Only the lowest common denominators are mercenaries, but we were left out of options. Fenrir was untraceable, our reputation had gone up in smoke, we had to do something where we could use our years of training, and mercenary work was it.

The problem with mercenary work is there are no morals behind it. We could be working for the military, we could be working for scumbags, whether we liked it or not. And most of the time I didn't like it. Most mercenary work is decided and helmed by soldiers who've gotten kicked out of the service, animals who have no honor. That wasn't what the Snow family was about, and I couldn't believe we were reduced to that.

Mercenary work is also dangerous work. The animals who run the jobs have no regard for the soldiers they send. Many tasks are suicide missions. I've seen plenty of mercenaries without limbs or eyes after a few months.

My brothers and I were able to endure only a couple assignments before we decided that we had had enough. On one assignment, we were appointed to guard a shipment of stolen goods for some smugglers. Guess who we ran into? The Alliance. They pummeled our small mercenary crew. The battle almost left Danzel without his hind legs.

On another assignment, we were told to take out some young drug cookers. Except, we weren't told how young they were. By the time we stormed their lab and bombarded it with energy shots, it was too late. We had killed a young group of suppliers that barely reached their adolescence. One was a mere pup. They were poor and desperate to make some creds. The big drug kingpin that hired us wanted all his competition squashed, regardless of how small they were.

It was my lowest point. What had the Snow family legacy become? Were we so hopeless that we'd morphed into child killers to survive? We couldn't bear to look ourselves in the mirror because we were ashamed. And through all this embarrassment, my fury boiled. One thing fueled me. One thing - the fact that Fenrir was responsible for all of this and I would get my revenge.

It was his fault our family had wasted away. We've fallen so low. He chose to abandon the mission, something that's unheard of from a member of the Snows. He never had the killer instinct, he didn't deserve to have the talent. I deserve it. I've done everything for this family, sacrificed will and body to make sure we were in the Brotherhood's graces. The long nights, the countless injuries, mission after mission, task after task, all of it was for our family honor.

Yet in one reckless decision, he threw all my hard work away. And why? To help some monster out? That's why he turned his back on us? Some science experiment is more important than upholding the family tradition?

He never knew what it meant to be the figurehead of the Snows. He didn't have the passion, the call of duty that the rest of us did. He just had the talent. Fenrir is nothing but an ungrateful, selfish punk, and on those dark days after we were banned, all I could think about was how I could find him.

The Brotherhood had no desire to track Fenrir down. They didn't want to waste the wolf power and credits. But I was willing to do it for them, for free. If I could present them with Fenrir's rotting carcass, then maybe our family would be given a second chance. I was hoping that by turning in the traitor, they'd see the Snows are worthy once more, especially if we were willing to capture our own brother in their name. That would show them where our loyalties lie.

For months we trained, perfecting our abilities to prepare for our pursuit of Fenrir. I learned new scents and my brothers reached their peaks physically. We wanted to be in top shape, because we knew we were taking on the best. Once we encountered Fenrir, there'd be no holding back. We had new weapons, new armor, and a plethora of enhanced gear.

Finding him was no easy task. He covered his tracks well. He changed accounts, contact information, even his paw prints were nowhere to be found. He hadn't been seen in his old hangouts, his friends, the few that he had, couldn't vouch for his whereabouts. It's like he had disappeared from the face of the Earth.

But I'm good at tracking. Fenrir wasn't perfect. He left bits of clues for me to find. A small purchase here, traces of fur there. To most beings, these clues would be insignificant, but to me, they were pieces to a very large puzzle. One piece of fur led to one conversation, which led to an interrogation, which led to a store where he bought supplies. He had few interactions with the outside world, but the ones he had were like chain links, leading me to his location.

My tenacity wouldn't let it go. I was unrelenting in my quest. There was seldom a moment when I wasn't thinking about the evidence I discovered. I analyzed every clue to make sure it would help me find him. It was my obsession. Even Raymus, Patrice, and Danzel were astounded by how dedicated I was. I would use all these pieces to find him, even if it killed me.

My investigation led me deeper and deeper into the forest until, almost two years later, we are here today. We've finally found his hideout, an inconspicuous cabin deep in the heart of the woodlands.

We arrived here in the morning and set up a stakeout from a distance to observe our target. I didn't see any sign of Fenrir, but I was sure that this was the cabin. I told my brothers to split up and encircle it while we waited for him to come out of his dwelling. All of us put on masking odors to make sure he wouldn't catch our scent. Fenrir could probably detect us a mile away with his nose, so we took no chances.

We squatted there for hours, waiting patiently for him to leave the cabin. I didn't want to ambush him in his home. Knowing Fenrir, the cabin might be rigged with traps, and running into an unknown hideout would surely get us killed. No, I wanted to draw him out and fight him on fair territory.

Still, my brothers are getting impatient. The time is now noon, and Fenrir still hasn't emerged from the house.

"Should I draw him out?" Raymus asks through his communicator. "You know, follow the plan and make some noise so that he can come our way?"

Raymus is the oldest of my three younger brothers. He's the one closest in age to Fenrir and I, and his maturity shows. He's careful but obedient, and very intelligent. He's the most pragmatic of the younglings and usually takes the lead when I need someone to help.

"No, not yet," I say. "We have to be certain that this is the place."

"I thought you said you knew for sure, sister," Danzel interrupts through his communicator. I am their leader, but my brothers like to question me. Danzel is the most vocal about his skepticism. He's arrogant and cocky, and thinks he should be in charge. He's usually the rallying cry, getting Raymus and Patrice to side with him. I suppose they don't think that a female is equipped to be the alpha. Idiots.

"Better safe than sorry," I say.

"Perhaps we're playing it too safe," Patrice says on the relay. He's the youngest of the three brothers and the most soft-hearted. He's much mellower than Danzel and Raymus, an easy going youngster who can be naïve, but also willing to do what is necessary for the family. Don't misjudge his tenderness for weakness, I know he'll kill without a moment's notice if I ask him to.

"Patience, young one," I tell him. "First, you have to set the trap before you attack."

Suddenly, a wolf comes from the cabin. It's him, Fenrir. He looks healthier than the last time I saw him, which was over a year ago. His coat is shiny, and he seems cleaner, leaner. I suppose running around in the woods has helped his shape. But it's not the physical changes that are obvious, it's his whole demeanor that makes him seem like a new wolf. He's actually smiling. It's weird. The only Fenrir I can imagine is a sulking one. This one looks like he's been brainwashed. He has a new step about him, filled with energy and vigor. His head doesn't hunch down, rather, he stands tall and proud. Everything about him, his posture, his wagging tail, his facial expression make me wonder if it's really him.

But it is.

"Looks like you're right," Raymus says. "He's here. Should we strike yet?"

"No, continue to wait for my cue," I say.

"Why?" Danzel argues. "We should attack now."

"No!" I say sternly. "If you make one move towards him, Cerberus help me, I will maul your face off."

There's an awkward silence among the intercoms.

"That's what I thought," I say.

We're safely observing him far away with our magnifying goggles on, protruding from our helmed weapons. Fenrir runs forward, away from the cabin, about fifty meters and starts to sniff the ground. I'm worried that he's gotten a hold of our scent, but he continues to survey his area, looking around vigilantly, but never making a move. We're safe.

My brothers begin to sidebar a conversation. I listen in while watching Fenrir's movements.

"What do you suppose he's doing?" Patrice asks me.

"Beats me," Danzel says.

"Perhaps he's searching for sustenance," Raymus says. "He's been living here for a while in secret, he's had to have been eating something."

"You mean he's hunting for his own food?" Patrice asks.

"Probably," Raymus says casually.

"Hardcore," Patrice responds.

"Geez, how far some of us have sunk," Danzel says. "Hey, do you suppose that thing he supposedly saved is here too?"

"It could be possible," Raymus says. "We can't get a clear view of the cabin, but she might be in there."

"Man, it's crazy that he left us for that freak," Danzel says.

"You think he really did?" Patrice asks.

"Like I said," Raymus interjects. "It's possible."

The mere thought that Fenrir has dumped us for this halfkind creature makes my blood boil. If what my brothers say is true, then Fenrir's actions are unforgivable. He's only known this halfkind for a fraction of his life, and he runs away with it and leaves our family in ruins. What an asshole.

Then again, Fenrir has always been a romantic. When he met Eve, he was inseparable from her. He lived and died by emotions. And when she passed away, his soul went with her. He was a moody wolf before he met her, but her death threw him over the edge. I could tell he hated everything around him, including our family. It's never been about us for Fenrir, it's only been about himself.

Fifteen minutes pass and nothing happens. Thirty minutes pass and he's still in the same spot. My brothers begin to grow antsy, their conversation goes from interesting to mindless. I continue to focus on Fenrir with unrivaled fortitude. Finally, an hour later, Fenrir is on the move again, back to his cabin.

"Damn," Patrice says on his headset. "He went back inside! Now what?"

"We continue to wait," I say.

"I'm done waiting, we need to act!" Danzel chimes in impatiently.

"No," I bark back. "Do you remember my threat?"

"Perhaps Danzel is right though," Raymus says. "We can't wait here forever. And look, the door is open. We should ambush him."

"I don't want to enter without knowing the full layout," I say.

"Maybe we can draw him out then," Patrice suggests.

"I say we do it now, or don't do it at all," an antsy Danzel responds.

Facing the collective pressure of my brothers, I have no choice but to relent. I don't want to cause any tension at this stage of the search.

"Fine," I say. "Raymus, create a diversion so that Fenrir can go after you. Once he's drawn out, we'll corner him and take him on."

"Got it," Raymus says.

I see him run toward the cabin and he brashly rubs his body against some bushes. The leaves brush against each other, creating a ruffling sound. Fenrir doesn't bite, so Raymus backs up and tries again at a different spot. Once again, nothing happens.

"He's not going for it," Danzel says.

"Just wait," I say. "Raymus, try it one more time. Do it hard."

Raymus shakes the branches so rough that twigs fall out. The noise is clearly audible, even to me. Instantaneously, Fenrir is drawn out. Raymus then backs away and makes some more noise so that Fenrir is exposed, completely vulnerable. He's now on the chase, in pursuit of Raymus's trail. Raymus runs in the other direction, the ultimate goal is to lead Fenrir to a place where we can attack him.

"All right," I say. "Fenrir is on Raymus's trail. Let's move out."

"Wait!" Patrice says. "What's that?"

I look back at the cabin and see… something. It's a creature I've never laid my eyes on before. It looks like a human from the distance. It stands on two legs, has two arms, and a head on top of its shoulders. It's not too tall, probably between five or six feet. It's wearing clothes. It definitely seems human, but as I look closer, it has the features of a cat. The fur, the pointy ears, the whiskers. Hell, there's even a tail sticking out of its pants.

"It looks like a halfkind," I say.

"A halfkind?" Patrice says shocked. "You mean *the* halfkind?"

"I don't know," I say. "I can't get a clear look."

"This is certainly unexpected," Danzel says. "The halfkind is here, Fenrir is in another direction. Do you want us to get both? Should we only focus on one? What do you want us to do, Fang?"

The game change happened so suddenly and I rush to make an audible. I didn't see this problem arising and with little time to respond, I can only muster out one response.

"Engage," I say.

Chapter 4 - Iris Lawton

Undercover

May 2, 3043 1:13 PM

"Let's see," I say to myself, "The deer has extra onions, just like Fenrir prefers, and the drinks are out. Everything is set, ready to eat, and I'm hungry. Why does that wolf always scurry off without warning?"

I prepared a feast for Fenrir while he was looking for deer or elk or whatever other meat he can scrounge, and now he's not here to enjoy it. Sometimes he can be so stubborn, and his impatience will be the end of me. However, I'm grateful he's around and I feel safe knowing how careful he is.

He's been able to provide for me with his hunting skills. I don't know how I would get my protein fix without him. All the kills he's made have afforded us enough food for the winter season, and now that spring is fading and summer is arriving, there'll be more on the way.

The cooling unit that he lugged out here has been a real help, too. We placed it underground to conserve space. I lift a floorboard and all our refrigeration necessities are in check. It's one of the things I needed in order to survive out here.

Setting up this cabin wasn't an easy task, especially when I first arrived in the middle of a dreary November. The coming winter was blustery and harsh. Fenrir was worried I wouldn't be able to last in such brutal conditions.

First things first, we had to get the provisions I needed for survival. Fenrir bought me a coat and some blankets to sleep on. He also got me an insta-item, not the portable ones like the kind Tiago tried to obtain in Primm, but a bigger one that could teleport in larger items. He hauled all these things miles deep into the intense winter weather, through thick snow and heavy winds, all to make sure I could survive. He was amazingly noble and I was eternally thankful.

After I got my insta-item, goods were considerably easier to get. Within the month, I had all I needed to live on my own. The insta-item is linked to Fenrir's account, and I make sure to get his approval before I decide to order anything. I am afraid he will be angry with me for using his creds, but he's made it clear that won't be an issue. He's more worried that whatever I order will be easily traceable. Fenrir has warned me that the Alliance or some other group might be on the lookout for me, and that they will try to find any link to my location. This includes purchases. Thus, I am wary of doing anything that might tip them off, and I make sure Fenrir helps me take the precautions needed to keep my privacy intact.

Fenrir also makes sure to supply me with weapons to protect myself, but I don't have the killer instinct like he does. We have a cache of both wolf and human armaments that I can use in case I need to, but I pray I won't.

When I moved here I was alone, but not completely. Fenrir would stop by, check up on me, sniff suspicious scents, all for my safety. His visits became more and more frequent. And then, when the news of his role in my escape broke out, he lived here, and it's been great ever since.

I smell the mix of chopped onions and herbs in our dishes.

"Needs a dash of pepper," I say as the aromas fill my senses. The meal is ready, but I make some after-served adjustments so that it's perfect. Fenrir likes his meats with a blend of flavors.

Making food for two different species is no easy task. I usually have to cook separate portions. Fenrir likes his meats raw, but with enough spices to kick it up a notch. Fenrir says that wolf cuisine is difficult to master, but I don't see why. You need meat, meat, and more meat. Throw in some things to entice the taste buds, and boom, you have a wolf meal ready to go. I, on the other hand, thanks to my semi-human anatomy, need my meats cooked. I can handle the rawness better than a human would, but the bacteria needs to be killed or I'll get sick. Besides, it tastes better.

There's still a lot about my composition and makeup that I don't know. When I lived in Primm, mother never took us to the doctor for obvious reasons. If we asked about our bodies, she would tell us the answers based on a human body without really dissecting the core of our physical structure.

But as I grew older, I noticed there were obvious things about me that were different from my human counterparts. I prefer to eat meat like a cat, and I have fur that allows me to tolerate colder weather. I have a strange mix of paw and fingers for hands, and my natural senses - sight, smell, hearing - are more heightened than an average human. I am in between a cat and human.

The same went for my siblings. Curtis had scales for skin, but long fingers like a human. Lombardi had his feathers, Leonard had a prehensile tongue. We all had traits that made us unique to our origins, but human at the same time.

Thinking about my family makes me remember how everything changed the night that Fenrir calls Operation Halfkinds. It only took a week on the run for me to watch firsthand my family break apart. The siblings that I had known over a lifetime morphed into beings I didn't recognize, the struggle made them act irrational and drastically different from their normal selves.

First there was Leonard, who couldn't take the shock and face the reality that Mom was dead. He was so stuck to her memory that he risked not only his life, but ours, to make sure she was given a proper send off. In times of extremes, you have to think about your safety first. He didn't know what dangers were out there and when he found out, it was too late. That lesson cost him his life.

Oscar was supposed to be a strong leader, but under the pressure, he folded. While Tiago was proactive about his plans, Oscar waned around and hid from the realities that were thrust upon us. His weak leadership showed until his death. I don't understand how someone could go from strong-willed to weak-minded in a matter of days, but it happened.

On the other end of the spectrum, Tiago changed so drastically that when I look back, I forget that he was my brother. When that night happened, I didn't know exactly what he did. But after I escaped, Fenrir revealed the truth. Tiago had committed several acts of betrayal. He was the one responsible for Leonard's death. He orchestrated the assault on Oscar's camp, on the camp I stayed in, to buy himself more time for his plan to go to the Moon. He took advantage of Curtis's depression and sent him on a suicide mission. My brother was always the hard one, the one who would know the things we didn't want to. Yet, I didn't think he'd be on such a warpath that he would sacrifice the weak in order to save the strong. That wasn't the Tiago I knew. The person he turned out to be on that night was evil.

Tiago had one saving grace about him. According to Fenrir, he wasn't the one who betrayed Isaac and I. It was Alex. When it came down to his last breath, Tiago would have rather died than give up my location. As I always suspected, it's because he thought I was special. He was the most convinced that I possessed some kind of precognitive power, and when he shunned us away, I gave him a look that let him know I saw something wrong with his plan. I guess when it came crumbling apart, he had no doubt I foresaw it, and that my power was too valuable to throw away.

A lot of crazy things happened between my family that I thought unfathomable. Looking back on it brings up bad memories. I can't even think about Isaac without…

…no, my mind can't go through that dark tunnel again.

I still have my visions here and there, but they're inconsistent and focus on insignificant occurrences. I can see things like the weather and minor events, such as Fenrir's reactions to my cooking, but I can't see anything big. Or at least I haven't yet. I also have some measure of control over the future. If I have a vision of Fenrir catching a deer in a certain area of the forest, I tell him, and, sure enough, he gets it. If he had gone where he originally intended to go, no deer would be had. So I suppose my visions are useful in aiding Fenrir on his hunts.

Still, everything is so subjective. I wish I could have the ability to look into it myself, instead of getting these random flashes. But it doesn't work that way, it never has. I hate uncertainty, since I've lived a lifetime of it. I want to see things clearly. I guess I have to accept that's the way it is.

At times, it's hard to keep my optimism. I'm away from Primm, away from that prison of a city, but I'm still underground, sheltered from the world. Mother isn't keeping me from going public, my own fear is. And for all the sacrifices I've made, for all the things I've gone through, I've ended up in the same exact place that I started. Nothing's changed but the scenery. It's a lot cleaner, a lot prettier, but it's still a cage.

Fenrir has the best intentions, I know he does, but I wonder how long will we be doing this? Is a lifetime undercover really my fate? There's so much I won't experience, so much I can't see. Perhaps uncertainty isn't what makes me worry, but, rather, certainty, for I already have my life set ahead of me. No surprises, nothing new to discover. The only thing that awaits is a life in the dark.

It's this world's fault. They've trapped me here, and it's a damn shame that living in the shadows is all I will know. I can dream about living free and among the masses, but my dreams mean nothing.

Thinking about it makes me question what dangers lie out there. Fenrir has gone over the various threats to my life. He's told me the Alliance has stopped actively looking for me, that they have other things to worry about, but I'm sure if they found one piece of my fur, they'd come running.

There is so much hate in this world. Humans hate animals, animals hate humans, and they all hate each other. If they could find something else to hate, something like me, they'd jump at the chance. And I represent the worst kind of hate, the hate brought by ignorance, the hate of the unknown.

I worry that I'll be snatched by those motivated with fear. It could be a mob, hunting me down like an outcast, ready to rip me from limb to limb. Or I'm scared I'll be picked off by a sniper from an elite force. They are irrational fears, I know, but they haunt my mind and scare the crap out of me.

I can't be bogged down with all this again. I've had the past couple of years to cope with my issues. I never really had many before. I was always optimistic, even though I was afraid. Mother made me feel safe, that despite how miserable the situation, I'd be okay. Fenrir has given me a shred of this. I feel secure with him. Though the deaths and the trauma have shaken my outlook on life, he makes me feel the way I used to feel. He'll do anything to help me survive, and I trust him.

I have to stay positive, for him. The fact that he's risking life and limb at this very moment speaks volumes about my friend.

I continue to put the finishing touches on our table setting. I have my fork and spoon set neatly next to my plate, and his silver bowl is placed squarely on the ground. My cup of water glimmers sunrays that escape into our cabin through the windows, and his water bowl reflects pools of light into my eyes. Everything is finished, and I sit at our setting waiting for him to come back.

I wait a few minutes and he hasn't arrived.

I wait a few more and still no sign of him.

I wait another set of minutes, and not even a snarl is heard. The wind blows an eerie cry against our cabin walls. An abrupt nervousness comes over my senses, and I look outside with steady eyes. What's taking him so long?

I take one step towards the open door to get a closer look. The trees sway in the distance, but no one is there. The only noise I catch is a single bird chirping as the wind continues to moan its dreadful chorus.

And then I hear it, the rustling that Fenrir chased after. It is no longer hundreds of feet away, it is in my front yard. I hear another one behind me, beyond the cabin walls, again outside. My heartbeat rises, and I feel the sounds enclosing on my position, suffocating my thoughts and pumping up my hysteria. But I don't see anything. Whatever the sound is, it's out of my view.

I bravely take another step forward. My footsteps create a slight thud that faintly echoes through our dwelling. To the right of me, on the way to the exit, I see one of the weapons Fenrir had gotten. It's an energy baton, concentrated light that retracts from its base to create a blunt striking object. I pick it up and arm it, a beam shoots out, ready for me to bludgeon anything that might bring harm.

With the weapon in hand, I take another few steps forward. I'm almost at the door and I grip the baton tightly. It feels like if I squeeze any firmer, the stick will crack in my hands. The rustling sound gets louder and more chaotic by the second. Something knows I'm heading their way.

With one final lunge, I leap outside and take a mighty swing at the air, hoping to scare off the would be attacker. To my surprise, I only see the trees, and the noise has ceased. I look left, then right, look up, then down, and nothing is there. A rush of exasperation flows through my body, and I let out a sigh.

"Guess all that was for nothing," I say to myself. "Time to-"

A jarring force pushes me forward, and I hit the ground face first. My eyes see nothing but darkness. The fall stuns me, my orientation becomes discombobulated. I can't tell where the grass starts and where the sky ends. But as seconds feel like minutes, my senses come back, and I realize that I'm lying on the dirt, face toward the floor. My arms are outstretched before me, pinned down by an entity that I cannot see. My legs feel stiff, like they're glued to the surface.

I struggle mightily to let myself loose, but my attempts are pitiful and in vain. Whatever has me nailed to the ground is incredibly heavy, and no matter how much strength I use, I can't move.

"Help!" I scream. "Fenrir!"

But it's no use. He's far away, and even if he could hear me, my pursuer is too close. I can hear him, her, whomever, from behind, walking towards me. I can't see what it is that has ensnared my body. It or they move lightly on their feet, treading through the cabin with grace and poise.

Panic overcomes me as the intruder inches closer. I try once again to flail my limbs in the hopes that something can come loose. But the trespasser now stands above me, and all I can think about is the end. I've journeyed to the edge of the world, hoping to find some peace, and it seems even out here, I can't be free.

Fenrir, thank you for everything.

With that last thought, I feel a sharp pain pinch me on my neck. Things become foggy. My vision hazes, and I become drowsy. My hearing disappears with every moment, but I can faintly make out the footsteps of the intruder. Though fuzzy, I'm able to perceive that it stands in front.

With my final ounce of strength, I look up and see a grey blur hover over my fading consciousness. And then I black out.

Chapter 5 - Fenrir Snow

Confrontation

May 2, 3042 1:27 PM

"Why can't I smell it?" I ask myself. When I approached the rustling noise, it ran. I could hear it scamper through the shrubbery. It is much faster than any deer I've encountered. There were a few animals that could move as swiftly as the one I am chasing, and I'm certain which one it is.

Wolves, specifically, a member of the Brotherhood's elite soldiers. They don't take failure lightly, and I'm sure they were less than thrilled when they heard I helped Iris and went underground. I wonder who they sent. Maybe it's my old rival, Auger, that jackass. That vet always said he would kill me. Or maybe it's Hearn. I heard he was an upcoming youngster who earned raves within the Brotherhood's inner circle. I'm not worried, though, whoever they send, I can handle.

I'm more concerned about how they found me. I did everything to cover my trail, and I made sure Iris was just as careful. Yet it didn't take long for a Brotherhood lackey to come my way.

No matter. When I reach my target, I'll have my weapon drawn ready for the kill. I don't care if there's one or ten of them, I'll do what it takes to make sure Iris is safe.

I'm close, real close. I can sense it. The target is tired and his quickness decreases by the second. He stops. In front of me stands a large wall of twigs and small trees, and I'm sure my mark is beyond this barrier. I still can't smell him, but it doesn't matter. My ears suit me just fine. The noises he makes tell the story. His heavy breathing is audible, his feet scratch against the ground and tell me where he is.

I try to devise a strategy, but I'm lost for an approach. I can't see anything beyond this wall of plants, and as I look around, there's nothing that would give me a clear advantage. The only thing I can do is a direct assault, and that's fine by me. I kneel down and ready myself for a jump.

One.

Two.

Three.

My hind legs jettison me past the thick grove. My head bursts through the branches creating a cloud of foliage and I land safely on the other side. I immediately regain my footing, shake off the leaves, and lift my head up to see who is there. The sight in front of me is definitely a surprise.

"Raymus," I say.

"Hello, Fenrir," he says.

"I didn't pick up your smell."

"We applied some scent masks.

"Makes sense. So the Brotherhood sent you? I'm a bit surprised, didn't think they'd resort to having families take each other out. Then again, I should've figured it would've been someone close to me."

"Brotherhood? What are you talking about?"

He looks confused by my assessment. I am equally perplexed by his reaction.

"They didn't send you?" I ask him.

"Send us?" he says in an offended tone. "Wow, Fang was right. You really don't understand what's happened, do you?"

Raymus is right about that. I haven't talked to any of my siblings in a long time. Any communication with them ceased once I started hiding with Iris. It was for her protection, my family can't be trusted. With Raymus's presence, my suspicions are justified.

"I suppose I haven't," I respond.

"Let me fill you in," he says. "Ever since your little escapade into the forest, the Brotherhood struck their judgment hard on us."

He barks and growls rapidly in wolf language. My wolf speak is rusty, as I've been speaking to Iris in human most of the time. Speaking wolf is no longer instinctive to me. I take some moments to compute his talk.

"Someone had to be responsible for your crimes," he says. "They decided to make an example of us to show the others that abandoning the Brotherhood is a serious offense. Our whole family has been stripped of our ranks, and now we're in shambles. And it's your fault. The Snows are in ruin because of you."

The news shocks me a bit. I didn't believe the Brotherhood would be so harsh. A rush of guilt spreads through my body as I think about the family members I have let down.

"I'm sorry brother, I didn't want that to happen," I say.

"Yeah, well, neither did we," he says. "They won't hire us anymore, we have nothing. No missions, no objectives, nothing for us to apply our skills. What are we to do now?"

"Serving the Brotherhood isn't your only purpose in life. Trust me, I know. Because of the way we were raised, you think that serving them is a priority. But it's not. They're a bunch of old farts that use entire families like ours. You have to get away from that, all of you. I used to be like you, but I've moved on."

What I say sparks anger in him. His eyes narrow and his teeth start to show.

"You were never like us!" Raymus says. "Fang pointed it out. All you did was mope around like a sad sack. You had no heart and could care less about our family traditions. No matter what you do, or what you say that might convince yourself otherwise, you never cared about the greater good of the Snows."

What he says is partially true. I never did care for my family's politics with the Brotherhood. I always thought that they used the Snows like puppets, but my desire to uphold our legacy prevented me from doing anything about it. It wasn't until Operation Halfkinds that I was set free. And I've never looked back. That didn't mean I didn't love my family and care for their welfare.

"I have and always will cherish you, Patrice, Danzel, and Fang," I say. "But I care enough to do something about it. Our family shouldn't be the Brotherhood's playthings. Aren't you tired of taking orders from them?"

He looks at me begrudgingly.

"We haven't taken orders from them in over a year," he says. "And I miss it everyday. So, no, I'm not tired."

My eyes droop and my heart sinks.

"Then I truly feel sorry for all of you," I say.

"We don't need your sympathy," he says. "Not anymore."

We stand there in silence, eye to eye in a stare down. It feels like it lasts for ages.

"So, shall we begin this then?" I ask.

"Not yet."

He lets out a sharp howl in the air, and like the swiftness of the wind, another wolf leaps from the forest and lands right next to Raymus.

"Danzel," I say.

Raymus looks shocked and anxious, as if something unexpected happened.

"Where are the other two?" he whispers to Danzel. His voice is lowered, but I can hear what he's saying.

"They got preoccupied with something," Danzel says.

"With what?"

Danzel looks at me and tries his best to be sly. He's not doing a very good job.

"I can't really divulge that information at this moment," he says as he stares at me. "I'll tell you later."

"Why?" Raymus persists. "What happened?"

"Seriously, shut up."

"You shut up! Tell me what's going on."

For goodness sake, what the hell is wrong with these two?

"Enough!" I yell. "What are you two yammering about?"

"Um, nothing," Danzel says with a guilty tone.

"Stop lying you idiot," I say. "Raymus asked where the other two are. Who are you referring to? Patrice? Fang?"

"Um…" Danzel mumbles.

"And what distraction are you talking about?" I persist.

"You idiot, you've told Fenrir enough already," Raymus admonishes.

"Don't call me an idiot," he says. "If you saw what we saw, you'd be talking about it, too."

"Where's Fang?" I shout at them fiercely. My bark surprises them and they look at me stiffly. Their ears point up and their tails remain frozen. I suppose even after all this time, they're still a little scared of the alpha in this family.

"Um, well," Danzel mutters.

"You're all bark and no bite, Danzel," Raymus says. "You'll see her soon enough, Fenrir. But you have your paws full anyway."

"Two against one?" I ask. "Seems hardly fair."

"What you did to us wasn't fair, either," Raymus responds.

"The only way we'll get our spot back in the Brotherhood is with your body on their steps," Danzel adds. "Sorry, brother, but you made your decision over a year ago, now it's our turn."

They swipe their tails and four thin, mechanical arms protrude from their helmet's side. The arms then expand out to three barrels a piece. This isn't a single cannon helmet like I have, it's much more sophisticated.

"Not voice activated?" I ask.

"Nope, there's a tail motion sensor in the back," Danzel responds. "And the guns have some homing capability and rapid fire. These aren't straight shooters like yours. It can switch back and forth between piercing mode and burst mode, creating mini energy bombs on the fly. We came prepared, and have a whole slew of other goodies with your name on it. Top of the line stuff, Fang spared no expense."

"It won't do you any good," I say.

"Whatever," Danzel says. "You ready?"

We look at each other intensely. No words are said for a few seconds, and we stand in silence as the wind blows against our fur.

"Let's go," I say. "Stun shot!"

I fire a blast straight in their direction and they scatter. Raymus goes left, Danzel goes right. It's not a heat bullet, but, rather, a paralyzer. It's an energy shot designed to knock out the victim, not kill him. They may want me dead, but these are my brothers, and I refuse to kill my own family.

My brothers, on the other hand, will. They fire shots from their helmet, four apiece, eight total, in my direction. I only have a split second to dodge the barrage of fire, so I run. A few trail behind me, and from the corner of my eye, I see a decrepit log. I pounce behind it with all my might and duck, only to see an explosion of bark above me. This crusty old piece of wood has saved my life.

I hear some gears interlock and I peer from behind the log to see what it is. Above each of my brothers' heads float two rotating disks of carbon metal.

"Chasers," I say to myself. These saucer like items hover in the air like a sentry until they detect the enemy. Then, as the name implies, they chase the target and once contact is made, it's boom-boom, bye-bye.

I can only stare at them in the short seconds that I have before they pick me up with their sensors. I have time for one shot. I better make it count. I look directly at one and focus.

"Fire," I say. I prefer voice activated shots instead of using the tail sensor. I'm much more accurate this way.

The energy shot flies out of my helmet and hits one of the disks. It harmlessly falls to the ground. Sometimes the old ways are the best. Raymus and Danzel look at each other in amazement.

"Damn, he hasn't lost it," Raymus says.

"Don't worry, we have one more left," Danzel says.

He's right. It's found me, and charges forward with incredible speed. Instinctively, I run the other way as it chases me through the forest. I jump over bushes, around trees, but the disk follows my every turn. It's getting closer and closer, there's no way I can outrun it. The only thing I can do is follow the last ditch plan I've made up. I see a large tree placed next to my brothers.

"Time for a return," I say. I dash towards Danzel and Raymus, running with full speed. They don't fire at me because they're too surprised by my actions. They think I'm going to tackle them, but I run right past the two to the tree behind them, leap towards it feet first, and with my front and hind legs push off the tree in mid-air. My triangle jump propels me in the other direction in front of Danzel and Raymus, and, in a fraction of a second, the disk collides with the tree behind me, causing a small explosion that sends my two brothers falling forward. The plan worked, the disk missed its mark.

I land on my feet and immediately turn my attention to my dazed siblings.

"Stun fire," I say looking at Danzel. A shot comes out my helmet and hits him square on his side. He shakes a little, and his eyes close. He's out cold. Raymus is still recovering from the explosion and doesn't have time to react.

"Stun fire," I say again. This shot hits him on his side, and he falls over. Just like that, my brothers have been subdued. It's time now for the next two. Fang and Patrice are no doubt nearby. I have to find them.

But something bothered me about what Raymus and Danzel said. Something about being preoccupied. Obviously, I'm their target, and I'm sure Fang would have ambushed me with a full team. It didn't make sense for her to attack two by two. What could have distracted her…

Oh, no! Iris! I need to get back to the cabin quick. I sprint to our home, thinking the absolute worst. What if Fang already got to her? Or what if she's captured Iris and is holding her hostage? The scenarios that run through my mind cause me to push harder. I have to get there.

Suddenly, something tackles me from the side. I tumble to the ground, only for my momentum to be stopped by a heavy body that pins me to the dirt floor. My legs are up and I tilt my head to the sky to see who it is. In my view is a snout and fangs.

"Patrice," I say.

"Hello, brother," he says. "Looks like we finally meet again. You know, since you left…"

"I'm going to be honest with you, Patrice, I don't have time for this. One quick question, I didn't know you were coming, and you could've sniped me any time. Why'd you attack me physically?"

He looks confused.

"Don't you realize that my weapon is pointed right at your face?" I ask. "Stun fire."

A shot comes out of my helmet, and hits him in the jaw. He keels over and is on the ground cold. Rookie mistake.

"Don't think that I'll be that stupid," a familiar voice says to me.

"Where is she?" I ask Fang.

"Who, your girlfriend? We'll talk about her later. Right now, we have something to settle. Why did you leave us with your mess?"

She looks at me with a mix of anger and desperation. I avoid her glare. I'm tired of answering questions, but I know I must respond.

"You've never, since we were pups, wondered why we must serve?" I ask. "Doesn't it bother you that we are loyal to a Brotherhood who doesn't care about us?"

"Speak for yourself," she says. "The Brotherhood has always treated the Snows well."

"They used me, Fang. They took advantage of my grief and exhausted me until I felt I had no soul. Going against them made me feel alive again. How can our family work for such heartless leaders?"

Her eyes get watery and she looks at me with rage.

"Don't act like you care about our family!" she barks. "It's only about you. It's always been about you. I don't know why you are constantly the center of attention. All you care about is yourself. You took away everything that this family held sacred and flushed it down the drain, to make yourself feel better. Don't you dare bring our heritage into this, you don't deserve to wear our name. You deserve to die, like a traitor!"

She swishes her tail rapidly and a swarm of shots come my way. I run to my right, behind some trees, and the ammo keeps coming. She's wasting power. Fang is fighting with her heart, not with her mind.

The firing stops and I look beyond the tree at Fang. She stands there calmly and unemotionally as she stares back. Without warning, an energy shot volleys from the ground near where I sit and into the air. It startles me and I hop from my concealment. Fang then fires at me, but in the nick of time I foresee her actions and jump out of the way. However, the shots still fire out of the ground, like lava spraying spit fires into the air.

"Newest stuff on the market," Fang says in the background. "They're called tunnelers. Basically, energy shots I fire at the floor. They burrow into the ground and fire upwards. The opponent won't know what's coming."

Luckily these things carry a scent, and I'm able to anticipate where they are. Guess Fang didn't think of that.

"Like I said, I don't have time for this," I say.

"I don't care about what you want anymore," Fang says readying another shot.

"Reflect screen," I whisper softly. A translucent light screen appears in front of me, nearly invisible to those who aren't close enough to see it. Fang fires a shot, right into the screen she can't see, and it fires back at her. Good thing I spent the creds on this wonder. Surprised by the trick I've pulled, she tries to leap out of the way, but her own shot hits her leg. She lets out a howl of pain.

"Coward!" she screams. She won't be running anytime soon.

"Sorry, Fang, but I need to see what you've done," I say.

I start my dash back home. A few tunnelers fire into the air from the ground below, but I evade them with ease. Nothing is going to stop me from getting to Iris, nothing.

Yet, it appears my worst fears have come true. When I get to the cabin, I look around and see Iris nowhere. The only thing that's visible is emptiness. I see her energy baton placed suspiciously at the front door. Some of her fur is scattered on the floor, but these are the only clues to her disappearance. Everything else in the cabin looks in place. There's nothing scattered messily on the ground, no signs of struggle. It's like she vanished into thin air.

I sniff the ground desperately to try to get a hint of something. I smell Iris, but I don't smell any of my siblings. It might have been the masking scent they wore, but my nose finds none of their odors. If they were here, they did a good job of hiding it.

Something else catches my nose, though. It's someone new. I can't put my paw on it, but it kind of smells like Iris, only rougher. The scent is different enough, but all too familiar. What is this?

"Lost your girlfriend?" someone asks me from behind. Fang limps her way to me.

"What did you do to her, Fang?" I bark.

"We didn't do anything."

"Liar!"

I arm my weapon and the barrel points out of my helmet. Her leg is slightly charred, and she's wincing in pain.

"I'm not lying," she says. "We thought we saw her outside. At that point, I had already instructed Danzel to go after you while Patrice and I stayed here. She, or someone we assumed was her, emerged from the bushes. It was hard to get a close view because our vantage point was from the side of the cabin. It then crept through the back, and moments later we heard her screaming your name. We rushed over to see the commotion, but by the time we got there, she was gone. Not a trace was left. We were as confused as you."

I look at Fang cautiously. For some strange reason, I think she's telling the truth.

"Too bad she wasn't there," Fang says. "We could've executed her, and that would've slapped some sense into you."

She crossed the line.

"Stun fire," I say. Just like the others, she falls to the floor.

They should be out for a few hours. Hopefully when they recover, they'll stop their pursuit, but I'm doubtful. That's the last of my worries, I need to find where Iris went. I sniff and sniff and sniff, but I find nothing other than the suspicious scent I caught earlier. Someone else was here. But that leads me to the ultimate question.

If Fang isn't responsible for this, who is?

Chapter 6 - Bastion

Encounter

May 2, 3043 1:15 PM

For the longest time, I thought I was alone. I was born in a HORUS medical room, in the outskirts of the Bay Area. It was the first and last time I ever saw my mother, she didn't want me. She collected her creds and ran for the hills the moment I popped out. I don't even know her name.

At least I had a few slivers of contact with her. I've never seen my father before. All I know is that he is or was a cat.

The only father I really have is Lionel Changer, leader of HORUS. I grew up during a time when there weren't many of us half-human creatures, halfkinds. I've been told the term is becoming a popular label for us. I prefer hybrids. In fact, when I was born, there were only a handful of us, Lucy included. Now there are roughly twenty, the abandoned children of whores who didn't want us. The technicians and scientist were my uncles, and Lionel was our guardian in this strange thing I call a family.

When we were young, the scientists were still figuring out what our anatomies were like. There were so many questions they had to answer. What were our dietary restrictions? What kind of immunizations did we need? What side effect would arise thanks to our "other half?" We were the first generation of hybrids, and there were many things that Lionel and his team of followers needed to discover until they were comfortable with what they knew.

Because of that, our childhood was interesting to say the least. We were test subjects. We ate non-divisive meals, foods with simple nutrients and bland taste to make sure there was nothing in our systems that would reject it. It was a matter of what a human could eat versus what a cat could eat. We had playtime when we were young, but that playtime usually involved some kind of skill exercise. They wanted to make sure we were equipped for whatever HORUS needed us to do when we were older.

Despite how callous it seems, Lionel made sure we had some childhood memories. When I say he is a father figure, I don't mean that in a loose term, I mean that he is my father. Lionel treats all of us like his own. When we were little, he read us stories and personally tucked us in. He spared no expense for our care. If we were sick or weren't feeling good, he got our lab techs to inspect us right away. Any medicines or equipment were paid out of his pocket. He was a rich man before he created HORUS, and he made sure to provide for us generously. And he wasn't cold about it, either. He didn't treat us like freaks, he made sure we got the attention we required.

Lucy and I were loyal to him, probably because we were groomed to be his protégés, but the others who weren't so lucky and wanted to leave. They would raise hell and argue with the lab techs. But when things got out of hand, Lionel would be there to placate everyone. Because he's done so much, none of them had the heart to mutiny. The minute he addressed the situation, all was well. He had that power over us because there's a mutual respect between his hybrid brood and himself. He had sacrificed so much time and money. We admired him, he was our patriarch.

And like any good dad, he made sure we were productive with ourselves. Our daily routine would be eat, learn, train, eat, learn, train, eat, spend some time with Lionel, and sleep. When we needed breaks, we took them. It wasn't slave labor or anything. It went like that during our youth and, to some extent, it still goes like that today.

Lucy and I were trained from the start to serve Lionel and HORUS's vision well. Our skill set was tuned to the advantages we were given from birth. Lionel made sure Lucy's brain was well stimulated. He was going to make her the cornerstone of research and development, and knew the powerful mind he inherited thanks to his studies on gene mixing between humans and chimps.

I, on the other hand, was suited to become Lionel's personal agent, like some kind of super ninja. I worked on building my physique to its peak potential. Everyday I would follow a strict regimen of rigorous exercise, maximizing my strength, speed, reflexes, and muscle movement. Lionel made sure I had all the newest gear to tackle my drills. He even designed some of my equipment.

I also got some help from the biotics division. Before Lionel went underground, he was a world renowned techno-bio genius, creating hundreds of biotic implant devices that are still being used today. That's how he got his fortune. And just because he went underground didn't mean he stopped development. Instead of creating breakthroughs for the public sector, he created it for HORUS. There are the uterus implants he invented which allowed our creation, but there's also the other stuff he's worked on. Leg and arm implants designed to heighten strength. Optical implants used to increase eyesight. Lung implants to expand air containment. Yes, Lionel made sure he had a whole slew of biotic advances that he and we could play with. And once Lucy came along, revolutions in the field increased tenfold. The world could never fathom the kind of stuff that Lionel and Lucy fostered; if they did, they'd be amazed.

These implants have helped me progress as a stealth agent to the point where I am damn near untouchable. I could move in broad daylight, jumping from shadow to shadow unseen. No noise would be made. I'd move so fast that you'd think it was the wind and nothing more. I can jump down from distances of twenty or thirty feet, land so lightly that a pin drop would be louder than me. I can sprint at speeds that outpace wolves, tigers, or any other predator and wouldn't waste even a single breath or drop of sweat. I'm that good.

Lionel has always seen my potential for greatness, and I've been championed as one of his favorites along with Lucy. He admires her for her brain and me for everything else. I guess you could consider me his teacher's pet. I remember the first time he called me "Agent Bastion." It was an honor. I felt like I had graduated into adulthood. It signified that I was no longer his student, that I was fully trained and ready to go.

Most of my early tasks were simple monitoring chores. I'd go in and check on targets that Lionel needed updates for. Then it progressed to tougher missions, such as infiltrating buildings and extracting information. I had to climb through ventilation systems, use code breakers to infiltrate properties, real spy stuff in order to get the files or hardware that Lionel needed. Creating implants isn't easy. Getting the resources or materials is no simple task, especially if you've disappeared from the face of the Earth.

I was always up for the job, and Lionel was proud of my work. And I was happy with it, too. I liked being the one that Lionel could depend on, it gave me a sense of accomplishment. The best thing was I never had to resort to bloodshed. Not one kill or injury has happened during my missions, and it's a fact that fills me with gratification. It's not my nature to be violent.

Still, as great as it was to be relied on, a part of me was sad. I felt alone among my peers. We were all considered brothers and sisters, but we weren't blood related. I had a different mother and father, Lucy had different parents, the rest did too. We looked different. I was half-cat, Lucy was half-chimp. Some of us were half-lion, others were half-pigs. We were demi-humans of different flavors and as hard as it was calling them my family, their appearances made it even tougher.

I was lonely growing up. I had Lionel, and to a very far extent Lucy, but I wasn't close to the others. Lucy and I were his favorites, and that came with a price. The others grew jealous of our prominent roles and isolation became a normal reaction. They didn't want to talk to me, hang with me, or even say hi.

Then, about ten years ago, Lionel let me in on a secret. There were other hybrids living in the world, away from HORUS central. Well, actually, it was one family, but a large one with eleven siblings. He told me that he had been monitoring them for some time, and that they lived with their mother. She was a prostitute who, unlike all the others, kept her children, and left HORUS to live on her own. This woman, Maya Lawton, thought she had gone completely dark, cutting ties with HORUS. She was wrong. No matter how hard you try, you can't escape Lionel's sight. He only let her think she escaped with her children. Lionel believed that those kids were still his property, and he wanted to make sure his goods were intact.

Yet, he didn't see the harm of letting these hybrids live off our facilities, as long as Maya kept a low profile. She did, and did it well. To Lionel, it was another experiment. He wanted to see the effects of these hybrids' development, living away from the care of HORUS. Lionel wanted to find out if living outside would make them more well-adjusted. Yet, he didn't completely trust them in Maya Lawton's care. She had cleaned up, but old habits die hard. Thus, he needed someone to check up on them once in a while, in secret. Of course, there was only one guy for the job. Me.

His instructions were simple, to observe them from a distance every once in a while, maybe once a month, maybe once a year, and report their status and my findings. I was given strict instructions not to interfere or make contact. The results of an experiment can be damaged if the environment is tainted.

I didn't think much of my assignment at first. I was fairly young in my career, if you want to call it that, and treated this case like any other. But then, when I went through their profile, something caught my eye. There were some cat hybrids among this family, two to be exact. And of those, one intrigued me. She looked like me, but there was something about her I couldn't turn away from. She was much younger at the time, but even at that age, the allure that radiated from her showed. I was compelled to learn more about her, and was eager to fulfill my assignment.

I visited that house in Primm several times throughout her life, and she had no idea I existed. I made sure to keep my distance as Lionel instructed.

They lived in an isolated house off some beaten path with no neighbors, no law enforcement, nothing. Getting around Primm was easy enough. Lionel had developed what he called a personal porter. It teleported me to a single programmed teleportation station, something Lionel called the rally point. Thus, whenever I went to Primm, I got there by conventional means, but when I was done, I was able to teleport to HORUS's own teleportation station, our rally point. It made half the trip easier.

I watched the family grow in age over the years. Iris was becoming a beautiful creature. From what I observed, she was a gentle one. Sometimes I'd watch her sit on her front porch, looking at the sky. I wondered what she was thinking, probably of a life outside her home. She looked lonely. She had a brother who was like her, a cat hybrid. But I could tell he didn't understand her pain. He cared for her, and would protect her, but that didn't mean he knew what she was going through.

It was during these times, I felt connected to her. We were kindred in a way. Both of us have been sheltered from the outside world, living underground like monsters, both of us yearned to be free. I like working for Lionel, don't get me wrong, but the prettiest cages are still cages in the end.

Lionel had a particular interest in her, too. He kept saying she was special, but I never understood what he meant. There were times when I tried to convince him to let me get her. I wanted to meet her, to tell her there was someone like her, someone who could relate. She wasn't safe in Primm, and if Lionel thought she was so important, she had to be protected. Yet, he objected. He said that her specialness would safeguard her, that my interference would frighten them, and that no good could become of it. I disagreed vehemently, but he assured me no harm would happen to her. Lionel hadn't failed me before, so I trusted him.

Still, I looked forward to the day when Iris and I would meet.

Then, many years later, something happened. Maya Lawton died and that alerted the Alliance of our existence. Tiago Lawton had no idea that by tipping off his brother Leonard's location, he unleashed Pandora's Box. The response was predictable. It was called Operation Halfkinds. A team of United Species Alliance hired squad members came to Primm with the goal of eliminating mother Lawton's children, and, unfortunately, that included Iris.

Once again, I was given the order to watch, but not intervene. I pleaded with Lionel to let me save them, but he refused. He knew they had no chance, but he wanted to test his experiment. For years, he let Maya raise these children while he raised us at HORUS. He was confident that if we were in their shoes, if the operatives were after us, we, Lucy and I, would come out triumphant thanks to our years of developing our skills. He wondered how Maya's parenthood would help her children survive. To him, these hybrids weren't his own, just something to toy with.

Except Iris. He was particularly interested in how she would do. He talked all those years about her specialness, and now it was time to see how special she really was. Lionel was sure that she would survive and her ability would help her get to safety. I was sure he had gone off the deep end. How could one defenseless hybrid possibly hope to outlive this assault from a trained team of soldiers? How could he gamble her life as if he was watching some kind of game being played?

I wanted to disobey, to help Iris at the very least. But I didn't. I was still in debt to the years of care that Lionel provided. I slunk around the shadows, and watched the carnage unfold without anyone knowing. I witnessed death after death as the Lawtons were killed mercilessly. I begrudgingly followed Lionel's orders, but if Iris died, it would be the last straw. And amazingly, he was right. In the end, through a remarkable sequence of events, she made it. She was the lone survivor and, like vapors into the air, she disappeared with Fenrir Snow the next night.

I did a sweep to clear out any evidence that the USASD might find about HORUS, though it was hard to be thorough on such a limited timeline. I then teleported back to headquarters and took a few months to prepare my briefing for Lionel. He seemed disappointed that Iris slipped away, but delighted she was alive. Now that Iris had no family and nowhere to go, Lionel wanted her to come where she belonged, in HORUS's facilities. He said Iris had outgrown what she learned in Primm, and it was time for him to personally study her. He's always had big plans for her, and she was released from Maya Lawton's clutches. We didn't need to get her here immediately, especially when the heat was still on her. But as long as she was safe, we would find her, no matter where she ran off to.

Almost three years later, I've finally found you, Iris Lawton. I've been waiting for this day for quite some time. HORUS never lost track of her location; let's just say we've been aware of it for some time. We have many connections, and figuring out where Iris was hiding wasn't too difficult. The only thing we needed to determine was when would we strike. We wanted to do it about a year ago, but her roommate, Fenrir Snow, had attracted too much attention once the cat got out of the bag, so to speak. With his betrayal and the failure of Operation Halfkind leaking out, we decided to call off our plans until the dust settled. Some time passed and eventually they forgot about Fenrir. The ruckus died. With him and Iris living untouched in the woods for a while, it was time to act.

It was a simple kidnapping mission. Once Fenrir was away from Iris, I'd swoop in, hit her with the knockout serum, and teleport back to the rally point, HORUS headquarters.

Nabbing her didn't seem to be difficult, getting to her was another story. I had to trek endless miles through dangerous Wolf's Den territory to get to the cabin. That meant teleporting to the a teleportation station, then going into the forest on foot to where they dwelled. The closest teleportation station was in a small town called Landin, which was still forty or so miles away from Iris's possible location.

And while doing all of this, I had to keep a low profile. I was covered up, concealing my face and body. Wolves aren't known for being hospitable creatures. They'd probably attack a freak like me without warning, so I had to find the most remote teleportation station receiver out there, so no soul would be encountered. Receivers work nonstop and I could arrive anytime. It was a matter of picking the right moment.

Luckily, when I arrived to the Wolf's Den, no one was nearby. I made my way towards the outskirts, into the woods. I equipped my air gliders, gravitational boots used to aid traveling long distances on foot. These allowed me to hover in the air and surf a few feet above ground. It wasn't exactly flying, but I didn't need to fly for this task, I only needed to get there.

The woods were quiet and uninhabited. I was in the desolate wild of Northern Canada, away from any populated city, so I didn't expect to see anything. But, about ten miles in, I sensed I wasn't alone. I heard noises about one hundred meters away from me. It wasn't the mindless chatter of an unintelligent animal. These things were communicating with each other, in a language I didn't recognize.

I immediately took the high ground, up a tree, and put on my surveillance gear to take a look around. I had x-ray lenses, noise amplifiers on my ears, even motion sensors at the base of the tree. I tweaked the settings on my equipment and homed in on my target. From my x-ray goggles, I could see four quadrupeds talking to each other. I couldn't discern what they were, just grey blurs. But then I put on my noise amplifiers and heard them speak. They were barking, growling, deep tones and rough sounds. There was no doubt about it, they were wolves.

But what were they doing out here? There were a million possibilities, but only one real explanation - they were out to get Fenrir Snow. The Brotherhood lost some power within the Alliance thanks to his actions, and they don't take such losses lightly.

But if they found Fenrir, they would find Iris. And if they found Iris, she would be dead, or captured. This was unacceptable. I needed to get to Iris before they did. My mission would be executed more swiftly than I anticipated. I had to run in and grab her, I didn't have time to talk to her.

I made my way to the cabin at an incredible pace, but the wolves were just as fast. It became a race of who could get there first. These wolves had tenacity. I climbed over trees, jumped back on the ground, used all my skills to get there in time. But as fast as I went, the wolves were right near me.

We arrived at the cabin around the same time, and to my surprise, they didn't go in guns blazing. They waited around, like a predator stalking its prey. Iris wasn't alone, Fenrir Snow was with her. That meant I couldn't run in and grab her, unless I wanted to go toe to toe with the wolf. And judging from what I read on his profile, it most likely wouldn't end so well for me. I figured if the wolves hunting him were patient, then I should be too.

So, I waited as they waited. They had no idea I was nearby, exactly like all those Alliance idiots had no idea I was around them during Operation Halfkinds. Fenrir stepped out of the cabin and these wolves still waited. They split themselves up and eyed him and Iris cautiously, but did not strike. Iris was alone in her home, it would have been the perfect opportunity to get her had it not been for all this outside interference.

Fenrir came back, and it was at this time the other wolves finally took action. They sent one of their teammates out into the forest to draw him away. He took the bait and went after the stray wolf. The rest were preparing to either go after him or into the cabin. I couldn't let them get near Iris, so I had to go forward with my plan. It's do or die time now.

I step out into the light from my concealment and stand to the side of the entrance of Iris's dwelling. I'm well aware that the wolves can see me, but I don't care. Once I get Iris and teleport away, there won't be anything for them to find.

I creep up near the rear window. Fortunately for me, Iris has been distracted in the front by a small animal that was messing around in the bushes. I open the window and slip in. Her back is facing me, and she has no idea what is behind her.

This is too easy. I take out my containment blaster and aim at her. An energy net should spray out of the gun and strap her to the ground. Then, a simple tranquilizer will put her to sleep while I get us out of here.

Before I shoot, I take one last look at her. She has no idea what is about to happen, or who I am, but I've known her most of her life. I thought of all those times I yearned to find someone like me, and now, finally after years of waiting, I'll get to introduce myself. A hint of excitement fills my body. I've been looking forward to this moment for a long, long time. She's coming home.

Sorry about this, Iris, I think to myself.

With a squeeze of the trigger, the net blasts open and forces her to the ground. She struggles mightily, but it's no use. Not even a rhino with enhance muscle strengtheners could burst out of that. It's pure energy, used to withstand forces beyond what a living organism can dish out.

She cries for help, and it makes me uncomfortable. I hope I haven't hurt her. I take out another gun, a tranquilizer, and shoot one into her neck. Her screams stop, she's out cold. The energy net disables and I haul her over my shoulder. The personal porter is a watch-like device that wraps around my wrist. I program a few adjustments and it activates. I make one quick call to headquarters to let them know I'm coming in. The personal porter then starts its process. A blinding light hits my eyes and, in a flash, Iris and I are thousands of miles away from the Wolf's Den.

I'm in a teleportation pod, HORUS's own custom one located in our transportation bay. I follow a series of tunnels that lead to our gym. I walk to the exit, the door slides open, and Lionel's already there to greet me and my package.

He's very excited to meet Iris. We all are.

Chapter 7 - Iris Lawton

Arrival

May 5, 3043 8:12 AM

I had a dream a few days ago. I felt out of place. Not in the sense that I was lost. Well, actually, I was literally lost because I didn't know where I was. Things looked familiar to me, but I couldn't put my finger on it. It wasn't about not recognizing my physical surroundings. And it wasn't about feeling like I belonged. I was in a forest. I've lived in the woods so long that I felt welcomed by any place like this, but not this time. No, this went beyond the location of my body, it was about the location of my mind.

The dream was an out of body experience. I couldn't move with my own free will. I wasn't controlling my limbs, they were being controlled for me. I was simply a passenger in a vessel, an observer looking through the eyes of someone else. Their point of view was my point of view. I could not feel what it was feeling, I could only see and hear. I was looking into a window of this beast's consciousness. Yet, what I saw was very familiar. It was a quadruped. I rarely ever had my head down so low, only when I crawled. And as I observed what this thing was doing, I saw that it had a solid coat of fur on its legs. I could only see the front ones, but I could tell they were strong. The muscle definition showed through the fur.

I tuned into what this thing was doing. From my point of view, it had its head buried toward the ground, grazing its face on the dirt. It took heavy breaths, coming out at rapid fire. It's as if the creature wasn't breathing, rather smelling. Or to be more accurate, sniffing.

"Damnit!" the animal growled, its voice coarse and raspy.

It scared me, but as I replayed it in my mind, I realized that I recognized that scowl. This host was familiar, and with my observations, it became very clear who it was. Fenrir! I was looking into his mind.

What was my friend doing? And how was it possible that I could see what he was seeing? Was I hallucinating? Was my mind playing tricks on me? At the time, I didn't know if I was awake or asleep.

I did think of the other possibility, that this was a vision. Perhaps I was looking into the future. But right then, I was holding on to my consciousness. I didn't have the clarity that I would have if I was fully awake. Usually my visions came to me only when I was alert.

Also, my visions never came in this variety. It was always in flashes, quick, detailed instances that attached to my memories. This was different, things were too spacey, too opaque for me to understand what was going on. And the visions have always been through my point of view, not someone else's. This wasn't normal, it was weird.

Fenrir's frustrated voice broke my hazy concentration.

"Where could she have gone? They couldn't have taken her far," he said to himself. Who is he talking about? And who took who from whom? He said she, the only she he would be referring to would be… me.

Images flashed through my head. I remembered everything. The empty cabin, falling to the ground and feeling pinned there. The footsteps, the sharp pinch on my neck, and that gray blur standing above me. I must have been kidnapped, and now Fenrir was desperately looking for my trail.

But why was I looking into this event now? Where was my body? Was I dead? Everything was so confusing.

I heard him yell in frustration once more.

"This is pointless, I have no idea where she is," he said despondently. "I only picked up a faint scent, nothing more. I could be following this road to nowhere for days. Iris, where are you?"

I've never seen that side of him before. Fenrir has always been a model of strength and bravery. His voice is sturdy, his confidence is assured. Yet at that moment, I saw a weakness, no, a sadness, that broke my heart. My friend was in pain. He was on the brink because he was worried about me. Our friendship meant that much, so much that it fractured his cast iron exterior.

I wanted to reach out to him, to tell him that things would be okay.

"Fenrir!" I yelled. "I'm okay! I'm a bit confused, but I'm in one piece. Don't be sad…!"

And at that moment, a recognizable rush came to me. My head felt like it was swelling and what I saw in front of me became muddled. Colors blended and shapes swayed, but in a matter of seconds, they reformed into something clear. It was an experience I knew too well. I was having a vision.

I was back in my body, looking through my own eyes. I couldn't control myself, but I observed my hands to make sure it was me, and the tiny hint of orange fur gave it away. Yup, it was me.

Before me stood a man and two creatures that looked very familiar. The man was middle-aged and wore a silver lab coat. It was really shiny, and I wondered if he was a doctor. He was Caucasian and had a curious look on his face. He also had a tablet and electropen in his hands for note taking. That's all I could gather from my quick glimpse.

The other two reminded me of my siblings. One appeared to be a chimp-human, very similar to how Candy looked. The other one was like me, kind of. It wasn't identical, and it looked like a male, but he was a half-cat, half-human creature. Only he wasn't orange, he was grey, like something I had seen before…

… the blur. It was him!

Why wasn't I panicking? Why wasn't I freaking out? I mean, my kidnapper stood in front of me, yet in this vision, I remained perfectly calm. I didn't get it.

"Where am I?" myself in the vision asked.

"You're in our headquarters," the man answered. "It's located in the outskirts of the Bay Area, probably fifteen miles from San Francisco."

An audible ringing hit my ears, and in a split second, the vision was gone. For a while, I saw nothing in front of me but darkness. While my out of body experience with Fenrir and my episode seeing the future was somewhat lucid, I went back to my state of haze and blur. Time lost its meaning and I was bombarded with images. I saw flashes and memories of my siblings, Tiago and Isaac, Oscar, Maddie, Leonard, Candy, Alex, Ace, Lombardi, and Curtis. The small cabin I called home floated by in my consciousness, as did the moment when Apollo Bradley had his gun to my head. And I saw Fenrir, seemingly lost in the woods looking for a missing me.

A light hits my face and my eyes open. The white glare leaks through my pupils and I squint to adjust to the brightness. I shake my head as I become more and more awake with every second. I feel that I'm lying down, on a reclined bed. I try to move my arms and legs, but I can't. Something's holding them down, and as I tilt my head, I see straps fastened tightly around my wrists and ankles. I'm pinned. I shake my arms and legs violently, but these straps are made out of woven kevlafabric. It's no use.

Now fully awake and slightly defeated, I look around at my surroundings. The floors are white, the walls are white, and the ceiling is white. The room is mostly empty and everything looks as clean as can be. There appears to be some medical equipment to the right of my bed and some automatic doors in front of me. There are no windows, though I feel like I'm being watched. I take some time to absorb what I see, but after a while, I know where I am. Though it was brief, this is the room from my vision.

The door slides open and three bodies walk through it. I glimpse them briefly, but it's pointless, I already know what they look like.

There's the human, an older man with his tablet and electropen, wearing the same shimmering lab coat that I saw earlier. He's slightly bald, but other than that looks healthy enough. He's rather average looking, not too handsome, but not too ugly by human standards. The skin on his face is smooth and well shaved, and his hair is a cool silver color. Judging from his appearance, he's probably approaching his century mark.

Then there's the chimp halfkind, the one who looks like Candy. Her look is feminine enough for me to know she isn't a male. Her attire gave her away. Her face is hairy, like Candy's, and her locks are long and flowing, like my sister's. She wears a skirt and has some sheik looking footwear. This chimp halfkind is as fashionable as Candy. She has a different edge to her, however. While Candy's choice of clothing was trendy and fun, this one's is professional and proper. Everything is crisp and straightened to perfection.

She has glasses and presents herself in a serious, almost cold demeanor. Her overall look is neatly put together. And her facial expressions are icy. You could tell Candy's exuberance for life with one glance, but on this one, I see nothing.

Finally, there is my abductor. He's half-cat alright, like me, but he's dressed in tactical gear. He must be some kind of special agent or something, and he certainly looks like he's come back from a kidnapping mission. He's tall and lean, and has big yellow eyes. He has pointed ears, yet he's bipedal and I can clearly see his hands. There appears to be a human sidearm on his hip, but it's hard to tell what kind of weapon it is. He's slightly more "cat" than I am. His demeanor is different from the chimp halfkind. While she looks all business, he looks anxious at my sight. He doesn't seem like the dark menacing blur that snatched me from my cabin, he almost looks gentle. Yet I won't let my eyes deceive me. I remain suspicious of him because he's the reason why I'm here.

The three of them look at me from the other side of the room. I stare back at them as an intense silence fills the air. This goes on for a while, and I become uncomfortable with three sets of eyes fixated on me. I look away.

Finally, one of them speaks. Thank goodness.

"What are we, a prison?" the man asks the other two. "Let's get these restraints off our invitee. But don't start a riot, Ms. Lawton. Any rash actions may require Bastion to demonstrate his skills."

He says it in a deep voice and hearty disposition, like a host entertaining a guest. I didn't expect him to have such a casual attitude. Yet he throws his threat at me so calmly that it sends a chill down my spine. The other two look at him calmly. The one that looks like me walks over to my restraints, and glides a transmitting device over it. The cuffs snap open and I am free.

I could've made a break, but I'm too scared to do anything. Even if I tried to dash, these three would overpower me, and I have no idea what dangers loom outside this room. So I sit steady, and hope that these creatures don't hurt me.

"How do you feel?" the man asks.

"I have a huge headache," I say, clutching my forehead.

"That's probably a side effect of the sedative," the man says. "Getting you was no easy task. It tested the limits of my child's, Bastion's, capabilities. But enough of that, let me introduce myself. I'm Lionel Changer, the founder of the fine organization that you're among, the Human Organization Reestablishing Untainted Society. These are my children, so to speak, Lucy and Bastion. I believe you've already met Bastion."

"Yes," I respond with a stark tone and heated eyes directed to Bastion. "You said children? You birthed them?"

"Not in the literal sense, but it was by my hand that they were created. In fact, to a lesser extent, you're my child too."

"What?" I say in disbelief.

"You see, our organization, HORUS as we call it, is what created your kind. You, your brothers and sisters, Lucy, Bastion, all hybrids exist thanks to my work with HORUS. If it wasn't for me, none of you would be here today."

"Hybrids?"

"I say hybrids, you say halfkinds."

"So, you're the reason why my mother was able to give birth to us?"

"Indeed. You sure are a smart one, Iris."

I never knew everything about my mother's past. I knew she was a prostitute, and I knew somehow she did the impossible and gave birth to us. I always wondered what made her unique, why she could do what others couldn't, but I never pressed her on it. As a teenager, it's awkward to confront your mother about this stuff. I didn't want to stir up any bad memories, so I left things unanswered. After Lionel's revelation, now I know.

"When your mother was younger, she was an extremely poor and desperate woman," he continues. "She needed some quick cash. We found her and determined she'd be the perfect candidate for our birthing implants, so she volunteered for the process and was rewarded with a nice sum of creds. She was already in the murky business of servicing non-humans. All she needed to do was collect samples, to put it nicely. She did her job, and we gave her the tools to collect what we wanted, the sperm, to be frank. We then used those samples to artificially inseminate her. The other prostitutes worked in the same manner."

"Artificially inseminate? I always thought it was done the old fashioned way, even though I don't want to imagine it," I say.

"Neither do we. I suppose because of their profession, you just assumed it to be so. How the prostitutes got their 'samples' we'll leave to them. They had the clientele and the motives to do so without raising any suspicion from the law or the Alliance."

"So, they weren't really prostitutes, but rather sperm collectors?"

"In a sense, yes, but they still had to prostitute in order to maintain our anonymity. If we had gone into the world and extracted the samples ourselves, the Alliance would no doubt rain fire on us."

He takes a brief moment to clear his throat.

"To answer the grand question, we artificially inseminated the host bodies," he says. "Copulation the natural way would be impossible with certain species. I mean, you've seen your brothers. An eagle and a human conceiving the old fashioned way? Don't be silly. Not even the wildest imaginations could figure out how that would work. It's icky business that I don't want to sully my hands in."

My mind goes to the nether region.

"I'm going to throw up just thinking about it," I say.

"You and me both," he says. "Anyway, back to the main point, we only wanted your mother's offspring, so once she gave birth to some human hybrids, we would sweep up the results. That's how it went with the other prostitutes. They deliver, we collect."

I look at the chimp hybrid Lucy, and the cat one, Bastion. If what Changer says is true, then my mother was part of this hybrid, halfkind baby mill.

"So, Lucy and Bastion, is it? You two are products of this process?" I ask them.

"Correct," Lucy says.

"Where were you raised?"

"They were raised here, within HORUS's walls," Changer interjects. "Like you should have been."

"I should have been?" I ask.

"Yes," he responds. "You see, of all the prostitutes in our little operation, none of them wanted to keep their children. We were very excited to have you all, but they were… unenthusiastic. The same was for your family. Your older brothers and sisters don't remember, but they actually spent some time here, as the protocol was for us to keep our products. However, the more children your mother had, the more she grew attached to them. We allowed her to be on the premise to interact with your brothers and sisters while you were infants. We even let her be the mother she wanted to be on our grounds. It was convenient for us, as the lab techs couldn't watch all of the hybrids beings produced, and we figured a mother's influence on the children would be positive. It was a peaceful co-existence. If things had gone to plan, she would've stayed within HORUS and given up the prostitution to be a den mother of sorts. We could have financed the life she wanted. But then something unexpected happened. You were born."

What does that mean? What did I do? From what he tells me, mother seemed to be happy under HORUS's roof. What about my birth changed all this?

"Excuse me?" I ask him.

"You see Iris, right from the start, we knew you were special," he says. "And we wanted to study you as much as we could. Naturally, your mother was afraid we'd turn you into a science project, dissecting your brain the first chance we got. She was fearful for your life, so while she was still pregnant with your youngest brother, Leonard, she took you and your family away from our grasp and hid in seclusion."

"Wait, if my older siblings were here before, why have I never heard of it?"

"Most of your siblings were too young to remember. Except maybe Tiago, he was five when Maya left, but even then, it's hard to say what he would have recollected about HORUS. I'm also not sure what your mother kept under wraps."

I remember the time when Tiago told Leonard about Mom's prostitute past. He got the scolding of a life time.

"You might be right about that. Mom never wanted us to talk about it," I say. "What do you mean when you said she thought she was out of your grasp though?"

He looks over to the cat hybrid.

"Bastion over here has been keeping tabs on you most of your life, ever since you were around ten," he says. "We wanted to make sure your mother was taking good care of you specifically, and we wanted to see your potential bloom. We could've stormed the house and taken you whenever we wanted, but we refrained because it would have caused too much trauma. We knew your mother's care was vital in your development. So we left her alone and let her raise her family, all while watching from afar."

"You've been monitoring me my whole life?" I ask looking directly at Bastion. He looks dumbstruck by my question, and is unable to blurt out a response.

"Indeed he has," Changer says.

"Then where were you when my family was being slaughtered by the Alliance?" I say angrily. "If you were watching, you could've stepped in and saved some of us!"

Bastion again is unable to respond. But he does look ashamed by my question.

"I told him not to interfere," Changer says, answering for him again. "We needed to keep a low profile at all costs. Don't want the Alliance to follow a trail to our headquarters, you see. And to be honest, your family was expendable. They didn't have what you had, and I knew you would come out on top. Your uniqueness helped you survive. In a way, I wanted to test out your capabilities, and you passed with flying colors. You're here, after all, alive and healthy."

"You bastard!" I yell. "You let them die."

"They had nothing to offer," he says. "Except your sister Candy. It would've been nice to have another great mind."

The anger boils inside my body. I want to tear this mad man apart. Guilt and frustration looms over my head. All of it was my fault. Mother left HORUS because of me, and Changer only wanted me alive. He didn't care about the others, about my brothers and sisters, about Isaac…

I couldn't hold it in any longer.

"Why?!" I scream at him, tears rolling down my eyes. "Why me? What makes me so special?"

"Let's not beat around bush," Lucy says bluntly. "We know about precognitive abilities."

She has a distinct speaking style. It's short sentences and pauses at every word. Her speech pattern is fragmented, and she appears to not use articles.

"Ah, yes, you'll have to forgive me for Lucy's harsh attitude, she's very fact oriented. She's also very intelligent," he says. "In fact, she's the one who figured out your condition."

"Yes," Lucy responds. "From birth, noticed odd patterns in brainwaves. Unlike anything seen. Younger at time, teenager, but able to analyze what anomaly meant. After months of research, concluded distinctive genetic makeup gave latent psychic abilities, precognition. After discovery, alerted Lionel more tests needed to understand potential. Tests might have endangered physical health. Infant body not able to handle it."

"Naturally, your mother didn't like this idea," Changer interrupts. "This is why she took you away from us."

"Progression quite fascinating," Lucy says. "Determined over past few days potential off charts."

"A few days?!" I say in a panic. "How long have I been out for?"

"Today is May 5th, been out since May 2nd, three days," Lucy says in a matter of fact tone. "Bastion gave strong tranquilizer."

I glare at Bastion with rage.

"You, how could you kidnap me like that?" I admonish. He doesn't say anything, and looks away from me shyly.

"It was the only way to bring you here," Changer says. "We've let you live with that wolf long enough. It was time to bring you home."

"How did I get here so fast?"

"I've developed technology on my own, far more advanced than what's on the market. I gave Bastion what I call a personal porter. Instead of going from station to station, the personal porter allows the user to directly port to a station from his or her location. Thus, after Bastion sedated you, he teleported to our personal station here at HORUS."

I feel helpless. With that kind of tech, we must be thousands of miles away from my home. But then I thought of him.

"Fenrir will come find me," I say. "And when he does, you'll have to deal with his wrath."

"Let him try," Changer says arrogantly. "The Alliance has been on our trail for years and they still don't have a clue where we are. I doubt your wolf friend is that good, and besides, what harm can one canine do?"

I suppose he's right. I'm probably stuck in the middle of nowhere, in some super-secret lair that can never be found. The fact that I may never see Fenrir again depresses me. I wish my friend was here, I'm scared. The once certain future I had has again been thrown into jeopardy. I change subjects to try to get my mind off my worries.

"So, what do you know about my powers?" I ask Lucy.

"Believe you have certain level of precognition," she responds.

"I could've told you that," I say sarcastically.

"Yes, but believe it has to do with genetic makeup. Notice trend that certain hybrids share similar traits. Example, I am chimp hybrid. Possess intelligence that far exceeds most humans or chimps. Do you know anyone like me?"

One name pops in my mind instantly.

"Candy," I say.

"Correct," Lucy says. "Chimp hybrids share trait of supreme intelligence. Noticed feline males possess characteristics of grace and speed. Counterpart Bastion is example."

"Or Ace," I say.

"Correct. Cheetah hybrid brother possessed similar traits."

"Wait, Isaac was a male feline hybrid, but he was anything but ultra-stealthy."

"Some excel more than others. But all possess potential to grow in individual areas."

I took a few moments to absorb the information.

"So, you think my psychic abilities are what female felines are given?" I ask.

"That is theory. However, do not know potential you have, need run more tests," she says.

"But you said they'll hurt me," I respond worriedly.

"Would have if still infant. Should be safe now."

"When you say potential, you mean there's more?"

"Correct. Precog abilities are sporadic? You cannot control them?"

It amazes me how much she knows without ever meeting me. I've known my brothers and sisters my entire life, and they hadn't figured out the things she did. She's definitely like Candy in the brains department.

"Yes, they happen at random," I say.

"I see," she says. "May be case now, but have potential to control with enough development. Chance of other abilities as well."

"Such as…?" I ask curiously.

"Theorize you can tap into others' psyches. If been around long enough, might absorb brainwaves emit. Ever experienced anything like that? Seeing through something else's consciousness?"

The dream. I was able to look through Fenrir's eyes so clearly. That had to be what Lucy is talking about. He was looking for me in that vision, and if I've really been out cold the whole time, it's possible I had that vision while I was asleep. I saw what he was seeing at that exact moment in time.

"No, I've never experienced anything like that," I lie. I want to understand the true nature of my powers before I give any kind of information.

"Unfortunate," Lucy says in a disappointed tone. "Certain calculations correct. Suppose you haven't developed that stage. Too bad, saw potential for other talents."

"Really? Like what?"

"Psychic communication, transmitting precognitive abilities."

I then thought of the other vision I had. In it, I saw myself sitting in a chair in a room much like this, speaking with a group of humans and hybrids much like this one. That was my future-telling powers at work. I saw this very moment.

Sometimes I wonder when I see a vision and I don't act on it, what will happen. In that vision, I asked where I was. But if I don't ask that question, is it really the future? Can I change it, or is it impossible? I've always been too much of a chicken to find out, and I'm tempted to keep my mouth shut.

Yet, Lucy mentioned that I'm getting new powers. I already had that out of body experience earlier. Somehow I psychically linked up with Fenrir. And I thought about the other things she mentioned. Could I really gain psychic capabilities along with my precognitive ones? And was there a way to combine the two?

Maybe that's why I had that vision where I asked about my location. Perhaps my subconscious was telling me that it's important to ask. It might help me in the end. I can't explain it, but I feel it's something I must do.

"Can I ask you all something?" I say.

"Sure," Changer says.

"Where am I?"

He looks at me peculiarly. The question is out of the blue, and he probably suspects I'm up to something. But like in my vision, he relents.

"You're in our headquarters," he answers. "It's located in the outskirts of the Bay Area, probably fifteen miles from San Francisco."

"Why do you want to know?" Bastion asks suspiciously. Finally he says something.

"It's okay, Bastion," Changer assures him. "There's no harm in telling. Anyway, we've had a lot of time to talk. Bastion has brought you a bag with a change of clothes and some breakfast. I'd advise you to dress and eat your food, we have a long day ahead of us. We'll leave you to your things and come back in half an hour."

"Hold on!" I say as I run to the door, but it shuts in my face. I'm alone. I take some time to think about what's happened. I've been captured by this renegade group, the cabin that was home and wolf I called my friend may be a distant memory forever.

Fenrir, I hope you heard me.

Chapter 8 - Fenrir Snow

Envy

May 2, 3043 2:02 PM

I've been at it for almost thirty minutes and haven't found much. No blood, no fur, no nothing, only some small holes on the floor and the door wide open just as I had left it. Iris is nowhere to be found.

Where could she have gone? If someone abducted her, it wouldn't have been so clean. The cabin was literally the same as it was when I left. And I taught her things. Even though she wasn't a hardened soldier like me, she would have at least put up a decent fight. Yet I found nothing to suggest it. It's like she vanished into thin air.

The only thing that I can use is this foreign scent I picked up. It's a very faint smell, but it's enough to latch onto a trail. It won't be easy to follow something so thin, but it's the only lead I have. I don't recognize who it is, yet it's definitely not one of my brothers or sister. No, this smell wasn't wolf at all, it was something else. In a way, it almost smells like Iris, but a little grimier than her strangely flowery essence.

The trace went out the back window, away from Fang and the others. Before I embarked on my quest, I went to check on their status.

They're all knocked out cold from my stun shots. It should keep them sedated for at least a few hours, which will give me an adequate head start. When they wake up, they'll eventually track me down again. Even if I hide my scent, it won't be good enough. They were raised to be the best, like me, and there are four of them. There's no way I can lose them without preparation, I can only hope to distance myself.

I go back to Fang and check on her health. I'm not too worried about my brothers because they were only hit with stuns, but my sister suffered a flesh wound when her shot reflected back at her. If the shot seared off enough flesh, it could be infected, which would be quite dangerous in a remote place like this.

The wound on her leg is blackened and smoking. It looks quite serious, and I must commend her on her toughness. She barely complained when the blast hit. Her shots were meant to kill, and if they had been fired at a closer range, it's quite possible her foot would've been blown off completely. I'll do what I can to bandage it.

They're after me, and they're not holding back, but that doesn't mean I'm not their older brother. Even though we have our differences, I'm hoping that it's only temporary, that I can convince them to get off this warpath. I don't want it to be family versus family fighting until the death. I may have done some things that have damaged the Snow legacy, but I will not end the Snows permanently. I am their brother and I must take care of them.

I go back into the cabin and with my teeth grab an emergency kit I have stored. I trot back to where Fang lies, set the box down, and press a button on the top. It folds open and an array of medical supplies are at my disposal. I can't heal Fang's wound completely, but I can, at the very least, prevent any infection. I just need to apply some medigel and put a bandage over the wound. That should kill any bacteria and help the area heal faster.

I take a swabbing cloth and use my teeth to grab the medigel capsule. With one squeeze, the gel squirts onto the cloth and I pick it up, making sure the gel doesn't make contact with my nose. I put the cloth to Fang's wounded area so that the medigel is heavily applied. I then snatch a retracting bandage from the kit and place it gently over the applied area. I lightly wrap my jaws around the bandage, which is around Fang's leg, and softly bite down to tighten it. I step back and take a look. Her leg has been treated, and a part of me is glad that I did something to help.

I quickly grab the kit and tuck it away in our cabin. With my brothers and sister neutralized, I direct my attention back to my search. I have the faint scent on my nose, and I decide my only shot is to follow it. It may lead me to where Iris and the kidnapper are. I follow the trail, which points me outside and away from the cabin. It could take me on a chase that may last miles, leading me far away from this place I've called home. This cabin will be a memory. With one look back, I think of Iris and say goodbye.

Many things run through my mind as I start my journey, the first being my family. I was very shocked when I encountered them. So much information had been dropped on me at one time. I didn't know my family had been in such dire straits, and I certainly wasn't aware that the Brotherhood excommunicated them. I was even more surprised that they wanted me dead.

I never thought there'd be a day when I'd be their target. My, how these times are strange. If I had known how rock bottom they had been, I would've helped them. I suppose I haven't been a very good brother since Eve died. I left them on their own to go on my death wish, mission hunt. Before, I was practically their mentor, the leader of the Snow family, the prodigy. All that changed in an instant. I couldn't deal with the loss and had to be left alone. I was selfish.

It got even worse after Operation Halfkinds. I completely abandoned them. I cut off communication and disowned everything the Brotherhood had taught me. Their values, their beliefs, meant nothing to me. I finally realized I was being used, the anger I felt over Eve's death was a weapon the Brotherhood wielded to control my actions. And if I was to go into hiding, I had to cut all ties, including my own blood. I knew it was something they would never understand, so I spared them the trouble and disappeared.

But I didn't know the Brotherhood would punish our whole family. After our confrontation, I now know I'm the reason the Snow name is has gone through turmoil. My selfishness has caused their grief. I made my choice, I chose Iris, but, in hindsight, was that the right one? I'm truly sorry for what I did, brothers, and I'm truly sorry to you, Fang.

I think of how Fang looked when I bandaged her. Even in a state of rest, she had that scowl on her face. Fang and I have always had a strained relationship. My brothers idolized me before I left, but Fang hated me from the start. I knew it was because she was jealous of what I had. I could do things that she couldn't, and I carried my talents around as if I was both blessed and cursed.

Fang thought I was ungrateful for my gifts and, in a sense, I was. My family had always prided ourselves on what we could offer the Brotherhood, and I was the one who could do the most for them. Like any good son, I was happy to make my family proud, but at the same time, as things became easier and easier, I lost the drive. I became bored with my work. As often happens with routine, I started to question what I was doing. Was this all my life would be? Was I going to be an errand boy for the Brotherhood forever?

Fang on the other hand desperately wanted that honor. Just like how I became full from oversaturation, Fang became hungrier and hungrier the more she had to live in my shadow. She was the second oldest, but the only female. She wanted to prove herself, but it was hard to do with a brother like me getting all the good assignments. This fueled her resentment.

I remember she worked so hard to make herself stand out, but she couldn't. She was, and still is, an excellent tracker and top-notch fighter, but she doesn't have the innate talent that I do. No matter how hard she trained and how much she educated herself, she couldn't get over the fact that I was better than her.

I remember one particular time she was working out. This was long before I left the family. She trained by tying weights to a sled and ran through the snow for hours. I joined her on one of those sessions. I hadn't been keeping my cardio up as much as she had, but I could manage. She did those kinds of exercises seven days a week for months, maybe even years. Yet, despite all her work, I outran and lasted longer than her. By the time she was ready to pass out, I wasn't even breathing hard. She looked at me in a tired state, with envious eyes as she lay defeated on the ground.

"How do you do it, Fenrir?" she asked.

"Do what?" I ask, pretending not to know what she's talking about.

"How do you run miles and miles in the harsh winter, with probably sixty to seventy pounds on your back and not feel like you're going to die?"

"I don't know, I guess it comes natural. But I'm not special or anything, I mean I think any one of us could do it."

My attempts to be humble annoyed her even more.

"Don't give me that crap!" she yelled at me sternly as she panted for air. "I've been at this… for months… and I'm still not close to you."

"Don't be so hard on yourself, sister," I said.

"It's not fair."

"What's not fair?"

I knew the answer, but I played dumb. I didn't want to rub it in her face. Fang looked at me sharply, trying to figure out my intentions.

"Just forget it," she said as she walked away coldly. Those kinds of interactions were the only ones I had with Fang.

I'm about fifteen miles into my mission, sniffing through the dirt. Unfortunately, the scent becomes harder and harder to identify with all the underbrush distracting my senses. I'm growing frustrated by the amount of focus I have to put into it.

"Where could she have gone!?" I say angrily as Iris floats in my mind. "This is pointless, I have no idea where she is. I only picked up a faint scent, nothing more. I could be following this road to nowhere for days. Iris, where are you?"

I pick up my spirits and continue on the trail. I think of Fang once again. The only time she let her jealousy go was when Eve died. It was a few days after Eve passed, and I was in mourning at home. I had been alone for four days straight and, to my surprise, Fang visited me with some food, her gesture to console me. But I was too heartbroken to let her in.

She rang the bell and scratched on the door for about thirty minutes, but I never came. The only thing I did was watch from the inside on the screen of my intercom, while she relentlessly tried to get me out. I wanted to go, but it was too much to deal with. I needed to be alone. Eventually she got tired, dropped the food on my doorstep, and left. But before she was out of my view, I saw her turn around and look at the door with the concern I didn't know she was capable of having.

I know it took a lot for my sister to do those small things. Looking back now, I wish I had opened the door for her and let her in. Maybe that trivial act could've changed the course of our relationship. But I guess it's too late... it's too late for a lot of things.

The Snows are engaged in a civil war, and my siblings and I are on opposite sides.

I'm finally near a dead end. About twenty to thirty meters away is a teleportation station. I had a feeling all roads would point to this.

"What do I do now?" I say to myself.

I can wait until off hours to use the teleportation station or perhaps sneak in and activate it. That's not the problem. The problem is figuring out where to go. The assailant used this station to travel from his home. That's where Iris is. If I was in the Brotherhood, I'd have access to the station's destination and arrivals log. But I'm a wanted fugitive, and my privileges have been revoked for a long, long time. There's no way I'd be able to figure out where the kidnapper ported to without giving myself up.

Then, something strange happens to me. I feel this odd sensation in my head, like someone is watching me. No it's more like someone is looking through my eyes. I can't really explain what it is, and it never happened to me before, but it's oddly familiar.

Suddenly, I feel a sharp jolt hit my brain. I close my eyes and when I open them, I'm not longer in the forest. I'm somewhere else, in a lab I think. White walls are everywhere. The room is well-lit, so much that I take some time to adjust. I see three blurry figures in front of me and, as my eyesight clears, I realize it's a man and two other creatures. Candy Lawton, is that you? And is that Isaac? No it can't be, this one has a grey tint to his fur. These are completely different beings.

I also realize I'm frozen. I see things clearly, as if I was looking through my own eyes, but when I try to move my legs, nothing happens. I feel paralyzed. And then I see it, below me are a set of hands. Hands, on a wolf. This is impossible. Where was I? What happened to my body?

Before I go into a full force panic, I look at the arms, and I recognize them right away. They're human like, but with an orange color of fur. I only know one creature like that. Iris. This was her body.

How did this happen? And knowing Iris, it wasn't about where I am, but rather it's about when I am.

"Where am I?" I hear a familiar voice ask. It's her.

"You're in our headquarters," the man answers. "It's located in the outskirts of the Bay Area, probably fifteen miles from San Francisco."

And as quickly as it happened, my vision goes black and I open my eyes, only to see the Canadian landscape in front of me. The teleportation station is still meters ahead. I'm back to where I started.

I stand there unmoving, unsure how to react to what has happened. Was I dreaming? No, because I wasn't sleeping. That doesn't happen to me. I think of the other possibility. I know she had these kinds of visions, but I wonder, Iris, are you responsible for this? Is this where you want me to go?

With no other clues to guide me, I take it as a sign from her. I don't know how she did it, but I think I saw one of her visions. I can only go on my suspicions and have nothing to back up my claim, but I have faith it was Iris.

The Bay Area, here I come.

Chapter 9 - Brock West

Prep

May 7, 3043 4:00 PM

"All right, fellas, I hope you got a good night's rest, because today is the day," I say. "Operation Horus is officially commencing."

We left the Bay Area Alliance Headquarters thirty minutes ago and we're on our way to our target. We should get there in fifteen minutes. The transport is a large armored hover tank capable of holding me, my crew, and any prisoners that we may capture on the way. The team arrived in San Francisco at different times, but they've been briefed and are ready to go.

They're my team, I've led them on countless missions through thick and thin. They've got my back, and I've got theirs. We're known as Company Manticore because we're one unit comprised of different animals. And I like it that way. If you have a team of only humans, they're limited by their human proficiencies. But a team as diverse as this is versatile on so many levels. We can scout air, land, and get through a variety of obstacles thanks to our adaptability. There are nine of us and each has a role to play.

The transport hits rough winds through mountainous terrain. We're in the heart of the forest. The base is somewhere in the middle of the woods on the outskirts of town, underground, hidden away from big city life. The fading sun tells me it'll be getting dark in a few hours. No houses anywhere. Good. I don't want any idiot civilians getting in my way.

Grodd Arbock is our pilot. He's a gorilla, a big one at that, but I suppose they're all big. And yes, there's a lion on our team, but the Gorilla Lion Conflict ended two years ago, and our team has worked together for years. Their allegiance to their kind is a non issue.

Arbock is built like a brick, muscles bulging through his fur, nice thick frame, and powerful arms. But that's not important. When you have a pilot, all that matters is that he can fly. Arbock has the reflexes of a fox, and I've seen him dodge, maneuver, and bulldoze through obstacles piloting hunks of junks. If you give that beast anything that has a steering wheel, he'll get you to safety. I've been on these kinds of missions with him for probably eight years. He's a good soldier, obedient, and competent.

"We're almost there, Captain," he says to me. "When we arrive, where do you want me to land the hover tank?"

"Take it ten miles outside," I tell him. "They have sentries, but they don't patrol more than five miles away from their headquarters. Ten miles should stop us right before any traps or monitors they have set up. We'll proceed on foot and take out their defenses covertly and then proceed to their base."

"Sounds like a plan. Once you guys start, I'll wait until you're ready to be extracted."

Our vehicle lowers to stay hidden under the canopy of trees. As we descend closer to the ground, I make sure my crew is ready.

My first stop is Arrow Ingle, the eagle. A mouthful I know, but he's the master of scouts, vital to our operation. His flight gives us an edge over any air sentinels they may have. He's swift in the sky, and can see miles away, probably the most reliable pair of eyes

I've ever met. He'll catch stuff I missed in my detailed reports. If there's a last minute change or hidden trap that I didn't anticipate, you can be sure Ingle will find it.

He's currently perched up in a cubby, tinkering with some of his gear. He has a pair of sight amplifying goggles and some light weight razor wings, special design in order to let him glide through the air faster. He also has some talon shooters on his legs, energy cannons that will allow him to fire in flight, in case he needs it.

"You know the plan, right, Ingle?" I say.

"Sure," he says confidently. "While you guys set up post, I'll lookout ahead. I'll scrutinize, survey, and make sure nothing is out of the ordinary. I'll also set up some of those code scramblers on the locks so Kanji can uncrack their systems when you guys reach the entrance. I'm sure they won't notice a little old bird like me."

"Excellent. Their base is underground, so you'll have to have a sharp eye to locate the entrance," I say. "Don't let us down Ingle, we're counting on you."

"Don't worry boss, I got this."

He's one of two scouts. We have the air covered, but underground is a maze left to be investigated. The HORUS complex is built like of an intricate labyrinth of tunnels. I plan to split my team into two, one for a direct frontal assault, and a covert team that can infiltrate below. Luckily, I have a crocodile who's an expert on this kind of stuff, Joe Waylon.

"Waylon," I say as I approach where he lies. "How are your preparations going?"

He's on a compcube looking over some holographic schematics, and barely registered what I said. I don't mind, I love it when a soldier is well prepared. He glances up and sees that I'm there.

"Sorry, Captain," he says. "I was going over the underground plans, didn't see you come over."

"What did you find out about the facility?" I ask.

"There are several underground entry points that we can use to penetrate the HORUS complex. It shouldn't be difficult to get where we want. I must say, their security is impressive, but not good enough."

"You have the pseudo streams?

"Yes. We can remotely hack into their feeds and mask ourselves from them. They'll see a prerecorded loop. Even when we're in their server room, they won't know we're there. As a bonus, we'll be able to mask you from their feeds, too. There could be a war going on above ground, and they won't even notice it because they only have their screens to rely on. Unfortunately, you'll still have to fight through their defenses, those are automatically triggered."

"Not a problem, I love a good tussle."

We both smirk.

"The good news is that John's hacking program not only allows me to mask ourselves from their feed, but it also disables any security alerts. In other words, they won't know that their defenses have gone off, so everything will be right as rain from those inside of HORUS headquarters," Waylon says.

"Excellent. After you enter the server rooms, what do you plan to do?" I ask.

"More hacking. We can cripple their communications and information from there. Once we're done, we'll set up the EMP's on their hardware and detonate on your commands. Then we'll enter the compound and start blasting away."

"Remember, only EMP their servers. The drives are located inside, and we want to extract those. It's part of my secondary mission. I repeat, make sure it's just the servers. We need to get some sensitive info, and I don't want you to incinerate it. The Alliance will be raining fire on us if we do, so be careful."

Waylon looks at me a bit cautiously, as if he's afraid to fail. His insecurity annoys me slightly.

"Understood," he says shakily. "Obviously Clipper will be with me, but who else?"

"Winde," I say. "He's the tech chimp and will be executing most of the hacking protocols. I want him to check their data before you blow it. He will be second in command when I'm not around, and you will not act until he gives the signal. Do you copy that?"

"Of course. I'll continue with my preparations, then."

Eli Winde is a chimp and extremely smart, probably the most intelligent on my squad. Chimps have that reputation. Our strategist, Bill John, is sharp, but Winde is sharper. That's no knock on John, it's only that Winde is that good. And besides, their expertises are different. John's a tactical expert, Winde is a technological ace. The chimp's our field knowledge officer, the one who answers questions on site, during the mission, when I cannot. He's a fast learner and quick to boot, and we need someone like him in new terrain. He can analyze new technology and devices. Chimps are usually good with toys, and Winde is no exception.

"You're going to be paired up with Waylon and Clipper on the bravo assault while my team will do the frontal," I tell him. "I need you investigating those servers like we talked about earlier. I've told Waylon that he has to wait until your signal before he acts. He'll give you some time to check them out, but remember you're on a schedule. Do you recall what you're looking for?"

"Yes," Winde responds.

"I'm sure the information the Alliance wants is stored within the headquarters, but you never know where facts pop up. So scrub and dig into any technology before you discard it. If anything looks like something the Alliance needs, don't hesitate to copy and extract it, understood?"

He nods. Winde isn't exactly a talkative chimp, but I know he doesn't need to say much. He'll get the job done. The same can be said of all my soldiers. We trust each other completely and have spent a lot of time becoming one cohesive unit. There have been several simulation missions and run-throughs to make sure nothing gets out of hand while we storm the gates of HORUS headquarters.

"We'll be there in five minutes," Arbock yells from the front.

I address the team as they prepare.

"You heard the ape," I say to them. "We're almost there. Prepare to set up stations once he parks."

I intend to walk to John, but Clipper, our explosives and demolitions bear, is on the way. He's going underground with Waylon and Winde. His sole purpose is to set up the EMP's and any other explosives needed. He's a dense bear, but intelligence isn't really required for his kind of job. But he's also the fiercest warrior I know, and even though combat isn't his specialty, he's quite proficient out on the field. He's a behemoth waiting to be unleashed. Just the sight of him scares a lot of helpless victims.

"Make sure those bombs are prepped," I say as I walk by him.

"Got it, Captain," he says eagerly.

I get to John and see him messing around on the console. He's a pig, and although their kind has a bad reputation, he is a very capable coordinator. I don't sense greed or politicking from him. There's a high duty compcube and a communication station at his disposal. He's our headquarters away from home, providing commentary and strategy to us while we are out in the heat of battle. He's the operator, mission command.

"Captain," John says to me. "I've mapped out the itinerary and coordinated the teams. The plan is pretty simple when it boils down to it. You, Kanji, Ingle, and Kimba will approach on foot head on. Kimba will have all the equipment you need. It should handle whatever they throw at you and, based on your reports, they have a lot to throw. Be prepared to take on sentries, proton cannons, and a plethora of other things. I don't have the specifics, but Kimba can provide you information on what you'll use to counter their defenses."

"Don't worry about it," I say. "I've gone over with Kimba our needs, I think we can handle whatever they have."

"Good. Once you make it to the entrance, Ingle should have already applied the scrambler on the doors. They lead underground where HORUS is hidden. Kanji can decode the locks and gain access to the front entrance and unlock most security protocols. Simultaneously, Winde and his team will tunnel underground to gain entrance to their perimeter and cut off communications within HORUS. They'll enter the server room and gain full access to their mainframe.

He can shut down and enslave their own drones. Clipper will then destroy it after Winde has obtained remote control. They can't reestablish their systems if their hardware is wiped out. The occupants will be like chickens with their heads cut off. With security protocols and their network at your total disposal, you should have an easy time eliminating anything that moves. Once both parties have entered and established securement, we'll all separate individually."

"Good. Operation HORUS should be fast and effective. I want you to make sure everyone follows the plan and they reach their target points on time. Understood? I give you full jurisdiction for this, if anyone complains, refer them to me."

John looks at me eagerly.

"Don't worry, Captain," he says. "They'll hit their goals on time."

"They better," I say sternly.

I walk away from John and finally approach the last two of my crew, Sol Kimba and Tatsu Kanji. Kimba is a lion and our arms expert. His mane has been chopped off, but he's still large and frightening to those who don't know him. He has a small scar above his left eye, a parting gift from a mission he completed long before I met him. When I understood what defenses HORUS had, I quickly deferred them to Kimba so he could set up his game plan on how to tackle it. He's usually good at finding the proper gear to handle problems, and with a hefty Alliance budget at his disposal, I'm sure he's found every effective remedy to whatever will come our way.

"Captain," he says to me. "Here's your Tang 618 Hydra Blaster, as you ordered."

He hands me a large human gun that has several buttons and switches. It looks like a kid's toy with so many devices, but I know this is top of the line stuff.

"I love multi weapon designs," I say. "Why carry five different weapons when you can have all in one?"

"Gotta agree with you," Kimba says. "You got your standard energy blaster, spitfires, grenade launchers, and plenty of other surprises in a nice compact package."

I look at his other stockpile of goodies. There are guns and melee weapons of different sizes strewn neatly against the wall and on the ground. He really went all out on this one. There's so much gear here that I don't use on a normal basis, but I'm sure it'll come in handy once the mission commences.

"The crew knows how to use this stuff, right?" Kimba asks me.

"We've gone through dozens of simulations and training. They tested their weapons firsthand, and I've personally approved it. What do you think?" I ask.

"Just making sure."

"Don't worry, Kimba, we're ready to use your gear."

He smirks a bit.

"Good. Then I guess they'll suit up once we stop," he says.

I leave him for now and get to Kanji, our security expert. He's the code breaker and will be opening the doors on the outside while Winde works on the inside. Kanji is a tiger, and from what I understand they are a cunning species. They usually get along with other feline counterparts like lions, cheetahs, and cats. For the most part, Kanji is a mild tempered individual. He's equipped with claws and a strong body, but he doesn't seem like a fighter to me. That's okay, we just need him to handle decryption.

"You have your protocols set?" I ask him. "Disabling security is our first priority in the initial phase of our plan."

"Of course, boss," he says enthusiastically.

He greets me warmly, which I admit is a nice change from all the gruff characters in my crew.

"Once we get to an access point, it'll be a piece of cake to enter their mainframe and halt their defense programs," Kanji says. "You won't have to worry about a thing after that, not outside, not inside. Make sure Ingle gets that scrambler attached on one of their routers."

"He'll get it done. I also have Winde on a plan to get admin rights to their network, so if he's successful, we can control their systems as well," I say.

"Really? That's pretty cool."

"Yeah, but you're going with me on the ground. I'm mainly concerned about the gauntlet of sentries and cannons we'll encounter in our first phase. It won't be easy, but after that it should be cake. Be prepared to fight."

He looks a little nervous that he'll have to do some combat.

"Uh, sure thing," Kanji says nervously.

"Don't worry," I say. "Ingle, Kimba, and myself will be with you. You don't have to be afraid."

He nods somberly.

"Yo, Cap," Arbock says as he interrupts our conversation. "We're here."

Arbock puts the tram to a complete stop and the doors open.

"Okay," I say addressing the group collectively. "We're here. Everyone lug the gear out and get the posts set up. Survey the area and make sure it's clean. This is where our mission control will be, so give John something good to work with. After that, start preparations to engage. Understood?"

"Yes sir!" they all bark in unison.

They each get off of the tram, carrying equipment and cases into this woody area of the Bay Area hills. It's a barren place out here, no signs of civilization to be found. This is the perfect spot for us to set camp.

Suddenly, my communicator goes off. I switch it on and see that General Rox is on the line. The Alliance has come to check out the situation. I find a secluded spot on the now empty tram and answer the call.

"Company Manticore," he says. "Can you read me?"

"Yes, general," I say. Rox is a dog, a Rottweiler, and a highly decorated war hero. He's been a council member on the Alliance for some time, and he's usually the dog who supervises covert missions like this.

"Captain West. I'm here to check on your status before you launch your assault this evening. How are things going?"

"Good. I've gone over with each team member their role in the plan."

"Excellent. Do they know the objective?"

"Of course. To terminate HORUS."

"Yes, and are you ready for your personal, special assignment?"

I look around to make sure no one is eavesdropping.

"Yes, I do," I say.

"Anyone on your team aware of it?" Rox says discreetly.

"Only Winde, my tech expert."

"That makes sense. But choose who you plan to divulge this information to carefully. This is classified to the highest command."

"Understood."

"Extermination of HORUS and its occupants is the number one priority, of course, but there's a great opportunity to extract a large deal of information from Lionel Changer's personal files. Make sure you download as much as you can. The Alliance is very interested in the things he has been working on."

"Understood. I'll get as much as possible."

General Rox looks pleased and excited.

"Naturally, you'll be rewarded handsomely. Ask whatever you want, and it will be yours if you are successful," he says. "It'll be a small price to pay for the kind of data that you've been tasked to get."

I nod silently.

"Then, I won't take anymore of your time," Rox says. "Good luck, Captain."

"Thank you General," I say. I turn off my communicator and turn around, only to be surprised by Kanji.

"Um, Captain," he says. "Who were you talking to?"

I look away and avoid eye contact.

"No one," I say.

"Um, okay," he says nervously. "Anyway, we're starting to set up camp. Do you want to come out and oversee?"

"Of course," I say.

Once we have things ready, we'll begin our assault. It's time to take down those freaks and stop Lionel Changer's madness.

Chapter 10 - Bastion

Orientation

May 5, 3043 10:03 AM

The door slides open and Lionel, Lucy, and I enter Iris's holding cell. Two hours have passed since her arrival. She's dressed in the clothes we supplied her. The food we gave her is gone.

"How do you like your outfit?" Lionel asks her.

"It's comfortable, I guess," she says apprehensively.

She still looks scared and unsure of our motives, despite Lionel's calm tone. I guess I would be too after learning what she learned.

"Feeling better? How are the headaches?" Lionel asks.

"They're still occurring here and there," Iris says.

"Hmm, we'll have Lucy take a look at you later. It's not from the sedative, they should've been gone by now."

Lionel looks at the empty bag of food.

"Looks like you devoured that. How did you like it?" Lionel asks.

"Doable," she says tersely.

"That's good. I understand that this situation must be stressful for you, but you not need to worry. We have no intentions of harming you. I make sure all my creations are well taken care of. Bastion can account for that."

She looks at me skeptically, glaring laser eyes in my direction. She's still angry because I was the one who abducted her. I look away uncomfortably in Lionel's direction, but he has his eyes wide open and is nodding his head. He wants me to say something.

"Uh, yes, Lionel has always been good to us," I say anxiously. "He's fed us, put a shelter over our head, and took us in when our real mothers and fathers abandoned us. If those aren't good intentions, I don't know what is."

Lionel then looks at Lucy in the same manner and she stares back at him with a frozen expression.

"Agreed," she says.

"Thank you, Bastion and Lucy," Lionel says. "As you can see, the others in this facility aren't worried about anything, so you shouldn't either."

Iris continues to look cynically at the three of us.

"If this place is so great, why did you have to kidnap me then?" she says furiously. "I had a nice life out in the woods with Fenrir and, without warning, you stripped me of that and took me to some fortress in the middle of the mountains, away from everything that I loved. How do you expect me to trust you?"

"First of all, we took you for your own protection," Lionel says in a defensive tone.

"Is that so?" Iris says. "Last time I checked, I was doing fine in the Wolf's Den. It was quiet, peaceful, and I felt safe under Fenrir's watch. I enjoyed it. I haven't run into trouble for the last three years, so it seems I was already well protected before you had to come and save me."

"Three years isn't that long of a time. All it takes is one wrong move, and you could have mercenaries, the Alliance, or any other number of dangers march right to your doorstep. You weren't as safe as you thought you were."

"Says you."

"Seems like you're confident about that. But did you know that there were four wolves waiting outside your cabin before Bastion took you?"

She looks astonished by the revelation, thunderstruck. The expression on her faces makes it clear that this is new information.

"Who?" she asks desperately.

"I'm not sure, but Bastion stated that there were four of them," Lionel says.

"I think they were agents of the Brotherhood of Wolves," I interrupt. "I'm not certain, I didn't really get a chance to talk to them, you know? But from the looks of it, they were definitely hunting something, and I suspect they were after either you or your buddy, Fenrir Snow. They were right outside your doorstep before I acted. If I hadn't gotten you, they might have taken you out."

"No, this can't be true," Iris says.

Iris slumps down to the floor. The cozy blanket of security she felt has suddenly disappeared. The rest of us stand there in silence as we watch her go into a state of utter shock.

She starts to cry a little. Lionel approaches, kneels down, takes a handkerchief out of his pocket, and hands it to her. She looks at it cautiously and in her moment of weakness, grabs it to wipe away the tears.

"It's okay, Iris," he says comfortingly. "I know that news was hard to hear, especially with everything you've been through in your life."

She fights off her tears and collects her composure.

"I can't believe I was so naïve," she says softly. "For some reason, I thought I'd be safe forever. I've been hiding in fear all my life. When I lived with mom, I was afraid of a world that would reject me. There wouldn't be a night when I didn't worry about a mob storming our house to massacre my family. In a way, it did kind of happen, and I'm the only one left alive."

"You mean Operation Halfkinds?" I ask.

Iris nods at me with teary and droopy eyes. It's the first time I see her without a scowl.

"After they died and Fenrir took me in, I wanted so badly to believe that it was over, that I could finally find a measure of happiness on this planet," she continues. "We lived in seclusion for such a long time that it seemed possible. Even if it was a longshot, I held on to this scenario with hope, but it looks like it was in vain. I'm still wanted. Your news makes me come to the realization that no matter how hard I try, I'll never be left alone. It's a truth that I want to run away from, but it follows me everywhere I go. I'm always going to be someone's target in a world that will never accept me."

"I'm sorry, that must be hard," Lionel says. "But here, among HORUS, I guarantee that you will be accepted. You're not a freak here, not a fugitive. You're an equal. Why don't you come with us and we can show you around. That's all we'll do, no tests or anything, I promise."

He extends his hand to Iris. She looks hesitant, and examines me and Lucy before doing anything. I flash her a tender smile, and with a cautious heart, she makes her leap. She grabs Lionel by the hand and hoists herself up.

"Okay, let's go," she says.

Lionel leads the way out of the room. Iris takes her first steps out of her cell and into HORUS's facilities. The three of us are ahead of her, and she walks slowly behind us, analyzing her surroundings, and pays close attention to our movements.

The halls are a bright white, clean, and smooth. There's not a single spec on the floor, and the room is chilly enough to give it a cool, crisp feeling.

We reach a door to our left, and Lionel places his hand on a scanner. The door slides open, leading to a corridor with many other doors inside of it. There are twenty of them, lined up against the wall, like a gallery. Lionel leads the way and opens one of the doors, showing Iris the room behind it.

This is my room. Why did Lionel have to pick my room? It's only been a few hours, and Iris now has a window into my personal life. Fantastic. Inside there's my bed, a small dresser, a desk, and some clothes messily strewn on the ground. Some of my gear is also on the floor, like my stealth suit, my knockout gun, and a variety of other small arms. If I had known that we were coming, I would have cleaned up. Iris probably thinks I'm a total slob now. How embarrassing.

"This area is the barracks," Lionel says. "It is where all my creations sleep and rest. This is Bastion's room. The previous hallway with all the doors leads to everyone else's personal rooms. There's a communal bathroom down the hall."

Iris takes a step back and looks at the room we were in earlier, with all the doors. She stares at them quietly, taking her time observing and pacing around as she grasps the information given to her. She's thinking about something, something that's familiar. I'm a bit curious by her reaction.

"Are you okay?" I ask.

Iris breaks out of her trance.

"Yeah, I'm fine," she says. "It's just that this place reminds me of my mom's house. When I lived in Primm, she kept us underground, and we got our own rooms. This hallway reminds me of the hallway that led to all those rooms. I guess I'm experiencing a bit of déjà vu."

"No worries," Lionel says. "It's a lot of information to take in. We'll have a room ready for you, and you'll have plenty of time to adjust. But in the meantime, we're going to continue our tour."

We exit through the way we came and end up back in the main hall. We pass through another few doors until Lionel stops in front of one that's larger than the others. He opens it and behind it lies a giant room. There are a few of the lab techs, I think it's Josh and Bobby, sitting down at large tables eating their grub. It must be a late breakfast for them. They look at the four of us briefly and continue with their meal.

"This is the cafeteria," Lionel says.

Iris takes a look around.

"It certainly is white, like everything else here," she says.

"The white gives it a clean feeling," he says. "Obviously, the cafeteria is where everyone eats, my workers and my creations alike. The hybrids actually mingle a lot with the technicians, I encourage a community-based atmosphere. I think it's important to have this interaction, since we're remote. Any socialization is good in my book. Here in the cafeteria, we have some cooks staffed, so feel free to order whatever you want."

Iris gazes at the uniformed workers who are eating their breakfast.

"How do you keep this place running and still stay secret for so long?" she asks.

"With rigid standards and requirements," Lionel responds. "I have some secret accounts in black market banks that I've put a lot of my money into. They fund everything you see here. When it comes time to get supplies such as lab equipment and food, well, let's say there are methods of getting those things discreetly."

"Interesting, but that's not what I meant. What I'm wondering is have these workers been here forever? Do they have a home away from here? How do you keep them from blowing your cover?"

"Oh, well, workers stay here on the premise. They have their own barracks. Our group is pretty small, there's only forty two workers and twenty three hybrids. If workers elect to leave, they are free to do so, but we run them through a quick mind wipe first."

Iris gawks at Lionel blankly. I suppose his relaxed tone disturbs her.

"Mind wipe?" she asks in shock.

"Yes, we erase their memories from when they started to when they leave," he says.

"Um, I didn't know tech like that exists, or if it's legal."

"Like our lab equipment and food, there's ways of getting that tech discreetly. And it isn't legal per se, but that's never become an issue. The workers rarely leave. We're doing some ground breaking stuff here at HORUS, and my employees are fully engaged in their research."

"I see."

I sense that Iris is skeptical. She has a smirk that says "bullshit."

"What Lionel says is true," I say. "The workers are treated very well here and are rewarded handsomely. We've never had anyone leave ever since HORUS started. And for the most part, us hybrids get along with the workers fine. Lionel isn't kidding when he says that it's all about community."

"Anyway, enough chat, let's continue to the next area," Lionel says.

As before, we walk out the way we came and go down the corridor. We take some right turns and left turns, traversing around the maze-like structure of HORUS headquarters. Even though there are signs, and I've been here most of my life, I admit that for a first timer like Iris, it must be confusing to keep track of where she's going.

We arrive at another door and it slides open. We reach a large indoor window and look into a room with several patient tables, biohazard boxes, and a variety of devices. There are some doctors on their compcubes researching and running diagnostic tests. Another one is looking over the bioscan results from Iris's physical exam, the one we did when she was first brought here.

"This is the medical bay," Lionel says. "It's the place where we do physicals on our hybrids and humans. We want to make sure everyone is in good health, and we have the top of the line equipment to treat our people. Lucy can fill you in on the details."

"Han Company Bioscanners along with operating drones," Lucy says in an abrupt manner. "Have biohazard suits, manual instruments, medical gels, marrow capsules, and other things."

Iris looks at her stupefied.

"I have no idea what you're talking about," Iris says bluntly.

"Don't expect you to," Lucy replies. "Am doing what Lionel instructed."

"Lucy here is our resident whiz kid. She's an expert in the sciences, and has a knack for biology and technology," Lionel says. "I personally tutored her myself. To simply put it, she's my star pupil."

"Spend much time in lab. If need medical assistance, don't hesitate to talk. Acknowledge come off chilly, but here to help."

"Anyway, I think we've spent enough time here, let's move on, shall we?"

We continue to walk down the hall a short distance. Right next door is the lab, our next stop. It looks similar to the medical bay except the equipment is different. This area is geared more for research and study as opposed to operations and bioscans. This place is considered the R&D area of HORUS. Lionel and Lucy spend most of their time here perfecting and crafting their breakthroughs, so it has the best of the best in terms of what he needs. His specialty is biotic implants, the same ones that allowed our creation.

"You could say this is your birth place," Lionel says.

"Excuse me?" Iris asks.

The two of them look through the indoor window at all the technicians busy at work. There's about ten of them, each researching a different project. Some are working on improving the uteral implants, others are working on arm and leg implants for strength. Everyone has their own thing to do.

"Well technically, your mother gave birth to you in the medical bay," Lionel says. "You don't remember, you were only here for a few months when she took you away. But this is where I developed the first models that made interspecies breeding possible. I spent a lot of time in this lab fostering my devices, and you could say it was here that the possibility of hybrids like yourselves was created."

"I see," Iris says quietly. "Looks like a busy place."

"It most certainly is. Let's go, though, not much that you'd be interested in here. We only have two stops left on our little orientation."

Past the medical bay and the lab is the gear room. Lionel opens the door and Iris peers in. This is where I spend most of my time. There's a myriad of training equipment at my disposal, and all my weapons and stealth aids are here. It's sort of a hybrid armory and exercise room for me to use.

"This is Bastion's favorite room," Lionel says.

Iris looks at me with amazement. I guess she's wowed that I'm able to use everything here, because there's quite a lot of things. She walks in and picks up an item to examine it. They look like your standard gloves.

"What is this?" she asks me.

"Weighted gloves," I say. "Basically, I put them on and once they are prepped, I can adjust how much the glove weighs by voice command. They can be as light as one pound, to as heavy as one hundred. I wear them when I shadow box and combat train. I usually stick to about eighty pounds or so."

"You're kidding."

"Nope. Here, I'll show you."

I take the gloves and put them on.

"Eighty pounds, please," I say.

The gloves beep and the sudden shift in weight causes my hands to drop. But I easily pick them back up and demonstrate a few hooks and uppercuts in the air. Iris steps back, but looks impressed. I love showing off, especially to someone as attractive as Iris.

"I can't believe you're that strong," she says. "I mean, no offense, but you don't look like much."

"Bastion has been training his whole life," Lionel says. "Even though he doesn't have a huge frame, his body is packed with pure muscle. He also has a few implants in him to help with his strength and speed. He's graceful and powerful, the perfect combination, my right hand man. When I need something difficult done, he does it."

"What kind of things?"

"That's between me and Bastion."

I take the gloves off, and turn off the power setting. They're light as a feather now.

"Here," I say to Iris, "you can take these if you ever want to exercise on your own."

"Uh, thanks," she flabbergasts. "So, that's it? He's your only defense?"

"No, we have plenty of drones and security measures in place," Lionel responds.

"But no soldiers? No bodyguards? Aren't you afraid of someone coming here to harm you?"

"No. We've remained off the grid for years. I don't think that's going to change anytime soon. Besides, we are a science facility, not a prison. Why bother paying guards and soldiers when you have machines doing it for you?"

"Um, I guess that makes sense."

"Good, I'm glad you comprehend. Okay, let's continue, we have one last stop."

We walk a few corridors down until we reach the end of the hall. There is a big sliding double door and Lionel opens it.

"This is the communal room," he says. "It's where the hybrids spend most of their time."

"It's huge," Iris says.

"The room is indeed very large," I say. "We have some entertainment streams on the monitor and games in the corner there. There's also a snack bar and some lounge chairs. At the end of the room, you'll see a door, which leads to our classrooms. It's where we learn our skills. Right now it's holiday, so most of us hybrids are relaxing and resting unless Lionel has an assignment for us. Usually, Lucy and I are too busy to spend our time here, but you'll find the others to be very friendly."

Iris observes the inhabitants. Some of them ignore her, and some pay notice. It must be weird for her to come to a room where there are creatures like her. Most of her life, she was under the impression that she and her family were the only ones, and when Operation Halfkinds happened, she was certain she was the last hybrid alive. Now she finds out she's not alone.

"I can't believe there are so many," she says. "It reminds me of home, it reminds me of Primm."

"I understand if you need some time to adjust," Lionel says.

She walks around and circles the room without talking to anyone else. The other hybrids are now paying attention to her, and they stare at her as she stares at them. She starts to notice that she's the center of attention and quickly comes back to where Lionel, Lucy, and I are standing.

"I haven't seen one window in this entire facility," Iris says.

"No use for windows when all you'll be able to see is the dirt," Lionel responds. Iris looks confused. "You see my dear, HORUS headquarters is completely underground. All of this is built below the Earth's surface. We wouldn't be much of a secret facility if we stuck out like a sore thumb. No, we have to maintain this front, so when I created this place, I built everything hidden from plain view."

Iris looks stunned, but not too surprised.

"There is one more thing I find strange, everyone here is either a human or hybrid," she observes. "During our tour, I didn't see a dog or cat or tiger or anything."

"Of course," Lionel says. "I don't want my glorious work getting muddled by an impure creature. Let society have those vagrants, but in HORUS, the human touch is always the best one. And you, my dear, you and my wonderful creations represent the next level our human greatness can achieve."

She looks confused by his comments. She doesn't know about Lionel's background, so his speech flies over her head.

"What do you mean, impure?" she asks.

Lucy whispers something in Lionel's ear. He looks a bit concerned, but his attention shifts back to Iris.

"Nothing," he says, blowing off her question. "We'll have plenty of time to talk later. I have to attend to some matters, Lucy and Bastion will be following me. In the meantime, you can stay here and get to know some of your fellow hybrids."

"Wait!" Iris yells. "I still have a lot of questions!"

"Don't worry, we will get to them. Just be patient. Bastion, Lucy, let's go."

Lionel leads the way out and we follow. I take one look at Iris to try to comfort her before the door shuts in my face. Lionel then turns to me.

"Now that she's in the communal room, I want you to monitor her," Lionel says. "See how she socializes with the others and note anything unusual or out of the ordinary. That is your task, understood?"

"Yes sir," I say.

"Good. Lucy and I need to prepare some of the tests. If you need us, we'll be in the lab."

They walk forward, and then turn to the left. I make my way to the monitor room to start my assignment.

Chapter 11 - Lionel Changer

Horus

May 5, 3043 10:30 AM

When I lived in the city decades ago, I usually took an afternoon stroll when my day was done. I'd walk to this one park that was five minutes from my house. On my way, I'd often encounter a dog or cheetah, or sometimes even a chimp, and they'd greet me a pleasant afternoon. I'd nod at them politely and continue on.

When I got to the park, I normally sat down and fed the pigeons. They weren't like their eagle counterparts. These birds were dumb as doornails. I'd have some bread, toss it to them, and watch them waddle about. They bobbed their heads and stared into space like the idiot creatures they were. I'd then look up and see a dog with his pups playing in the grass. Sometimes there'd be cats too, and on rare occasions an eagle would perch on a tree and rest after a busy work day, much like I did. The animals were all friendly to each other, and they were nice enough to me. I'd sit back and think about how it came to be that these creatures were living harmoniously in the open as my equals.

And the more afternoon walks I went on, and the more I observed and thought about it, I soon realized I hated it. The mere notion that these things were on my level, the human level, brought a deep disgust within me. These things were my peers? How revolting.

I've always had a fervent hatred for so-called 'intelligent' animals. They were made because of an over ambitious science project. The very notion of their existence is bizarre. Humans should be the only ones in charge of society. It shouldn't be shared with these abominations. That's the way things ought to be, that's what's natural.

I can only wonder what it was like before they took over, before humans were stupid enough to go through with the Ark Project, before that fiasco known as the Ark Rebellion. I've seen the history streams about the time before the Ark, when humans ruled the world. I saw us as a species thriving, finally living in a peace that had eluded us for our entire existence. A thousand years ago, it seemed impossible that there'd be a day when all of the world's conflicts were gone and we lived with each other in harmony. Us humans are capable of amazing things. In a few centuries, something that seemed fictional became the truth.

Our paradise had been realized and, even more amazing, it had gone beyond our wildest expectations. Before the Ark Project, we were at the top of our game. Major illnesses had been cured, cutting edge teleportation developments were being made, and our environment had been cleaned up. We didn't fight over which flag we bore, we lived under one. Us humans lived in a perfect society, a utopia where our only limit was the ends of the universe. I wish I could've lived during this time. It was the greatest time to be a human being. But then we did something very human, we fucked ourselves over.

The aftermath of the Ark Project and Ark Rebellion left the balance of the world in shambles. The emergence of intelligent species led to an implosion. No longer could humans thrive like we had been doing, no longer could we work to our true potential because things had changed. Humans had to worry about their new enemies, and everything we wished to accomplish went out the door.

That new breakthrough in cold fusion energy? That had to be put on hold because our human government had to set a campaign to stabilize the fronts between warring species. That small cryogenic firm that was destined to push medical advances to the next level? It turned into a weapons company because war had become profitable again. And the bounty of resources: credits, artificial materials, fields of genetically perfected crops? They weren't just for humans anymore. All the animals wanted a piece of the pie. They felt it was owed to them after the years of suffrage they experienced under the human regime. What a bunch of shit.

I examine history and wonder what we would've done as a human race if it hadn't been for those aberrations. It seems technology and human progression has either gone down or remained at a standstill after the Ark Project and Rebellion happened. We could've had so much greatness, created a world that truly fit what our ancestors imagined the thirty-first century to be. It's nothing like that. We humans have fallen short of our goals and our potential, and it's all our fault. The dogs. The cats. The wolves. The tigers. I hate them all, every dirty, four-legged, winged, trunk-swaying, hairy, long-armed asshole I see. Every time I watch one of these things walk down the street, I'm reminded of what they've taken away from my kind.

I believe in a world that's right, a world that is pure and cleansed from the animal scum around me. It's the philosophy I was taught when I was young, and one that has shaped me into the person I am today.

I was always considered a prodigy growing up. I don't deny it. I lived in the deserts of New Mexico, in a remote house away from the city. It was a small community, probably considered technologically backwards, but my parents made sure I was surrounded by the latest learning tools and gear. They recognized the brains I had, and did as much as they could to nurture my gifts. They supplied me with the knowledge so my abilities could thrive even in the wasteland under the sun.

I had a knack for robotics and an even greater one for biology, so my parents guided me to combine the two. By the time I was eight, I was dabbling in biotic experiments. I cut the wings off of chickens and was able to reconstruct it with some basic robotic parts. They were crude looking, and didn't have much finesse, but it was still impressive for a child.

When I turned twelve, I sold my first patent. It was for eye contacts that grafted themselves onto your eye. That would give a person instant clarity. They'd automatically adjust to your level of near or far sightedness, making it a permanent fix for the rest of your life. That was my first breakthrough, the thing that put me on the map. I made my first credit haul off that simple design, and in an instant I went from being an average kid in the desert to being a figurehead in a new wave of biotic designers.

When I turned eighteen, Implantus, the small company that would make me my fortune, started up. We specialized in designing biotics that were tailor-made for human use. Implantus could allow a person who was born with no limbs, diagnosed with a weak heart, and had half his brain blown out from an accident function as a normal human being. All that would be needed were some arm, leg, cardiac, and cranium biotics implanted into said patient. They were artificial robotics that looked and felt like the real thing. That person could walk down the street and no one would suspect that their body wasn't the genuine thing. That's the kind of stuff I developed, the stuff that many medical facilities use today. Implantus was the first company to provide products of such high quality that it became the standard.

I never forgot my roots as my company got larger. My ancestors lost a lot of land, and some of them their lives, during the Event and the Ark Rebellion. The animals did it. They have never brought any good to the Changers, and my parents made sure I knew that. We were stolen from. My inventions would serve humanity and only humanity, because they're the only ones who deserved it.

I only had one motto, biotics made by humans, for humans, only. It wasn't a public motto, and we didn't outwardly endorse any human supremacist group, but people knew our standing. We were a small company, but we were successful and groundbreaking. Any group with that kind of reputation is bound to get scrutinized by the public eye.

The world got wind of what we were doing, and that's when "minor" observations were made. The first was that our company only hired humans. I never established a final, human only hiring policy, but I wanted to make sure that my employees were the best. Quite frankly, humans are the best. I didn't want my life's work being handled by the mangy paws of a dog or wolf.

The second thing was that I only made biotics for humans. I had no lion legs or enhanced frog eyes, no chimp ear implants or artificial cheetah hearts. Even as my company got more successful, and the demand for animal biotics became greater, I stood my ground. Animal groups protested and picketed, and I did nothing. My reputation was a small price to pay in order to maintain my values.

Other copycat companies eventually redesigned my tech and made animal options available. I launched massive lawsuits against these companies, but I'd always lose. The courts said that they weren't really copying anything, and that the reimagining of inventions has been going on for centuries. But I think I lost because I was fighting a one-man battle against a world that didn't see the truth, that animals didn't deserve any of our help, that humanity should help itself.

We were still cutting edge when it came to human biotics, but I soon grew tired of the public scrutiny. The amount of condemnation I felt from society took a toll on me. I was viewed a bigot simply because I wouldn't acknowledge those science experiments. I felt that my genius deserved to do more.

It was the year 2990 when I started my new plan. I had already mastered the world of biomechanical engineering, it was time to do something else. But I couldn't think of what. Then, one day, I saw a child playing with a pup and a cub. They were engaged in a friendly race in the park that I frequented. I saw the three of them take their mark and set. The child's mother yelled 'go' and the three were off. The dog and lion sprinted forward and, in a matter of seconds, the child was in their dust. It was unfair, the dog and wolf were gifted with natural abilities that the child was not. And now, they had intelligence to boot. How could that child ever compete with those animals? As I thought about it, it was the same with humans. The animals were getting smarter, and in a few short millennia, with the combination of their physical and mental capabilities, us humans would be left behind like that child.

That's when I got an idea. I was going to create something to even the odds. Before, I helped humanity with my developments. Now, it was time to push it to the next level. We weren't going to get shoved aside, we were going to take the next step towards evolution, and it would be through my work. If humankind wanted a chance at the future, we had to adapt and gain the advantages of our neighbors. If we could run faster, get stronger, and most importantly, become smarter than our animal peers, then there would be nothing to worry about. Humanity could not only regain their footing on this world, but crush any other threat to it. I had to start the catalyst in order to protect our kind from the animal threat that had emerged.

My first approach was to integrate genetic recombination, directly altering strands of DNA to artificially engineer the human hybrids I was envisioning. Yet, this proved more difficult than I thought. The process seemed simple enough, all I had to do was encode a human DNA strand with a target animal's one, then use that as the basis of my biological engineering. I should've realized, though, that there's a reason that after hundreds of years, it still hadn't been done. The problem was that there was no base between the two genetic blueprints. A human's makeup and another animal's were completely different and as many similarities as there were, I found a million differences. It was like trying to combine a hovercar and a teleporter into one cohesive unit without turning it into Frankenstein's monster. I needed a concrete base that could be built upon and since this was something new, there was none.

All my final products would turn out like a combination of masses instead of the smooth end result that I had imagined. My approach was too blunt. I was forcing my hand at creation. None of it was natural, and the results showed. Unfortunately, the products of my experiments suffered. They barely lived past a few days, and many of my subjects had to be disposed of. It pained me to know I caused such suffering to my own constructions.

The donors were another matter. Most of the source subjects were homeless animals that wouldn't be missed. Dogs, bears, lions, they all served my cause well, and all didn't survive the splicing process. I didn't care, they're just animals. Not a human was sacrificed, only the vile masses were.

Thus, I had to come up with a way to make the blending more effortless and less forced. It had to be natural. There are some things that can't be created artificially, it needs a combination of manmade and inherent progression. I reworked my plans and decided my hybrids could be created if some nurturing and birthing was involved. It was unheard of and seemed farfetched. Everyone I talked to thought it was science fiction instead of fact, but I would prove them wrong.

I spent years and years researching, thinking of every possible theory, and testing every possible outcome. Finally, by 2999, I had the pieces in place to finally start. HORUS headquarters was mapped out. Implantus had already been sold off years ago, allowing me to have a healthy sum of creds to work with. I had vanished from the public eye. Some people thought I was dead, others thought I changed identities. I got rid of any public records and made sure I was off the grid. If I was going to start building the foundation to HORUS, it had to be secret. Genetic experimentation like this would surely catch the eye of the Alliance, and I had no intention of being in stasis in a prison pod. Everything was off the books, and I was good at being discrete.

By 3002, HORUS headquarters was fully operational, ready for development. I hired brilliant minds within my circle and made sure they shared my vision while maintaining an oath of secrecy. Many of those employees are still here today, and the ones that aren't, well let's say I took the extra steps needed to ensure they wouldn't tell anyone. This was the team that developed the staple of hybrid creation, the uterus implants. The first prototype was a synconium device lined against the uteral walls that was a mini-genetic recombinater during the birthing stages. It acted during the early stages to make a fetus between the two species possible. Then, it tweaked the development of the fetus while it was growing, adapting it to its surroundings, to make sure the fetus would survive inside the mother's womb. With the technology prototyped, clinical trials were ready to begin.

We looked for volunteers, but not everyone was jumping at the chance to give birth to a hybrid. That's why we went to the prostitutes. They were hopeless enough to do anything for creds, and their profession made them the perfect fit to collect the sperm we needed for insemination.

Our first subject was Isabella Starla. She was a woman in her fifties, very beautiful, with long brown hair and clear skin. She had been a prostitute for about ten years, and was struggling with drug addiction. One word described her - desperate. From the black market listings, we saw that she serviced non-humans and contacted her with our proposal. We gave her all the details, the implants and the birthing process. She was revolted by the mere idea, but when she saw the creds we were offering, she couldn't resist.

Per her agreement, she had to remain with HORUS until the birth was done to make sure her drug habit and poor upkeep wouldn't affect our creations. She also agreed to undergo a mind wipe so she couldn't remember who we were and where we were located. The last thing I needed was some crazy prostitute blowing our cover.

Since she was our first experiment, we didn't know what to expect. We told her to try to get a chimp client, since we were thinking that the similar genetic structure would yield a higher success rate. She didn't listen. The first hybrid fetus was a from a dog donor. We didn't think the little guy would survive, but to our surprise, Starla gave birth to a healthy half human, half dog hybrid. His name was Zorro. My lab technicians wanted to call him Subject Zero, but I added some flair to it. After he was born, Starla was done. We gave her a mind wipe and let her be on her way. It's a pity, though, because I heard two years later, she died of synconium poisoning. That's what the stuff will do to you, and we're working on making it one hundred percent safe. Lucy has been tinkering on an improved version, and I think it may end the synconium poisonings our subjects have been hit with. It's too bad Starla was the first subject, she might have made it if she had gotten one of the later models of implants.

Zorro is the oldest of my creations and, sadly, probably the most useless. In terms of speed, strength, and intelligence, he's only slightly above human. And now he's older than he actually is. The poor hybrid is aging at a rapid pace. Those weren't the results I expected when I envisioned a perfect specimen. That's how it always goes when it comes to testing. You build your prototype, and then you improve upon it. And that's what I did. Slowly but surely, I saw the skills and abilities of my hybrids grow. With every birth, with every new creation, they came out faster, stronger, and smarter. Some could outrun cheetahs, others could glide through the air. The years of research paid off. My children demonstrated the true potential of my gene mixing dreams. And you don't see any rapid agers now.

I was especially blessed with Lucy and Bastion. One has intelligence far surpassing any human I've seen, dare I say even smarter than me. The other moves more gracefully than any cat or canine out there, and could bulldoze a rhino or gorilla if he wanted. They are the pinnacle that I hope become the standard for the future generations of hybrids. As the years go by, they'll be equipped with more biotics to increase their aptitude.

Yet, despite what those two have shown me, I would never have imagined beyond my wildest dreams what Iris Lawton is capable of. I only thought the hybrids would take on enhanced traits of the animals they stole their genetics from, but I didn't think we'd see a mutation that went beyond that. She is the first to show precognitive abilities and in the right hands, mine, that is a wonderful weapon to wield.

I didn't think much of Maya Lawton when she came here. She was a prostitute like any other, but what separated her from the rest was the compassion she showed to her hybrid children. She refused the mind wipes and wanted the possibility of interacting with her little ones. I found it odd, but then again, she always wanted to be a mother, but with her sordid past, that was difficult. Maybe she wanted children who were like her, outcasts of society.

Since Maya didn't want to go through with the mind wipes, we offered to let her live at HORUS headquarters. We needed her to provide a motherly touch for her children and the abandoned hybrids. The agreement worked out fine. She didn't cause trouble, and was well behaved. The staff liked her, and I liked her. She was friendly, and had a pleasant way about her.

One thing concerned me, she didn't understand that the hybrids were mine. She truly believed they were hers, and I had a sneaking suspicion this would be the undoing of our working relationship. Low and behold, I was proven right when Iris was born. Maya refused to let us experiment on Iris once we got wind that she had innate precognitive abilities. Without warning, she slipped away from HORUS headquarters along with her children.

I suppose our security measures weren't that well equipped at the time. That's changed. I wasn't worried though, Maya wasn't going to tell the world about us, she had too much to lose. What I was worried about was my property. I didn't want to lose Iris, but by that time, she had grown attached to her mother. Any separation would have traumatized her. So I let Maya play house while sending Bastion to keep an eye out on them, waiting for the day when I could reclaim Iris for myself. But before that could happen, Operation Halfkinds was launched. Iris's life was now in danger, and I had to come to a decision - send Bastion to rescue her and risk getting exposed, or wait and see what happens. I chose the latter. I knew her powers would help her somehow, and I wasn't ready to let the world know about HORUS. Bastion strongly objected, but I made my choice and stuck with it. Looks like things worked out. Iris survived, and now here she is, back where it all started, her true home.

She is the key to my plan. I am already the master of a new power thanks to my hybrids, but she changes the game. Iris opens the door to many other possibilities. Precognition is just the start. I can see my hybrids playing host to a number of other powers. Telekinesis, telepathy, pyrokinesis, morphing, the list goes on and on as to what opportunities lie within their DNA. Thanks to me, humankind will be able to take back the throne, armed with weapons the world has never seen.

All we need to do is understand what lies in Iris's wondrous anatomy. I'm sure if we research enough, poke and prod and record every observation, every detailed finding, we'll not only replicate her abilities, but build upon them. There is no limit to what we can do. We've waited for Iris long enough, and now it's time to reap the rewards of our patience.

My ultimate goal has always been to steer humanity back to the top. The hybrids are a first step. How ironic that in my quest to perfect human beings, I have come to rely on their worst enemies. But it's a small nuance that I will overlook if it allows us to restore things to the way it was before. I want to make the

Event, the Ark Project, the Ark Rebellion a simple blip in history, a rare accident that never should have occurred. Thousands of years from now, when humans have restored the balance and control the world with an array of abilities, they'll look back and laugh that there were animals who lived with them as equals. They'll think of those times as a dark age, when we stooped so low. And they'll remember me and my work, the man who brought humanity back from the brink.

We've built the foundation. My prodigies, Lucy and Bastion, have shown what they're capable of. We'll continue to perfect the process so that over time, the hybrids will be less of a hybrid and be more of a superhuman. Iris will be the cornerstone of my plan, the mother to future generations of highly evolved humans. That is why she is so important, that is why she is special.

Chapter 12 - Fang Snow Trail

May 2, 3043 4:53 PM

"Wake up, dumbass," I say to Patrice.

He's still knocked out from the stun shot, but it should be wearing off by this time. Sure enough, I'm right, his head starts moving.

"Ugh, what happened?" he asks as he struggles to get to his feet.

"We've been out for almost three hours," I say. "Fenrir, it seems that I've underestimated you."

"He took out all of us?"

"That appears to be the case."

Patrice looks astonished.

"Wow, he's been out of action for a while, and he still has the skills to incapacitate four wolves. Pretty amazing," Patrice says.

"I would hardly say it was amazing," I say. "He defeated you in a very ordinary fashion. A blast to the head. Pssht. How could you expose yourself so carelessly? Don't give him credit for your stupidity."

Patrice looks embarrassed and disappointed by my remarks. Perhaps I am too hard on him.

"Anyway, it appears that Fenrir is long gone. I've scouted the area nearby and I don't see him," I say. "He must've left this place hours ago."

"I see," Patrice says.

He surveys the landscape, looking into the woods and horizon. He takes a few sniffs of the ground. Something captures his attention, and his eyes fixate on it. Before I can say anything, I realize Patrice is looking at me.

"Fang, your leg!" he says.

"Oh yes, that..."

When I woke up, I felt the pain immediately when I attempted to stand. It wasn't crippling, but it was enough to make me wince. I remembered Fenrir being sly and using a reflector to deflect my shot right at me. The blast scorched my fur and sent a sharp pain through my body. What I don't remember is bandaging it. The wound was already covered up perfectly when I came to.

"Is it bad?" Patrice asks.

"I'll live," I say. "It's a flesh wound."

"You did a nice job wrapping it up, though," Patrice says. "Looks like you even got some medigel on there. I didn't know we had some."

I didn't do it, but I know who did. I suppose I should thank Fenrir when I see him, but I know that won't happen.

"Forget about it. Let's go investigate," I say dismissively. "Fenrir's cabin is over there, we can see if there's anything that will help us with our search."

"What about Danzel and Raymus?" Patrice asks.

"We'll go get them afterwards."

We walk back from where I came and enter the cabin. Patrice starts sniffing the ground, and I survey my surroundings. There's a small kitchen connected to the main room. I see a human-sized bed and Fenrir's wolf cushion. Cooking supplies are strewn about on a raised table, and three compcubes are scattered nearby. In the corner is a large insta-item, which is how he got everything out here. There's also a foot-high stand with some sparse tactical equipment on it, which I'm guessing is Fenrir's work station. There is some food in storage and discarded bones on the floor. It's a bit messy, but livable.

"You picking up anything?" I ask Patrice.

"I smell two faint scents of foreign bodies. And Fenrir's scent is all around this cabin," he says.

"It's the two foreign bodies I'm interested in because they'll lead us to Fenrir. You don't recognize them?"

"No. And they're really hard to detect."

"Let me try."

I'm the better tracker anyway. I burrow my nose to the floor and sniff. The scent is familiar, like that of a regular cat, but something smells off. It's a salty smell, kind of grimy. It's that of a human. I knew what halfkinds were all about, and I knew they were part human and part cat or whatever, but I didn't think it would translate to their scent. The peculiar thing is that both entities smell similar to each other. I always thought Iris Lawton was the last of her kind, but this other body is proving me wrong.

"They're the same," I tell Patrice.

"What do you mean?" he asks.

"The two mystery bodies, they have similar scents. It seems that there were two halfkinds here."

"So Fenrir housed both of them?"

"I'm not sure, let me smell some more."

In the center of the room, the scent branches off. One scent appears to be all over the place. Around the kitchen, around the human-sized bed, around the front door. The ages of the various scents vary, so whomever owns the first one has been living here for some time. It must be Iris's.

The other scent is more direct. It doesn't appear anywhere else but in one straight line, from the back of the cabin to the front. This one must belong to the intruder we saw when we were on the stake out, the one we mistook for Iris. It only had business here and didn't linger around. I suspect this other halfkind was sent from an outside source, because I can tell it didn't mess around.

The bizarre thing is that its trail disappears when it gets to the front door. I'm able to follow it until a certain point, and then it vanishes into thin air. The scent that I think is Iris's also disappears. I feel that this was some kind of abduction case, because both parties are gone, but how they left so abruptly confuses me.

Then again, my focus isn't on the halfkinds, my focus is on Fenrir. After he took us out, he didn't spend much time here. I smell a few faint traces of him, but he left in a hurry, probably to find Iris.

"The two halfkinds don't matter," I tell Patrice. "We're only here for Fenrir, and from what I detect, he's gone."

"Can you trace his scent?" Patrice asks me.

"Yes, I have a scent booster, so it'll help me. It's everywhere here, tracking him won't be too difficult, even through the woodsy terrain. Let's see if Raymus and Danzel have recovered."

My communicator opens up.

"Danzel, Raymus, are you there?" I ask. There's no response.

"Do you think Fenrir took them out, too?" Patrice asks.

"Let's find out."

We stroll out of the cabin, back into the forest. I command the scent amplifier to equip itself. The device slides from my helmed weapon and puts a screen in front of my nose. Wolves are usually resistant to this kind of technology. It's a pride issue, we like to rely on ourselves. But as much as I hate using it, I need this tech for my search. Finding Fenrir over all this terrain requires sophisticated equipment, and I have to adapt.

I use the amplifier to pick up where Danzel and Raymus scurried off to. I trek furiously through the woods, and Patrice follows behind me. Their scent is strong, and I don't go more than fifteen minutes until I see two wolves out cold on the ground.

Patrice and I approach them and nudge their bodies with our noses. They're breathing fine, but the stun shot has put them in an effective slumber.

"Looks like Fenrir got to them," Patrice says as we stand above Danzel.

"We need them to wake up," I say.

"And how do we do that?"

"Watch. Shock."

A thin metal baton protrudes from my helmet. A spark flies from the tip. I lower my head so that the electrified end points to Danzel's abdomen. Then, I thrust forward.

Instantaneously, Danzel yells out a yelp and jumps to his feet. He's feeling a mix of pain and bewilderment to his rude awakening. At first, he's unaware at what transpired, but then he sees my shock baton sticking toward his face.

"The hell is wrong with you!?" he yells at me.

I turn toward Patrice.

“It worked,” I say calmly. “Go over and do the same to Raymus.”

He looks at me and then looks at the fuming Danzel.

“Are you sure?” he says meekly.

“I’m sure,” I say sternly. “Go.”

He turns away sheepishly as if I sent him on a death march.

“What’s your problem, Fang?” Danzel asks angrily.

“You needed to wake up. It was the easiest way,” I say nonchalantly.

“You could’ve been gentler.”

“I wasn’t.”

Danzel looks around.

“How long have I been out for?” he asks.

“About three hours. I woke up first, and then Patrice. We came for you guys after we scouted Fenrir’s cabin,” I say.

“And where is he now?”

In the background, I hear Patrice apologizing to a knocked out Raymus as he gives him a shock. Raymus’s howl echoes through the forest.

“Long gone,” I say, answering Danzel’s question.

“Great,” Danzel says.

“Don’t worry, I have his scent, we should be able to continue the trail once we get moving.”

“Where do you think he went?”

“Iris Lawton is nowhere to be found. It appears another halfkind was involved in her disappearance. Fenrir has most likely has gone after them.”

Danzel looks startled by the news.

“Is that so?” he says. “Didn’t think there were more of them out there.”

"There are, and it appears they've departed with Iris somewhere," I reply.

Raymus and Patrice make their way to where we are.

"Thanks a lot, Fang," Raymus says.

"I'm glad I could help," I say smugly.

"Anyways, Patrice has informed me about the magical, disappearing halfkind," he says. "Where do we go next?"

"The halfkind is a secondary priority," I say. "If we eliminate her, good, it'll only further our case to rejoin the Brotherhood, but she's a bonus for now. Fenrir is our main goal, and I have his scent. We'll follow wherever he's gone to. We've only been out a few hours, so it's still fresh."

"What if he's hidden it?" Patrice asks.

"He hasn't," I say. "With the four of us on the case, we'll get to him in time."

"And what if he's used a teleporter?" Danzel asks.

"We may be out of the Brotherhood, but they haven't expired our rights," I say. "Wherever he teleports to, we'll find it in the record logs. There isn't anywhere he can hide."

They all look at each other in agreement, and then look at me. It's an odd feeling, being treated like the leader, but a nice one too.

"Let's move out!" I yell. "It's time to reclaim our glory."

Chapter 13 - Iris Lawton

Resemblances

May 5, 3043 11:01 AM

"So you're the one who the uppers are raving about," a gravelly voice says to me. I'm in the 'communal room,' as Lionel calls it, where all the other hybrids are congregating. It's a large room with a lot of activities going on. There are probably about twenty or so of them in here, which is more than I've ever seen in my life. Before I arrived at HORUS, and after Operation Halfkinds, I thought I was alone. Bastion and Lucy's existence surprised me, but I'm not prepared for this.

"Um, I guess so?" I say with a raised voice.

"Hmm, I've seen a lot of hybrids, and honestly I don't understand what the commotion is about," the creature says to me.

Like all hybrids, he has a human base, but this one looks more like his animal counterpart than any of the others. From what I can tell upon first glance, he's part dog. The furry tail that wags from his seat is a dead giveaway, and his nose protrudes like snout. His tongue is long and flat, and his nose is blackened, wet, and cold. He has fur like a dog. It's a faint dirty white color with large black spots. The color lets me know that he's part dog, and not wolf. His canine features are very distinctive and, at this point, I've been around enough of them to spot these characteristics with ease.

That's not to say that he looks completely like a dog, his human features are still there. He's bipedal, like all the other hybrids I see. He has opposable thumbs like a primate. His fur is visible, but it's not thick like a dog's, and the outline of his fat can be seen clearly. His ears are notably abnormal. On the inside, they have the grooves and cartilage of a human, but the skin hangs over, creating a floppy effect that I would see on a Beagle. His eyes are much larger than a dog, but they look droopy and sullen.

Overall, he looks pretty old. His fur is crusty and his teeth are discolored. He moves around on a hover chair and has a large hump on his back. He looks frail and weak, and the hoarseness of his voice makes things worse.

"What's your name, youngster?" he says to me.

"Iris," I respond. "What's yours?"

"Zorro. It's nice to meet you."

"It's nice to meet you, too."

I look around and watch the variety of hybrids in the room. Most are sitting down on couches and chairs talking to each other, some are watching video streams of sports or sitcoms. Others are playing games on screens. It's a very leisurely environment and, for the most part, they appear to be enjoying themselves.

"So this is halfkinds headquarters, huh?" I ask Zorro.

"It is, though we prefer being called hybrids. We've been told halfkinds is a somewhat derogatory term that some in the outside world call us," he says.

"Oh, sorry."

"Don't worry about it."

"So, is this what you do all day? Just relax and hang around?"

"Today is an off day, but usually we follow a strict schedule."

"And what is that?"

"Sleep, eat, study and learn, eat, rest, sleep, then we do it all over again."

Everyone looks like they are relishing the free time.

"You all look so… comfortable," I say.

"For the most part we are," he says. "But sometimes looks can be deceiving."

"What does that mean?"

He looks around nervously.

"Forget I said anything."

Watching all these hybrids socializing, interacting, in one place at one time is perplexing. Lately, I've been overloaded with so many shockers. Secret facilities, prostitution mills, psychic revelations. Whatever else I learn, I can only roll with the punches and expect the unexpected.

Yet, despite everything that's new, things seem oddly familiar. The rigid schedule of work and rest is something I've experienced firsthand. My mother put us through the same thing. I wonder if this is where she learned it. The group gatherings and social interactions, treating each other like they're brothers and sisters is also another environment I've been accustomed to. The dorms look exactly like the underground rooms that I slept in during my childhood.

It's not only the environment that feels like déjà vu, it's also the hybrids that I'm surrounded by. In the distance, there's what appears to be a frog hybrid. Leonard. To the right, I see a cheetah hybrid. Ace. There's even a large, bulky hybrid reading a tablet, and he has a horn sticking from his face. Alex. It's like I never left Primm, that my family is still here, a mish mash of human and animals mixed to make a cohesive unit.

Some of the parallels are uncanny. I've already seen the strong resemblance Lucy has to Candy, even though her demeanor is different. Her looks and intelligence made me do a double take when I first saw her.

The more I look at this collective of hybrids, the more I think about my dead siblings. I miss them dearly. I hide it from Fenrir well, but there isn't a day that goes by when I don't think about how they perished and why it happened. I refuse to bring it up to Fenrir because I know he's ashamed of his part in Operation Halfkinds. He did end Lombardi's life after all, though it was the only kill he made that evening. I forgive him for that because I know he was following orders and was still confused with himself when it happened. I believe he's seen the errors of his ways, I just hope he believes it, too.

For seventeen years, my siblings were the only creatures I knew. We were kept secret from society, but we had each other's company. They all had something about them that I remember fondly. Oscar was kind, but that, unfortunately, was his downfall. It's unfair that he paid the price for his naivety. He protected those who couldn't be protected, the Leonards, Maddies, and Lombardis of this planet. I sorely miss having a positive influence like that around.

On the other end of the spectrum, there was Curtis. He had all the negativity that Oscar didn't. He was depressed, angry, and suicidal. But behind that tortured soul was someone who was misunderstood. He loved us, and sacrificed himself for what he thought was the greater good. I don't think I'll ever meet someone who is as complex as he was, a beautiful creature who was willing to die for his brothers and sisters, but wanted to end the miserable existence of his life. Such characters are hard to come by, and I miss his thoughtfulness and loyalty.

I even shed tears over Tiago and his followers, Alex and Ace. The actions of one night don't deserve a lifetime of condemnation. He was scared, stressed, and thought rashly, but that didn't mean he was evil. He made the decisions that he thought were right, the tough ones that helped him survive. And to be honest, he almost made it. As crazy as his plan was, he came pretty close to the freedom that had eluded us all those years.

I'm still monitoring these hybrids, and I realize I was wrong before. This isn't my family. I am a stranger in their home. No one can replace my brothers and sisters. My mother was one of a kind. Upon hearing Lionel's revelations, I have a new respect for what she did. I didn't understand her then, but I understand her now.

And Isaac…I can't even think about him without breaking down. So, I won't.

"Ugh," I groan.

"Are you okay?" Zorro asks.

I clutch my forehead. The headaches seem to be getting worse. My brain is throbbing and it feels like it's going to explode. But I have to pull it together. I shake my head and try to focus.

"I'm fine," I say, brushing off his concern. "So, you look like you've been here a long time."

I'm referring to his fragile appearance. The other hybrids in the facility look young, even more so than me, and I'm only twenty. But Zorro looks ancient.

"I'm actually not that much older than you," he says.

"Really? You look like you're over a hundred," I say.

"Try thirty three."

I look at him in astonishment. He looks prehistoric, there's no way he could be so young.

"What happened?" I ask him.

"It's the price you pay for being the first of your kind," he says. "I am the prototype hybrid. The process was far from perfect at the time, but, by a miracle, it worked. I came out a young, healthy baby. But as I got older, it showed, dramatically. I age at a faster rate than everyone else, something that the lab scientists and Lionel didn't expect to happen. I suppose I should be grateful I'm still alive."

"Am I going to suffer the same fate?"

"I don't think so. You're thirteen years younger than me. Lionel has improved the process greatly over those years. He's enhanced his techniques, learning from his mistakes, learning from me. They've solved the aging issue a while back. I'm guessing your lifespan will last one hundred twenty years or so."

Though I feel bad for him, I'm a bit relieved.

"How do you like it at HORUS so far?" he asks.

"To be honest, I haven't been here long enough to make a decision, though I don't appreciate being abducted from my home," I say. "Can't say they're going to earn my trust that way."

"If it makes you feel better, the uppers generally treat us well. They feed us, clothe us, and house us. Lionel gave us life. I don't have a complaint about our living conditions. I enjoy it here."

"But he keeps you locked within this complex, like a prisoner."

"Trust me kid, it could be a lot worse. You've seen what's out there, what the world does to creatures like us? I mean I've heard things about you, that the Alliance hunted down your family. Lionel is protecting us from those horrible beings."

"I've feel like I've heard this conversation over and over again."

It's true what I say. Zorro doesn't have to lecture me about the dangers of the world, I've experienced them first hand.

"So, why are we here?" I ask him.

"What do you mean?" he replies.

"I mean, why did Lionel create hybrids? We're underground, there are black market deals being made, and I'm sure this place is privately funded. What's his ultimate goal? Why would he spend all this money? Surely someone who has been around since the beginning has some information."

"Nope, I don't."

Zorro scans the room suspiciously to make sure no one is eavesdropping on our conversation.

"I really don't know, but I heard he used to be some big human supremacist or something," he says quietly. "Maybe hybrids are part of his ideology. It's a rumor, though, nothing's for certain. He only tells Bastion and Lucy his plans, so other than that, the rest of us hybrids are kept in the dark."

"And you're okay with that?" I ask him in an upset tone.

"Look, what Lionel wants to do is none of my business. If he wants to create some new world order, that's his plan. Nothing I can do about it. It is what it is. I'm too old to be useful."

"So, you do think he has some hidden agenda?"

"I wouldn't be surprised. He treats Lucy and Bastion like a prince and princess. I mean, they are the best at what they do. And he always talks to Lucy about perfecting this, teaching the younger hybrids that, monitoring so and so's progression. With talk like that, of course there's stuff going on that's bigger than me. But I don't care, my days are numbered."

I think about Lucy and Bastion, how they're separated from the group. They were with Lionel when I woke up, following him at every step. When he left me here, the two of them went with him. I don't think they mingle with these hybrids very much. They're given preferential treatment because they're Lionel's right hand cronies. Like a mind reader, Zorro knows what I'm thinking about.

"I've take it you've met Lucy and Bastion," he says.

"Yes, they showed me around the facility," I say.

"Those two are lucky. They get to hang out with Lionel all day and do some real work, while the rest of us lounge about here like nobodies. I'm pretty sure Lionel has hand-picked them to be his successors. That Lucy is a genius, and Bastion moves like a goddamn super hero."

"He's not so great. That jackass was the one who kidnapped me."

Zorro lets out a chuckle.

"He is good at that kind of stuff," he says. "He usually does all of Lionel's dirty work. And Lucy does all of the real shady stuff."

"Shady stuff?"

"I guess I'm spouting off at the mouth. I don't really have facts, just rumors. But from what I've heard, she is second in command of the biotics developments."

"Biotics? You mean like organic-technological stuff?"

"That's it. So you've heard of them?"

"Here and there, but I'm not an expert on it."

"Basically, it's tech that they surgically implant in you to enhance your body. Lucy is the one who has helped Lionel perfect the whole breeding process, and I hear they're working on some other things, real advanced, real classified."

"You don't know what they're up to?"

"Does the word 'classified' mean anything to you?"

His sarcasm is a bit off-putting. I give a hint of my disgust, and he quickly realizes his rudeness.

"Sorry about that, didn't mean to be so annoying," he says. "But I really don't know what they're up to. That doesn't mean I don't have my suspicions and, honestly, I think what they're scheming has to do with is you."

"With me?!?!" I yell in astonishment. I'm so loud that the other hybrids stop to take a look at the scene.

"Keep it down!"

"Sorry. I wasn't expecting that."

"Anyway, the reason I say that is because for a while, Lionel would make references to the great Iris Lawton. Then the gossip started to brew among us, with different hybrids saying different things. Some suspected you were a mutant, the others said you could shoot lasers out of your eyes. Naturally, I rolled my eyes at a lot of this talk, but among all the commotion, one thing was for certain, that you would be the key to his future plans."

"This can't be right, me? I'm sure you're mistaking me for someone else."

"I don't know anyone else named Iris. You can't be utterly clueless, though. There has to be something about you that would validate these speculations."

Then it hit me. My powers. Lionel mentioned them earlier this morning, and by the looks on his and Lucy's faces, it was pretty obvious they were interested in it. Precognition is an ability that's unheard of, I may be the only thing on this world that possesses it. Yet, my powers are marginal at best. They happen at random, I can't control it, and when it does work, I never see anything important. I had a vision of what the weather is going to be. Big whoop. I don't think Lionel has any use for a glorified meteorologist.

But Zorro is waiting for my response.

"I guess I can tell the future, kind of," I say awkwardly.

"The future?" Zorro exclaims.

This catches the attention of the surrounding hybrids. They start to circle me with interest. I get a closer look at them, and they indeed look younger than Zorro. It's hard to gauge their ages because there's such a large variety of make ups in the crowd. Some are half-dogs, others half-elephants, some have reptilian appearances, some have bird-like appearances. They come in many different shapes and sizes, though as wildly diverse as they are, there's still that similar human quality that unites them.

Their demeanor is inquisitive, wide-eyed and attentive, as if I am some kind of guru that needs to be heard. The questions start to shoot out at rapid fire.

"You can see the future?" one bear hybrid asks.

"Um, kind of," I respond, trying to avoid the answer. "I can see bits and pieces of it, but never a complete picture."

"So you can predict events?" another asks, building off the previous question. This time it's the rhino hybrid that looks similar to Alex.

"Um, well, more like I can see visions, but it's never on my own will, they come randomly," I say.

"I heard you can control the future, make things happen before they happen," one pig hybrid says.

"That's also a kind of," I say. "I can make decisions based on my visions, but I wouldn't really say I'm controlling anything."

"Does it hurt when you see the future?" a reptilian looking hybrid asks me.

"Not really, but I have been getting these major headaches lately," I say. I try to be courteous and polite in my answers, but I'm a bit overwhelmed by the sudden assault of questions.

"What's the outside world like?" a lion hybrid asks, changing the subject.

"Um, it's nice, I guess?" I say. "I haven't actually had the chance to see much of it. I've been in hiding most of my life, like you."

My lackluster answers don't impress them. I sense their impatience. They look skeptical, almost upset by my responses. They were expecting much more, especially from someone who was deemed the key to Lionel's plans.

Yet, it's not fair. I can't provide them with the answers. They probably think I'm a world traveler, the only hybrid to see Earth from outside of HORUS headquarters. In reality, I'm an average hybrid caught in the middle of this craziness. I'm no God, no oracle who can tell them what they need to know. I'm far from that.

Lucky for me, I'm saved by the bell, or genius to be more exact. The communal room door opens, and from it comes Lucy. She sports the same emotionless look that has become her trademark. As she approaches, the other hybrids back away and return to what they were doing before. It's an odd reaction, and it makes me nervous.

"Hello Zorro," she says to him. He's the only one that's different from the others. He's stayed put the whole time.

"Hello Lucy," he says.

"How are implants going?" she asks. "Feeling younger?"

Zorro eases up a little. I couldn't tell if Lucy was making a sarcastic jab, or if it is genuine concern, but that comment has some of the pleasantness that was sorely missing in my previous exchanges.

"Can't say that I am," Zorro says bitterly.

"Assure you doing everything can to stop aging," Lucy says.

Lucy then turns to me.

"Iris Lawton, need your time."

"To do what?" I ask

"Run tests on brain patterns. Need to know limits of powers and effects may have on body. Procedure painless, only check-up."

"Sure it is. It's always 'only this' or 'only that.' Like how my abduction was 'only done' for my well-being?"

"It was."

I don't know if she caught the disdain in my voice when I said it, or if she's ignoring me. She's quite difficult to read.

"Any case, need you to come with me. Please cooperate," she says.

"Like I have a choice," I say.

"Do have choice. Come , or will stun and make you come."

She looks dead serious about her statement.

"Okay, I'm coming," I say begrudgingly.

I turn to Zorro and say goodbye. I'm hoping to see him again, he's a nice hybrid to talk to, but I don't know what Lucy and Lionel have planned for me. I still have zero trust in them, and a dark dread looms over my head. I have a feeling something bad is going to happen.

Damnit, why don't my visions work when I need them to?

Chapter 14 - Lucy

Subject

May 5, 3043 12:43 PM

Specimen, Iris Lawton, prepped. Status stable. Currently cranial detectors placed above head allowing monitor of brainwave status. Screen shows equipment functioning normally. Possible glitches register less than one percent. Procedure safe.

Subject calm, awake. Has been here for one hour. Sedatives not needed. Physical scan of body shows healthy. Organs and cardiovascular systems working. Fat is low, but muscle definition below average. Will recommend higher fiber and fat diet. Subject also vitamin deficient. Since living with wolf, Fenrir Snow, Lawton has likely been eating variety of meats. Must realize needs to consume adequate amount of vegetables to balance nutritional needs of human make up. Will reinforce this in future months. Already included healthy foods this morning in installation pack. Unsure if Lawton consumed out of choice or hunger. Follow up and investigate later.

Lawton lacks serious wounds since encounter with Alliance. Appears to have escaped unscathed. Impressive. Odds of survival against Alliance soldiers low. Changer suspects precognitive abilities aided her. Agree, though high amount of luck also factor.

Been studying Lawton for long time, relying on Bastion's status reports. Had no contact with subject, yet details from accounts impressive. Thoroughness most likely result of semi-obsessive fixation with Lawton. Will need to do full psychoanalysis on Bastion to ensure not fanatical. Devotion to Iris alarming. Cannot separate mission from emotional investment. Attachments inappropriate.

Lawton has been cooperative. Negative attitude annoyance, not hindrance. Projects undesirable feelings towards Changer, Bastion, I. Is understandable. Surprised has not been more hostile.

After escorting her from communal room to medical bay, gave full itinerary of check-up. First I conducted physical exam to check health. Then moved on to brain scan to observe mental capabilities, both intelligence and precognitive. Subject currently sits relaxed in medical chair.

Lawton appears to be only one with special powers. Though I have superior intellect, and Bastion has perfected body to peak of limits, rest of hybrids have not demonstrated anything unique. Some have enhanced senses, durable exteriors as result of animal gene mixing, but most above average. Process still young, will continue to work on creating perfect specimens.

Lawton very smart. Aptitude tests not needed, scan shows activity coming from brain and cognitive progression. High intelligence likely correlated to precognitive abilities. Will need to further study. Nice to have actual subject here, cannot rely on status reports from Bastion. Need physical interaction to get accurate results.

Have learned a lot from past hour. Based on readings and biometrics, hypothesize that Iris can receive bursts of psychic resonance, creating channels to various points in time. High brain activity and abnormal functioning allow her to use bursts to open windows to future. Calls these visions. Comparable to catching radio wave, where wave gives direct link to certain time. Lawton's mind acts as receiver to waves, brain acts as processor to lay out coherent messages. Does not have control over this, only occur in random spurts.

How her brain is able to do this in first place? Unsure, but unique genetic structure has allowed it. Perhaps has to do with feline attributes? Or an anomaly during birth? Too many possibilities to conclude answer. Goal will be to emulate this in future generations of hybrids and improve. Possibilities endless, may be able to exploit gifts to produce new ones. Telekinesis, telepathy, astral projection not out of question.

Interview needed to get more complete analysis. Stepping away from command console to approach Lawton. Biometric drones stop scanning. Stares at approach with mix of anger and fear. Cold demeanor and science coat do not create comforting atmosphere. Irrelevant, I am not concerned with emotions.

"How are you feeling?" I ask Lawton.

"Fine," she responds.

"Have completed physical analysis. Now time to ask few questions concerning condition."

"My condition?"

"Yes, status as precog. Do you know what that means?"

I offend her. Not sure why she has emotional reaction. It amuses me.

"Of course," she says.

"Good," I respond. "Please answer questions honestly. Process will be over quickly. First, describe what happens during precognitive stage."

She pauses to think about answer.

"First things black out a little," she says. "Then I usually see some kind of event happen, and that tells me that whatever I see is going to happen. I can't control what I see or when I see it."

"Interesting."

Everything hypothesized correct. Take notes on tablet as she talks.

"Do visions ever change?" I ask her.

"What do you mean change?" she asks.

"If you see vision, able to act upon it? Able to change future?"

"That I don't know."

"Explain."

"For example, sometimes I see an empty hunting ground for Fenrir-"

"You mean wolf, Fenrir Snow?"

"Yes, Fenrir Snow. As I was saying, I tell Fenrir not to hunt there. So he hunts in a different area. Now, what I don't know is what if I had never told him this? Would he have hunted there anyway? And if he did, would I have seen it as a vision, him being at that hunting ground? It's hard for me to determine if my actions had created that vision, or if that was the vision the whole time."

"This is consistent? Can never change what you see?"

Lawton pauses and thinks again. Looks confused. Deduce Lawton does not know nature of powers.

"Sometimes I can," she continues. "Like when I was small, I saw in a vision my family getting crushed by a falling tree. But after the vision I warned them and they moved away safely before the tree could get to them. So, I guess in that sense, I did change the future because I saw something that didn't happen in the end."

"Understanding of powers hazy," I say. "Conclude have ability to change future, but not confident."

Lawton looks surprised by remarks. Can tell this is subject that she does not talk about frequently. Would have known how to verbalize abilities better. Seems flustered.

"I suppose you're right," she says. "I guess I never really thought about that."

"To understand something, must talk about it," I respond.

"So, what is your diagnosis?"

"Unsure, will need to analyze and consult with Changer before can give definite answer. Next question, any pain related to abilities?"

"I get a headache here and there, but…"

She pauses.

"…that's it."

"Ah, yes," I say. "How are those coming? Subsided?"

Lawton takes moments to answer question.

"Yes. They're gone."

Suspect she is lying. Readings indicate brain activity has been spiking. Tell-tale sign for migraines. Curious why she is lying.

"Have you experienced multiple visions for same event?" I ask her.

"Excuse me?" she says.

"Multiple visions, alternate paths based on degrees of decision making."

"You mean like alternate realities?"

"Yes, but on smaller scale."

"Um, no?"

"I see. Those are all questions I have for you."

She looks at me in stunned manner.

"That's it?" she asks.

"Yes, will not waste time with chit chat. Any questions for me?"

"Um, no."

"Very well. Have gathered all information for now. Bastion will escort back to communal room."

I open communicator and Bastion pops on holographic screen.

"Bastion, please escort Lawton back to room," I say. "I have completed examination."

Moments later, Bastion arrives and takes her away. Lawton gives puzzled glance and leaves. Suddenly, get beep from communicator. Changer appears on holo-screen.

"Lucy, I understand you're done," he says. "Please meet me in my office."

Turn around and walk to Changer's office. It is different from others. Walls and floors are not white, instead furnished with expensive carpeting and antique shelves. Several holographic displays are on walls, live feeds of different rooms around HORUS.

"So, how did it go?" he asks me.

"Lawton was cooperative," I say. "Have all data I need."

"So, do you think she's ready?"

Changer refers to prototype been working on - nano neuro amplifiers, designed to heighten brain activity. Tested them on some subjects, have shown very minor psychic abilities. Changer believes prototype can be applied to Lawton in order to enhance growing powers.

"Not out of question, and can retrofit to adjust to biology," I say. "Need to study information gathered to make sure she will survive operation, but am confident implants will help speed development, even raise capabilities further. Quite possible she will inherit new powers. Examples: telepathy and telekinesis. Retrofitting implants should be simple process. Have already examined physiology prior to arrival."

"How long will that take, to make your adjustments? If these brain implants do what you say they can, then I want action to be done immediately. The faster we can see what limits Iris can reach, the better."

"With data I have, full day's work should be enough. Already done most preparations prior to arrival."

"And you think they're safe?"

"With knowledge and expertise, always safe."

Changer looks at me with curious expression.

"How were you able to create a design without having her here for a physical examination?" he asks.

"Used Bastion as model," I say. "Both have similar physiologies, developed implants around him with intent of using on Lawton. One hundred percent sure they will work."

Changer smiles at confidence.

"Good," he says. "Work all you can Lucy and get the operation ready. I'll want to start in the next few days. Is that enough time?"

"Strict deadline, but should be able to get it done. Forewarning, time to recover from surgery is fast, no more than day, but process will be painful. Okay with this?"

"Yes. A little pain won't hurt Iris in the long run. Once she understands what you're doing for her, it will be nothing."

Changer presses buttons on desk and holographic rendering projects in air. Image of latest model of uteral biotic implants.

"Is she ready for this?" he asks.

"Negative," I say. "Although process has improved since implementation, uteral implants still dangerous. Do not recommend using them on Lawton. In addition, have not made model for Lawton's biology, that will take time."

"I see. How's your progress on that?"

"Improving. Soon synconium problem will be non-existent. Then can start model for cat hybrid. Could not use Bastion to jump start development, he is male and uteral implants only designed for females."

Changer looks disappointed by news.

"And you are sure she can't reproduce the natural way? These implants are needed?" he asks.

"Correct," I say. "Impossible for hybrids to crossbreed with each other. For now, hybrids can only be produced through human hosts. The biology of each hybrid unique, must make plans for universal uteral implant. No time table for when this will be possible."

"That should be our primary goal. First we understand Iris's powers, then we get her to breed. Combine the two, and she will be the mother of a generation of super-powered hybrids. All this rests on your shoulders Lucy, you've far surpassed the skills I possess. I've taught you everything I know. You are the only one equipped to continue my legacy."

"Thank you."

"For now, let's focus on one thing at a time. Start your work on those neuro biotics. We'll want to make Iris is as powerful as can be, and this will be the start of it. Our target for operation will be first thing on May 7. Understood?"

"Yes. Morning ideal, will give Lawton enough time to recover by evening."

"Good. That is all then, Lucy, get to work."

"Understood."

I turn around and exit office. Distractions must not be encountered, work must be completed.

Chapter 15 - Fenrir Snow

Eve

May 7, 3043 6:10 PM

I'm here, in the Bay Area, just outside the city. There's nothing but trees, chirping birds, and rustling leaves. The woodsy setting reminds me of the Wolf's Den, only warmer. In the distance, the bright glare of the sun hits my fur. It will be setting soon, and I want to move quickly before it gets dark.

I've been on Iris's trail for five days and barely used my nose. I've been able to get here through a series of strange occurrences. First there was the vision I saw, the one that told me to go to San Francisco. Then there's this. I don't know how to explain it, it's like a mental radar. I have this sixth sense that I'm following. It's not a voice or an image, it's this instinct, like I'm drawn to a certain location, even though I can't exactly pinpoint where I'm going. I just kind of know, and as I get closer and closer, the gut feeling gets stronger and stronger. At this point, I can tell I'm very close.

Is this Iris's doing? Do her powers go beyond telling the future? Is she a beacon, sending out a psychic signal that I can receive? I never really got a clear understanding of what she could do, but it seems to me her powers are evolving. I know this intuition I have is because of her. It has to be.

I want to believe that because it lets me know she's still alive. She's sending me a message and can only do that if she's safe. But a cast of doubt clouds my mind. What if I'm on a fool's errand? What if this instinct is completely wrong and Iris is rotting face down in the ground in some wasteland? What if this gut feeling I have is a combination of deliriousness and desperation? I could be on an imaginary trail, losing my mind, wasting my time.

No, I can't let this gloom hover over me like darkness infecting my brain. I must move forward, at least for her sake.

I don't know what about her makes me compelled to save her. Perhaps it's because she saved me from the grueling hell that was my service. I would have never been free from the Brotherhood's grasp unless I found a reason to go. And to be honest, I don't miss it one bit. I'm happy with how things turned out. Iris has been a great creature to live with. She's attentive to all my needs. And it's nice having someone to take care of instead of having to kill. No more do I feel burdened with the horrible things I've done. I've made a peace with myself that I've been trying to accomplish for years.

Yet, it looks like fate has reared its ugly head back in my direction. Here I am, plunging myself into the depths of the unknown, and when I get there, I'll probably have to kill again. Even worse, my targets may be my very own brothers and sister.

I can't believe how crazy things have gotten. This grizzled wolf can't find any solace in this messed up world.

I need to focus on Iris, I need to know my priorities. Over the past years, she's been a part of my life, and now, without her, I feel stripped of purpose. I haven't felt complete in a long while, not since Eve. Those were great times for me, and every second I am with Iris reminds me of a life I used to love. The two of them are so similar that being with Iris immediately puts me in that happy place.

Obviously they don't look alike, but when I dig past that, Iris has an aura about her that is much like my late wife.

Eve met me the same way Iris met me, as a broken wolf on a warpath to my grave. Before I met Eve, I was a relatively green member of the Brotherhood's personal task force. Not to brag, but I was by far one of the most talented recruits they've ever had. They could expect no less from the famous Snow family. That's why they threw me in the fire right away.

I was assigned grueling operation after grueling operation, many that required a high level of experience that I did not have. The first ones were particularly brutal, each time I barely escaped from death's cold clutches. Luckily for me, I had some good mentors that educated me in the way of the Brotherhood's warriors. I learned new skills that couldn't be taught in training. I had to adapt on the field, or die trying.

With more and more missions under my belt, my star soared through the Brotherhood stratosphere. Yet, the only rewards I reaped were tougher operations. I was still young, and was eager to please my superiors, so I took my assignments, no questions asked. My body could handle it, my mind could, and the credits were great. Why stop?

And then, things became dark. Soon, I wasn't being assigned to simple skirmishes or drug busts, I was being sent on eliminations, as the Brotherhood called it. They told me that I was sweeping away any unwanted rivals some of the superiors had, that it was standard protocol to do these jobs. Yet, after the first killing, I realized what I had become, a cold hearted assassin.

My targets were never wolves, but the faces of my victims remained in my mind nonetheless. Their screams and pleas to be spared echo through my ears, even today. I didn't understand why these rivals were on the Brotherhood's hit list. In fact, I didn't understand a lot. I never knew any information about my targets, just their location. For all I know, I probably killed the innocent.

At that point, I had been tainted. I became a heartless machine, a puppet dangling by the strings, and I gave no resistance whatsoever. I let them work me like an old drone until that's what I became. I felt no joy in what I did, felt no accomplishment. After a while, I lost my soul, and the only way for me to be free was to die. I signed up for the worst of the worst kinds of jobs the Brotherhood threw at me, hoping that my life would be ended. But my skills betrayed me, every time I came out of an assignment, I came out alive. The only thing moving me forward was the hope that one day I wouldn't. I wanted to change, but I couldn't.

And then I met her. It wasn't like some cheesy movie, but it was coincidence. I met her at a bank. She was looking up my account and she asked for my number. I gave her my communicator number, but she was asking for my account number. We had a good laugh and carried on with business, but in the end I did give her my contact info. We went on our first date and never looked back.

Eve was unlike any wolf I knew. She hadn't been exposed to the world of Brotherhood higher-ups. She didn't care for military operations, family honor, or any of that horseshit. I liked it. The best way to put it was that she was a civilian, not a soldier. For a wolf that comes from a strong military background and only knew other high ranking officials within the Brotherhood's inner circle, she was a breath of fresh air.

Eve was an orphan, a young pup left on the streets and raised in a center. She worked for everything she had. Nothing was handed down to her, unlike me and my siblings. The Snows had a reputation to uphold, she had none. This attracted me to her. I felt carefree when around her. The heavy burden I constantly felt was lifted when I was with her. Like as I was with Iris, when I was with Eve, the problems floated away.

None of these things would be important if she didn't have the personality to back it up. She was a joy to be around. Eve did things that showed me she loved me, as opposed to the way I was raised, where you just assume your clan does. My family, brothers, sister, mother, and father, they were never really affectionate. I was told what love was, not shown. Eve was the first wolf I knew that displayed it. She paid attention to all the little idiosyncrasies that made me, me. Eve knew what foods I liked, what movies I liked to watch, what made me mad, what made me happy. She was the only wolf who knew these things.

All my life, I've felt alone, that no matter how many wolves I was surrounded by, it meant little. I was literally a lone wolf. Eve was the only one who had the key to my secrets, the only one who treasured them. I didn't feel alone anymore, I felt kindred to her, and made an emotional bond I thought I never could.

Eve had this spunk about her that I wasn't used to. I've been around wolves who only told me what I wanted to hear. I think it's because a lot of my peers knew my reputation as a hardcore soldier and ruthless killer. My presence scared others. Yet, Eve wasn't afraid. When we first met, she barely understood what I did for a living. I tried to keep a stonewall demeanor around her, putting up my guard as much as I could. She saw through that and challenged me in many ways. It was a first for me and I enjoyed it. She dug deep to get to know the wolf I was. Even when she uncovered the horrifying truth behind my work, she sought to change me. It sounds cliché, but she did.

She was the sole reason I was able to get out of my downward spiral. I didn't go into missions wondering if I was going to live or die because I didn't take those kinds of jobs anymore. I wanted to live for her. Naturally, the Brotherhood didn't like the idea of losing their elite weapon because he turned into a love sick fool. But I didn't give a shit, I was finally happy. She broke me from their spell.

But then one day, without warning, I learned she got some kind of mysterious disease, that she was terminal, and there would be no cure. The news hit me like a cheap shot to the head. We had only been married for a short while, and the whole time I knew her, she never showed any signs that she was sick. She ate well and took care of herself. It was bad luck, she caught something going around that was fatal to wolves.

It was called Smith's Disease, named after patient zero, one Robert Smith. Humans were the original carriers of this virus, but it was harmless to them. In fact, it was non-lethal to most animals. The only species that it affected was ours, and when a wolf was infected, the virus acted fast. First, within a week, a wolf's hair would thin to the point that clumps would fall out. Then a few days later, their eyes would turn red, and the infected would cough blood. Then on the final day, their heart would stop beating.

I watched Eve go through all of this, day by dreadful day, second by painful second. Her shimmering coat shriveled away. Her eyes became redder than blood. And her voice, the one that spoke so beautifully to me, only coughed noises. She was in agony, but she was also in quarantine. I couldn't be close to her, not even during her dying breath. I watched, from a distance, as her body violently shook and stopped moving. Months later, the virus was cured by top Brotherhood scientists, but what's done was done. My Eve was gone.

She died on a Sunday. I buried her a week later.

It's the humans' fault, all of it. They were the carrier of the disease, the ones that created the sickness. There were even rumors that it was artificially manufactured by them, as a way to weed out the other intelligent species in a way that could absolve them from responsibility. I mean, how could it only kill wolves while our other canine counterpart, the dogs, were unharmed? It sounds sinister, fishy, and evil. It sounds human.

Earth must have been a paradise before those naked apes came and messed things up with their inventions, and their weapons, and their conviction. The filth and corruption they've done to this planet is sickening. They took and took and took, until they could not take anymore. Then they try to restore Mother Nature to its former glory so that it could survive their destruction. Pitiful.

They've made this world unnatural. Their high rise buildings are an eyesore on the once majestic landscapes that used to be there.

Even now, after they were dumb enough to even the playing field, they consume society with their greed. The disease they gave Eve is a metaphor for what they are, a plague to this world. What does a plague do? Bring death and destruction. In their short existence, what have humans done? The same thing. Every time I see one of those two legged monsters striding around, I can't help but think what a horrible creature he or she is. If I had it my way, I would bring them the same kind of devastation that they have brought to my kind. It's personal, but I don't give a shit.

I've had these feelings for a long time since Eve died. It wasn't only them, I hated this world. That's why I signed back up to the force, so I could take out my aggression on faceless enemies. Yet, whatever I did was pointless, I still felt empty and hollow without her. The loop was closed. I was the Brotherhood reaper once again.

Odd that it was my rage that brought me into contact with Iris. I realize the irony that while I hold a human hating doctrine, I have fallen in love with something that is part of them. But at her core, Iris is anything but a human. She may have some of the DNA, but she lacks the inherent evil that comes with their kind.

I find it amazing that I've met someone like that again. She has Eve's kindness, her attention to detail. Iris was shy at first, but after my many visits, she opened up and has become the only thing that I care about. Much like Eve, she has pulled me from the depths and made me realize that, as much as I denied it, life is worth living, that there is some good hidden beneath this pandemonium.

I thought I'd be alone forever, that her death was a surefire sign that some wolves are destined to know only themselves. What I didn't realize, is that things change, fate is not always set for you.

Through her compassion and kindheartedness, Iris is now the holder. I'm not going to let her slip away. It can't happen again. I don't know much about my enemy, but I don't care. I'll kill anything that gets in my way so that Iris has a chance to live. My opponent is my opponent, their bodies faceless. And though I may regret it down the line, my family is no more, they are simply threats to Iris's life.

The mental signal seems to be getting stronger. With every step I take, I feel closer to her. I don't have anything to guide me, my intuition is strong enough.

The woods of the Great West are quiet, too quiet. I look in the distance and watch the sun fall. I can't recall the last time I've seen a sight like this, it's quite mesmerizing. If only Iris were here with me.

Zip!

Something flies by me at great speed, causing a small explosion on a rock nearby. I'm blinded, but just temporarily. I quickly run behind a nearby tree for cover.

Whiz!

I'm being attacked. More shots are being fired. I don't have to see who the culprit is. I already know. Fang, you've come for your rematch, haven't you?

Chapter 16 - Fang Snow

Grudge

May 7, 3043 6:20 PM

It's been a never ending journey tracking Fenrir down to this point. First, we followed his scent through miles of Northern Canadian wilderness until we got to the teleportation station. I'm surprised he got out of the Den so easily, but then again, I've learned not to underestimate him.

Once inside the station, my brothers kept a low profile while I accessed the Brotherhood's central network to figure out where Fenrir was going. After some digging and log reviews, I realized he was headed towards the Bay Area. I wondered what business he had there, but there was no time to waste. We quickly paid our fare and went through the bright lights of the teleporter.

When we got to the other side, I could still smell traces of him here and there. I used those traces to follow a trail, through the city, and into the outskirts. I had to be relentless if I wanted to stick to it, because the longer I waited, the more and more his scent would fade away.

Fenrir did everything on foot, which is fortunate for us. We probably could have tracked him even if he went on a transport, but this makes things easier. I suppose he didn't want to be traceable, so he went completely off the grid. Being out in the open, using creds to make purchases, would no doubt lead to someone noticing. The chance is small, but I know Fenrir. He's always extra careful. Hell, I even bet he thought twice before making that trip on the teleporter. I guess in that case, he had no choice.

His trail led us outside the city, to the mountainous areas that border the Pacific coast. I felt at home there, the tall redwood trees and canopy they created reminded me of the Wolf's Den.

Back in Canada, I live in the Snows' hometown of Helken. It's one of the bigger wolf cities, and you seldom run into areas like this. As I think about it, I understand why Fenrir secluded himself to the forest. It wasn't only for security purposes, I think a part of him enjoyed that environment. I can see why as I spent time in these types of places during our search for him.

The sun is starting to set, and I'm exhausted. Since we started this chase, we barely took any breaks, halting only for short food stops and rest. I know Raymus, Danzel, and Patrice are starting to grow tired of this pursuit. I've been pushing them harder and harder along the way, and I wouldn't be surprised if a mutiny formed. They look beat and irate, but we were getting so close to Fenrir that we couldn't stop for anything.

Then, we finally caught up to him.

In the distance, I spotted Fenrir. He was alone, all we had to do was wait for him to be vulnerable and strike. I wanted to catch him as off guard as possible, so we stalked him, putting on scent blockers so his suspicions wouldn't be raised. It took a while, he was as unyielding as we were in his pursuit. Why was he out here, anyway? I can't imagine Iris being taken to the middle of nowhere, and from the looks of it, civilization wasn't to be found for a while. Fenrir knew something that I didn't. He wasn't lost, he looked like he was exactly where he wanted to be.

Finally, he's come to a stop. I signal my brothers to form a perimeter so we can surround him, north, south, east, and west. We'll create a trap. They move covertly through the brush and twigs to their marks.

"Positioned," Danzel says through his communicator.

"I'm here," responds Raymus.

"Ditto," Patrice says.

"Good," I say, addressing them all. "I have a clear line at Fenrir from my spot. He's about fifty meters away. I think I can hit him. Snipe."

Out from my helmed weapon comes a sniper barrel. A sight scope adjusts in front of my eyes, the cross hair locates and targets Fenrir. Even with all this aid, I still have to fire a skilled enough shot to get a clean hit. His back is turned to me, I can't get a headshot, but all I need to do for now is injure him. I'm the only one I trust with this and I want to be the one who collects the kill.

I watch him observing the horizon, probably gazing at the sunset. It catches my eyes too. I turn my attention back to Fenrir. I take a deep breath in and a deep breath out.

"Fire," I say.

The shot careens out of my weapon and directly hits… a rock next to Fenrir. He becomes startled by it, staggering a bit from the bright flash of the impact. However, before I can blast another one, he comes to his senses and runs for cover. I hastily fire another shot, but it's too late, he knows we're here. Shit, this was not what I wanted, so much for the element of surprise.

Fenrir takes a peak behind his cover as he tries to figure out where we're coming from. We still have position to our advantage, and I can tell it confuses him.

"Everyone, fire from all directions," I say from my communicator.

"Affirmative," they say in unison.

A stream of ammunition flies from the shadows, beyond the trees, right on Fenrir's location. Dust and dirt scatter into the air, creating a cloud of debris so thick, that not even I could see through it. A minute passes, and the veil of grime starts to expand to the point that it reaches my brothers and I.

"Cease fire," I cough out as specs of soil fly into my mouth.

"I can't see anything," Danzel says.

"Me neither," Raymus retorts.

"Everyone, stay put until all this settles down," I say.

We hold our positions and wait it out. Slowly but surely, the cloud starts to dissipate until I can once again see. I quickly look at where our gunfire was concentrated, only to see a small crater. No body, no blood, no evidence of him.

But then, my eyes catch something to the right of it, a grey mass of fur with a helmet on his head. Fenrir. Damnit, how did I know that was going to happen?

Something that looks like a metal canister pops out of his helmed weapon and flies into the air. I tilt my head up to see what it is, but before I could make it out, it explodes. A bright flash causes me to look away. Streams of energy scatter from the core toward the ground.

"Crap," I tell the others over the communicator, "it's scatter rain. Everyone, duck for cover."

Scatter rain is like a firework. It gets propelled into the air, and disperses pure energy into the sky. The energy floats down from above, like a rain of lights, and burns anything in its path. If we don't find something to hide under, we're literally toast.

Luckily for me, I see a boulder formation a few meters away. I dart my way to it and slide under an opening so that my body is completely covered from the incoming hail of energy. I peer from beneath it and watch as small trees and brush get demolished by the flares. One streak slices a branch, and I watch it crash to the ground.

"Damn, Fenrir," I say to myself, "didn't know you had that kind of firepower on you."

A transmission arrives to my communicator.

"Fang, where are you?" Raymus asks.

"About ten meters from my original location," I respond. "Where are the others?"

"We're hiding until the shit blows over!" Patrice exclaims. "Shouldn't be much longer."

"Where's Danzel?" I ask.

"I don't know," Raymus responds. "I think he's in a clearer area. The scatter rain's ammunition floated away from him. He's not in danger."

"Good," I say. "Wait a minute, what's that?"

A strong force blows through the forest. Its aura is blue and gold and charges straight in Fenrir's direction.

"Danzel," I say to myself, "what the hell are you doing?"

Actually, I know exactly what he's doing. A few days before we started our mission, Danzel came home with a big smile on his face. He had finished a visit to some weapon upgraders. I asked him what new armament he got grafted onto his helmed weapon.

Scatter spheres? Energy drones? Perhaps some plasma mines?

No, he got none of those. Instead, he purchased something called the Blue Bullhead. The minute he said it, I rolled my eyes. I knew exactly what a Blue Bullhead was, an energy layer that surrounds your head, which increases strength when gaining momentum. It allows you to rush at your enemy head on so you can bulldoze anything in your way. The energy surrounds your head and body, allowing you to be protected from collateral impact. It's more or less a glorified, energy shielded helmet that is specifically designed for charging.

It certainly looks cool and intimidating. Things fly in the air, and all you can make out is this ball of mass heading your direction. Despite the bells and whistles, it's not practical. You have to make physical contact with your target, and Fenrir is extremely elusive. You can't simply locate and run over him.

Still, I'm a bit surprised because Danzel is coming at Fenrir in top speed, and Fenrir looks flabbergasted. He's not moving or putting himself in a defensive position. He just stands there as Danzel's train of destruction heads his way. Maybe Danzel's crazy weapon will actually hit him.

But, I'm wrong. At the last second, Fenrir casually slides out of the way, and Danzel runs right into a tree. The Blue Bullhead does its job, as Danzel is able to topple it over with no injury to himself. Impressive.

Still, he's missed Fenrir completely. Fenrir pounces on Danzel savagely and takes a large bite towards his neck. Danzel swiftly turns over and rolls, pinning Fenrir on the dirt, both of their backs face the ground. Danzel jumps to his feet to bite Fenrir. The only place he can chomp down is on his face or neck, the rest of Fenrir's body is covered in armor.

Danzel isn't fast enough, though. Fenrir summersaults forward, using his momentum to crash into Danzel. Fenrir has him dazed, and does something that I thought he'd never do.

"Fire," Fenrir says as a shot comes out directly at Danzel's leg. It's blown off completely, and blood gushes out of the stump that used to be his foot. Danzel writhes in pain, rolling around and howling, all while Fenrir looks upon him coldly.

"Is this what you want?" he yells to us in his native tongue. "The time for mercy is over, Fang. If you want to play hardball, then let's play hardball. But I don't want to take any of my sibling's lives. Let this be a lesson to all of you, do not cross me again, because these are the consequences you will face."

I watch as Danzel agonizingly retreats into the woods. He's still whimpering, and his injury leaves a thick trail of red on the dirt and grass. I realize that we are more out of our league than ever, and I don't know if I should keep going. Our lives are more important than our legacy.

But before I can bark an order to retreat, an eruption of energy and plasma fires from below ground into the air. Tunnelers. One of my brothers must've launched them when Danzel got injured. I see a wolf leap from the bushes, launching a hail of gunfire at Fenrir. Raymus.

Unsurprisingly, Fenrir dodges the geyser of force coming from the tunnelers and easily evades Raymus's shots. I'm not sure why Raymus chose to go with this strategy. The tunnelers didn't work before, so what made him think they were going to work this time?

Still, Raymus does have the upper hand, as Fenrir is seriously out-gunned. Fenrir leaps behind a rock for fortification. At this point, Fenrir can only arm his single barrel, and he pathetically lets some ammo loose at Raymus. Raymus dodges that, and it appears they're at a stalemate. Both exchange a few more rounds, but neither gets a good hit on one another.

That's when Fenrir changes tactics. He ceases fire, and takes a moment of deep thought as he hides behind his cover. Raymus looks at him cautiously, wondering what his next move will be. Then, as quickly as he jumped behind it, he soars over the boulder and dashes to my brother. Raymus looks surprised by the brash decision, and is unprepared for a direct assault. Fenrir knocks him to his side. But something else flies off of Raymus, his helmed weapon. That was the real reason for the charge, Fenrir wanted to disarm him.

Raymus is now looking straight at Fenrir's barrel, but I know Raymus has something else up his sleeve. He taps his feet to the ground, and a metal alloy wraps them. Before our mission, Raymus had installed some leg implants. Upon activation, they jut out from his legs and ensnare them to create a durable exo-armor that Raymus can use to strike him.

I'm not a big fan of melee tactics. Why hit something when you can shoot it? I thought his implants were useless, much like the Blue Bullhead, but perhaps I was wrong. It certainly gives Raymus an advantage here.

Immediately, Raymus whips his body around, allowing his hind legs to mule kick Fenrir in the stomach. Fenrir must feel like a sledgehammer had hit him. Those implants are strong, and one kick could've easily knocked Fenrir out if Raymus hadn't hit Fenrir's body armor.

Raymus takes another violent kick, this time at Fenrir's rear. It once again connects on Fenrir's body armor, and it once again causes Fenrir a great deal of pain. A few more smacks, and its lights out for Fenrir. Raymus rears back and prepares one final swipe to Fenrir's head. With a mighty swing, he releases from his stance and his front paw travels violently through the air.

But, it misses. Fenrir ducks under it, thrusts his head into Raymus's body, and pushes my brother backward. He loses his footing and tumbles over, right to where Fenrir wanted him to be, over a tunneler. In a flash, Raymus gets hit with the geyser and goes flying into the air. He crashes a few feet away, alive, but knocked out. Two down, two to go, just like before. It's déjà vu.

Or not. I'm startled as Fenrir lets out a giant howl. Had I been paying attention to the background, I would've noticed Patrice sneaking up behind Fenrir as he was dueling it out with Raymus. He got a deep bite on the back of Fenrir's neck the moment he pushed Raymus, tearing into the flesh like a thick steak. Fenrir violently tries to shake Patrice off, but his grip is firm, and Patrice merely rides Fenrir's struggle.

Fenrir falls to his feet as Patrice chomps down another vicious bite. This time he's not letting go, and Fenrir howls into the sky. It appears Fenrir is going to lose, but, in a desperate moment, Fenrir lunges back slamming his and Patrice's body to the boulder Fenrir was using for cover. Surprisingly, Patrice still doesn't let go.

Fenrir lunges again with a slam, but nothing happens.

He does it again, and Patrice bites down harder. Fenrir yells out another cry for pain. However, I can tell the repeated smashes are wearing Patrice down. If he doesn't let go, he's going to pass out.

Patrice knows it too, and with one quick movement of his jaw, he turns his head and rips out a large chunk of Fenrir's flesh. Blood oozes out of the wound, and I see Patrice spit out hunks of fur and muscle. Fenrir looks subdued with blood trickling down his forehead. He's probably in some of the greatest pain he's ever experienced.

However, my idiot brother has left himself exposed again. His head is right in front of Fenrir's helmed weapon. With a simple phrase, Patrice could be dead. I see Fenrir open is mouth, about to motion the words that will end Patrice's life. And that's when I go into action.

"Fire," I say. A whiz hurls out of my head, and right into Fenrir's helmet. His weapon zaps and in an instant, Fenrir's on the ground shaking.

I didn't fire a standard energy shot, but an electro disrupter instead. It's a mini EMP, concentrated, allowing electric scrambling at a target, in this case, Fenrir's weapon. The helmet goes haywire, and Fenrir feels the electric shocks that spreads from its frazzled mainframe. His brain is literally frying.

I walk closer to him. The barrel from my helmet is pointed right at him. He's helpless, in pain and stunned. One shot can end his misery and restore the Snow family back to glory. Yet, I hesitate. I lived in his shadow all my life, using our rivalry to fuel my drive. All the training, all the limit pushing, and I wasn't even close to his level. He's been my greatest enemy, but also the only one who cared. He wasn't a bad older brother, he was a good one. I look at the bandage on my leg, a wound he cleaned up even though we had made it clear that we wanted him dead. We are family, that's why he did what he did. Yet, we are family, and here I am doing what I'm about to do.

This makes no sense. Is this what I want? I look at the destruction that surrounds me, injured brother after injured brother. Danzel will have to walk with an artificial leg. For the rest of his life, Raymus may have scars from the burns of the tunneler. And Patrice, our youngest, almost died. Fenrir's life is now in my judgment. Is this the price for honor? Would my father, my ancestors, want this to happen?

I look at Fenrir one last time before I call to fire. My voice is shaking. All the hate that I felt earlier this week is gone, the only thing that's left is hesitation.

Fenrir's still shaking on the ground. But, strangely, his front leg isn't moving as erratically as the others. It's like he has control of it. He's nudging it against the ground, as if he's pounding on something. And that's when I realize it, he's not banging his leg, he's banging something on his leg to the ground. It's a small black box, something that looks familiar.

Shit. A marble shooter and he armed it. A dozen blue energy spheres flood the ground, and I yell for Patrice to move. We run away from Fenrir like rats from a fire. I hear some booms, and mounds of dirt explode to the sky. I leap toward the tree that Raymus knocked down. A careening rock hits my head, and knocks my helmed weapon off in mid-air. I can't go back for it, because when I land, I'm already behind the log.

Things settle down. I emerge from my hiding spot to look at the aftermath. Patrice slowly gets back to his feet as well. I run over to where I had Fenrir trapped, and he is gone. Damnit. I sniff the ground and see a trail of blood. He must've ran off as fast as he could after the blast. He was released from my hold the moment my helmed weapon flew off. No matter, he's injured. We'll catch up to him, but I look at my two brothers, Raymus and Danzel. They've have been grievously injured. They've been through hell, and I'm in disbelief that Fenrir would have gone to such extremes. Patrice approaches me.

"We have to tend to them," he says.

It will take a few hours until they're at least in shape to continue.

"We'll have to cauterize Danzel's wound and put an impromptu artificial foot on him. It's not permanent, but at least he'll be able to walk for the time being. For Raymus, find some burn cream and apply it. All the stuff you'll need is in the medical pack," I say.

Patrice looks at me with confused eyes. "What are you saying? We need to go to a hospital now."

"If we do that, we'll lose his trail."

"So?"

I observe my brothers. They're in rough shape, but if I push them hard enough, we can keep going.

"I hesitated earlier," I say. "I had a chance to end Fenrir and I didn't. I don't know why, but I did. I guess a part of me realized that he's our brother. But then, as I see what he's done to Danzel and Raymus, what he's done to you, I realize something."

"What's that?" Patrice asks.

"He's no longer our family. A real brother wouldn't do that to his kin. That halfkind is more important to him than us."

I sniff his blood. It smells fresh.

"Do what you can with Danzel and Patrice," I say. "We'll take some time to rest it out, but we're not going to stop now. Their wounds will heal, and Fenrir will pay for what he's done to us. Do you understand?"

With a fearful look on his face, Patrice nods his head.

"Good," I say.

Chapter 17 - Bastion

Monitor

May 5, 3043 2:03 PM

The door to the communal room is open, and Iris walks through it.

"Here you go," I say in the most comforting tone I can muster. "You must be very tired after Lucy's examination. For now, you'll spend some time here, but in a half hour I'll stop by and will escort you to your room. Does that sound okay?"

She doesn't answer. She still has the same sour, irate facial expression. Actually, it goes beyond that, Iris looks like she wants to rip my head off. I think out of all us at HORUS, she hates me the most.

"Hey, I know you must be pretty pissed off and scared," I say in the same calm voice. "You don't have a clue what's going on, and you probably think Lionel, me, Lucy, HORUS in general, are monsters for kidnapping you. I mean, we took you away from that nice life you had in the Wolf's Den. But trust me, we're here to help. I'm not asking you to like us, I'm asking you to understand that we have good intentions."

Still, she doesn't respond. I let out a sigh. It seems no matter what I say, it won't help.

"Looks like your mind is made up, just know I meant what I said," I say.

She quietly walks into the communal room and the door closes. I go the opposite direction and turn around to a corner, walk up a ramp, and into a small room at the end of the hall. We hadn't passed by it earlier, but this is the monitor room, a place where the walls are adorned with live feeds from every corridor in HORUS headquarters. As Lionel's elite, I help out with security.

The feeds show activity from the perimeter and the room also has controls to the defense mechanisms. We haven't had to use those, ever, and I don't foresee a need to use them anytime soon. No one's stumbled upon this place. Lionel is very diligent in making sure we stay underground. It would take a tenacious animal to track us down. So far, no agency, not even the Alliance, has sent anyone with such ferocity. A part of me worries that one day such a creature will come, but for now, that's the last thing on my mind.

Lionel has given me clear instructions to observe Iris as she stays in the communal room. I'm to report anything suspicious, but so far Iris has given me little reason to be on high alert. For a hybrid in her position, she is actually surprisingly calm. Sure she's pissed off as hell, but I don't sense much fear in her. If a normal being were kidnapped from their home and captured by an underground organization, I'm sure they would lose their mind. Not Iris, though, she has been perfectly rational. Her stability only adds to her mysterious aura.

She gives off this presence, like she knows stuff. I'm not only talking about the future either, I mean in all aspects. We haven't had a clear definition on what she can do, instead we only know bits and pieces. She only knows bits and pieces. Yet, she's demonstrated a variety of peculiar traits. I guess that's what makes her so mystifying, her possibilities seem endless.

I see her sitting down on a couch, by herself. The others don't approach her. They cautiously mind their own business as Iris nervously looks around, aware at the commotion she is causing. I suppose rumors have started to fly between my fellow hybrids. I don't think any of them truly know what's going on, what plans are in store for Iris. Hell, I don't know everything. I suspect that even Lucy, as much as Lionel shares with her, only learns of things piece by piece. Only Lionel knows the master plan.

Still, everyone, hybrids and humans, know that big things are coming up with her. And that probably scares them. A hybrid with such potential brings a lot of hullabaloo among the common masses. I think they're fearful of Iris because they know Lionel holds her in such high regard. She is someone not to be messed with, a prized jewel that is untouched.

Lionel sometimes goes on these ambiguous rants in front of the others when it comes to Iris. He uses words like 'powers', 'evolution', and 'future.' From his description, images of a mythical goddess are conjured. I'm sure they're scared of what she can do. As I said before, they don't know her potential, they know she can do things. What those things are exactly remain in the dark, but I'm sure their imaginations run wild.

Iris's question and answer session did little to clear the confusion either as she stumbled through her answers. It probably added to it.

One of the hybrids approaches her. I see him on my feed as he hovers over to Iris with his giant chair. Zorro. They were chatting earlier, and it seems Iris has had good rapport with the old geezer.

He's a nice fellow, it's a shame that he's aging so rapidly. He isn't gifted like me or Lucy, or even the others, but he has wisdom and wit that comes naturally. He also doesn't let you forget about his ancient appearance, but he has a good sense of humor about it. Despite his curmudgeonly exterior, I'm fond of him.

Yet, I also know that as the elder statesman, he tends to cause trouble. He is the reason there is a very small divide between the 'elite' hybrids like Lucy and myself, and the 'normal' ones like him. I heard his discussion with Iris earlier, about how he thinks we are prince and princess. I can't say I agree with him on that one, we're just the ones that help Lionel the most. If we have the ability to shine, why shouldn't we? I think he's a little jealous because he ended up with the raw deal.

"So, did they mess with your brain?" Zorro says jokingly, though I sense a level of seriousness behind the sarcasm.

"No, not really," Iris says warmly. Her demeanor around him is much different than me.

"What did they do to you?"

"I think only a physical. She scanned me, asked a few questions, that's about it."

"Oh."

His terse response causes a bit of alarm within Iris.

"Did you want to add something else to that? It seems like you didn't say everything on your mind," Iris says.

"Um, it's nothing," Zorro says.

Zorro looks up and down, left and right. He lowers his head, as if he's about to whisper something in Iris's ear. I zoom in on my feed and strengthen the audio.

"It's just that when that chimp examines you, she usually has a purpose behind it," Zorro says. "Normal physical checks can be done by any of the lab techs, but the fact that she personally did it is kind of weird."

"Really?" Iris says in an astonished tone. "I thought she checks out everyone."

Zorro shakes his head.

"She checks me quite often because she's trying to work on the anti-aging stuff," Zorro says as discreetly as possible. "If she's checking on you, it's probably because she's planning to do something, and soon."

Iris reacts to this news with a nervous smile.

"What kind of things do you think she's doing?" she asks.

"I don't know," he says. "I mean don't get me wrong, she might be there to help. Maybe you have a sickness or something. How have you been feeling?"

"For the most part okay, but I've had some non-stop migraines since coming here."

"Migraines? Non-stop? Has it ever happened before?"

"Um, not really. I've never experienced headaches this long. They're throbbing, and they happen in a steady rhythm. It's almost like a constant beeping in my head, like an uninterrupted signal is being sent. That's the best I can explain it."

Zorro sits back in his chair to think.

"I'm sure Lucy is investigating it," Zorro says.

"I guess," Iris says. "I'm as stumped as you are."

That makes the three of us. I wonder what Lionel is up to. Knowing him, and knowing Lucy, this might have something to do with biotics, but what could she be implanting in Iris? Even though this has to do with their experiments, I'm usually not left this much out of the loop. What are they hiding from me? I'll have to find out.

Perhaps they are working on something to help Iris. I mean, she did have those headaches, and she's been talking about them since her arrival. I hope that's what they have in store. Anything to help Iris would be great, because I don't want any harm to come to her.

Lucy thinks I'm borderline obsessed, but they don't understand what it's like to find someone like yourself. We're hybrids, but none of my peers are cat hybrids like Iris. She's my true kind, and we are literally a match for each other.

Is that why Lucy and Lionel are keeping me in the dark? They're afraid I'll interfere?

I look at the clock and I haven't realized time has flown by so quickly. It's almost 2:30, and Lionel has instructed me to lead Iris to her quarters.

I head down to the communal room and approach her. The other hybrids look at me with the same caution they do with Iris. This is the slight divide I talk about. I always suspect that the others fear Lucy and me to some degree.

"Time to rest," I say to Iris in a peaceful voice. She still looks at me with a death glare.

"Sorry Zorro," she says to him, "but the grunt tells me I have to go. I'll be sure to talk to you some more later."

Zorro smiles and returns the gesture.

"No problem my dear, I'm looking forward to it," he says.

I look at Zorro and give him a brief nod.

"Zorro," I say.

"Bastion," he replies.

Iris and I walk out the room and we make our way to her lodging. She remains as silent as ever, and instead of pressing conversation I decide to take the unspoken route as well. Neither of us utter a peep during our stroll.

We arrive at the barracks and I show her to her room. The door opens, she walks in, and I turn around.

I expect the door to close, but it doesn't. Instead I hear her voice call me.

"Bastion," Iris says. She still looks pissed off, but has less of a scowl. "What do you guys plan to do with me? I've heard things from the others, and I'm a little concerned. I want a straightforward answer."

I stop in my tracks and think of what to say.

"To tell you the truth," I say, "I don't completely know the details behind Lucy and Lionel's scientific plans. I do know that you're going to be a centerpiece in Lionel's master stroke, that's probably why he had Lucy do a physical on you."

"Why is that? Why does everything hinge on me?"

"Because you're special," I say convincingly. "I know that word gets tossed around so frequently, but it's true. You can tell the future, that by itself is something to behold."

"That's it?" Iris says skeptically. "Lionel's only using me for my abilities? I'm another one of his freaks that he can control."

"Don't call yourself a freak. We are Lionel's finest creations. We aren't monsters, we're the next step. And Lionel is here to guide us, not control us."

Iris looks at me squarely, eye to eye.

"You sure about that?" she says.

"Of course."

But Iris continues to look at me until things become awkward. I feel uncomfortable with the confrontation, and her question hits me hard.

"No doubt in my mind," I say insecurely.

"I see," she says. "Well I am going to rest now. Thank you for being honest with me."

The door closes in front of my face and I walk away to exit the barracks, but before I leave the corridor, I look back at Iris's room. I think about her blunt question. The simple inquiry rattles me and all I can think to myself is that Lionel has always been right. She is special.

Chapter 18 - Lionel Changer

Mediate

May 5, 3043 2:35 PM

"What is meeting for?" Lucy asks as she walks into my office. She looks a bit irritated. I probably interrupted her during her work.

"It's to discuss the upcoming surgery we have planned for Iris," I say.

"Nothing to discuss. Surgery planned on May 7. Details reviewed. In middle of planning, meeting preventing me from doing work. It is annoying."

Lucy is as blunt and focused as ever, that's why she's one of my favorites.

"I understand, Lucy," I say. "I'm busy, too, but I need to have this meeting to make sure all of us are on the same page."

"All of us?" she asks inquisitively.

At that moment, Bastion walks into the room, looking as confused about it as Lucy.

"You called, sir," he says.

Bastion is punctual and a loyal follower. That's why he's one of my other favorites.

"Why is he here?" Lucy asks defensively.

"Meeting about scientific procedure, only discussed between us. Subject is hybrid that Bastion has been orbiting with diligence."

Bastion looks at Lucy with confusion.

"Sometimes, I don't get what you're talking about," he says.

"Listen up you two, the reason I called this meeting is to have one final check out before we go through with the procedure," I say.

"Procedure?" Bastion says in a surprised tone.

"Ah, yes, not informed," Lucy says. "Finished examination. Concluded Iris Lawton's brain activity off charts. Precognition definite, psychic abilities mild, telekinesis not outside possibilities. In order to enhance powers, amplify, neurological implants must be installed. Procedure painful, but safe. Recovery swift. Iris Lawton perfect candidate for biotics, designed off your physiology."

"Implants, brain surgery? What are you talking about, Lucy?"

"In order to learn and exploit powers, must operate soon. Target time two days."

"Operate?"

Bastion looks at me with angry eyes. He realizes what's going on.

"You're experimenting on her?!" he yells.

"Yes," Lucy answers for me. "Faster we act, faster can explore potential."

"And you said this procedure will be harmless? But you also said it'll be painful. How painful?"

"The procedure safe, but always are risks. Potential pain… hard to describe," Lucy explains.

"What exactly are you going to do?"

Lucy looks at me to get approval before going into the details. I look at her reassuringly to let her know it's okay to divulge.

"Two incisions, symmetrical holes no larger than one millimeter. Piercing side of cranium, allowing careful insertion of biotics. Will have surgical drones to assist to assure preciseness of cuts," Lucy says.

"Okay, I guess that doesn't sound so bad," Bastion says.

"After incisions are made, surgical drones will use two injection needles, six inches to directly penetrate brain. Needles deposit nanotech implants into grey matter, activate. Other drones vacuum excess blood coming from patient's head."

I see Bastion grimace at the thought of the needles entering her brain while also picturing the drones sucking away her blood.

"Implants will respond," Lucy says. "Patient feels immense distress during time, as activation done by small electrical pulses. Direct stimulation needed."

"Well, at least she will be sedated," Bastion says.

"Negative. Sedation may weaken brain activity. Need to be at optimal threshold during procedure for nanite implants to start up."

"You expect Iris to undergo that much pain willingly?"

"Subject's commitment optional. Any concerns taken lightly. Procedure safe. Pain may not be tolerable, but subject will survive."

"Pain won't be tolerable? And you accept it?"

"Yes, implants are for benefit, greater good served. That is price she, we, must pay. But these matters irrelevant."

"Irrelevant? What are you talking about?"

I see the anger boiling in Bastion. Our secretive plans for Iris have left a bad taste in his mouth. His voice is steadily rising, his eyes narrow further and further. His hands are clenched in fists, as if he's ready to punch Lucy in the face. He's emotionally invested now, this can't be good.

"Not need be concerned what happens to Lawton," Lucy says. "Merely following plans. Never objected before. Lawton clouded mind. Signs obvious. Blinded by obsession."

"Obsession?" Bastion responds in a shocked tone. He breaths get heavier and heavier. "You think I'm obsessed?"

"Vitals rising, antagonism showing, movements erratic, reaction defensive. Signs of unhealthy fixation."

"Fixation? I don't know what you're talking about."

"Denial useless. Spend surplus time reading files, observing. Desired attachment obvious. Do not understand how one can be enamored by one they have just met. Bonds confusing, irrational."

"Not everything is about rationality!" Bastion yells. "Why do you feel everything needs an explanation? It's not an equation that needs to be solved. You may know a lot of things, but I can't fathom how you don't understand that."

"Confusion mutual."

Lucy says it with a smile, but Bastion hardly looks amused. He looks desperate, and I decide to step in.

"Bastion," I say. "I have to call you out on it. The first day I told you about Iris, those many, many years ago, I could see in your eyes that you were drawn to her. I know that's why you accepted all those monitoring missions, why you were so eager to serve my interests towards Iris Lawton. You're attracted to her."

"That's... that's absurd!" he says trying to hide the obvious truth.

"No, it's okay to admit it. I can see why. You're part feline, she's part feline, it only makes sense to think you two are kindred."

Bastion's anger slowly calms down and shame enters the fold. That's it Bastion, let your guard down, tell me the truth.

"I can understand where you're coming from. We often search this world looking for someone like us, someone who can understand us," I say. "Surely, as a hybrid, this hits close to home because you are but a few in a world of billions."

Bastion remains silent.

"But surely you must've known that this would be coming," I say. "I've been talking for years about how Iris is the key to my final goal, how her abilities could spring forth powers in future generations of hybrids. In order to reach those goals, sacrifices must be made. I guarantee you she will be okay after the procedure and, in the long run, implants like these will help her."

I walk over and touch Bastion's arm.

"Just look at what they've done for you," I tell him. "Mine and Lucy's biotic designs have given you strength, agility, physical prowess that goes beyond your limits. They're in your arms, legs, even soul. Imagine what we can do with a hybrid like Iris."

Bastion looks confused. He wants to protest more, but he's holding back.

"Have you forgotten what HORUS is about? It's about development, improving the human race so that we can take what is ours. We are the future, you are the future, Iris is the future. We can't make those giant leaps if we hold back. Development is made through blood, sweat, and tears."

"I…I… I don't know," Bastion says softly. "Of course I want to remain true to your vision, Lionel, but I can't explain it. There's something about her that I'm drawn to. I know it's clouded my loyalty a bit, but I'm so mixed up inside. I want to make sure that she'll be safe. I'm compelled to protect her."

"In the long run she will be, and you will. Years from now, when we've accomplished everything we worked for, we'll look back on this day and not an ounce of regret will come from our decisions. I've raised you, cared for you, and I haven't let you down. I won't start now. And I guarantee Iris will be by your side. She's warming up to our facilities. She'll be one of us in no time."

A long sigh comes from him, and after some hesitation, he finally releases a response.

"Okay Lionel, I'm with you," he says.

"I never had any doubt," I respond. "The procedure will occur on May 7. Is that okay?"

Bastion nods his head.

"Good. That's all then, you're free to leave."

Bastion turns around and exits my office. Lucy then approaches me.

"Shouldn't be involved," she says.

"That's all right," I say. "He needed to know eventually. The earlier we get rid of these distractions, the better. Continue with your preparation, May 7 is in only two days. With her implants in, we'll look toward the future. Nothing is going to stop us."

Chapter 19 - Brock West

Nightfall

May 7, 3043 7:17 PM

A cool breeze flows past my body. The sun had set an hour ago, so there's nothing but a pre summer night sky and the faint dim of lights set up in our camp. I always love this feeling before a mission. It's a calm time. Our prep work is done, equipment is set, the game plan has been reviewed, there's nothing left to do but relax and enjoy the final hour before the mayhem.

Half my team is scattered about, making final preparations for the frontal assault. The other half is underground. Arbock has our transport parked nearby. Once we're ready, he'll be on standby to make any emergency pick-ups during the mission.

John is set up at a portable command console. He'll be our eyes and ears during this mission, and he has the equipment to do so. The pig will be firing off instructions, map detail, and a bevy of other calls as he guides us through our operation.

Kanji is going through his code breakers and inspects his encryption devices. I'm depending on him to get us through the entrance quickly. Ingle is in the air, scouting, and on his way to installing the scramblers, which will assist Kanji in his task. Teamwork, that's what it's all about.

Kimba has the necessary arms ready to go. He's given us full training, and I'm familiar with what to use and when to use it. Each weapon is special tailored to our physique. Some are made for lions and tigers like

Kimba and Kanji, others for birds like Ingle the eagle, some for gators like Waylon, and so on.

The underground team has already started their task, and is the closest to HORUS headquarters. That reminds me, I need to check in on their status.

"Winde, this is West, do you copy?" I ask. I see his chimp face appear on the screen.

"Yes, I'm here," he says.

"State your team's position."

"We're currently ten meters away from the server room. I've already hacked into their security feeds and applied the masks. No one will know we're there, unless it's a wrong place, wrong time kind of situation. Security alerts have also been disabled."

"How has it been getting down there?"

"Slow. We've avoided any sensors thanks to John's maps, but tunneling has taken longer than I expected. The laser drill has been downright buggy, and Waylon has been using it for almost two hours now. No worries, we're getting there. Once we arrive at the compound, I expect that we'll run into the perimeter wall. Clipper has brought his silent explosives for that job. We'll be in the server room in probably thirty minutes. Once we get in, communications and drone control will be ours."

"Good. Scramble their communications once you're there and set off the EMP. I'll give you the go when you can enter the rest of the premise and start your cleaning. Take out every living creature you see, got it?"

"Yes sir," Winde says without hesitation.

"Excellent, and remember…"

"Leave the drives alone. I know, I know."

"Just making sure. This is West, out."

In the sky I see Ingle approach our camp. It looks like he's completed the task.

"How'd it go?" I ask. "See anything suspicious?"

"Other than the dozens of laser turrets, plasma cannons, and what I think is a gravity gun, nothing seems to be out of the ordinary," Ingle says sarcastically.

"You scared?"

"I repeat myself, a gravity gun. Not all of us like challenges as much as you do."

"You should be used to it by now after all these years. Did you find the entrance?"

"Sure did. It's literally a hole in the ground."

"And the scrambler?"

"It's installed."

"Nice work Ingle."

I signal to the others and motion for them to come. Arbock, Kimba, Kanji, and John arrive where Ingle and I are situated. A gorilla, lion, tiger, pig, eagle, and a human gather around a campfire. Sounds like the set up for a bad joke.

"All right, the time is almost half past seven, our assault is going to start in a little less than an hour. That's thirty minutes to make your final arrangements before we storm the compound," I say. "Winde's team is already below ground, ready to scramble their servers. They plan to execute the EMP and bomb their way in. It'll be a simultaneous attack, one that will surprise them and cause mass disorder from within. Winde's team will be coming from behind, we'll be coming from the front. We're taking on scientists and freaks, not soldiers. I don't foresee any major threats to our safety except their security drones and turrets. This sweep will be relentless and efficient, I don't want to see one survivor. That's a direct order from General Rox."

I take a look at John.

"You ready to call this?" I ask him.

"I'm ready. Since the day we were assigned this task, I've studied and prepared. My execution plan is flawless. Bring on this side show and I'll show them why you can't play God."

His snout is moist, but the expression on his face is cold and ruthless. He's ready. I then look at Ingle, Kimba, and Kanji, my ground crew.

"Ingle, good job on the scrambler, ready to scout some more?" I ask.

"Yes sir!" Ingle says with enthusiasm.

"Kimba, your weapons ready for us to use?"

"Yes. You shouldn't even have to ask," he roars.

"And Kanji, are your codes all lined out?"

"Um, yes," he says. Unlike the others, he seems nervous.

"Scared?" I ask.

"Um, just worried about the field. This mission is the kind that we've never faced before. Our opponent is a complete mystery."

"Whether you know your opponent or not is irrelevant. Anything can be killed, and today we'll be doing a lot of it. You're worried that a bunch of civilians can take us down? You're silly. Don't be afraid. Be ready to act."

Kanji looks at me with confidence.

"Yes… Yes sir!" he roars.

We are approaching the start line, and they need to be inspired, they need to be fierce, they need to have the warrior's mentality. I am their leader, I must be the voice that speaks their mind.

"Listen up crew," I say. "This is the second time the Alliance has sent a team on a halfkind mission. The first time, that team failed. This time, the enemy will fall, the monsters, the mutants, the creatures that don't deserve to live. Halfkinds. Their leader, Lionel Changer, intends to change the game. He is a dangerous man, an intelligent one, and most lethal, a man with an ideology. These are the worst kinds of humans. Men who see themselves as visionaries have no morals. He wants to breed an army of freaks, and the Alliance has sent us to stop him. We are honored by this assignment, and I don't intend to fail the Alliance like that pussy, Commander Trevor, did. There's no holding back, we storm the gates, we enter the compound, and we incinerate them in order to protect the world from Changer's insanity."

I activate a hologram with Changer's image.

"This is our target, his facility is his stronghold. We will take him down at all costs! Do you hear me?!"

"Yes sir!" they all chant in unison.

"Make me proud boys, make me proud!"

Our chants echo into the sky like a wall of sound. Lionel Changer has no idea we're after him. He can't hear our roars now, but guaranteed, he'll hear it soon enough. The smoking barrel of my gun will be the last thing he sees. I have no doubt about it.

Chapter 20 - Lucy

Evolution

May 7, 3043 6:00 AM

Morning of operation has arrived. All last week spent formulating, analyzing, making final preparations to obtain successful result. Calculations completed, probability of failure less than one percent. Had additional check-ins with Lawton, took more scans with bioscanner, looked for anything might cause complications. Found none. Conducted neurological tests and recorded measurements. Brain function of Lawton retains impressiveness, not slowed down. Still complains about migraines, conclusions not found. Issue minor, implant surgery top priority.

Woke up thirty minutes ago. Normal desired amount of sleep not fulfilled. Instead of trying to fall back to sleep, decided to shower. Bath was refreshing. Will be alert during this vital procedure. Looking forward to doing work.

Finished breakfast few minutes ago. Ate oatmeal and cut bananas. Sugar, fiber needed for healthy digestive system. Now walking to medical bay to set up station. Hours of prep work needs to be done. Drones must be programmed, equipment must be tested, instruments will be sterilized.

Pause. Have forgotten important documents in quarters. They are results of Lawton's vitals check from yesterday, most recent copy. Not critical to review these, but recommended. Must not overlook any details. Currently making way back to quarters.

Thinking about what Bastion said in argument that occurred May 5. Something regarding lack of comprehension over my lack of understanding towards sentimental feelings involving Iris Lawton. Exact statement was 'not everything is about rationality.'

Am perplexed by comments. Without rationality, existence would be anarchy. Facts and rules needed to have lucid understanding of world. One must logically know environment to gain knowledge to facts and create understanding to surroundings. Understanding of surroundings leads to adaptation. Adaptation leads to survival. Survival leads to thriving, and thriving leads to evolution. For existence to exist, evolution must continue progressing toward better steps. Command chain backbone for lifeline of every species. Everything is about rationality, catalyst for this process.

Lawton's powers cannot be enhanced without procedure. Risks minimal, only damage is psychological. Recovery from mental scars unimportant compared to grander picture. Lawton will resist to untrusted personnel committing operation, will have to do against will. Unfortunate she is emotionally unfit to understand benefits bestowed. Predicting much resistance, but in time, will appreciate efforts.

Bastion against this. Fueled by emotions. They are pointless, only cloud greater good. Many argue about moral ambiguity of ends versus means. I see no argument. If end output is greater than input from means, then ends always justify means. Those who cannot see this lack intelligence. Creatures who have capability to comprehend should make decisions for them. In this case, Lawton must have decision made for her by me.

Bastion's concerns perpetuate from short sightedness. They go hand in hand. Compassion is weakness. Always prevents the next step.

Bastions worries for Lawton illogical. She will be alive after procedure, recovered within few hours, have assured risk is low, what could cause him to be resistant to implants? Procedure will help facilitate and amplify Lawton's powers. Claims to be looking out for Lawton's well-being. In actuality, preventing it.

Perhaps this is my weakness. Sometimes when I speak, I see fear in eyes. He is looking at monster. Intelligent beings have morals and ethics. I do not have these feelings, often makes me alienated from others. Social integration and dependence unfortunate requirement in development. Do not possess skills in these areas, hampers my potential. Lack of innate talents in this area frustrating. Are not things I can learn through study.

Not something concerned about. Changer understands what must do to get what wants. Sacrifices necessary, always will be. Am glad Changer knows this. Not surprising. It is philosophy he has engrained from start, the only one I believe.

Do notice sympathy he has towards Bastion's opinions. During argument, Changer heard both sides, gave neutral response. If Changer was true to cause, would have agreed with me completely, but did not. He acknowledged Bastion's need for emotional fulfillment, empathized with him. Unsure if he is playing to sympathies or if earnest opinion. I am skeptical but reaction may be genuine.

Not surprised if this is case. After all, such feelings are regarded as 'human.' This trait is of his species and shared by Bastion. Peculiar that I am half human and lack it. Changer is proud of human traits, because he is human supremacist. I have studied history feeds and understand social struggle that humans cast upon themselves. Changer's upbringing and personality is example of divide that tears world apart between man and rest of intelligent domain. There is much resentment that humans have against peers. They were creatures in prime, new hope to next step. Now they are merely fraction of it.

I am now at quarters. I grab measurements and make way back to medical bay. I have wasted five minutes, do not expect to lose more.

Changer wishes to put humans back in place, to evolve mankind to level where they are superior once again. This is noble quest, at least from perspective of humans. He does it for their kind. Yet, find his dream scenario foolish. Too narrow in vision. To only serve interests of humans leads nowhere. Has taught me to serve greater good, but isolating himself to human agenda not for greater good. Vision will lead to anarchy, divide, first within human society, and then rest. He is already viewed as outcast by human peers, campaign attracts negative connotations. Like Bastion, he is bound by emotions. That will be undoing.

Yet, play along and pretend to follow plans. Have something far greater on agenda, need to transfer his knowledge to me.

Changer will lead me to breakthroughs unfathomable. Want to learn what I can from him so that when he dies, and project is in my hands, I propel work into stratosphere. Changer wants to do this for benefit of humans, I am doing this for benefit of all creatures. Imagine world where this struggle we call survival banished, where every creature is one. No more will lions and gorillas fight, wolves and humans at arms. Competition brings nothing but ruin to planet. In order for Earth to survive as whole, we must eliminate fight. If every creature is one our objectives will be same.

I use humans as example. Before event, they were heading towards utopia. Diseases cured, technological advances coming, world at peak of height. How were they able to achieve this? Unification. Became solidified. Countries broke down barriers, languages transformed to universal one, differences put aside. Perfection created under single direction.

That all changed after the animals became threat. Progress stalled. Technology, biology, breakthroughs, and science that would have moved further did not. New competition prevented world from going forward.

Yet, should not ignore past. Humans were on to something. So now only solution to get back to golden era is unify. However, differences far too great. Humans able to bond together because they are same, other species are not. Propose that if all animals were combined, from hybrids to chimeras, then stage will be set for civilization to evolve back to original status quo. When every creature is one, then fighting will stop, progress will continue. This is way things should have been. I will get evolution back on track.

Changer has proved hybrids possible. Now is time to expand, mix more than two. Goals are different, but process same. Obtain tools from Changer, and then work toward vision, which is far superior than his. When all is one, and one is all, only direction to go is up.

Don't mind working under Changer, teaches me much. But in end, have my own calling to follow.

First things first. Before leaps are made, steps are taken. Must see what comes of these implants, what secrets Lawton holds to exploit and pass down to future generations. Starts with her, she has been branded as unique. Looking forward to continuing work so that she will be one of many, and will work toward goal of unified society rid of petty differences species have with each other.

Arrive at medical bay. A lot of work to be done, but operation will be conducted on time.

Eventually average creature will be developed into perfect specimen. I will be creator, and they will create, and creations will create and so on. This is first step to new evolution, justification of means takes to get there. Do not do this for glory. No selfish agenda. Do this because future demands it. Perfect species will be created.

Chapter 21 - Iris Lawton

Invaded

May 7, 3043 7:52 AM

The house is empty, but new. The floors are polished, the walls are clean, and there's not a speck of dust to be found. The air is cool, like a crisp, autumn morning. I don't recall how I got here, but as I survey the area, I feel like I've been here before. It's not only familiar, but a welcoming, like family. I look back from the porch into the house that I grew up in. The front door, the large room inside, even the kitchen look the same yet fresher. This is definitely my old house, and it's never looked better.

I see the sunset from the very same porch that I sat on a countless number of times in Primm. Even now, after all I've been through, it brings a calm that very few things can. I feel safe by myself. There's no family or Fenrir to ensure my security, but it doesn't matter. This is all I need, this is all I ever needed.

The night sky stretches past the horizon at an accelerated pace. In mere minutes, the stars shine and the blue and green hue of the moon radiates to the Earth. It's another sight I often took for granted back home. I never realized how beautiful every individual star was, and the culmination of it all is breathtaking.

Something's different. Everything is so clear. Usually, the night sky is blanketed with the haze from the city lights, making the stars barely visible. But now, I can see every single glint with a lucidity that I never thought possible. This is better than anything I've seen in the Wolf's Den.

My cradle, my home, my sense of belonging, it feels so nice to have you all back.

"Wondrous, isn't it?" a very familiar voice says behind me.

I quickly turn around and I am floored. A figure stands before me, a little taller, a little leaner, but he is no stranger. He was, is, one of the most important creatures in my life.

"Isaac," I say as I'm ready to burst into tears.

"Hello sister," he says to me.

"I must be imagining things, is this real?"

He reaches out his hand to touch mine. I grasp it firmly with all my might.

"Yes sister," he says, "this is very real."

"How?" I ask. "How is this possible?!"

"I can't answer those questions. We don't have much time to talk."

"Why not? Where am I? When am I?"

"You're home."

"I can see that, but this place shouldn't exist. I burned down our house three years ago."

"Yes, but I recreated it for this moment. Are you happy to see me? I've missed you."

Tears roll down my eyes. I can't fight it anymore. I embrace him, something I haven't done in such a long time.

"I've missed you too," I say.

We release from our hug and stand there in silence. It's touching, the kind of moment where you don't need words to progress time. Instead, you wish time would stop.

But then, Isaac's expression changes. He's no longer looks happy, but apprehensive. Something has hit his mind and the growing concern is written all over his face.

"I sense something is wrong, Iris," he says.

"Wrong? What are you talking about?" I say.

I'm half puzzled at the sudden change in conversation, and half surprised that he's able to read me so well. I shouldn't be, he knew me the best. I am worried. I can sense something bad is going to happen, like I did when I was in Primm the night of the assault. There are no visions, just gut feelings, and while I can't claim any supernatural powers are responsible, my gut feelings are usually right.

Yet, I'm in denial.

"Nothing's wrong," I say.

"Are you sure?" Isaac presses on. When he was alive, or is he alive now, he had a one of a kind expression that let me know the only thing on his mind was my safety. This is what I see now. It pierces me, makes me lose my guard.

"Something's going to happen Isaac, I don't know what exactly, but I feel like my life is in danger," I say.

"You're always afraid of the future," he says. "Always afraid that something is going to happen. What about something good happening? What about your visions? Do you see anything there?"

"It doesn't work like that, you know it," I say.

"I do, but I'm trying to tell you don't be afraid. What comes will come, and you'll be fine."

"But it's so hard to think that way when you're alone. I have no one left. All of you are dead."

"You aren't alone. What about Fenrir?"

I remain quiet and hesitate to respond.

"It's not the same," I say. "Family is irreplaceable."

"I understand that," he says. "Just try to be more optimistic. It's okay to be scared, but don't let it consume you. Don't let it control your actions. Be fearless."

"But…"

"I'm sorry, Iris, I told you I don't have much time. I have to go now."

"Go? Go where?"

"Here."

A bright flash blinds my eyes and I close them. A few moments later they open and I'm greeted with a view of my bed. Damn, it was a dream, yet as cliché as it sounds, it was so real. I wish it was. I didn't realize how much I missed my brother.

I suppose it's something I try not to think about often. When my brother died, a part of me did. I could feel the energy shot go through his head and exit his skull when I watched that dog kill him. Months had passed, and I still replayed those exact few seconds over and over again, like an infinite loop of personal hell.

"I should have killed you when I had the chance," I remember my brother say. I wish he had. Apollo Bradley murdered him, and if I could foresee what would have happened, if my visions could have kicked in like they do, I could have prevented. Or maybe I couldn't have. Why can't my abilities be more concrete?

Even now, I think about all those times we've spent together, Isaac and I. We were our own little pair. He had my back in a way that my other brothers and sisters didn't. He didn't fall in line with Tiago, nor with Oscar. He certainly didn't care who he had to stand up to, Alex, Ace, Oscar, to make sure that my priorities would be best served. He was the protector that I didn't deserve.

And I should've been able to save him. Since arriving at HORUS, all I've heard is talk about how I'm special. Yet, how important can I be if I can't even protect the ones I love? My powers are tailor made to help creatures in the situation that Isaac was in. But I remained helpless the moment the shot flew out of the barrel. He was dead, I did nothing. Isaac's death is my greatest failure.

That's why I worry about the future so much. I can see into it, but it remains so unpredictable. If it wasn't, Isaac would be alive.

Fenrir is there, and always will be, but I am still alone. The only person who could have convinced me otherwise is dead. He tried to show me in my dream. But that's all dreams are, make believe. Reality is a place where those dreams are killed. It's a place where your family is slaughtered in front of your very eyes for reasons you don't comprehend, a place where you get kidnapped and used for your powers, a place where you're isolated, depressed, angry. I wish I could throw reality away and stay in my dreams forever.

Unfortunately, I must deal with reality first hand. Today I'm getting another check-up, hopefully to help subside the migraines I've been having for a week now. They've been growing fainter, but I've never had anything last this long. It's not really a pain, more like an annoyance. Hopefully, Lucy has good news for me. I don't trust her intentions, but Zorro seems to think that she's helping me out. Let's hope he's right.

I get out of bed and look on the clock, it's 8:00. Lucy said she would stop by at 8:15. I better hurry and get dressed. They left me some food, which I admit isn't half bad. Their cooks know their stuff. Unfortunately, I have no time to savor it, so I gobble it up like a duck and head to the bathroom to clean up.

I'm in the middle of washing my hands when I hear a ring.

"Ready for check-up?" Lucy says over an intercom.

I turn off the sink and head toward the door. It slides open and there she is, shiny lab coat and all.

"Yes, I'm ready," I say. "Hope you can fix these headaches. They've been dying down, but it's still happening. Do you think…"

"Please, no talking," she interrupts me. She's surprisingly rude, even more so than before. I look at her and she doesn't even notice me staring. Instead, her eyes are looking straight forward, with unflinching resolve.

I decide not to talk because I start to have an eerie sense flow through me. It's not my standard future fear mongering. This is different, this is short term. I sense something strange, something dangerous is coming up.

We walk past a few halls and arrive at the medical bay. The doors open and, low and behold, Lionel and Bastion are standing there, waiting for me.

"Why are you two here?" I ask. "This is merely a check-up."

Lucy takes her place next to Lionel and neither of the three are smiling. Their faces are all serious.

"This isn't a check-up, is it?" I say as I realize what's going on.

"In a sense, no," Lionel says. "We're not here to cure your headaches."

"What are you going to do?"

"Give you some real power."

"Excuse me?"

I'm confused by his statement. Real power? What does that even mean?

"Plan to make two incisions, or more accurately, drill holes, into cranium to allow access for direct neural payload insertion," Lucy says. "Nano implants."

"Whoa, slow down. Incisions? Like cuts? What the hell is going on?!" I yell.

"Let me rephrase that," Lionel says. "What Lucy means is that we're going to perform a small procedure on you. It'll be short, you'll recover quickly, and most importantly, it's very safe."

"What procedure? And why?"

"To put it delicately, it's a simple nano implant that we'll install into your brain. This procedure will amplify your powers in ways we can't even imagine."

"Sounds like a science experiment. I'm not some lab rat for you to dissect."

"Didn't you hear me? It will amplify your powers."

"I don't care!"

Lionel pauses, takes out a damp cloth and wipes his hands with it. He puts it back in his pocket and then looks directly at me.

"Do you know what our implants will do for you?" he asks.

"I don't care," I repeat.

"Of course you say that, at least for now. Your powers are, unstable, to put it lightly. You can't control them, nor can you control what you see. They're also evolving. You've been able to do things that you haven't done before. Those headaches you're having? We think they're sending off light psychic signals. Telepathy, Iris. Yet, it's faint. What my implants will do is make these signals stronger, make your precognition more reliable. It's not simply about increasing your abilities, it's about control. You won't have random spurts, you'll be able to be in command of those spurts. You'll be able to see visions at will, know when things happen with pinpoint accuracy. No more confusing, vague flashes. It'll be crystal clear. And the best part? It'll be instant. The procedure will allow you to control these things like a muscle, right away. Don't you want that?"

I don't even hesitate.

"No," I say.

"Think about it," Lionel continues, "What if you had these powers earlier? Perhaps you could've saved someone, no some people. Those close to your heart? Hybrids, perhaps?"

His comment infuriates me.

"Leave my family out of this!" I scream.

"I'm being completely rational," he says. "If you had the power I talk about, you could've seen everything. You would have known your enemy, known when they were coming, and planned out a way to not only save yourself, but each other. The greatest mercenaries and military personnel would be no match for such power. You would have been invincible, and with that invincibility, you could've protected the family you love. But now they are dead and here you are, being given a chance to make things right."

His words hit me hard. He's right. As much as I hate him, as much as I hate this group for everything they've done, I can't deny the fact that if I had this potential, power that outclasses everything on this planet, power that only I can wield, the Lawtons might still be alive. I would've done anything to save my family, to save Isaac. If this was then, and I knew my family's lives were endangered, this wouldn't even be a dilemma. I'd take his offer in a heartbeat.

But the thing is, that was then, this is now. I can't change the past. Isaac is dead and dealing with the devil won't bring him back.

"No, I don't want it," I say.

He lets out a long sigh.

"I see, I hoped you would've seen the way," he says. "Bastion."

I'm expecting another tranquilizer but nothing happens. I look at Lionel, and he's as confused as me.

"Bastion!" he repeats in anger. "Do what you're told."

Bastion is hesitating to obey his master. Something is preventing him from making his move.

Yet, I've spoken too soon.

"Sorry, Iris," he says. From the side of his hip, he pulls out a fire arm and in less than a second he shoots something my way. I feel a prick on my stomach, and all of a sudden I feel…sleepy.

I try to hold on to my thoughts…but I became…tired…fatigued…. and I … drift from consciousness…

… Isaac… Fenrir… where are you…?

"Iris Lawton, respond," a robotic voice faintly calls out to me.

My thoughts are a bit hazy, and I'm slowly coming back into the fold. I'm lying down on a cold, smooth surface. I shake my head and blink constantly to make myself more alert. The darkness that blurred my visions fades away and I see a bright light in front of me. It's white, almost blinding. I can't see much else, only a blank ceiling ahead of me.

"Iris Lawton, please respond," I hear again more clearly. It's coming from speakers nearby. "Tranquilizer was too strong, behind schedule."

"Huh? What?" I say as I try to get up. I can't move my arms, in fact, I can't move anything. I use the small amount of energy I have to try to raise them, but nothing happens. I feel a tight grip at my wrists, and another one at my ankles. I can't believe it, I'm tied down to this table.

"She appears to be waking up," another voice says. I recognize it, Lionel Changer. And the other one I heard is Lucy.

"Why am I strapped down?!" I scream.

"You were uncooperative," Lucy says.

"Let me go!"

"Head restraints aren't in place."

I hear a zipping sound burst from both sides of my head and suddenly a strap wraps over my neck, almost choking me. Another one projects and it securely fastens my forehead. Now I can't move anything. I struggle hard, but it's futile. I'm bolted down from head to toe.

"Begin procedure," Lucy says.

A high pitched drilling noise blares in my ears. I wish I could cover them, but I soon discover it's the least of my worries. It comes close and closer, and my imagination runs wild. What could be coming my way? My temples are getting hotter. The object generates a tremendous amount of heat.

And then, contact. An incredibly strong, painful pinch comes from the sides of my head. I hear, feel the wound generating as something penetrates through the outer layer of my skull. It pierces my temples and slowly digs past the bone and flesh. My instinct is to throw up, and I try, but it's all a dry heave as my arms start shaking to control the pain. I scream out in terror, but nothing happens. Not a single yell is heard from my mouth. My nose picks up the scent of my own skin burning.

Every second is agonizing beyond belief, and as the probes go deeper and deeper into my head, a wall of agony flows through my body. Images flash through my mind as I lose control. My fingers twitch, my legs shake, my eyelids flutter. The digging continues until it reaches my brain, and I swear, I can feel the probes nestle within the grey matter. I once again drive heave, so much that blood spews from my mouth. A surgery drone hovers over and vacuums it up while the process continues.

This is by far the worst experience of my life. Worse than the kidnapping, worse than Operation Halfkinds, worse than my mother's death.

I'm about to pass out, but before I give up, the drilling stops. Adrenaline shoots in and oddly enough, I relax a little. In this small moment, my pain subsides, and I find a bit of peace from the madness. It's the eye of the storm.

But it starts all over again.

"Initiate implant procedure," I hear over the intercom. Pain surges through my body again and it originates from my head. This feeling is different from the other experience. I imagine a bunch of ants burrowing into my head, every movement directly stimulating a pain receptor. My brain is being invaded. I feel a sharp nip here, another nip there, all occurring within my skull. It's hard to describe it, the experience is new to me. Drilling holes in the head is one thing, to have something occur directly to your brain is another.

I just know it's ten times more painful than the experience I had a few minutes ago.

I definitely throw up this time. Right as rain though, the drone cleans up my vomit. My body continues to convulse violently, and my vision blurs out.

"Stay awake!" I hear Lucy's voice on the intercom yell. A drone hovers over me and gives me an electric shock. My eyes open wide as I spit out blood, again. But it's no use. My vision is still blacking out. I feel another jolt through my body, courtesy of the drone. It doesn't matter. I lay there convulsing, twitching, with probes in my brain, as the scene fades away from me. I wonder if this is my last thought. Nothing but machines and hot lights above me, not a single soul to hold my hand.

… You were wrong Isaac, I will always be alone…

… Fenrir… Isaac…

"Isaac!" I yell. I sit straight up. The restraints are off. I'm no longer on an operating table. In fact, as I look around, I realize I'm back in my quarters, on my bed. Though dazed, I sit up and get off to walk toward a mirror. I look at my reflection and see the damage done. My forehead is completely bandaged up, and the temples are spotted red. Dark red. That's where the penetration must have happened. I carefully reach for the bandage to touch the wound, but the instant I do, a sting emits from it. It's sore, definitely a flesh wound. The strange part is that it sinks in. It doesn't look that bad. They drilled holes into my head, did something to my mind, but what? Those little bugs I imagined felt too real to be a hallucination.

Yet, despite the wound, I do feel surprisingly better. My head hurts, but the migraines are gone. And I feel… more clairvoyant because of it. My mind feels fresh, clear, focused.

It hits me. Those headaches, I had them because I was trying to send out a message. A psychic one, one that was telling someone or something important information… my location… I was sending it to…

… Fenrir. He knows where I am, he's been following the signal I've been sending out.

"But how did I know that? " I say to myself. "What did they do to me?"

The clock reads about ten before eight. I've been out for almost the whole day. The door opens and an unwelcome visitor walks in. Bastion.

"What the fuck are you doing here?" I yell.

"Um, Lionel has sent me to do a follow up on your surgery," Bastion says.

"Surgery? Don't you mean forcible entry?"

He looks even more uncomfortable.

"Um, I'm here to ask questions. I didn't perform the operation, Lucy did," he says.

"And where is she?" I ask.

"With Lionel."

"You're as guilty as they are. You didn't seem to have a problem with drugging and strapping me to the table, did you?"

Flustered, he goes on with his stupid checklist.

"Question One," he says, "how do you feel?"

I give him a dumbfounded stare.

"You serious?" I ask.

"Um, let's skip to the next question. Have the wounds from your temple stopped bleeding?" he asks.

I take some time to calm myself down. I take a deep breath in, and one out, then proceed to answer.

"Yes," I say. "There's still some spotting on the bandage, but I opened them and it looks like most of the blood has dried."

"Good," Bastion says sheepishly. "I'll let Lucy know that you need a change in wrappings. Next question, have your headaches stopped?"

"Yes."

"Do you care to elaborate on that?"

"No."

It looks like he wants to press the matter further, but he relents.

"Okay, next question," he says. "Is there anything peculiar that happened during the procedure that you'd like to report?"

"You mean besides the drilling in my head, the sensation of something crawling in my brain, the vomiting, coughing blood, and the excruciating pain?" I say sarcastically. "Other than that, everything was peachy."

"Um, that must have been… uncomfortable."

"Really? You think, asshole?"

At this point the conversation becomes incredibly awkward. Obviously, he is ill equipped to handled my unbridled fury, and I'm in no mood to answer a bunch of silly questions.

"Can I say something off the record?" he asks me.

"No, you can't," I respond. "But you're going to anyway, right?"

He ignores my comment and continues.

"I can't stress this enough, but what we did, it was to help you," he says.

"Oh god, here we go again," I say sardonically. "How the hell do you expect me to believe or even care about anything you say after what I've been through?"

He's silent.

"Do you know what that's like?" I scream at him. "To be drugged, strapped to some cold slated table and have these machines dissect your brain all while you lay there helplessly? Do you have any idea? If you did, then all the power in the world would be meaningless to you."

"But we have good intentions," he says shamefacedly.

"Stop right there, stop right there! Anything you say is digging you deeper and deeper into a hole."

"It's true!" he blurts out. "If Lucy's calculations are correct, you should have already experienced a fraction of the power you'll develop. Can you imagine the kind of enhancements we've bestowed on you?"

"Goodness, it's like you guys don't know how to say anything else. Let me make it very clear what I think about power. I. Don't. Give. A shit!"

"But… but… what if you had your power when…"

"Don't you dare say it!"

It's the loudest I've yelled at him, and my eyes get watery.

"We're merely saying, Iris, from what Lucy has estimated, you'll have an array of abilities at your disposal," he says. "You'll be able to control your visions with pinpoint accuracy, possibly gain some telepathy. The sky's the limit on what you can do."

"I don't know how many times I have to say it. I truly do not…"

"Let me ask you this then," Bastion says, interrupting me. "Since you've recovered, have you experienced anything different? Are you more aware of anything, have you seen any visions, done something that you haven't been able to do before?"

I think about my earlier clairvoyance. It was instant power. There's no way I could've known my headaches were linked to guiding Fenrir here.

"No," I lie.

"Are you sure about that?" he asks. It's like he knows I'm not telling the truth.

"I'm sure."

He looks very unconvinced. I'm not the greatest liar in the world, so I guess he sees through my act. Or maybe I'm using telepathy to read his mind. Figuring this out is rather trippy.

"Okay, well in case you've said that, I've been instructed to ask you one more question," Bastion says.

"What?" I say curtly.

"Look into the future."

"Huh?"

"Look into it. See if you can view a vision."

"It doesn't work like that. They come to me at unpredictable times. I can't look into it like I'm looking through a window."

"Maybe you can do it now."

"I can't."

It looks like 'no' isn't going to be an answer he'll accept. Maybe if I fake it, I can get him to shut up.

"Fine," I say. "What do I do exactly?"

"Lucy said your power should come to you naturally," he says. "I suppose you can close your eyes and focus on the seeing something. Perhaps a vision will pop up."

I look at him skeptically.

"That's it? I'm only supposed to close my eyes and think about it, and something will magically appear?" I ask.

"I guess. That's what Lucy said," he says.

"Are you sure that's how it works?"

"Well they're your powers. Shouldn't you know? I think it would come naturally…"

"Don't give me attitude. You're already teetering over a thin line."

"Just try it."

"Fine."

I close my eyes and concentrate. And concentrate. And concentrate. And nothing happens.

"This is stupid," I say. Bastion is unrelenting, though.

"Keep trying," he says.

Once more I close my eyes to do it again. I focus and focus. I clench my eyes tightly, and frown until it feels like a vein is going to pop from my forehead. I grit my teeth and tighten my face. It must look like I'm constipated.

I feel dumb. I'm about to tell Bastion how silly this is until a ringing vibrates in my ears. I become deaf to my surroundings and within my closed eyes, I start to see images form.

I… I'm having a vision, and this time I controlled it.

I see bright lights and smoke. Explosions flash in front of me, and the blue lights of energy shots whiz by. There are animals of various kinds armed with weapons, firing into different directions. A tiger. A lion. A croc. A bird. They are vague shapes, yet at the same time, I can see them so clearly.

And then I see a human. He's large and has weapons in both hands. Tactical armor hugs his body, a small beard hangs from his chin. He has a shaved head, and fierce eyes. There's a twisted smile on his face as he's firing off weapons right in front of me. And he shoots with little discrimination. Energy shots empty from his gun dozens by the seconds. He attacks with violent aggression, and his presence shakes me to the bone. I don't know who this man is, but I'm already petrified of him.

He vanishes before me, and now I see drones floating about, firing shots as well. Faint screams fill my ears. It sounds like disarray, terror.

The drones disappear and, in their place, dead bodies arise. They are humans, lying face down in pools of their own blood. All of them look familiar and most of them are wearing shiny lab coats that have been stained red. Each one of them has a scared, hopeless expression frozen onto their lifeless faces. They died in terror, violent deaths and fearful last moments.

The scene shifts to another group of bodies. These too have been slaughtered. But they are not humans, they are hybrids. Half-man and half-animals. They have the same horrified expression that the humans did. Some lie face down, others lie on their backs. None have weapons. They are all unarmed, innocent bystanders that happened to get in the way of a destructive tornado.

I recognize one of them. He's old looking, spotted white and black. His head is slumped down, body drooped on a hover chair. Zorro.

I realize what this vision is, an assault. Dread overtakes me. My eyes immediately open in panic, and a confused Bastion is startled.

"What's wrong? What did you see? Did it work?"

For a brief second I don't say anything. But I make myself utter out a single statement.

"Yes," I say.

"What did you see?" he asks.

I can't describe everything to Bastion, there was too much going on. How could I tell him about the attackers, the dead bodies, his fellow hybrids who will become corpses? My description won't do it any justice.

"A lot of death," I respond.

"Huh?" he says perplexed.

Suddenly, we hear an explosion echo in the background. The ground rumbles and my bed shakes.

"What was that?" he asks. But I know the answer to his question.

"Oh no," I say. "It's happening again."

"What is?"

I don't utter a peep and remain locked in fear. I sit there dumbfounded. The only thing I can think about is the impending doom that's coming.

Chapter 22 - Brock West

Entry

May 7, 3043 8:00 PM

"Winde, how's your team looking?" I ask.

"We're inside the communications room, ready to send their system haywire. Their network will go down and the residents will know there's been a breach," Winde says.

"And the hacks?"

"They're successful. Best part is they have no idea we're here. The false streams worked. They only see the loop. We covered our tracks well. Their security measures are disabled and are in our hands. We can turn their tech on them. There's only one thing…"

"What?"

"They have a separate defense system that manages the perimeter. I couldn't get access to that, so if you're going to go through the front, you'll have to mow down their outside fortifications."

"Shit. That won't be easy. How long would it take for you to hack into that?"

"I wasn't prepared for it, so I would have to decrypt things on the fly. It could take five minutes, it could take five days."

"Fucking shit, Winde! We don't have time for this nonsense."

I take a moment to think about the plan. Any changes in schedule are too risky, everything has to be followed to a tee.

"We're going to forego that then," I say. "Kimba, Kanji, Ingle, and I will proceed ahead. Do you have your charges ready?"

"Yes, Clipper has set them," Winde says.

"Okay then. I'm counting on that bear. Set them to detonate in one minute, then enter the compound. Also scramble their communications now."

"Yes sir. Once we do this, they'll know we're here. Any masks that we applied will be gone."

"Good, I want them to know. Follow the plan, and we'll meet you inside. This is West out."

We stand at the perimeter, a tiger, a lion, an eagle, and me, outside of the marked territory where Lionel Changer's wave of turrets, mines, and drones await. It's been almost three years spent researching, planning, checking every fact, every detail in order for this moment, this evening. Tonight is the night where all my hard work will pay off, tonight is the night HORUS and Lionel Changer will pay for their genetic crimes against animal-kind.

"We're going to have to do this the hard way," I tell my squad.

"Winde couldn't disable the perimeter defenses?" Kanji asks.

"No. But not to worry, they shouldn't be too hard to get by. With Kimba's weapons, we should be like a storm mowing down paper houses. We have all our gear, we're ready to go. Ingle, you will remain in the sky and offer air support. The rest of us will charge head on. About one hundred yards from here, there's a small shack-looking building. It's thin, it's old, it's basically nothing. But that's our target, for that piece of shit is the door that will lead us to our objective. We get there, we get to HORUS. Ingle has already placed a scrambler on it, Kanji, you ready to break some codes?"

"Yes."

"Good. Then let's make a straight dash. Remember, there's four stages of defense set up around the perimeter. No fear, no slowing down. We are prepared, let's finish this!"

"Yes sir!" they yell in unison.

"Showtime!" I scream.

Ingle flies above while the rest of us start sprinting. Naturally, Kanji and Kimba out run me. We encounter the first line of defense. Energy turrets rise from the ground and start firing. I see a hail of blue and yellow lights coming my way.

"Bioshields, initiate!" Kimba yells.

My view distorts a bit, and I can see light bend, creating a translucent screen that encases my body. The same happens to Kimba and Kanji, and I look to the sky to see it on Ingle as well. The defense budget I lobbied for really came through this time. Body armor is nice, but a clear shield that covers you from head to toe is nicer.

It's a neat little gadget that he picked up. The force field is concentrated light, a solid shield of energy. It's strong enough to absorb and deflect any gunfire that comes our way. The drawback is that they only work on projectiles. Bioshields are ineffective against melee attacks.

All of us are equipped with them, the only thing we needed to do was wrap one of our appendages with a band that Kimba provided.

I watch as the shots harmlessly fly in other directions upon impact. They bounce off my shield like rain on a smooth surface. Some hit harder than others, and they jolt me a little, but there's no harm done. We come to a close enough range to clean out the turrets, so I kneel down calmly as the enemy fire hits the force field and prepare my weapons.

Kimba and Kanji do the same as well. They both have harnesses on them with dual cannons and ammunition property changers, standard feline weapons. Both lay down, in prowl stance as they focus on their targets.

"Kimba, you take the turrets on the north, Kanji, you have the northeast ones, I'll take the turrets directly in front of me," I say. "Our plan is to use our big ammo and blast away. Fire at any gun we see."

"Understood, sir. I'm going to use the heavy duty plasma shots that I've programmed into my harness," Kimba says.

"I'll have mine equipped as well, but in spray mode," Kanji adds.

"Okay then, set your weapons and fire!"

We unleash our barrage of shots at our marks. A small hole opens in our bioshields so that they can get through. Turret after turret gets blown apart, our gunfire shredding through them like tissues. I home on each of my targets and watch one after another get blasted to smithereens. Kanji and Kimba do the same. We fire with pinpoint accuracy. The caliber of our energy shots out match the weak ammunition that comes from the turrets. Changer may have had plenty of them to secure his fort, but our weapons are too powerful. In less than five minutes, they have been decimated, and I'm shocked that a supposedly advanced facility has such shitty defenses. Guess they were really counting on the whole secrecy thing.

Next on the battle plan are mines. According to my specs, they're beyond the turrets. These I can't blast away, it's too hard to track them one by one, and many are buried way beneath the ground. We can't exactly walk through the field either, even with the bioshields on. They're not designed to take that kind of impact.

I'll have to rely on the ace up my sleeve.

"Ingle, it's your turn," I say through my communicator.

The three of us look up and see him swoop down towards our position.

He will be acting as a mini carpet bomber so that he can set off the mines and provide a clear pathway. He's equipped with Tunneling Electric Expanders, or TEE's. They're the size of peas. The way they work is you drop it from the sky, watch them dig a bit into the ground, and set off an electric charge, perfect for wiping out any nuisances that may be lurking beneath the surface. In this case, it's the mines. The electricity that spreads from the TEE's will detonate them instantaneously.

"Ready to drop the payloads," Ingle says to me.

"Do it," I respond.

I see him jet across the land in a straight line, dropping a trail of TEE's. They pick up speed and crash the ground, making contact in less than a few seconds. They start their work, burrowing under the dirt. Once below, the TEE's detonate. I hear some buzzing and a small rumble and in cadence the mines go off in the order the TEE's fell on top of them.

Dust and grime disperse into the air. I wave my hands to fan it away and get a clear view. I am relieved, there's nothing but a decimated landscape in front of me. The mines are non-existent.

But in case I'm wrong…

"Kimba, run a scan," I say.

A device pops from his harness and the sensor light blinks. It's long and thin, and makes a few audible beeps. A holoscreen pops in his view and he studies it carefully, looking for any explosives that Ingle missed.

"It's clear," he says.

"Excellent, on to stage three," I say.

"Um, you mean that?" Kanji asks nervously.

"Yes, I mean that."

He's referring to the gravity guns. That's pure flair right there, not really practical in terms of weaponry. It's still dangerous though, and the sight of them at work is enough to freak out any trained soldier.

"Don't worry, Kanji," I say. "Kimba has it covered, right?"

"Of course," Kimba responds.

"Let's go."

Instead of a charge, we approach cautiously. I'm not sure what to expect of these. Turrets are straightforward. I've seen a million of them, and I know how to handle it. But gravity guns are a mystery. They'll throw you into the air for miles until you're up so high that oxygen becomes a luxury. Might be fun.

The moment we're in range, four cannons spring from the ground and aim in our direction. We only have a split second to react.

"Watch out!" I yell.

The cannons fire a huge circular, purple blast that lights up the night sky. It's slow, but massive. All three of us split into different directions, and the shot misses, hitting a rotting log that was behind us. I watch as it rumbles. It must weigh well over two hundred pounds, but it starts to levitate. It slips higher and higher, picking up acceleration until it completely floats into the air, like a balloon. Into the sky it goes until the branch is out of my sight, all in a matter of seconds.

"What do you have for this?" I shout to Kimba.

"Polarity mines with S-graded attraction levels," he says.

"These guns are made of metal?"

"Something like that."

"Smart move."

Another gravity gun repositions itself in our direction. From Kimba's harness pops out a metal cylinder. The weapon fires and Kimba launches the mine right in the trajectory of the blast. The cannon's shot hits the cylinder and it starts to float away aimlessly, exactly like the log. However, the magnetism kicks in and negates the gun's effect. Instead, it draws itself towards the cannon, slow at first, but then faster and faster until it latches onto the gravity gun's side.

A bright flare erupts from the cannon, and I shield my eyes. As it dies down, I look at where the gravity gun stood, now in shambles. Kimba's weaponry did the trick again.

"Fire on the other three!" I yell.

Three of the same cylinders emerge from the harness and Kimba volleys them to the remaining gravity guns. They latch on like the first one, and explode in a fiery blaze.

"All style and no substance," I say about the gravity guns.

"Indeed," Kimba says. "So what's the last wave?"

"John, did you hear Kimba's question?" I say to the pig over my communicator. His face shows on my holoscreen.

"Drones," John says.

"Are you serious?" I ask in a stunned tone.

"Yes."

"After all that, we have to face some puny drones. I mean for inside battles, they might do the job, but outside, it's a field day for us. Their firepower is too weak and we outrange them. What was Charger thinking?"

"He's a scientist, not a general. Besides, he probably didn't think anything would get through the first three waves."

From under the ground, the drones rise out, about twenty of them. They look like miniature hovercrafts with wings. I see guns mounted on both sides, but they're low caliber and won't hit us unless they can get closer. They won't.

"So," I say to Kimba, "what do you have for this occasion"

"How about scatter rain?" Kimba asks.

"Too outdated, give me something new."

"Oh, how about some Sonic Pulse Barriers?"

"SPB's? Now you're talking."

An SPB is basically an undetectable fence you can plant on the fly. Shoot two poles on the ground, and the space between is your safeguard. Anything that goes through it will get fried. And when I say undetectable, I mean it. Thermal, electric, even microcell scanners have been known to be ineffective against this tech.

"All right, set it up," I tell him.

Two small javelins, no longer than four inches, fire from his harness in opposite directions. They shoot ahead of us, and stand twenty feet from each other. The javelins are still attached to Kimba's harness by strings. Kimba activates a trigger with his tail and the javelins expand, reaching a height of ten feet or so. He then flashes the sonic impulse on, and I hear a light beeping. It's armed. If I were to walk through the gap between the poles, I'd be incinerated into dust.

The drones come at us aimlessly. They only identify the target. There's no thought behind their actions. They hover slowly and I can see their guns in ready position, probably preparing to shoot us as they draw closer. But they hit the barrier. A static noise bursts into our ears, and I see sparks geyser up above, only to free fall back to the ground. Metal flies, wires and pieces of the drones get ripped apart. Bangs happen in unison as all twenty drones crash through the SPB together. They crumble right before our eyes in a giant spectacle. And all we had to do was stand there.

"That was pretty cool," I say to Kimba.

"Glad you enjoyed the light show," he says as he disarms the SPB's. They fold back to their original size, and retract into his harness.

Ingle soars down and joins the rest of the group where we stand. We've arrived at the entrance. It looks like a makeshift shed made out of rusted metal. It's no larger than twelve by twelve feet and it wobbles back and forth through the wind. I don't think much of it until I take a look inside and see that the whole thing is a decoy. On the floor lies a very sophisticated sliding door. It's smooth, cold, and flat. I see an eye and hand scanner, as well as a voice recognition keypad.

Also in my view is a small node no bigger than a button. This was placed here by Ingle earlier this evening.

"Okay, Kanji, you're up. I see Ingle already planted the scrambler. It's been downloading codes and uploading hacks since its installation. That little baby will help you expedite your job. Do your thing," I say.

"Sure thing, boss, shouldn't take more than a few minutes," he says.

What appears to be a prodding stick protrudes from his harness. It latches onto the scrambler, extracting the information Ingle's device has obtained. A holoscreen is conjured in front of Kanji and he scans the readings. He uses his tail to control a part of a harness that's linked to the graphical interface. The master is at work, decrypting everything, breaking code on the fly in hopes that the door will open.

I stand there nervously, but within seconds it slides ajar.

"It's done," he says.

"Good work, Kanji, good work," I say.

At this point we have nothing to worry about. Winde has already assured us that all the security protocols are not only disabled, but at our disposal. I want to get this job done quick and easy, so the four of us rush down the stairs and enter the underground facility. We've entered the motherland.

There's a lot of white everywhere. The doors are white, the halls are white, the ceiling is white, the floor is white. It gave the place a clean feeling, one fitting for a mad scientist. I don't see anyone though. We've rushed past the main hall, so I was expecting to see a straggler or two, but there's no one.

Yet, I've spoken too soon. A man in a lab coat runs by us. The four of us go after him. He was in such a rush that he ran completely by us without noticing. He faces away from my team. I normally don't like shooting people in the back, but I suppose this will do.

I raise my gun, aim, and shoot. I hit him directly in the leg, and he spirals down to the floor, screaming 'what the fuck' as he crashes on his face. I think the blast surprised the hell out of him. He recovers fast enough to turn his back over and looks at the four of us. He's going to shit bricks.

"What the hell?" he says, voice trembling. "What is this?"

"This is an assault on HORUS headquarters, sponsored by the Alliance," I say.

"What? The Alliance? Shit. This can't be good."

"I'd say it isn't. What's your name?"

Apprehension flushes over his face and body. He starts to shake: fingers, arms, even in the leg that I shot up. Either he's too scared to answer, or refuses to do so.

"Listen, pal," I say. "I could either torture you to get it or I could kill you right now. What's your name?"

"Um, Aaron. Aaron Le Mothe," he says quivering.

"I'm here on official Alliance orders, and you can probably piece together why. What I need to know is where the others are. We've entered this premise, walked through the main halls, and we haven't seen a single soul. You guys are somewhere, and I need to know, per my mission, where every living creature in HORUS is located."

"Um, um..."

This is getting nowhere and I'm wasting valuable time. I have to take it up a notch. I raise my foot high in the air, and stamp down hard, very hard, on the poor sap's wound. He shrieks in agony, like a baby without his pacifier, while I raise my foot again. One won't do the trick, it has to be continuous. But he sees this and knows what's happening. He breaks. Some people are easier to convince than others.

"Don't do it!" he pleads. "I'll… tell you want you want… anything. Just get me to a doctor, please!"

"I can't help you out unless you help me," I say. "I want you to answer my questions as precise as possible. First one, where are the others?"

"By others do you mean the hybrids or the people. Because there's a difference between the two. Hybrids…" he continues.

I raise my boot up and slam it to the ground in the same place as I did before. He instinctively clutches it and rolls on the ground screaming.

"God damn, I need a location, not a fucking novella. Now let me ask again, where is everyone?" I ask.

He's sluggishly recovering from the pain and focuses enough to answer the question.

"The humans are in the cafeteria, the hybrids are in the communal room," he squeaks out.

"Why are they there?" I ask.

"It's protocol. Our communications and security programs went berserk ten minutes ago. Our drones are malfunctioning, and we can't get a hold of each other. In emergencies like these, the meeting spot is in the cafeteria or communal room, but most of the other humans are in the cafeteria. It's supposed to be a safety zone. That's where I was headed until you shot me."

"And how many are there?"

"Um, I don't know, I'm kind of new here. I think it's about forty or fifty humans and twenty something hybrids."

"And where are these rooms?"

He looks at me stunned.

"I'm not telling you, you're going to slaughter them," he says.

"John, you hear this?" I ask him on my communicator.

"Three steps ahead of you, I'm sliding a holoscreen your way. It's a map I hacked when I extracted information from the scrambler. That'll have the schematics of the whole building," John says. "Sending them to your interface."

The diagrams show on my communicator's holoscreen. I study the floor plan and now know where I'm going.

"Thanks for the info, Aaron," I say, "but we won't be needing you anymore."

I point my gun at him and I see for a brief second an expression of fear and hopelessness. I can read it in his eyes how royally screwed he knows he is. I pull the trigger and watch the energy shot fly out, right into his face. His head collapses on him and blood splatters everywhere, like a popped water balloon. Nuts, some of it got on my pants. I'll have to rewash them now.

"Let's keep moving," I calmly say as we walk by Aaron's corpse and towards the cafeteria.

"Hold it right there," a voice says to me. No creature is nearby. The noise comes from the walls.

"Who is this?" I ask bewilderedly.

"This… this is Lionel Changer," he says.

"We cut your communications, how are you able to speak through the comms?"

"I'm using my private line. I've been able to see everything unfold. It's wired differently from the internal communications systems you disabled."

"How do I know it's you?"

A holoscreen appears in front of me, projected from the walls. I inspect the face that displays from it.

"Lionel Changer, it is you," I say.

"Who are you or who sent you?" he asks, cutting the bullshit small talk. "Mercenaries? An old enemy?"

"I'm Special Forces Agent Brock West, serving for the United Species Alliance."

"How did you find me? No one's known our existence for years."

"It took a while. I've been on the case since Operation Halfkinds ended, non-stop around the clock. Any trace of evidence, news, images linked to HORUS, I found it and pieced things together like a puzzle until I had a complete picture of your location. With that kind of persistence, I can find anything. You really thought you could hide from the Alliance? Nowadays, you can't hide from anything."

"I… I had no idea you were coming. Nothing was set off until the communications were disabled. I was clueless."

"Like I said, I did my due diligence. Masks, or prerecorded feeds, were sent to your stream. We were battling your defenses outside. It was quite a fight, but you didn't see us. Instead you saw that everything was okay through your security monitors until it was too late. It was only until you switched to your private line was when you saw the truth. We had to make sure we had surprise to our advantage. Every preventive measure you would've taken, we had it covered. I probably know this facility better than most of the people here. Years of research will do that for you."

He appears terrified and nervous by my answer, and takes some time to think about the situation.

"What does the Alliance want from me?" he asks.

"To exterminate HORUS and anyone associated to it. Your work here is done," I say.

"But why? I assume you know everything about me. Don't you know I'm fighting on your side?"

"Excuse me?"

"You're a human. So am I. We're brothers in a world that should be ours. There was a time, long ago, when we were at the top. But these insidious, four-legged monsters have taken everything away from our species. How can you work with them? The Alliance? Nothing more than a bunch of humans who have lost the way. I'm engineering a way for us to get back in the game."

"I'm nothing like you. You are a monster. Interspecies breeding. Running a stable of unbalanced hookers. You think you're saving humanity? No human would ever approve of your actions. We are not brothers, and a billion other humans would say the same. You are a criminal, committing crimes not only against the Alliance, but against nature itself. That's why they've sent me, I'm going to end this."

He's speechless.

"How can you even associate yourself with those animal science experiments? Those freaks?" he asks.

"You're dense, aren't you?" I say authoritatively. "Don't you get it? We, human beings, are the freaks. Look at us, we're weak, slow, useless. Without our intelligence we'd be nothing. We're lucky nature gave us such a gift, because we'd be wiped out without it. We were the only ones who got the brains. And look at how we've squandered it for most of our existence. Pollution, death, destruction. These animals aren't science experiments, these animals, my peers, are what nature has done to correct itself."

"You're indoctrinated."

"You're behind the curve."

He looks at me through his holoscreen with despair.

"What happens next?" he asks.

"Within these headquarters lies your followers and creations," I say. "I'm going to kill them, and then I'm going to kill you. See you soon."

"No wait, please. They're innocent. Leave them alone, leave me alone. It's my life's work, it can't end like this, it can't..."

I ignore his pleas and continue walking to the cafeteria.

"C'mon boys," I say to Kanji, Ingle, and Kimba. "Our targets are beyond these walls. Winde, if you can hear me, try to disable the private line."

"That might be tricky," Winde says from his communicator.

"Just do it."

I follow John's schematics to the cafeteria. There isn't a human around, so Aaron must have been telling the truth. We pass by some of the other rooms. One appears to be a medical station. Another looks to be a research and development center. Tablets, scanners, holograms all crowd the small area. Both are completely cleared out, and despite how much junk is in each, the emptiness gives the facility a hallow feeling.

We're close, but twenty or thirty feet away from the cafeteria, some security drones block our path. They are motionless, hovering in the air like brain dead birds.

"Winde, there are drones in our way," I say over our communicators.

"Yeah, but they're unresponsive, right?" he responds.

"Yes."

"Hold on, let me fix that."

The drones activate and hover toward our direction.

"They're on now," he says. "All the drones are linked to your communicator and will respond to your commands."

"Good. Follow me," I say to the drones.

I walk past them, and they start trailing me. We reach two large sliding doors with a sign above that says 'cafeteria.' We're here. The doors open and beyond them stand a group of fifty or so humans of various backgrounds and attires. Cooks, scientists, doctors, maintenance workers, the collective are in this room. They are the cogs and gears that run HORUS's operation. They look tired, angry, frustrated, confused, but most of all, scared. A flurry of questions fly my way.

"Who are you?"

"Why are you here?"

"What happened? I was working and the alarms went off!"

"What's the emergency, what happened to our network? Why has it been disabled?"

"So many questions…" I say to myself.

"What do you want to do, sir?" Kimba asks.

I think of the perfect answer, and then it comes to me.

"Let's use the drones on them," I say. "That way, we conserve our firepower."

My team nods approvingly.

"Drones, fire on the targets ahead," I say.

The group of people stand back, astonished by the turn of events. Some don't have time to comprehend what has happened or who I am. Others know, and think they have a chance to fight back. A few brace for impact.

The drones unleash their volley of energy shots into the mass of people. A whirlwind of shrill screams echo within the confines. The rapid fire of the drones' guns create a steady rhythm of bangs. The ammo rips through every worker's body, tearing their skin into pieces, and demolishing their skulls with every headshot. Their bodies quake violently, and their limbs flap in the air like string in a windy draft. Blood splatters and paint the walls red. Some specks fly in our direction, but we use the bioshields to keep ourselves clean.

One injured worker manages to temporarily escape the path of destruction. He crawls on the floor, toward me. I simply look at him, and a drone blasts one shot straight through his cranium. Pieces of his brain rocket from his head into other workers who have already fallen slain.

Within seconds, the drones have done their work efficiently. About fifty people stood before me alive, now every single one of them is a corpse beneath my feet. The smoke clears and my team is left towering above them.

"That was easy," Kimba says.

"Sure was. This is turning out to be a cakewalk," I say. "Nice change of pace. Wish we could track down scientists more often."

"Where do we go next?" Kanji asks.

I look at the carcasses that lie before me, bloodied, disemboweled, and dismembered. Some have mortified expressions on their dead faces, others have no face at all.

"This is a warm up," I say. "We've taken care of the help, now it's time to go to phase two."

"The halfkinds?" Kanji asks.

"Yeah. Let's go."

We walk away from the cafeteria and head towards the communal room. The dead members of HORUS will be left for the flies.

Chapter 23 - Lionel Changer

Reduction

May 7, 3043 8:20 PM

"Looks like the operation was a success," I say to Lucy as we sit in my office looking over Iris's results.

"Biological, neural readings indicate so. Need confirm with Bastion after completes survey," Lucy says.

"Agreed. His findings will be vital. I hope Iris answers honestly about any new developments she's experienced."

"Doubtful. Resents us."

"Not to worry, she'll come around. I think at this point, Bastion should be done. I'll contact him."

I tap the side of my head to activate my communicator and expect him to answer, but, to my surprise, nothing happens. I tap it again, but it is non-responsive.

"What in blazes," I say. "That's odd, my communicator isn't working. Can you try yours, Lucy?"

She does as she's told, but has the same result.

"Ineffective," she says. "Will check logs."

Lucy runs the diagnostic program and reads the holoscreens that appear in front of her. Going through various folders and protocols, she is able to find the answer.

"Network down," she says.

"That can't be, the network hasn't gone down since I broke ground on this place. That must be a mistake."

She looks at her readings one more time.

"No mistake," she says.

"If that's the case, then the workers should know there's an emergency. They should all be heading to the cafeteria. Security feeds!" I command.

The feeds appear in front of me and I examine them furiously. It appears the workers are going about their normal routine. I switch the view to above ground and see the perimeter hasn't been breached. My turrets, guns, mines, and drones haven't been triggered, so I'm a bit confused. Everything looks right as rain.

"There has to be something wrong," I say as I stand there perplexed by the communications failure.

"On standard feed," Lucy says. "Have private line. Use that one."

"No, that shouldn't matter. If everything here looks normal, than everything on my private feed should be the same."

"Try."

"Okay. Switch to private feeds!"

The holoscreen changes the picture and, to my utter shock, what I see before me is completely different. I'm still looking at the above ground feed, but everything is decimated. My precious defenses have been blown to bits. The turrets I placed are not there, my mines have been detonated, my drones obliterated. Even my gravity guns weren't standing upright. Who did this?

More importantly, how did I have no clue that this happened? The standard feeds showed that everything was okay, yet this one clearly displays the damage that has been done. No security alerts went off, no warnings, it's as if someone walked in and disabled everything.

Which makes me realize that whoever did this isn't there anymore, they're probably inside! I quickly change the feed to the inner halls and there I see the culprits. There's a human, an eagle, a tiger, and a lion. They walk through the halls, curiously looking around for something. They must have just entered.

Another feed shows another group entering from the opposite side of my headquarters. It consists of a crocodile, a chimp, and a bear. They've blasted through the walls, so they must've tunneled their way down here. It still doesn't explain how they were able to get through my security. But I observe the two groups and notice they're all uniformed and wearing heavy duty armor and weapons. These guys aren't normal intruders, these creatures are professionals. I wonder who sent them.

I then check the other rooms. The medical bay and lab seem to be empty. The cafeteria is filled with my employees. The hybrids are in the communal room, as protocol instructs them to. And I breathe a sigh of relief as Iris is with Bastion, still in her room at the barracks. If anyone can protect Iris, it's Bastion.

I hear a blast come from the other feed. My attention was focused on the others that I didn't see what happened exactly. I only see one of our newer guys, Aaron, rolling in agony on the ground, holding his leg while the other four stand over him.

They ask him questions but he is too flustered to answer them directly. The human stomps on his injured leg and the poor guy screams. I gasp at the brutality being displayed. This man is torturing my employee. Aaron's a lab tech that I recently hired and doesn't deserve this kind of treatment. He's probably scared and doesn't know why or what is happening.

The soldier asks where the others are, and I'm hoping Aaron doesn't spill the beans. Sadly, it's too much to take, and my worker tells him. It makes me wonder what this soldier wants to do with us.

But then I see it with my very eyes. As soon as the soldier gets his information, he takes out his gun and blasts Aaron in the head. I see his skull hit the ground and shake violently until he is lifeless. One of my men has been executed in front of my eyes. I'm rocked to my core.

"Lucy, does my private feed also have a communications link?" I ask.

"Yes," she says.

"Switch me on."

Lucy tinkers with her diagnostics screens.

"You are live."

"Hold it right there," I say to the group of murderers. The man looks around at the walls. I appear to have startled him.

"Who is this?" he asks with curiosity.

"This… this is Lionel Changer."

The man asks me how I've been able to talk to him because he says his team is the one responsible for cutting the standard line. I explain to him about my private line and the conversation goes from there. After a few pleasantries, I learn who has sent him - the United Species Alliance. Of course it would be them. My activities are highly illegal for the laws they've set, it was only a matter of time until they sent someone.

I always thought I've kept high standards when it came to protecting my secrecy, but as this man, Brock West, explains how he found us, I start to realize that there's always someone better than you out there. He's found me and no matter what I've done to hide myself, he's been able to uncover it all.

And he's well prepared for his assault. He tells me about his masks and pre-recorded feeds, and I start to feel stupid over how easily duped I was, how weak my defenses are, and how vulnerable HORUS really is. All this time, I've been searching for the next step of human evolution, and I failed to fortify the place I was doing it in. I'm such a fool.

I try to convince him that everything I've done was for him, for humankind, but he simply scoffs at my suggestion like he's brainwashed Alliance mind would. That fascist group of animal loving traitors has truly turned this world into a madhouse. I can't believe we would even associate ourselves with these lowly creatures, let alone create a working government with them. Those spineless cowards throw away any notion of what it means to be human.

After our conversation is done, Brock West leaves me with a parting message.

"Within these headquarters lies your followers and creations," he says. "I'm going to kill them, and then I'm going to kill you. See you soon."

He's going to execute them all. The people that I call my family will be murdered in cold blood by the government. He can't, they can't! We've done nothing wrong and we're going to die for it! This is sick. I won't allow it!

"No wait, please. They're innocent. Leave them alone, leave me alone. It's my life's work, it can't end like this, it can't end like this!" I plead, but he ignores me and continues to walk away.

My communication is cut, I can only see him from my feeds, and he's heading to the cafeteria where all my employees are. I desperately think of a way to prevent the oncoming slaughter. There aren't any interior turrets set up, and I didn't hire security personal. That's because I have drones. The drones! They can stop Brock West.

They're already in his way, blocking his path. Lucy looks at me blankly as I fumble through my desk to find the security controls for the drones and when I get them, I triumphantly hold them in my hands. Perhaps they can stop this Brock West. Yet, as I try to activate them, nothing happens. I stamp my thumbs on buttons and look at my interfaces, but nothing. I don't understand, they should be following my orders, but they hover in front of his team mindlessly. They should be blasting him to bits!

And then I see Brock West say something and the drones move. He orally commands them, they're under his spell. He must have hacked them in the same way that his team hacked all my communications and security. I'm powerless.

The cafeteria doors open and West stands in front of my workers with a cold gaze on his face. My people look back at him, confused and afraid. They're my brothers in arms in this struggle against the rest of the world. They're the good guys like me, preaching what is right. And now I'm helpless to save them.

He enters, the drones arm, and before my very eyes, almost all of the HORUS employees are slaughtered. Several are riddled with holes and burst out blood like popped tomatoes. Others try to run, only to have limbs and heads blown clear off, all while their bodies keep going because their nerves haven't caught up to them. Others have their skin charred and it bubbles like hot lava. What I am witnessing is a brutal mass killing, and

I can do nothing but turn my eyes away from the rampage.

The noises are extremely disturbing. It's a chorus of wails and splatter. I can recognize every single employee as they die their horrible death. One scream sounds like Alan, one of our top cooks, another sounds like Wang, our maintenance guy.

It feels like an eternity, but minutes later, the noise stops. Brock West has completed his task, he's killed a large chunk of my workers. When he's done, he simply walks away coldly, like a machine, onto his next target.

I look back on my feed and see the mass of slain bodies. Lifeless eyes are wide open, faces frozen in fear. Skin and clothes are coated red. There's some twitching here and there, but that's as far as things go. None of these men and women died with dignity. I will never forget their last moments.

The future I planned, my legacy, is now gone. Everything I've worked for was killed when all those souls were extinguished. These people were the foundations, the building blocks of what I planned. They were a collection of the brightest and most talented minds I could assemble, and now they are food for the rats. As I look at their butchered bodies, I shed some tears.

But then it occurs to me, the bad news isn't over yet. I observe where he's going and it fills me with terror. He orders the eagle to go in another direction, but him, the tiger, and the lion stay together. West is headed to the communal room, the same place where our hybrids are gathered, as protocol demands.

I immediately head for the door to intercept them, but, then, surprisingly, Lucy holds me back.

"Going where?" she asks.

"To stop them," I say.

"Chances of survival minimal. Hostiles armed, you are not. Demise assured."

"I don't care. I have to save them."

"Cannot. Can only save self."

"Out of my way!"

I shove her to the side. She slams against one of the walls and falls down. I immediately feel guilty, so I rush to her side. I offer my hand and get her back on her feet. She takes it and stands upright.

"Lionel Changer," Lucy says, "must listen. They are gone. Will not survive. Understand am being blunt, but we can live. Escape, rebuild, continue goals."

"No, I refuse," I say.

"Inside, know you cannot. This is setback. Must survive to further development. Go to hybrids, will die, work incomplete, effort in vain. May sound difficult, but must live at expense of others. Is for greater good."

I am furious at the words coming out of her mouth. How can she be so cold? Does she have no human side to her?

But as I step back, I realize she is right. There's no way we can fight against this group. We are outmuscled and outgunned. If I go after Brock West and his team, I'm a dead man. If I flee, I'll live to fight another day. I can start again, but only if I take that chance. I'm sorry my children, but work still needs to be done.

"What is decision?" Lucy asks.

I pause and think about what to say.

"We can use the transportation bay," I say.

"Yes, teleporters provide means to escape," Lucy says.

"I agree. I have a small, unmanned, private back up facility on a tiny island in the Pacific. It's a place to stay hidden and survive, but, you're right, if we escape there, we can rebuild and start over again. It took me over forty years to get this place running, and I don't care if it'll take another forty, but I will get humans their redemption. I still have the credits and resources from Implantus to do so. This will be a minor setback."

Lucy smiles.

"Yes, minor setback," she says. "All it is."

I look back at the feed. Brock West is now at the communal room with his team. The doors are shut, and that's all I choose to see. I turn off my private feed that directly links to inside the room.

There are no drones, it's just him and his weapons. The door opens and I can hear the panicked yells of my hybrids as they see the team and their array of guns and explosives. Questions are hurled at West, much like my employees did. And like before, he answers with a hail of gunfire. Blood curdling screams echo in my ears. Cries for help and pleas for mercy fail to move West, he continues shooting.

"I'm sorry, my children," I say, tears rolling down my eyes. "I can't help you anymore."

I don't want them to think that in their last moments I abandoned them. I don't use the term child lightly. They were my creations. I loved them, and hearing their calls for help will surely haunt my soul forever.

But we must do what we must do to survive. I regretfully shut off the feed in mid slaughter and look at Lucy.

"Iris and Bastion are still at the barracks," I say. "We must ensure her safety and meet with them so we can escape together. She will continue to be an integral part of my plan. This is non-negotiable."

"Understood," Lucy says. "Appears Alliance unaware of Lawton, Bastion. Can try to intercept safely."

I still see the two in another feed. She remains in her room while Bastion cautiously scopes the area to see what is going on. They have no idea the danger they're in, but I know Bastion is ready for this. He's been doing stealth missions for me all his life, and his physical prowess is extraordinary. I have faith that he will keep her safe.

But then, something catches my eye. It's the eagle, and he's headed straight their way. It may look like a silly bird, but it's actually a flying armory. Bastion has nothing on him, no weapon at all. I hope he and Iris live long enough for us to reach him.

I run to one of the closets in the roomy office. I open the door, and within it are energy pistols neatly stacked on shelves. I've always had these stored here, though I never thought I'd have to use them. Lucy and I both look at each other with some apprehension. Neither of us are prepared to go into combat.

I close my eyes and think one last time of my hybrids' screams.

"For the greater good," I say to myself. "For the greater good."

Chapter 24 - Fenrir Snow

Wounds

May 7, 3043 8:31 PM

I cleaned the wound as best as I could, but it was a second-rate job. Without the physical capability to reach the torn flesh, the best I could do was squirt some of the healing gel on a sterile surface and roll around on it. In times like these, I wish I had thumbs.

I thought I was done for the moment Fang electrified my brain and I was put into a seizure-inducing paralysis. I was shaking uncontrollably, about to pass out, with only a small amount of control over my body. She had me right in her reach, and when I saw her approaching with her weapon armed, I knew it was over. Yet, she hesitated. Something caused her to pause. I'm not sure what exactly. Maybe even the weakest familial bonds are hard to break.

I had to act fast. She wavered, but it didn't mean she wasn't going to still kill me. Fortunately, I had my trusty marble shooters attached on my front leg. Through the quaking, I was able to use every single muscle to bang my leg on the ground, in hopes that it would trigger the box. And it did. In a few seconds, the marbles leaked from the container like, well, marbles, scattering across the ground toward Fang and Patrice. The two of them scattered away from me in haste.

I guess I'm the luckiest wolf in the world. Not only did the little bombs not destroy me, but it also knocked Fang's helmed weapon off her head. Her electric hold on me was gone, and I was free from her control. The bombs provided a diversion, but I had to act fast before the dust cleared. I used the rush and excitement to fuel my body as I picked myself off the ground and bolted in the opposite direction. I ignored the pain, ignored my wounds, so I could escape with my life.

Five hundred meters later, I was in the clear.

I was panting for breath as I took a small rest to allow my body to catch up with itself. Blood was dripping down my neck, through my fur, leaking onto the ground. Even now, a few hours later, it continues to trickle. I have no doubt created a trail for the others to follow. I imagine they too are recovering from our battle, but knowing Fang and her tenacity, they're back on my case.

Or maybe not. I roughed two of my brothers up pretty badly. Danzel is missing a leg now, Raymus is probably burnt all over. I didn't want to do it, but I had to. Things have gotten out of hand and, at this point in the game, it's kill or be killed. I'm backed against a wall. If I hesitated like Fang, I'd be dead.

I shouldn't have secluded myself from them. I should've been a better older brother and kept in contact. They're in this mess because of me. So desperate they are to continue the family legacy. Yet, if I had been there for them, maybe their rage would've gone away, maybe getting in favor with the Brotherhood would be less important.

I hope that my brothers are okay, but I'm forced to come to the realization that at the pace things are going, we'll probably kill each other. The Snow family may be no more. I can't think about it, it's only going to distract me. When the time comes, I'll worry about it then, but right now, worries do nothing for me.

Thinking about my brothers' wounds also reminds me of the wounds that I've suffered. Patrice took a large chunk off my neck, ripped out from his strong jaws. Thank goodness it's not fatal, the gel should take care of any infection that might occur.

I guess I should be happy he didn't take a leg or anything that would hinder me. It's a flesh wound, and I can still walk, run, jump, and use my abilities without any handicap. The only drawback is that it hurts like hell whenever I do those things. I feel like every time I move a muscle, the pain nerves shoot out from that spot. I can't even stand without feeling agony.

That's not the only area where it's sore. I fought four of my siblings, one after another, and the pushing, falling, biting, charging, and kicking has left myself stained with bruises that my thick fur cover. I've been put through the gauntlet, not once, but twice, and I know there is more to come. Just thinking about it makes me dread taking another beating.

The electric cage on my head didn't help either. High voltage flowed through every part of my body, and it left me a convulsing mess until I was able to escape. I still feel the effects now. My tail has been twitching on its own, so I had to turn off the back sensors on my helmed weapon or I might accidently fire something. My jaw feels funny too, like it's numb, and my eyes blink more than they used too. Damn stun weapons.

I've been on this journey for more than a week now. I've laid low and been running on little sleep. I can't risk the rest knowing that my family is on my tail. I've been wired on awakeners, trying to energize myself in any way possible.

All the chems in the world haven't been keeping me motivated as much as Iris has. The thought that she's in danger makes me want to move faster. I can't fail Iris now.

This intuition I have, this mental beacon, I know it's her, it has to be. A sense is guiding me, nothing concrete, but it's stronger than anything I've ever felt before. I know I'm right, my gut is stronger than fact. I don't need a map, Iris is telling me in her own way where she is.

The communication has been dying in the past hours, and I wonder if something's happened to her. I still know where to go, but I don't feel her sending me signals. I'm worried. I hope she is safe.

It's now half past eight, and I think I'm here. There's a hill I need to get over, but after that, I'll be there. I don't know what to expect. Maybe some kind of large facility, maybe nothing. I have a feeling she's being held underground.

Over the hill I go, and before me is a barren landscape of broken tech. There are drones split in half, turrets and energy defenses that have been demolished completely. It's a field of scattered metals, electronics, and weapons. The shear amount of debris is impressive, the fact that someone or something mowed through it all is even more so.

I don't see one casualty amidst the destruction. Any normal creature would have been crushed by this array of weaponry. Yet, whoever took this head on did it in stride. They came through clean.

I'm confused, how could this have happened? As I look closer though, I see an opening to the ground. It's a small door, opened widely, with stairs leading below. And traces of smoke are coming out of it.

Fear rushes through me as I see the bits and ashes rise from it. Someone has gotten here already, someone bad.

I have to hurry, Iris's life depends on me.

Chapter 25 - Iris Lawton

Foresight

May 7, 3043 8:32 PM

Bastion peers his head out of the doorway and looks around.

"I think it's clear," he says. "We should be okay."

We've been staying in the barracks since we heard the explosions. Bastion noticed his communicator went down. He contemplated meeting the others in the communal room, but decided against it given the danger we sense. Bastion tells me he's been on many missions for Lionel, seen many things, and can tell when something is going wrong.

This situation gives me flashbacks to Primm on the night of Operation Halfkinds, particularly when Oscar, Maddie, Isaac, and I broke off from Tiago's group and found refuge in the Spades and Diamond Casino. I never felt comfortable when we were hiding there. I had that premonition that we weren't safe. Isaac tried to assure me that Oscar knew what he was doing, and that he would do everything to protect me. Isaac subsided my fears, but I never completely felt secured.

Look how that turned out. Guess I was right.

Bastion trying to keep me safe as a group of intruders storm the facility is like déjà vu. He's like Isaac right now, another cat hybrid who's looking out for my safety. It seems like it's more than duty with Bastion. While I can tell Lucy views me as nothing more than work, I get the feeling Bastion thinks differently. It's hard to read what his intentions are.

I haven't seen any visions pertaining to the end of this night. Even when I try, and even with my 'upgrades,' I still see nothing. I wonder if this is a good or bad thing. Yet, I don't want to focus too much on the future, I should focus on the present. Right now, Bastion is deciding what we need to do.

"We have to get to Lionel," he says. "Iris you need to come with me. I'm the only one who can keep you safe."

I'm still pretty apprehensive with relying on my kidnappers; they knocked me out and performed unwanted surgery. Yet, right now, I don't have much of a choice, and I don't know what threats are lurking around the corner. Bastion was well trained enough to snatch me unnoticed, he's probably my best line of defense at this point.

"Okay," I say hesitantly. "I'll go with you for now."

He walks out of the barracks on light feet, and I follow. We hug the walls, and crouch close to the floor. The halls are eerily quiet. I've only been here a week, but every day that I have, these halls were bustling. I would run into lab technicians, workers, even another hybrid or two. But now they've fallen so silent that you could hear a pin drop and it would echo through the corridors.

"Where is everyone?" I whisper to Bastion.

"Probably in the communal room or cafeteria," he responds. "That's where we're supposed to congregate when the communications go down or there's been a security breach. With that explosion and the network failing, that's the surefire spot the hybrids and workers would go."

"Everyone's there safe and sound?"

"They should be."

"Why don't we head there too then?"

"I'd rather meet up with Lionel. I want to understand what's going on as soon as possible, and Lionel will tell me that. Besides, he'll probably need my help while he sorts out this mess."

"Fair enough. Things seem so creepy with the place so empty."

"Tell me about it. I've been here all my life and I've never seen anything like this."

Suddenly, we hear something in the distance. It's a light flapping noise. I can tell it's getting closer and closer. I don't know what to expect, but I become more frightened as it approaches. In a moment of weakness, I jump behind Bastion and clutch his shoulders.

Swoop, swoop, swoop. The halls are still empty, and the seconds feel like an eternity as I wait.

Out from the corner emerges the culprit, an eagle, armored, and menacing. Miniature guns adorn his wings and a handful of bombs and metal canisters hang from his body. His talons are equipped with large, sharp daggers. His body is completely uniformed, black. Only his face is partly exposed, but there's a helmet that covers his eyes. He looks like a winged merchant of death.

He may not be that big, but he's fast and his weapons make him deadly. He wears a uniform that I'm all too familiar with at this point. He's from the Alliance. I start to see flashbacks of my family members getting slaughtered, Oscar getting shot, Maddie being blasted away, Isaac slumped on the ground lifeless. I stand there frozen.

Bastion, on the other hand, grabs my arm and bolts in the opposite direction. We start running for our lives.

"I see two hostiles!" he yells in human over his communicator. I'm surprised he speaks human, not his bird language, but I guess human is the standard among Alliance soldiers. "They're running away, I'm going after them."

With Bastion leading the way, we sprint through the hallways, running by many rooms and corridors. The eagle tails us ferociously. It'll only be a matter of seconds until we're in his sights and within firing range. We make it around the corner, out of view from the eagle. Bastion desperately looks for a place where we can hide. He sees a door, quickly opens it, and pulls me in. The door then slides to close.

It's small in here, and dark. I feel a little stuffy, and Bastion's body presses against mine because we're so squished together. I think we're in a closet of some sort.

"Where are we?" I whisper to Bastion.

"Utility closet," he says.

"We're going to hide here?"

"Do you have any better ideas?"

"No."

"Then, yes, we are."

I can't see outside, the door is solid, but I can hear the eagle talk to himself.

"Where did they go?" he asks. "They couldn't have gotten far. I mean they weren't running that fast."

He pauses a little bit, and Bastion and I stand there in silence. I'm scared out of my mind.

"Bastion," I whisper, "does this door have an auto sensor?"

"What do you mean?" he asks.

"I mean, the moment this bird flies by us the door will open, and then we'll be in deep shit."

"Fuck, you're right."

"We can't stand here then, we have to do something."

Bastion takes some time to think and doesn't answer.

"Well," he says, "he's a bird, how dangerous could he be? We're in a closed space, he can't fly anywhere, and I'm at an advantage. I've taken on way worse than this creature."

"But he's armed," I say. "You're not."

"If I'm fast enough, I could get the drop on him. I only need one good swipe to send him across the room. If I'm quick, he won't even have a chance to shoot his weapon."

My head starts to ring and I feel a small migraine. The dark closet becomes illuminated. I see a large ball of light coming to me like a giant burst of white fire. The brightness causes me to squint and eventually I shut my eyes completely.

When I open them, I realize I'm not in a utility closet anymore, I'm outside, in the hallway. And in front of me is Bastion standing directly in front of the eagle. They're eyeing each other, the tension seems thick.

"How'd I get here Bastion?" I ask him. But he does not react. He can't hear me. A vision, this is what I see, a glimpse into the future. I guess we decided for Bastion to take the eagle one on one.

He starts charging at the eagle with full speed. The eagle does the same. I feel like I'm watching an action movie, two foes giving everything they got to take each other down. Bastion leaps in the air and swings at the bird, but the eagle is nimble and dodges his attack, flying around his arm and right behind him.

As fast as it started, the fight is over. The eagle shoots a large spray of plasma at Bastion, and I watch in horror as Bastion's fur and skin light on fire while his clothes literally melt off his body. He tumbles and rolls around in agony, his screams echo through the hallways while the bird looks on emotionlessly. Within a few short seconds, he lies dead on the ground.

It then occurs to me that I might still be around and, oddly enough, when I look to my right, I see myself in the closet, frightened and helpless. It's an alternate me. The bird seems to notice, and flies his way towards my alternate-self as she can do nothing but watch her life pass before her eyes. The last thing I hear is a dreadful wail. They are my screams, shrill, and tormented.

"No!" I say.

"Quiet!" Bastion says to me. "The bird is going to find us."

To my astonishment, the room is dark. And I feel squished again. And Bastion is still alive! I'm back in the utility closet. Sometimes, my visions seem so lifelike that it's a surprise to me when reality comes back into play.

"Okay," Bastion says, "I'm going to see if I can stop this bird."

I'm still wearing off the effects of my vision but I remember what I saw.

"No, don't do it," I say.

"Why not?" he asks.

"I had a vision of you and the eagle fighting. It didn't turn out so well."

"But we can't stay here. We'll be found out at any moment. If we don't move fast, we're done for. What do you suggest we do?"

Once more, I feel that ringing in my head.

"Ugh, not again," I say. "How many of these am I going to have?"

At least this time, I know there's a vision coming. I already saw my own demise earlier, so maybe I'm looking into the future past that? In a world where I don't exist? I don't understand how I could see time beyond my own life. Yet, I also don't understand how I can see the future in the first place.

Once again I see someone standing in front of the eagle, in the same exact spot where I saw Bastion stand in my prior vision. I can only see this being's back. It's slender, and is definitely a hybrid. It has pointed ears, an orange complexion…

Wait a minute, that's me! But I died in the last vision, how am I alive in this one? I think about the previous one I had, with Bastion and the eagle, and I observe this one. The circumstances are exactly the same. Same positions, same eagle, same hallway. I turn and even see the utility closet wide open. And Bastion is there. Wait, Bastion is there? But I was there last time. And now I'm standing in front of the eagle this time.

Now I get it. I'm not looking ahead in the future, I'm looking at an alternate one. The last vision was to show what would happen if Bastion attacked the eagle. This one is showing me what would happen if I launched an assault.

I can look at multiple instances of the future? I never could do this before. Every time I saw some future event, it was one time. I could never replay the same event and watch things unfold with different variables. This is a breakthrough, I not only know the future, but all futures.

So, this is the power that nut, Changer, was talking about. And because I've had a number of other odd things happen, I start to think this may only be a preview of what's to come.

Before I get too excited, first things first, I need to see how this vision goes down. I see myself charge at the eagle, much like how Bastion did. The eagle does the same and it looks like we're about to collide. But at the last moment, my alternate-self ducks under him and continues to bolt forward. The eagle does a quick loop to turn about face and persists on his chase. My alternate-self runs faster, towards a wall.

What am I doing? That's a dead end! I look cornered now. My alternate-self turns around, and faces an eagle that's at point blank range. The eagle doesn't say anything. He hovers in the air like a silent assassin and I can tell this is going to end badly for me. Guess you can chalk this up in the 'Iris dies' column.

He takes his shot, but, to my surprise, my alternate self makes a quick move and slides right under him. She goes head first, right as his wall of plasma exits out of the mounted weapons on his wings. My alternate-self goes far enough where she is four feet behind him, and I hear a shriek. The events went by so fast, and I was so focused on myself that I couldn't clearly see what happened to the eagle. He's injured. He squawks some inaudible sounds, flutters his wings wildly in the air, and falls to the floor, a smoking mess. I'm completely confused by what has occurred.

He's completely charred. His wings look burnt and some parts of his uniform are engulfed in flames. Some of his weapons start to crackle and pop, causing mini explosions to patter around his body. He flails around violently, but within a matter of seconds, he stops moving. He's dead.

I take some time to think about what I saw, to piece together the clues in order to get the complete picture. I begin to realize that the eagle was directly facing a wall, and when my alternate-self made her maneuver, the plasma missed and hit it directly. This caused the piping lava-like energy to splatter all over the industrial strength partition and bounce back on him. In an instant, the plasma did its work and wrapped him in a tomb of fire. The armor he wore probably trapped the heat, roasting him alive as if he was stuck in an oven.

The vision ends. Like before, my mind is warped back into the tiny utility closet. As I recover, I let out a light groan.

"You okay?" Bastion asks. "I think you blanked out there for a moment. I was asking you all these questions and you didn't respond."

"I'm fine, just give me a second. I had another vision," I say.

"Another one? Did you initiate it?"

"No, it just happened."

"What did you see?"

The eagle's death, my daring moves, a way to escape. It all comes back to me, and I feel a rush of excitement envisioning it.

"Watch," I say. I move away from him and step toward the closet door. He abruptly grabs my arm.

"What are you doing? You want to get yourself killed?" he asks.

"No, I'm actually doing the opposite."

I swat my arm away from his. I exit the closet and spill into the hallway, in plain sight of the Alliance eagle. He's about thirty feet away from me, and sizes me up in an intimidating fashion. Airborne and ready to strike, he flaps his wings to maintain his position as we stare each other down like I saw in my vision.

He makes his move and starts charging for me. His guns are pointed at me, so I head forward as well. My movements mimic what I saw in my vision. I sprint right at him. I don't flinch, and I quickly duck and run right past him. He looks frazzled by the unexpected maneuver, but he quickly turns the opposite direction and continues his pursuit.

I've made it all the way to the end wall, I turn around so my back rubs against it, and I look straight at the eagle, who continues to zip in my direction. Watching something happen is much different than experiencing it. I remember my vision clearly, the running to the wall and being trapped there, but now I feel a rush of adrenaline shoot through my body. I breathe heavily and my muscles tense. Part of me wants to remain petrified. The other part of me wants to act on the rush that I feel.

My palms caress the smooth wall, the back of my head slightly bangs against it. A million things float through my mind, but I only have a few seconds to do something before I'm toast. I saw a vision where I saved the day. It is the future, but it's not set in stone. If I don't act, is it really the future? Perhaps if I stay here, I will die. My vision wouldn't be wrong, it's just one that I didn't see. I mean, I only saw two alternate futures, what if there are millions? What if I saw the wrong one?

The bird is now less than ten feet away. The gun barrels on his wings start to glow. The plasma is releasing.

Ah, fuck it.

The lava-like substance sprays from his weapon. I jump forward and slide underneath him before it makes contact. It then splashes on the wall and a small wave of it covers him. He was so focused on me that he lost his awareness to his surroundings. Just like I saw before, his scorched body thrashes in the air, and then plummets down. It takes a few moments, but he eventually dies after burning to a crisp.

Bastion comes out from the utility closet. He's witnessed the whole thing and looks awestruck.

"How, how did you do that?" Bastion asks.

"I saw his death earlier in a vision," I say. "This is how it played out."

"I can't believe all that happened. It was amazing."

"Nah, it was luck."

"Luck, or power?"

I roll my eyes at Bastion.

"Let's not start that again," I say. "Besides, we need to find Lionel."

"You're right," he says. "After thinking about it, he actually might be in the communal room. That's where all the other hybrids are supposed to be, it's highly possible he went to check on them. I think we should head there. I'm not sure where the eagle's buddies are, but I'm hoping the communal room is safe. Do you sense anything odd about that room?"

I close my eyes and concentrate. I focus on the communal room as if I know what I'm doing. I don't sense any danger, but something does seem off.

"I'm getting this eerie, creepy feeling," I say. "But I don't sense any danger from there. It's only my intuition."

"Good enough," Bastion says. "Hopefully, Lionel will be there. It's not too far from here, we better hurry. We'll need to keep a low profile. I know this facility and I'm light on my feet, so follow me."

Bastion steps in front of me a leads the way. The previous minutes are still on my mind. I don't know the full nature of my powers, but whenever I feel an intuition, a sense, I'm probably right about it. And my precognition definitely has improved. I guess whatever they did to me kind of worked.

Alternate futures, what a mind trip.

Chapter 26 - Fang Snow

Perdition

May 7, 3043 8:45 PM

Drip. Drip. Drip. It's Fenrir's trail of blood I follow. We're so close to him that I can smell victory approaching. And when we do get to him, it'll be his throat that I rip. No more hesitation. I had Fenrir in my clutches and I stopped. This could've been over. Yet, that moment of doubt allowed him to get away. If I do it again, I might not be so lucky. It could cost me my life. Just look at my brothers.

With his leg missing and no hospitals nearby, Patrice and I fashioned Danzel a 'temporary appendage' from our medical kit. It's basically a patchwork mechanical leg of low quality, used for a short-term solution. He can walk, even lightly run with his alloyed leg, but it's not as responsive or durable as a real bio-mechanical implant. Danzel was lucky that Fenrir had a clean hit on him. His missing leg could've been easily infected had Fenrir not been so efficient. Instead, the leg was blasted off rather neatly, and the plasma from his energy shot inadvertently cauterized it.

Our medical kit has spare appendages, ones designed for wolves. The matter of fixing him was relatively simple. We only had to attach his mechanical leg to a nerve ending, so it was an implant to his stump. The process was painful and Danzel howled into the moon. Imagine having an arm cut off, then jamming something in the wound. That's what happened to Danzel. Still, once it was attached and we cleaned up the mess, Danzel could walk again. He wasn't one hundred percent healthy, but this would do.

Raymus also obtained some serious injuries during his scuffle with Fenrir. A tunneler erupted right below him, burning fur and flesh as he was flung into the air by the mighty force of the shot. It went through his armor and large chunks of his torso were hit. The fur was burnt instantaneously upon contact with the tunneler. On those bare parts, you could see the freshly crisped pieces of flesh as a result of the extreme heat of the tunneler. Parts of his once glorious coat has now been reduced to ashes.

Still, like Danzel, he was semi-fortunate. He didn't have any facial burns, and, while I can't say he's completely healthy, his injuries are for the most part superficial. He'll live. Our medical kit had some ointment that we applied directly to his charred skin, and within an hour, I could see its positive effects.

Their wounds are non-fatal, and I need their help to take on Fenrir. If we lose any minutes, we could easily lose the trail. I told them we'd continue our pursuit, and Danzel and Raymus were downright furious. They wanted their medical needs to be addressed by professionals instead of the quick fixes Patrice and I applied.

"You've gone mad," Danzel said as he looked at his artificial leg.

"Do you see what's happened to us?" Raymus protested as he shook off his burnt strands of fur from his coat. "Is your journey of retribution the only thing that matters now?"

I didn't understand it. I wasn't the one who blasted Danzel's foot off. And I certainly wasn't the one who pushed Raymus into his own tunneler. It was all

Fenrir's doing. Yet there I was, defending my own orders against defeated and irate siblings. Through sweat and blood, this chase has been about restoring our honor and winning the Snows a place back in the Brotherhood's hearts. How did I become the bad guy?

"Have you forgotten who did this to you?" I barked back at them. "Do you remember the mercenary work? Do you remember going on countless missions like this, taking unnecessary risks day in and day out, because we were banished by our own kind? Or have your flesh wounds made you lose your memory?"

"You're out of line!" Raymus said, grimacing as he growled back at me. "You aren't the one that's scarred for life."

"I'm not, but if I did, I'd want to get even," I responded.

Raymus and Danzel stood there, thinking about their desires while Patrice and I looked on edge.

"We're hurt, Fang," Danzel said. "I can walk, but I'm in no condition to do this."

"Neither am I," Raymus said.

"I understand that," I said, "but you're still battle ready. Fenrir's changed, he would've never done this to you before he met that halfkind. He's no longer our brother, that part died in him the moment he decided to abandon us to the Brotherhood's judgment."

"Fang, that's a bit harsh," Patrice said. "He's our blood."

"Let it go, all of you," I said. "I remember Fenrir, he was a good brother. He took care of us, he loved us. And never in a million years would I think that he would have done what he did today. Our brother is no more. All this time, we've been struggling with the concept that he's the enemy. But as I look at your leg,

Danzel, and at your burns, Raymus, I can see clearly whose side he's on. We must find him."

I looked at Danzel.

"You'll never have your real leg again," I said.

I then looked at Raymus.

"Your burns will stay with you until the day you die," I say. "Aren't you angry? Don't you want revenge?"

Neither of them said anything in response, but they look at their wounds, and a rush of emotions were expressed on their faces. Grief, sadness, self pity, anger, and hate.

"You're right Fang," Raymus said. "The Fenrir I knew would never have done this. He's dead."

"Those are the brothers I know," I said smiling.

That was earlier this evening. We took some time to rest and started off on the chase again around seven. Fenrir left an easy enough trail to follow. I don't think he was being obvious about it, he's just headed to his destination in a hurry. I doubt he had the time to cover his tracks.

It is now almost nine and we are about to reach a hill. Fenrir appears to have slowed down, and I feel we are close. I sniff the air carefully. The rusting scent of metal and cut redwood invade my senses. It also smells like smoke and hints of plasma. Something is wrong, my nose knows it.

"What do you smell?" Patrice asks me.

I ignore his question and run over the hill. There lies a valley of obliteration, broken drones and turrets scatter the grass field. A tidal wave of annihilation swept through this area. There's so many dismantled gadgets and gears that it makes me a little nervous. I wonder if Fenrir did this.

But I can't be silly. There's no way one lone wolf could've amassed this destruction. My brother may have combat prowess, but this is too much for him. This looks like the work of an army, a well prepared army.

My brothers have caught up to me and they see what I see. Stunned, they look at each other, and then me for guidance.

"This isn't Fenrir," I say.

"Agreed," Raymus responds.

"So, what do we do now?" Patrice asks.

I scan the area for anything that might be a lead. I don't see Fenrir anywhere, nor do I see any other signs of life. This barren wasteland appears to be all that's here.

But then my eyes catch something in this mess. It's an unclosed door that leads to an area below. It's a bit dark, but I see some light and smoke creeping its way out. Something is down there.

"Do you see what I see?" I ask the others.

They scan the area but nothing registers.

"No," Patrice says.

"Me neither," Danzel comments.

Raymus continues to look. He crouches down and examines the landscape like a detective looking for a clue. Something startles him and he stands up.

"I see it," he says.

The others look harder, and see what we're talking about.

"That's where we're heading?" Raymus asks.

"It's the only place Fenrir could've gone to," I say.

"But what about all this junk lying about?" Patrice asks.

"Yes, someone else was around," Danzel adds. "And from the looks of it, they're here for serious business."

What is this place that Fenrir has brought us to? Why did it attract so much attention? Is this some kind of government facility? Maybe it's an unground criminal headquarter?

"We can't worry about whoever else is here," I say. "If we see anything suspicious, we'll get out of the way. Judging from all the broken turrets and drones, this place is a big deal. And a big deal means a big headquarters. If we need to, we can find cover so that we don't encounter anything else. Our goal is to hunt down Fenrir, that's all. We won't get involved in anyone else's business."

The others look at me, and they seem a little tense by this wildcard that has been thrown our way. I'm afraid too, but I think if we stay vigilant about our secrecy, it won't be an issue.

"All right brothers, are you ready to head in?" I ask. They nod. We make our way to the open door and trek down the slope like lost souls heading toward the gates of hell.

Chapter 27 - Fenrir Snow

Dogfight

May 7, 3043 8:45 PM

I've entered the premise. I'm still sore all over, but the gels I applied help soothe the pain. Things don't seem right. I haven't been here that long, maybe no more than ten minutes, but I've yet to hear a peep. I don't know what this place is supposed to be, but from what I've seen so far, it shouldn't be empty.

I walk by rooms that looked like labs and next to them is what appears to be a medical station. Some machines are still on, and the rooms have an unorganized feel to them. Someone or something left this place in a hurry. It makes me wonder what happened and if it caused an evacuation. The smoke outside suggests this.

The instruments and equipment appear to be tailored for humans and nothing else. I don't believe there's an animal presence. It's strange that there is none, why is this place human only? I do know that there are humans in this world who still do illegal genetic experiments. That's why I suspected Eve's death was some kind of human cover up. This place looks secretive enough to confirm my suspicions.

This facility is also quite large. As I walk around white hall after white hall, I start to get confused where I am. That says a lot if an expert tracker like myself can't get a handle on directions. I can only wonder how far this facility stretches below.

I sniff the ground, and start to look for clues on Iris's whereabouts. Her psychic senses have stopped coming in, so I'll have to do things the old fashion way. I know she's here, though. I detect small traces of her smell. The ground is littered with a variety of aromas, but I can sift through all of them to detect Iris's. I discovered her smell when I stepped in, and I was one hundred percent relieved to know I was in the right place. I hope she's safe, because this place looks dangerous.

My nose continues on the floor for Iris's trail, but it's scattered. I don't detect a concrete path, rather, I smell movements in every direction. That means she's been around here for quite some time, not just once. That's a good sign. She's been walking around this place, and isn't holed up in some cell.

I continue to walk through the halls when I pick up another smell. Something is burnt; like charred flesh. The smoke becomes thicker as I walk deeper through the halls. There's been an attack here, and I desperately hope that it's not on her.

I hurry to the source of the smoke. My mind thinks of terrible things, such as Iris's body blackened, ashy, and smoldering from plasma burns. Please, don't let it be her, please.

It's not. I arrive at an open room, a large one. There are several dining tables and a kitchen set up on the opposite side. Trash incinerators, plates, cups, human food utensils, and liquid dispensers litter the room messily. That's not what I notice. What I notice are the dozens of dead bodies on the floor.

Every single one of these corpses are human. The blood is fresh and the burns are, too. The smell of death is strong here. I can smell it in the puddles of blood that cover the ground and smear the walls, I can smell it in the bodies that have been roasted alive. This was the work of high grade energy weapons. It must've been painful, scary, but also happened very quickly. I can tell these people died around the same time because of the freshness of their wounds. It's like they were rounded up here and massacred.

As I look at their attire, the humans have different backgrounds. Some are wearing lab coats, so they must've been scientists. Others are wearing workman clothes, and others look like chefs. They all appear rather indistinct though. I don't see one person of importance among the dead.

Not all of them are easy to identify. I can't even see the faces of some people because it's missing. Arms are gone, legs are gone, whole midsections have holes in them. The type of aggression taken out on these people was brutal. Even though I harbor ill feelings towards humans, I'm still put off by what I see here. It's disturbing. I don't see weapons or signs of resistance. No fight was put up. These people were executed.

I don't see Iris either. I am relieved. Yet, so many questions remain unanswered. If she's not here, then where is she? Who were these people, and what did they do to warrant such gruesome deaths? And lastly, what did this underground organization want with Iris?

I think about the pieces I have to put this puzzle together. A group of rogue geneticists who want the world's only halfkind… Wait, how did they know about the existence of the world's only halfkind? From my knowledge, information on Operation Halfkinds was never made available to the general public. Only confidential circles knew about it. If they specifically kidnapped her, then they had to know about her first. And if they knew about her first, they had to know about halfkinds, which leads me to suspect one thing: this group had their hand in creating them.

When I was on the halfkind mission, I was aware that Maya Lawton had birthing implants installed in her. Yet, I was never given any information where those implants originated from, and Iris's knowledge concerning her mother's ability to give birth to cross species creatures was hazy. Now, as I stand here within the walls of these secret grounds, the picture is becoming much clearer. This place is probably responsible for Iris's birth, and they took her to reclaim what was theirs. It all makes sense now.

But what about the bodies? My detective work doesn't explain that. Who would want to kill these people? I guess the answer is everyone. These kinds of experiments are universally frowned upon. An assault could have been launched by any number of law enforcement groups. This place wasn't easy to discover, though. I needed a psychic signal to find it, and I doubt any other being had that kind of luxury. It probably took a lot of resources to launch an attack like this. I guess the question isn't who invaded this place, but who has the means to.

There's only one answer I can think of - the Alliance. The minute they found out about halfkinds, they sent a team, one that I was a part of. Now that they've found what seems to be the headquarters, they're doing the same. And judging from the way that these people died, they're not holding back.

Shit, I have to hurry. I quickly run away from the cafeteria and scamper to ground that I haven't covered yet. I'm hoping I'll stumble into Iris. But right after I turn the corner, I stop in my tracks. In my way stands another creature, and it isn't her.

It's a crocodile. He's wearing Alliance issued armor. My suspicions are right, it was them who launched this raid. The croc wears what they call an omni-shell. It looks like a turtle shell, capable of protecting their midsection. It stores a gaggle of weapons that they control with specific muscle movements on their arms and legs. When they're geared up, crocs look like miniature tanks.

The croc looks at me with curious eyes. He's probably as shocked as I am to see the sight in front of him.

"A wolf?" the croc says to himself. "What is he doing here?"

"I'd ask the same of you," I reply in human. He looks a bit shocked that I can comprehend and speak the language proficiently.

"A human-speaking wolf? Are you a soldier?"

"It appears you are."

He notices that I'm eyeing his uniform and armor.

"You state correctly," he says. "This is ground scout Joe Waylon, representative of the United Species Alliance."

"What are you doing here?" I ask him. I know the answer, but I want to confirm it.

"It's official Alliance business. Completely classified."

"That's all you can tell me?"

"Afraid so."

"It's just you, then?"

He lets out a light laugh.

"Hardly," he says. "I'm here with my team members."

"That's what I figured," I say. "I know you said it's classified, but I understand you're here because of a halfkind."

"Halfkind?" He's floored. "How do you know what that is?"

I've completely caught him off guard. He wasn't expecting me to know about halfkinds or anything concerning their mission.

"Let's say I have an inside source," I respond. "I know what the protocol is. I saw what you and your team did to those humans in the cafeteria. They're all dead. You've come here to exterminate everyone, haven't you?"

He doesn't answer at first. The ground scout is confused about how I know this information. He can barely muster out a response.

"Who, who are you?" he asks.

"My name is…"

Without warning, a gun rises from his omni-shell and fires a shot at me. What a cheap move, he's a dirty player.

I'm lucky and fast enough to jump out of the way. I should've seen this coming a mile away. He was trying to draw my defenses down with talk, and I almost fell for it.

As soon as I land, I turn around and start charging at him, firing off shots from my helmet.

"Fire, fire, fire!" I yell as three powerful bursts of energy flow from my weapon. Unfortunately, the croc has a bioshield. My shots deflect and harmlessly fly in other directions. Running at full sprint also throws off my aim, and he moves around too much for me to get a clear sight. Even when I thought I had an open headshot, it hits the shield.

He returns fire, but he's too slow and inaccurate with his aim. I'm a great gunner, and he's not a very good one. Dodging his ammo is a cakewalk compared to Fang and my brothers. Still, with his bioshield protecting him and his erratic movements, I continue to have a tough time getting anywhere. We are at a draw.

The only way I can get past the bioshield is through physical contact. He's fast for his size, but I'm just plain fast. If I can get close enough to him, I can destroy the wrist activator and disable the shield. Getting there shouldn't be too difficult, he's only thirty feet away, and he's missed everything already. One full sprint should allow me to get within striking distance. I can't get too close. If he's able to nab me with his jaws, as primal as it is, my body will be crushed within seconds. Don't want that to happen.

I take my runners start and go headstrong at him. Predictably, he shoots at me, and predictably, I avoid it effortlessly. With one giant leap in the air, I pounce at him.

I emphasize the giant leap because I don't realize how far I jumped. I wanted to get within five or so feet, but I jump further than that, right within striking range for him. His mighty jaws are one snap away from my face or legs, and if I don't react quickly when I land, I'll be trapped.

He sees me approaching and lunches forward, jaws wide open. Shit. Time to bust out the moves. Right when I land, he thrusts his head forward and the jaws snap, but right before it closes, I swiftly take another hop forward. My legs and head are clear of his grasp by the time he shuts his mouth. I made it.

But not really. When I land from my second jump, I'm right on top of him. Literally. I stand on his back, over the omni-shell, pinning him down.

"Get off of me!" he yells.

I see he's about to roll to loosen himself free. If he does so, I'll be the one held down. I hastily find an exposed part of his neck and bite down as hard as I can. Ugh, it's tough and feels like I'm chomping on bark. I clamp down with more force and I think I break his skin. He lets out a bellow and stops his roll.

He isn't giving up. He continues to thrash around, but I persist to hold my chomp down until he becomes tired. My head bounces up and down with his neck. My body is still trapped on his back. The wounds I obtained from my encounter with Fang are opening again thanks to Joe Waylon's struggle. I get flung wildly with only my bite securing me as he moves. My jaw starts to get tired and I realize I can't hold on for much longer.

That's when I see it. His wrist activator is in clear view. Destroy that, and I destroy the bioshield. I prepare myself for one final lunge with my jaws.

One.

Two.

Three.

I loosen my mandible from his neck and go straight for activator. I chomp down hard and fast, but something unexpected happens.

"Ow!"

I've been zapped. A shock runs through my body and I reactively jump off him. I look at his armor and its glowing. Of course, he must've had some kind of electric shield. My body was on his back, on his omni-shell, and the second he activated it, electric currents made contact with me. Firing off the taser must've ben his last, desperate move to release me. Damn, I sure have been zapped a lot today.

I'm dazed and a bit stunned, but his shock wasn't as strong as Fang's. I'm not completely disabled, and am coherent enough to see him aiming another gun at me. I'm still reeling from his attack and he figures this is the perfect time to kill me.

The croc has a sadistic smile on his face. The gun that protrudes from his omni-shell isn't a standard energy blaster. The barrel looks huge, ten times larger than what he was using earlier. I'm guessing it's some kind of plasma grenade.

Yet, he's so eager to fire he doesn't notice the bioshield activator that I destroyed moments ago. These Alliance assholes always show off when they shouldn't.

"Fire," I say.

The shot comes out of my helmet, and I see it travel from my head directly to his gun. Upon impact, the shot detonates whatever missile or bomb he had in store for me. A bright flare of green and turquoise flies in the air and the explosion rings in my ears. I wince away, shielding my eyes from the spectacle of flame and sound.

The aftermath of the blast fills the room. Smoke starts to spread, and I cough it out. It takes a few seconds for it to dissipate, but when it's done, the only thing I see is the corpse of the croc. His omni-shell has been obliterated, and his back is a bloody, scrambled mess. At least he died a quick death.

I approach him and sniff around. He's a goner all right, but I don't find any clues. This asshole was definitely Alliance, and the way he fired first means that he and his team isn't joking. I wonder how many squadmates he has. With what I saw in the cafeteria, there may be an army shipped out to take down this facility.

The Alliance isn't joking this time. Agent Joe Waylon was a hard fucker to defeat. He had the most upgraded tech, weapons, and equipment. The Alliance paid top dollar for everything. And I imagine the rest of his team will be no different. The Alliance has probably learned from last time. Instead of sending a bunch of head cases who've never worked together, they've sent the real deal.

With these new threats, I worry that Iris won't be safe for long. If I could barely manage a creature like this, how can she? I must hurry, or the next corpse I see may be my dear friend's.

Chapter 28 - Lucy

Logical

May 7, 3043 8:45 PM

In Lionel Changer's office. Should have exited sooner, but needed to clear things out. Data must be scrubbed, information retained. Changer's work too important to lose, backup must be created.

Problem though. Too much data to download in small amount of time. Scrubbing may not be viable, danger imminent. Twenty minutes passed. More we wait, more our lives are threatened. Been encrypting, deleting, moving files to separate server. Protocols, programs not functioning, encodings failing. Quite possible that someone, perhaps intruders, figured way to shut us down, prevent from fulfilling this task.

"Fuck, I can't do anything!" Changer yells. "They've locked me out. Encryption protocols, deletion, I don't have access to do so."

"Those are minor," Lucy says. "Still have access to copy? Data is valuable, must be saved."

"They have me locked out of that too."

"Intruders targeting security settings. May be unaware of mine. Security clearance not as high as yours, but have read access. Possible for me to retain information. Please let me try."

Changer steps away from compcube and I log in. Must be quick, go through different screens until I reach Lionel's root folder.

"Dump all contents in main drive to datacube?" I ask.

"Yes, do it," he says.

Success, clearance has worked.

"Good thinking Lucy," he says. "With all that's going through my mind, I wouldn't have come up with the idea to try your access levels."

"Always good to have more than one mind on task," I say. "Have made one copy. Do not have capability to delete and scrub data. This is unfortunate, but time is running out, cannot afford to wait around."

"You're right. All the security feeds have been shut down. Looks like their programmer has cut them, including my private one. I don't know where Special Agent West or his crew is. But, lucky for us, they haven't gotten here yet. It won't be long before they are. We must move."

"Agreed. Transportation bay not far from here. Situation delicate, walking exposed in halls guarantees death. Must be silent."

"Yes. And Iris?"

"Hopefully Bastion taking her there too. Unfortunate cannot communicate with her."

"Unfortunate indeed."

Datacube rings and ejects from compcube. Upload complete. Grab and hand to Changer. Snatches and observes small device.

"All my life's work is in here," he says. "Every file, every document, every blueprint in this little cube. Amazing."

Getting sentimental. Don't have time. Tug on arm.

"Must go," I say. Snaps out of trance.

"Yes, yes, you're right," he says.

Walk toward closet and grab three energy pistols. Have never used firearm, but cannot be too difficult. Challenge lies in controlling adrenaline levels in order to remain focused.

Changer opens doors and looks out. Peer my head as well. Halls are empty, entry safe. Exit with energy guns in hands.

To get to transportation bay, must walk through halls and reach storage room. Large warehouse holds unused equipment. Food, clothes, and indoor vehicles. Once we get past storage room, we take right to gymnasium. Within gymnasium is secret compartment on ground which leads to tunnel. It is long, winding corridor, spanning close to one hundred yards. At end of tunnel is transportation bay. Reason Changer wanted bay to be separated from rest of facility is escape. Had transportation bay been close to facility or in obvious location, it would allow pursuers to continue chase. With secrecy and detachment from main facility, have enough time to escape without being caught.

Transportation bay is room filled with many teleporters. Working machines simple. Power them on, and set to auto shutdown mode. With this activated, instant we teleport out, porters will shut down and clear out logs. No trail left to help enemies locate post-teleportation.

Storage and shipping room is couple of halls away. To there is straight line. However, many intersecting hallways en route to target location. When HORUS was busy, collisions happened. Person run into another person perpendicular to direction.

Facility is empty, but no way to see who is around corner. If enemies are silent, they will apply sneak attack and we will be dispatched. Intruders have demonstrated killings of colleagues and hybrids. Watching fellow hybrids die was upsetting to Changer and I. Though lack capability to comprehend emotional reaction, part of me felt sadness. Not good at expressing feelings, but they exist.

Changer thinks differently. Suspects he sees me as robotic, persuading him from taking action while creations were murdered. Simply told him that actions lacked logic. To confront attackers is suicide. Had a near zero percent probability of surviving. What I spoke was truth. No point in having everyone including him die, must survive to continue work. Decision is difficult, understandably so, but reasonable.

Am glad Changer decided to hear me. Also glad that he has copy of data. Starting from beginning would be problematic, now have information to pick up where left off. Incident only minor setback.

Walk almost a hundred feet when we hear noise. Are thumps, coming at rapid succession. Sounds of footsteps. Not walking, running.

Someone approaches. Our backs hug wall. Changer draws gun, pointing it at corner. I do same. Neither have experience with firearms. Only half know what I'm doing. Seems simple enough. Point and click.

Fear rushing through veins. Thought emotions were under control, but basic instinct force I underestimate.

Sound gets louder, louder, louder, and then someone appears before us. Point our weapons. He looks stunned at appearance and frightened by guns.

"Don't shoot!" he yells. Bastion, it is Bastion.

"You're alive!" Changer exclaims. Embraces Bastion with hug. I look behind two and see Lawton.

"And so is Lawton," I say. "Chances of this happening are extremely low."

"We were on our way to your office," Bastion says.

"Ah, explanation," I respond.

"In either case, we must continue," Changer says.

"Continue where?" Bastion asks.

"We're going to the transportation bay," Changer says. "We have to leave post haste. If we don't, the Alliance will kill us. I'm so glad you two are alive though. I can't believe we ran into each other like this. Where have you been, anyway?"

Chapter 29 - Iris Lawton

Massacre

May 7, 3043 8:45 PM

We walk cautiously to the communal room. It's quite far, about a five minute walk. This place is massive, and I actually have to commend Lionel Changer for constructing it all underground.

I have my senses, but that doesn't mean our journey to the communal room is going to be safe. We could easily be ambushed, and there's no way that, without any weapons, Bastion and I can defend ourselves. I don't know what these soldiers want, but they're from the Alliance. That bird shot first, asked later. The second we encounter someone, we're done for.

We walk through the halls as silently as we can. Bastion is much better at this than me. His heels are raised, and he moves his legs with strict control. He's graceful, walking across the floor like, well, a cat, and I can't help but be impressed by his dexterity. And to top it all off, he's fast. Speed isn't being sacrificed for covertness.

I on the other hand can barely keep up. I stumble behind him, clumsily trying to keep up with his pace. My footsteps are not light, they're heavy and stiff. I try my hardest to maintain the amount of grace Bastion displays, but it's futile. The harder I try, the more I trip over myself. I almost slip and fall, only to catch myself at the last second. Bastion angrily turns around.

"Keep it down," he whispers.

"Sorry," I apologize, "I'm not as sneaky as you."

"This kind of stuff comes natural to me. Don't try to copy me, go at your own pace."

I shift my movements and walk like I normally would, only softer. I'm no longer goofily tripping over myself. I'm not as fast as Bastion, but I'm keeping up.

"Thanks for the advice," I say.

"Don't mention it," he says. "I want to make sure you're safe."

It's kind of weird when he says that. He's known me for less than a week, yet he always says stuff like how he wants to protect me and look after me. It's creepy. Yet, he's the only line of defense I have against any attackers right now, so I better stay close to him no matter what nonsense spews out of his mouth.

Suddenly, he stops in his tracks. He puts his arm in front of me and it prevents any further passage.

"Someone's coming," he says.

I stop walking and listen in. In the distance, I hear footsteps.

"You're right," I say. My fear starts to elevate but I prevent myself from panicking. "What do we do?"

"Just stay put," he says. "I think it's coming from the parallel hall. Might be another solider. I'm going to peak my head out to take a look."

Bastion looks around the corner and immediately he pulls his head back.

"Shit, it's an Alliance member," he whispers.

"Oh no," I shudder, "what does he look like?"

"It's a chimp. He has a bunch of high tech gear on him."

"What's the plan?"

"We're too underpowered to attack; I don't think we can take him head on. Have you seen any visions?"

"No."

"Damnit, that sucks."

"Hey cut me some slack, I got this power today. You can't expect me to be a master at it already."

"Sorry. All we can do is stay here and pray that he doesn't come near us."

Bastion raises his head, and inches his ear closer to the approaching noise. He motions for me to stay quiet.

I can hear the chimp talking to someone, and he speaks in human.

"This is Winde," he says. "I've searched the premises and haven't found any other personnel."

"Are you sure?" another voice says. It must be the other side of the communicator. "We found another straggler after we killed the halfkinds. Some scientist, Mark Allen or something. It wasn't Changer. Our crew can't seem to locate him. His office is empty. We've decided to split up, so everyone is alone for the time being."

"Where are you now, Kimba?"

"I'm alone surveying the halls, and you?"

"Near the barracks, I think. This place is like a maze. After we entered through the blast point, we scattered out as well. By the way, have you heard from Ingle?"

"No, not yet. Someone should check up on him."

He pauses again, and we hear him scratching himself.

"Anyway, I think I'm done here," the chimp says. "If I walk forward, I'll hit the communal room, right?"

"Yeah, but there's nothing there," the other voice says. "We already cleaned the place out. You should probably turn back."

"Okay, this is Winde out."

We wait a few moments and the footsteps become fainter and fainter. Bastion looks around the corner and the soldier is gone.

We start walking again, but Bastion looks mighty paranoid. I see his head anxiously tilt up and down at the floor and ceiling.

"We're almost there," he says, "but something doesn't feel right."

"What?" I ask.

"I'm not sure, I think I hear something."

"Another soldier?"

I pause and try to listen to what he's talking about.

"I don't hear anything," I say.

"Shh," he says

He walks nearer, with the same careful precision he used earlier. We approach the end of the hallway, and there's a fork, with one path leading right, another leading left. I follow Bastion closely, so close I'm almost touching him.

We reach the end of the fork and see where it leads. On the left it's a dead end, a blank wall. It's still relatively spotless, all white and everything. No damage has been done. On the right lies a door. In fact, it's the door that leads to the communal room. We're here, and it's closed shut.

I don't know what lies beyond them. It's still very quiet, too quiet. Bastion goes toward it, as do I. My heartbeats get stronger and faster. My legs start to wobble, and my arms shake uncontrollably. I don't even realize it, but my hands hold Bastion's waist. I don't care, I'm too paralyzed by fear to resist. All I see is this stupid, harmless double white door, but for some reason I am frightened to death of what lies beyond it.

"The door will open once we're a few feet further," Bastion says. He looks at me with reassuring eyes. "Are you ready?"

I nervously look back at him.

"Yes," I say.

"Okay, then here we go."

We both step forward and a haze of smoke greets our eyes. It's foggy inside, and I have a hard time seeing through the thickness. I wave my hands repeatedly to fan it away, and slowly, it starts to scatter. The open door ventilates the room. Smoke seeps out, clearing the vicinity.

"Oh my…" Bastion says with a stunned tone.

I'm still behind him and can't see what he sees.

"What is it?" I ask.

There's no point asking. The second I peer my head over his shoulder, I am in full view of the damage that has been done. There, lying in lakes of their own blood, are all the hybrids that I've become acquainted with. Walls are smeared with red, green, and dark substances, the splattered remains of my once alive colleagues.

Some hybrids look like they died together, as I see a few bodies stacked on top of one another. It's as if they were trying to shield each other from their attackers, but in the end it was futile. Others weren't so lucky I can tell they were fully exposed to the hail of ammunition that laid them to waste. Their corpses are so mutilated and torn apart, that I can't tell what they were. Was this one that I see on the floor a lion hybrid? Was this one a reptile hybrid? Was this a bird hybrid? I guess it doesn't matter.

Bastion runs towards his fallen comrades. I see him kneel down next to one, a wolf hybrid, and he raises its limp body from the ground. The bits of grey fur that overlap this hybrid's skin are painted crimson. A hand is blown off, and holes cover his body like a piece of cheese. Bastion holds it tight. It seems he was close to this one.

"His name was Hunter," he says looking at me with tears in his eyes. "We were supposed to work out tomorrow in the gym."

That's all Bastion can muster. He continues to hold his friend tightly. I leave him to mourn over his fallen brother.

I myself am filled with an incredible sense of sorrow. This is like Primm, all the senseless killing, and for what reason? It's never been clear to me. The Alliance wants us dead because we're abominations, but what have we done? Really, what have we done? We've never attacked anyone, never started wars or spread diseases, which is more than I can say for those other species. Humans have done those things, dogs, cats, gorillas, have as well. In fact, there's not a single intelligent species who has a cleaner slate than us hybrids. We've done nothing.

Those bastards are the abominations, horrible creatures who commit evil acts like the ones I've experienced. Humans, rhinos, elephants, whatever, they're all the same. There's not an innocent one among them all.

This world, the Alliance, I hate them. Since I was a little girl, I was raised to fear everything beyond our home. My mother painted the world as a place filled with heartless souls ready to snatch us from her and murder us in front of her very eyes. We all doubted her, but little did we know how foolish we were.

Then that fateful night, I watched as my brothers and sisters were hunted down like rabbits and picked off one by one. It came down to Isaac and I, and that wasn't enough. Their final soldier had to finish the job. The shot exiting my brother's head, that's an image I will remember for the rest of my life. It was gut wrenching, it was haunting, it was completely senseless.

And now I am here, almost three years later and nothing has changed. What I see solidifies everything I've thought about the Alliance. They are the personification of all that is lost and unholy. They are an immoral monster, always hungry for bloodshed, but never satisfied. It doesn't matter if they wipe out every hybrid on this planet, they'll never stop. They'll find something else to pick on, something else to hunt until they'll have no one to fight but each other. I hope that day comes, even if it means the destruction of the world. As long as they are done, I'll be happy.

I walk among the dead and search for a face that I might know, but, to be honest, I don't know any of them. I was here for such a short time that I can't make a connection to these lifeless bodies. That doesn't change anything. In a the past, I thought I was the last of my kind, and then I met them. The experience was surreal. It was a mixture of excitement and apprehension. I didn't know how things would be meeting more of my kind. And now, it seems I may indeed be one of the last hybrids. So many possibilities with my discovered kin could have happened, but it's washed away forever.

I finally see someone I do recognize. His body is contorted, bent over backward in an impossible position. His face is bloody, and his torso has been completely shot up. Next to him lies the broken hoverchair that he relied on so heavily.

"Zorro?" I say as I kneel down next to him. I use my arms to scoop his body on mine. His wrinkled skin and shaggy bits of fur rub against my shoulders. His eyes are closed and he looks peaceful, but when I look at his wounds, I can tell it was a violent death.

I use my hands to wipe some of the blood off his face. We only talked a few times, but they were the most enjoyable conversations I've had in a while. His wisdom and dry wit comforted me while I got used to this strange place called HORUS.

He had this kind way about him, funny, and caring. The Alliance thought he was a threat? That's why he had to be murdered in such a grisly fashion? He was so weak he relied on a hoverchair. Did he really deserve this execution?

"Did he?!" I yell.

Bastion snaps out of his trance and lets go of his friend.

"Hey, we have to stay quiet," he says as he tries to put on a tough front. He quickly wipes off the tears from his eyes.

"Sorry," I say. "This... this is so messed up."

Bastion looks at Hunter.

"I know," he says with his eyes on the ground. He shakes his head, lets in a sniffle, and then looks back at me with a stern face. "But there's nothing we can do here. We have to get to Lionel now."

"What? After all you've seen, that's all you care about?" I say reactively.

I look at him with piercing eyes, but what I see cracks my stone heart. My words have cut through him like a dagger. In front of me stands a hybrid trying the best he can to remain vigilant, to stay focused on the task of getting us out alive. It kills him inside to leave this scene, but he knows it's necessary.

"I'm, I'm sorry," I apologize. "This is all very hard to digest."

"I understand," he says, and I believe him.

"You're right. We can't do anything now. Let's go to Lionel."

He nods his head, and I grasp his hand, leading him out of the communal room. We take one last look at the sea of the dead, and the door shuts.

"We need to be careful," Bastion says somberly.

"Are you going to be okay?" I ask him.

"Yeah, I'm fine. Don't worry about it."

I don't press into it any further.

"We have to hurry," Bastion says. "You don't mind jogging do you?"

"No, but what about stealth?" I ask.

"At this point, fuck it. We're running out of time."

He leads the way like he did before and I tread behind him. Both of us are running, and while he can remain silent effortlessly, I work hard not to make noise. We're extremely fortunate because we don't encounter anything along the way.

Shockingly though, right when we go past a corner, someone is there with a gun pointing straight at us.

"Don't shoot!" Bastion yells.

The culprit drops his aim, and both of us are relieved. It's Changer and Lucy. We exchange greetings, and Changer gives Bastion a hug. He happily accepts it. Lionel has no idea what we've been through, and as I look at Bastion let out a smile, I can tell the embrace heals a part of his broken soul.

"Where have you been, anyway?" Changer asks.

What could we tell him about what we experienced? As if words could do justice the amount of grief and anger we felt absorbing the aftermath of the massacre. Bastion and I look at each other and decide not to say a single word about it. Sometimes, there's no way to answer the simple questions.

Chapter 30 - Bastion

Storage

May 7, 3043 9:01 PM

"Iris Lawton, how are surgical wounds healing? Should only be minor nuisance now," Lucy says.

"Yes, they're minor all right," Iris says sardonically.

"Do not understand sarcasm. Deduce that I am correct. Recovering at impressive rate."

"Well, that's great."

She has the same mocking voice as before. Before Lucy changed the subject, Lionel was explaining to us his plans to go to the transportation bay. We have to go through the storage room and get to the gym. There lies a panel on the ground that connects to the transportation bay tunnels.

"So, we're leaving this place for good?" I ask.

"We don't have much choice," Lionel says sadly. "My employees and creations have been eradicated. This facility will soon be property of the Alliance. However, there's a backup facility on an island in the Pacific we can flee to. It's not as state of the art as this place, but it will be good enough for a temporary home."

Lionel takes out a small data cube from his pocket and shows it to us.

"My life's work is in here," he says. "We can rebuild. I don't care if it takes a century, we will continue our mission. And our best chance of survival, heck, our only chance, is to escape. There's no way we can fight these Alliance cronies. We have to go."

Lionel looks directly at Iris.

"That means all of us," he says. "You have to come too."

"Like hell I am!" her voice bursts out. "You expect me to leave in a hurry, and stay on your magical island forever? I had a nice life, a great one, and after a few days it's gone. It's entirely your fault. Why would I go with you?"

"Probability of living at less than five percent if stay," Lucy says.

"Shut up, monkey girl," Iris says.

"Actually, chimp is ape. Should call me ape girl."

All of us stand there awkwardly by Iris's unwillingness to cooperate. Of course it's Lucy who breaks the silence.

"Not experienced shift in powers?" Lucy asks bluntly.

"Um, no," Iris says hesitantly.

"Don't lie, Iris," I say. "You took out an Alliance soldier today."

Both Lionel and Lucy look a bit surprised by the revelation.

"What do you mean 'took out'?" Lionel asks.

"She was able to look into not one but many futures and saw one where the Alliance soldier stalking us was defeated," I explain. "She acted upon that vision, and here we are, still alive."

"Is this true, Iris?" Lionel asks. She grudgingly nods.

"Point proven, powers, surgery, all beneficial," Lucy says.

"You keep saying that, but I don't care! I won't leave, I won't!" she yells with tears flowing down her eyes. "I just want to be left alone. I want my life back."

She's breaking down and I can understand. She always wanted to live a normal life, but fate doesn't have that in store for her. Wherever she goes, wherever she hides, someone will come. She attracts this unwanted attention. She doesn't ask for it, it's her nature to have people chase her because of what she is, a hybrid, a halfkind, whatever. And she has power most mortals only dream of.

But for her own sake, she can't give up now. If she stays here, she'll die, and I can't let that happen to her.

"Iris, I know you don't like me," I say. "But, I like you. I don't have a stake in this like Lionel or Lucy does. I'm not a scientist, I don't wish to experiment you or use your powers. I want to see you safe. I want to see you live."

"I don't understand," she says angrily. "Why?"

"Don't you get it? We're the same. And I don't mean that because we are hybrids, I mean that because we are kindred. I don't look like Lucy, I don't look like Lionel, I look like you and you look like me. We are the last of our kind, hell if we include Lucy, we are the last hybrids on this Earth. You've spent most of your life thinking you were alone, and now you're not. I saw you talk to Zorro. You enjoyed it. You seemed happy even when you thought things were so messed up. I think you were happy because you were able to talk to someone like you."

She continues to sob and looks away from me.

"I know what it's like to feel alone," I say. "It sucks. And I know it may seem like you don't trust us, but is that the truth? Are you so stubborn that you'd rather die than live? Nothing can replace what you've lost, but you've already lost it. You can't unmake time. The only thing you can do is band together. We are your genetic brothers and sisters. We may not be the family you want, but we are the family you need. Please, for your own safety, come with us."

She looks around and sees there's nowhere left to go. She can't runaway this time. And then she looks at the three of us. I can tell she's still furious, that rage boils inside her, but I can also tell she knows that I'm right.

Defeated and tired from everything she decides to give in.

"I guess I have no choice," she says. "I'll go with you, but it's only in order to survive. It's temporary. Once this mess is sorted out, I'm leaving."

The three of us look at each other cautiously.

"That's fine," Lionel says. "We will not force you to stay with us, you have my word. As a token of my trust, take these, you'll be needing them."

He hands us each a gun. I look at mine and Iris looks at hers.

"Let's go," Lionel says.

The four of us, weapons in hand, walk through the halls silently, toward the storage room. We're lucky because it's close by. I take the lead, peering over any corners to make sure we're safe. We don't encounter anyone or anything on the way, and in minutes we reach the storage hangar.

"Next door is the gym," I say. "Once we're in, there's a small panel on the ground we can lift to access the transportation bay tunnels. Are you all ready to go?"

They look at me and nod. I step forward and the double doors automatically slide open. The storage room is quite long and wide. It always has a cooler temperature than the other rooms because of its size.

It's not well-lighted, and has more of a grey shade than white.

Even though the room is larger, it feels more cramped and compact because of the various equipment stored here. Insta-items, medical supplies, food, and liquids are a few of the things that we house. Almost all the items are held within large containers. There are also some weapons, but most of that is kept in my private armory, which is on the other side of the building. I won't have anything but a few energy guns. I wish we kept some of my stealth equipment or explosives here, it would've come in handy.

All the items are pushed against the walls neatly, creating a clear path to the opposite side of the room. Over there is a door which leads directly to the gym.

"C'mon," I say to the others, "we have to hurry."

All four of us start sprinting to the door. Yet, as we get close to it, something doesn't feel right.

The door opens, and from it comes an Alliance soldier. It's a bear, a very, very large black bear. He has a body harness, which holds all his weapons, and a combat helmet on. Underneath his harness is body armor which completely covers his torso, legs, and arms.

He has the usual energy cannons that a tank build like him would have and combustible devices hanging from his armor. Some of the cannons have large calibers, which could be a grenade or bomb launcher.

"Hostiles!" he yells.

A turret on his harness rises. He's not wasting anytime.

"Move out of the way!" I scream. I grab Iris and push her away from the possible trajectory of fire. Lucy flees behind a storage container.

But Lionel, he's not used to combat. I dare say this is the first time he's come across a soldier like this. He looks a bit frozen and confused as the turret starts to fire. I try to run to him after shoving Iris, but I'm not fast enough. Four or five energy shots fly out of the bear's gun and hits Lionel in the arms and chest. His torso rattles, and his legs fall limply as my lunge makes contact. Together we fall to the ground and both of our bodies slide behind a container.

The storage units are pretty durable, and they'll provide a few seconds of cover before the bear continues his assault. I use this opportunity to check on Lionel. His chest and arms are leaking blood, and some fills his mouth. He starts choking on it and reactively spits some out. I open up his shirt to see the damage done. There are two holes on his shoulder and forearm, and another on his chest. His injuries look pretty critical.

His body shakes and his eyes start to close.

"Damnit, Lionel, don't do this!" I yell. "You have to stay focused. Keep those eyes open."

They bulge out and look at me. He starts nodding his head, struggling to keep it steady.

"Yes… yes," he says slowly. His hand grasps mine firmly. "Must stay… alive. Must continue… our work."

I look over to Lucy, who is still hiding behind a nearby container. Both of us are obscured from the bear's field of vision. I motion her over, and she quickly scurries my way. She immediately tends to Lionel's wounds.

"Injuries critical," she says. "Must apply medical care, no pharmaceuticals available."

"What about in one of these containers?" I say desperately.

"Yes, possible stored here. Must search."

"Well do it. He's going to die if you don't do something. Do you understand? He's going to die!"

"Understood."

She sneaks away further through the storage units. I see the bear inching closer to us. I guess it's just me and him.

From behind the container, I rise, delivering a storm of energy shots with my guns. I fire and fire and fire, yet they do nothing. All I see happening is the shots harmlessly colliding into a barrier in front of him while he remains unscathed from my attack. There's something protecting him, like an invisible shield that absorbs my ammunition.

Meanwhile, I hear him talking to someone over a communicator.

"West, this is Clipper," he says. "I've located the main target. Changer is here."

"Where?" I hear another voice ask him.

"In the storage room."

"Damnit, I'm on the other side of the building. It'll take me at least ten minutes to get there. Keep him busy. Contain him at all costs, do you hear me? All costs."

"Got it. This is Clipper, out."

The bear returns my fire with the same gun that he shot Lionel with. I hastily duck while the bullets hit the other side of the container. It won't hold up for long. I need to act fast.

The only way I can take him is head on. Hopefully that little shield he has only absorbs energy projectiles.

I think I'm fast enough to dodge his blasts. Only one way to find out.

From behind my concealment, I emerge. I stow my gun and charge at him with full speed. He switches his turrets and a small, flat antenna like stick rises on his harness. It fires a disc tracker, energy blades that have homing capabilities. These things take some time to charge up, but when they're ready, it's incredibly tricky to avoid them.

This is my chance to strike. Already running in full motion, and only a few feet away from him, I leap with all my strength to deliver a flying punch.

But then the energy shot is armed, and before I can deliver my initial blow it fires, tracking me down and hits my bicep. The blast causes me to be off balance and I spin around in mid-air. I try to land on my feet, but I stumble and tumble forward, right in front of him. I am exposed.

I quickly reach for the gun that's in my pocket, but before I do, he raises his arm and swipes his claws across my chest. My clothes rip like paper, and I look down to see three large cuts. Immediately, the stinging of the wounds sets in, and I curl and clutch my chest with my hands. It's a pain unlike any other, like someone is constantly taking a knife and slashing it across my body. I can tell the lacerations run deep because every pulse that I beat comes more and more blood from the openings. I lift my hands to see that my palms are painted red. I start coughing profusely, and my mindset becomes a little hazy, probably because of all the blood loss.

I am coherent enough to see the bear raise another arm, probably to strike a fatal blow. With one, last drastic attempt, I pull the gun from my pocket, aim it at his head, and start firing. The shots do exactly what they did before, and I watch with despair as my bullets are absorbed harmlessly into his shield. I guess this is it.

I close my eyes and wait for it, but, like thunder, I hear a large roar right in front of me. I open my eyes to see the bear's mouth wide open, emitting a growl. His eyes are closed and his posture is tense. He's in pain.

But how? My eyes search for an explanation among the confusion, and when they finally trail to behind his body, everything becomes clear.

There's a wolf standing there with a large chunk of bear flesh in his mouth. He spits it out and continues his assault, pouncing on the bear's back while the mammoth creature is dazed. He has a firm grip on the bear's harness and rides him like a wild bull. The bear tussles and turns, bucks and twists, but the wolf remains strong.

As I look closer, the wolf isn't just holding on to dear life, he's actually inching to the bear's wrist. It's tough to tell what from my angle, all I see is the wild flinging of bodies, but the wolf is targeting something near the bear's hand.

After almost a minute, the wolf finally tears something off. He is thrown from the bear's arm and the creature staggers around to recover. The bear looks a bit discombobulated and tired. The struggle with the wolf has worn him out.

The wolf spits a small, electronic wristband. There are wires and circuits branching out from it, strains that have been ripped off cleanly. I wonder what was the purpose of this device.

The wolf says something to me. At this point I'm very weak and have a hard time hearing what he's saying. But through the ringing in my ears and blurred vision, I can hear him faintly.

"His shield's down," he screams. "Shoot him!"

Did he talk human? I can barely comprehend his command, but the last phrase speaks to me. I point my gun at the bear and fire a stream of shots. They hit him wildly in several places. Some tear through his arms, others fly right through his head. Parts of his body turn red in a flash. My finger pulls and pulls and pulls on the trigger, and by the time I'm done, thirty or forty blue and green energy bullets have been fired into the creature.

I stop my onslaught, and the bear limply falls to the ground. It's over, I've defeated him. Yet, it feels like I'm the one who has been defeated. Black spots appear in front of my eyes, and things become even blurrier than before. I try to stand up on my own two feet, but the weight of my body collapses on them, and I hit the floor with a thud.

I turn over on the other side, my back on the ground, my head looking up and around. I see Lucy to my right, trying desperately to keep Lionel alive. I hope she can, I hope he'll be okay, he has to be.

I then look at Iris, who has risen from her hiding spot. She looks at me with a bit of terror. My wounds still bleed on my chest. I don't know how much blood I've lost, but I certainly don't feel too good. I wonder if I'm going to pass out, or even worse, I wonder if this is what it feels like to die.

I hope I live. I still have to see what could be with her.

Finally, I turn my head to the wolf. I don't know who he is, my mind doesn't have the energy to make the connections. The only thought I can muster is that I owe this wolf my life, and I am grateful.

"Thank you," I say to him.

With heavy breaths, I concentrate on staying alive, but as I hard as I try, I can't fight any longer. I slip away into darkness.

Chapter 31 – Lionel Changer

Legacy

May 7, 3043 9:19 PM

I let out a cough and a spurt of blood shoots into the air. At this point, everything on my body is red. Lucy tries frantically to patch me up. She's normally calm and cool, even when she conducts surgeries, but this time, she looks frazzled.

"How… does it… look?" I ask, struggling to say my words.

"Condition critical. Punctures and in lungs. Attempting to close wounds, repair damage, outlook not optimistic. Too many injuries," she says bluntly, yet with a hint of softness that I'm not accustomed too. Lucy is normally so unemotional that this kind of behavior catches me off guard. It's poignant.

"Lucy… do you need… anything? I… can help…"

"Only thing needed is relax. Complications arise if patient struggles."

She was able to find the necessary supplies while Bastion was battling the bear soldier. Medigels, scanners, laser sealers, and a vast array of other equipment are at her disposal. Yet, I feel it's over. That bear did quite the number on me. I know what organs were shot up, and she cannot fix the unfixable. I won't be living much longer.

I look around and see Iris and the wolf tending to Bastion. I saw him take a vicious swipe. It looked pretty serious, as he was bleeding profusely. He's unconscious but breathing. That's a relief. He fought off the intruder, blasting him left and right in order to save us. I couldn't be prouder.

He probably wouldn't have made it if it wasn't for this mysterious wolf. The creature looks vaguely familiar. I think I know him from somewhere, though I admit I would rather be caught dead than associate myself with such a creature. But I suppose I should thank him for saving the others.

He appears to have medical knowledge as well. Him and Iris are working together to stabilize Bastion. The both of them immediately attended to him the moment the bear was dead. Iris gathered the necessary drugs and instruments and the wolf instructed her on what to do. They seem to know each other, and I notice he's speaking human to her.

"How…is he…?" I ask them.

"He's going to live," the wolf says. "He's passed out from the blood loss, but the claw missed out on anything vital. We closed the wounds and have a blood pack attached to him. He won't be awake anytime soon, but Iris and I have him stabilized."

I am relieved. It looked a lot worse than what the wolf describes, but it appears Iris's friend knows what he's doing.

"Who… are you?" I ask him.

"This, this is Fenrir Snow," Iris says, answering for him.

Ah, so he made it here. I knew I recognized him from somewhere, but these wolves are often hard to tell apart.

"How did you… find us…," I ask him.

He looks at Iris, and then looks at me.

"Let's say I knew where to go," he responds.

Judging from the glance he gave at Iris, I'm guessing she had something to do with it. She probably was able to communicate with him somehow, and given what we know about her mental capabilities, I wouldn't be surprised.

I'm actually quite happy. This information confirms everything I've believed about her. She is the key. I may not make it, but my vision, my ultimate goals, they can still be fulfilled. The main players still live, Lucy, Bastion, and Iris. If they can make it out alive, my death won't be in vain.

"You… all of you… you must go," I say.

"No. Still working," Lucy says.

I use my hands to bat her arms away, and she looks a bit shocked.

"You don't… have…the time," I say. "Reinforcements, they're… coming."

I turn over to cough up some blood. I then look at Lucy who looks at me gravely.

"Continue… my work," I say.

I reach for my pockets and take out the datacube. It has all my files and specs. Models for birthing implants, psychic nano tech, body enhancers, every idea and schematic I've ever made resides in this handheld unit. I hold it up to Lucy and place it in her hands.

"You are the… future," I say. "You must be… the one… to rebuild… to complete my… vision. You… have always… been… my… protégé. Now… it's time… to be… my… successor."

A single tear rolls from her eyes as she looks at me. Lucy has never felt this kind of sadness before. I'm not sure if she can comprehend what she's feeling, but as I see that one teardrop fall to the ground, I become truly touched.

"You are mentor. Thankful to know you. Everything because of you. Cannot repay for wealth of knowledge given. Legacy will continue, perfect species will be created," she says.

Perfect species, the statement resonates to me. Is she referring to the human race? This must be the case, Lucy and I share the same goals. But I don't know what she means by that exact phrase. Besides, at this point, it's too late to find out more. No matter what she does, I am still glad because progress will continue.

"Iris… I need to tell you… one last thing," I say.

She walks towards me and kneels down.

"I know… you disagree… with what I've done, but… this is just the beginning… for you," I say to her. "I've… given you a gift… use it well. Take care of… Bastion… leave… this place… the transportation bay is… up ahead."

Iris nods and looks at me stoically. She doesn't say a word, yet the glances we exchange say more than enough. She walks back to Fenrir Snow and Bastion, and hoists Bastion on Snow's back. They secure him and start walking to the door. The two of them take one last look at me, as I struggle to stay alive, and exit. Lucy then stands, puts the datacube in her pocket and heads towards the door.

"Goodbye… Lucy," I say.

"Goodbye," she says, taking one final glimpse at my frail body before she turns around and exits from my sight.

All my children and extended family members are dead. The last members of HORUS are on their way out. Years of my hard work have gone up in flames. All those countless nights, all the excitement I felt when I mapped out my plans, have vanished among the violence and gunfire. Things happened so fast that I didn't have the time to understand the gravity of my loss until now. Since I was a little boy, the only thing I hoped for was that humans could regain this world. As the years went by and I built my implant empire, I still had this dream. Then it became a reality, HORUS was built. Any accomplishments I had at Implantus were trumped by the things I've done here. Implantus was a way to make the means, HORUS was the place where my passion strived.

So this is how things end. It's been an interesting ride through evolution and experimentation, it's too bad I paid the ultimate price for my deeds. If only those humans in the Alliance could comprehend what I was trying to do. Did they need to take such swift action? Couldn't we have worked something out? I don't know if what I did warranted this kind of retaliation.

Perhaps I should've prepared myself for something like this. I thought I was invincible, that they would never find me. My secrecy was something I've tried to guard so well. I thought I set up some good defenses. I guess it wasn't good enough.

It doesn't really matter. In the back of my mind I always knew that someday, someone would find me. That's why I had that back up facility made. The Alliance has always been relentless about stopping any genetic experimentation after that damned Event, and with my human oriented aspirations, this probably put them on high alert. It's too bad, I could've made some serious breakthroughs.

Minutes pass, and I hope at this point the others have reached the transportation bay. My thoughts are interrupted when someone enters through the door. I tilt my head slowly, agonizingly, to see who it is. It's a man I recognize, a tall, huge man.

"Brock West," I say to myself.

He's by himself and starts walking, but stops in his tracks when he sees his slain comrade on the floor. He kneels over and inspects the body. He removes the bear's harness and helmet to get a clear view, surveying the damage with an emotionless gaze. He then takes off his jacket, and drapes it over the bear's head.

"You were a good soldier, Clipper," he says.

He stands up and walks to me. I can't help but be fearful for what this man is going to do. The door closes behind him with a thud leaving the two of us alone as my despair fills the room.

Chapter 32 - Brock West

Blast

May 7, 3043 9:30 PM

Three of my soldiers are dead. I got the communication about Ingle and Waylon ten minutes ago, and saw what happened to Clipper. We underestimated the fight HORUS would bring. I thought everyone would be safe.

I suppose it doesn't matter. I got what I came for. Lionel Changer lies on the floor everywhere bloody mess. The man is shaking profusely. He raises his arms to me but struggles in doing so. Coughs come strong, each one spray chunks of crimson on the ground. His complexion is pale white.

Clipper got a few shots off before he died, and it has messed Changer up pretty good. He's brought Changer inches away from death, pathetically grasping on to moments of life. Now I'm here to finish the job.

Something is peculiar. There are surgical tools scattered about, as if someone was working on him. But I look around and don't see anyone. Lionel probably was repairing himself, because we've checked every other room and found no one. HORUS should be cleared out, but things have been moving rather quickly, so perhaps there's someone we're missing. I don't care though, Changer has always been the main objective, and now that I have him, I'm not going to worry about anything else. We'll do one final sweep later.

I stand above Lionel Changer and he looks at me despondently. His time has come, and I am his grim reaper. I live for moments like this, knowing that I've done a good job and that the enemy is at my complete mercy. I've worked hard for this, spending months and months, even years, researching everything about this man so that the Alliance could cripple his operation and bring his downfall. They trust me and I deliver. As I see Changer in this weak moment, knowing that every mad experiment and genetic atrocity he's worked on has been destroyed, I can't help but feel proud. Boy, does victory taste sweet.

I take out a small energy cannon and get it primed. Lionel watches me charge the weapon and in a feeble attempt to get me to stop, he shouts something inaudible. I inch closer to make sense of his gasps.

"What did you say?" I ask arrogantly.

"W…w….wait," he breaths out.

I burst out a hearty laugh.

"Wait?" I say. "Come to state one more of your lunatic philosophies? To convince me what you're doing is right? Don't even start. Your pleas for mercy won't help. Never did and never will."

"But.. b…but…we… are… both humans. Brothers."

I look at him with a smirk.

"Sorry, you're talking to the wrong guy."

With those words, I point my cannon at his head and pull the trigger. The blast echoes through the open space of the storage room. It causes an immediate explosion of bone, flesh, and brains as bits burst from his shattered head, flying in every other direction. His face becomes pushed to the back of his skull. When it's all said and done, I see nothing but a red mess, like strawberry pie, smushed onto the ground with smoke rising into the air.

I put my hand cannon back into my holster and turn on my communicator.

"John, this is West," I say. The pig pops up on a hologram in front of me.

"Brock," he says. "Where are you?"

"In a storage room. I've found Lionel Changer."

"Really?"

"Yes. He's dead. Target has been eliminated. He was already injured when I got here. Seems like Clipper got to him first."

"And where is he?"

"Dead, also. Probably killed by Changer."

"I see."

"We've eliminated the hostiles. The main objective has been fulfilled. Lionel Changer is dead, and HORUS is extinct. We'll get a science team here for cleanup and I'm going to order one more sweep, but for now it looks like it's mission accomplished."

"Agreed."

"Tell the others to do one final run through of the facility, and then we'll pack it up and go."

"Understood. Excellent job, Brock."

The hologram disappears and I make my way to the exit. Changer's headless body remains on the floor. Excellent job indeed.

Chapter 33 - Fenrir Snow

Tunnel

May 7, 3043 9:36 PM

This halfkind has passed out from all the blood loss. He's also built like a brick and I get the task of lugging him around through these tunnels. Congratulations, I've won the prize.

Iris looks amused.

"Something funny?" I say jokingly.

"Oh, nothing. You sure you don't need help?" she asks.

"Positive."

It's strange. We haven't seen each other since she's been kidnapped, yet despite all we've been through up to this point, we're still able to laugh about things as if nothing happened. I guess that's the kind of relationship we have. We're old friends who can find something to enjoy even in the direst of circumstances.

After we left the storage room, we rushed to the gym. There, Iris's, um, friend, Lucy, located an inconspicuous, loose panel on the ground. It blended in so well with the rest of the floor that the naked eye probably couldn't find it. She opened it and the three of us, along with Bastion on my back, jumped down below. The panel then closed on us. Hopefully, those Alliance soldiers won't track us here.

When I landed, I saw a long stretched tunnel. It's a bit different from the above floors. The walls here are a muddy brown, not completely white like the other rooms. The lighting is dark, and it's much colder. Lucy informs us that the transportation bay is at the end of the hallway. It's supposed to be a large room with a few teleporters. The fact that we have to access it with a hidden panel in the gym suggests that it's not a commonly accessed place. Probably only a few people have the clearance to use it, but it seems this chimp woman knows what she's doing.

"How do you know what to do?" I ask Lucy.

"Have operated before," she says. "Bastion most frequent, but been trained how to run teleporters for emergency."

"You know what you're doing?"

"Of course. Question stupid."

She responds in an abrupt, inconsiderate manner.

"Your friend is kind of rude," I whisper to Iris.

"Don't even get me started," she says.

While we walk down the tunnel, she pauses and takes a look at me.

"You, you're hurt! What happened?" she says. I guess since we were in such a hurry earlier, she didn't have time to see my wounds. The medigel I applied has blotted a lot of the blood, but I still look like a mess.

"I had a run in with my family," I say.

It occurs to me that during our years living together, I never really talked about my brothers and sisters. Iris is vaguely aware of their existence, but has no idea of the bad blood between us.

"Your siblings did this to you?" she asks. "But why?"

"For reasons too long and complicated to talk about right now. Let's say we don't see eye to eye," I say.

"Is it because of me?"

"No, it's completely my fault."

"So, are they okay?"

I think about Danzel's leg and Raymus's encounter with the tunneler.

"They'll live," I say. "Don't worry about it. I don't think they'll be coming after me anymore after what happened in our last run in."

Iris seems to know what that means. She surmises that this isn't the best topic to talk about and stops her questioning.

"I'm glad you're safe," she says.

"And I'm glad you are," I say.

Even though I know the danger that surrounds us, I feel some happiness. I've journeyed thousands of miles following only my instincts in order to find my kidnapped friend. I've battled my way here, fought family and Alliance soldiers. When her scent became stronger, and I found her and her companions in the storage room fighting for their lives, I had to react fast, or else every step that I took would have been in vain. I was sore and bruised from so many battles, but the mere sight of Iris motivated me to go into action.

And when it was all said and done, and the enemy had been dispatched, I was relieved. There are few moments in my life that can top that feeling of being reunited with Iris. I couldn't believe it happened. I had no concrete evidence where she was. The only thing I had was hope guiding me. But when she physically appeared, I felt like I was living a dream. In a million years, I would have never believed that I could find her using only my gut, but that reunion crushed my skepticism.

It was surreal.

"I can't believe you're here," she says casually.

I'm a surprised by her statement.

"Wasn't it you who told me where to go?" I ask. "I felt something in my head, some mental communication. It was a calling that told me your location, where I could find you. I thought you had something to do with it."

"I think I did," she says, though she appears as confused as I am. "I don't know. I had these headaches, like the worst in my entire life. Yet, when I had them, I felt something, a heightened awareness. I didn't do it voluntarily, more subconsciously, but I knew that I was speaking to you somehow. I knew I was telling you to come find me. I suppose, seeing you in the flesh confirms all this. Even though I didn't purposely do it, I cried to you for help."

"But how?"

"I… I don't know."

That's when I pay attention and see the bandage on her head. I thought it was a headband or something, I wasn't really paying attention. Now that I look more closely, I see there are spots of blood on it.

"What did they do to you?" I say in a protective growl.

Iris looks hesitant to respond.

"C'mon, Iris, tell me," I press on.

She's about to say something when suddenly, Lucy interrupts us.

"We're here," she says.

There is a towering steel colored door in front of us. Lucy approaches it and a laser scans her. The door slides open and we walk through.

The transportation bay is large, certainly bigger than some of the other rooms, but nothing too grand. It has the same mud coloring as the tunnels, but it's slightly better lit. There appears to be a console, which is the control panel to get the teleporters working, and on the other side are the teleporters.

What's really eye catching is a large glowing sphere in the center. It's blue and bright, like a miniature star. It's also well protected with high density glass. I've seen this before in other teleportation stations.

"This is your power generator?" I ask Lucy.

"One of many," she says. "Will be used for teleporters. Already running, need to program routines and teleporter will be operational. Place Bastion next to teleporters."

I walk over to where they are situated and call Iris over.

"Can you help me unstrap him?" I ask her.

"Sure," she says.

She walks over to me and unhooks Bastion from my back. That feels so much better. I loosen up my muscles a little.

"Now that we're alone here, I want to know, what did they do to you?" I ask.

"Um, don't worry about it," Iris says.

"Iris, you were bleeding. I see the stains on your bandages."

Iris puts her hand over the wound and rubs it a little. She looks at her palms and then looks at me.

"Fenrir," Iris says, "I… I've gained some powers."

"You mean your precognition?" I ask.

"Beyond that. I can sense things, people's thoughts, and their emotions. I faintly know when things are happening in present time. And now, I can see more than one future, multiple ones. It's weird. I can choose my destiny and know exactly how it'll play out from a plethora of visions that I see. I don't have total control over it yet. I'm pretty green, but what I've done today is unlike anything I've experienced. They took what I could do and amplified it."

I don't fully understand what she's talking about. I have an idea, but her explanation leaves me slightly confused.

"But, what did they do exactly?" I ask.

"They, they drilled into my head, I think," she stutters out. "And, they filled my brain with these machines, these microscopic implants."

This sounds crazy.

"That tech doesn't exist," I say.

"It does here," she responds softly.

I can tell she's still traumatized by what happened. Just like how she relented earlier, I halt the interrogation. We'll have plenty of time to talk about this later.

"What's the plan now?" I ask her. "Where does this teleporter take us?"

"To some back up facility Changer had in the Pacific," she says.

"And we're going to stay there with these two?"

"Hell no."

Iris's expression changes from calm to angry. That question lights a fire in her eyes that I seldom see.

"I'd rather die than stay with these two assholes," she says with scorn. "They want to use me like a pawn. It's not going to happen. We're leaving. Even if they take us prisoner, I won't stand for it. If we need to fight our way from their clutches, I don't mind. A shot to their heads is a bargain for us to return to the way it was."

It's nice to see that she still has the passion I've grown accustomed to, but this is a bit excessive for the Iris I know. I view her as a kind soul, unfit to harm a fly. This new extreme I see is such a departure from the norm that it frightens me. What has this place done to the Iris I love?

"Isn't that a bit harsh?" I ask her.

"You were once a soldier," she says, "and you always knew what needed to be done. What I said is the same. It needs to be done."

I look at her reassuringly.

"You know I will support you," I say. "We will return back to our old life, I promise."

She looks at me with watery eyes and smiles.

"And I believe you," she says.

Lucy's voice interrupts our conversation. I hear a violent rumble and I see both teleporters emit bright yellow lights.

"The teleporter is ready," Lucy says. "Programmed it to deactivate and erase logs once we are through. No one will follow. Should also be another command console on other side in case need manual shut down. Ready?"

We both nod.

"Good. Carry Bastion," she instructs.

At that instant, I smell something funny. It's a pungent smell, yet a familiar one. I recognize it, even though it's a bit off. It's the scent that has been following me everywhere these past few days.

"No, not now. Damnit, not now!" I say to myself.

"Fenrir?" Iris asks.

I hear a brisk zip and a bright blue light fly past me, right into Iris's arm. A sharp wail comes from her mouth. The force of the impact pushes her back, and she goes tumbling to the ground.

"Iris!" I yell.

She's hurt. She instantaneously clutches the wound on her bicep and reactively gets up to a sitting position. I turn back and nudge Iris to help her stand on her own. Lucy frantically runs toward the teleporter, as do Iris and I. Before I make it there, I drag a nearby metal container by the handle and place it in front of the machines to create a temporary shield, right near where I sat down Bastion. The four of us are concealed behind the metal box, wedged in between it and the operating teleporter.

"All three of you need to get out of here," I say.

"Who's attacking us?" Iris asks. She grits her teeth in order to get past the pain.

"Someone I know too well. Anyway, Lucy, Iris, drag Bastion and go through the teleporter, I'll follow you after I take care of this."

"Understood," Lucy says.

She grabs Bastion's body and rolls it into the teleporter. A small flash enters my eyes. I close them and when they reopen, Bastion is gone. Lucy then approaches it, but before she enters she turns around to face us.

"Goodbye," she says. The chimp halfkind enters the light and disappears.

"You need to go," I say to Iris.

"No, I'm staying here," she says. She grabs her gun and points it forward, beyond our fortification.

"You need to go!" I growl. "Your arm is injured."

"No! I'm not leaving you," she says.

Damnit Iris, why do you have to be so stubborn? I'm trained for this, I've been fighting all my life. You are not ready. You don't know this enemy like I do, it's not personal for you.

It's too late. From the darkness of the shadowy tunnels, four figures emerge. Raymus, Danzel, Patrice, and Fang. So this is how it's going to go down, huh, Fang? Very well then. It's time to put this family feud to rest.

Chapter 34 - Fang Snow

Fog

May 7, 3043 9:51 PM

How did we get to this point? I suppose the literal answer is that after we recovered from the second battle, the four of us followed Fenrir's trail to this underground facility. Danzel and Raymus are healed enough and, hopefully, we all can withstand one more confrontation with Fenrir.

Once we got inside, we followed his scent. His dripping blood was easy enough to detect. This place sure had a lot of it spilled in the past hours. We walked by the dead humans in the cafeteria. It was shocking to see such a sight. Someone else was here because it didn't look like Fenrir's work, it was the work of professionals. We certainly didn't want to run into them, the last thing we needed was to be caught in a firefight against a group of soldiers.

Luckily the facility was so large that there was enough space to stay covert. We didn't encounter anyone, but, if we did, we could hide.

Following Fenrir also prevented any run-ins. Since we trailed right behind him, he dispatched any enemies before they got to us. This proved true with the crocodile he killed. As a bonus, if he got injured during these melees, we could swoop in and finally end things. I'm glad it didn't come to that, I never like taking a coward's way out.

We watched him go into the room with the exercise machines. His party entered these tunnels using the secret door. We could've ambushed him right there and then, but it wouldn't be too wise to attract such attention. They went to an underground corridor, concealed from the rest of the facility. If we wanted to do things privately, we would have to ambush him in the tunnels.

And that's how we got here.

But, perhaps I'm not answering my original question. How did I really get here? At what point did we decide that killing Fenrir would bring our family back from the brink? I suppose I thought the Brotherhood would have loved to see one of their renegade disciples brought to justice. Murdering our own brother would prove to the Brotherhood whose side we are on. That's why they excommunicated us, because of Fenrir. Bringing him to justice would no doubt restore our reputation.

But would it really? Does the Brotherhood even care? Is their approval worth our own sibling's life? Somewhere along the way I started to doubt this. I hesitated when I had a clear shot. He was still family. Yet, after what I've seen him do to the others, and thinking about our history, how low he's brought the Snow family name, I realize I can't hesitate anymore. Fenrir will be dead, we'll have our peace, and order will be restored. No more indecision, no more doubts, it's time to take him out once and for all.

In the distance, I see a bright glowing light. Its source is a pod. At first, I'm unsure what it is, but then I look closer and see it's a teleporter. They have them here? That's impossible. A brown, human-like being is at the control panel. Another one looks unconscious, placed gently in front of the pods. Finally, I see Fenrir and that halfkind, Iris. They're planning to make an escape! If we don't act, they'll be gone forever.

"Brothers! It's time to attack!" I yell at them.

My brothers, especially Raymus and Danzel, are exhausted and sore, but, now, more than ever, they are ready to fight. Legs are gone, fur is charred, but they want nothing more than to seek revenge for what they've lost.

We charge towards Fenrir's party. He appears to have no idea that we're coming, until I see him sniff in the air. The blockers have worn off, our scent must be strong. Before he can react, I aim carefully at Fenrir's head.

"Fire," I say.

The shot jets wildly out of my weapon, but it misses. Instead of hitting Fenrir, it errantly goes into Iris Lawton's arm. She flies backward while the others react. They start running toward the pod while Fenrir grabs a piece of metal for cover. The brown halfkind drags her friend through the teleporter, and he disappears. She then follows behind into the light.

Fenrir stands firm. I suppose he intends to finish things once and for all, no more running. And it looks like his little girlfriend is joining him too.

"Fire all that you have!" I command to my brothers. They release their shots and I hear clinks and clanks colliding into Fenrir's makeshift wall. None of them connect, but we'll be there soon enough and Fenrir will have nowhere to hide.

The bullets continue to unleash on Fenrir, but he does nothing. He's taking his time. I haven't seen him fire one energy bullet. Fenrir's plotting something and as my brothers run ahead, I slow my pace to observe what he's planning.

After a few more seconds, Fenrir makes his move. From behind his cover, a small metal ball is flung in the air, landing directly in front of my brothers. It bounces on the ground for a short time and starts beeping.

"Bomb!" Danzel yells.

The three of them scatter about but I hold my position. I knew what it was the moment I saw it, and it's no bomb.

The beeping stops and a cloud of smoke expands from the ball's openings. It's a mellyst cloud, thick, shadowy haze made to impair vision. Basically, it's a smoke screen amplified to ten, a fog that removes clarity. I can't see anything, not even my brothers. Even worse, it's scented. Using my nose is out of the picture. Smart move, brother.

I'm sure Fenrir can see though. That's how mellyst clouds work. The user is equipped with special visual filters on his helmed weapon that helps them see through the mist. They're best used in confined places, like this one. In an open area, the cloud would dissipate. If we're not careful, the four of us will be sitting ducks.

The room becomes dead quiet. The mellyst ball has stopped its release, and all I can hear is the heavy breathing of my brothers. I move my head around to pick up any sounds I can detect.

In front of me, to my left, come some fast footsteps. They pitter patter rapidly. I brace myself for an oncoming attack, but I realize the sound is too far. If it's Fenrir, I'm not in range of him.

The zipping sound of an energy shot is heard, and a yelp echoes in the air. Before things went dark, Patrice was to my left.

"Brother!" I yell. "Patrice! Are you there?"

There is no response. I stand there shaking, wondering if Fenrir plans to sneak up on me like that.

I hear scampering, and once again, it comes from in front of me. The sound travels across, from my left to my right. In a matter of seconds, it stops. I pause, waiting for something to happen.

Another whiz is fired, and another squeal rings in my ears.

"Danzel?" I say. "Are you hurt?"

That had to be him. He was standing right where the cry came from. Two of us are down, and I can only use my imagination to visualize things. Did Fenrir really kill them? Or did he stun them?

"Someone answer me!" I growl. "Raymus, you're still there, right? Raymus?"

My call is answered with another shot of ammo firing and another howl. Then silence. I'm the only one left.

I pace myself slowly, continuing in the direction that I think Fenrir is in. We were going forward before, so that's where I'm headed. Still, I feel like a prisoner walking to their execution, the darkness and thickness of the cloud obscures me from seeing my executioner. I don't know if Fenrir is in front or behind me. He's moved around this area like the wind, taking out my brothers with ease.

The only thing I can do is remain on high alert. I pay attention to my surroundings, but I only hear my breathing. I must not be afraid, no matter how deceptive Fenrir may be. I will stand strong even if he sneaks from behind to shoot.

From my right, I hear it. The galloping of Fenrir's legs approaches my way and I only have a split second to see a bright, blue light glowing from the cloud. It's an energy shot. I leap out of the way and it misses me by inches.

But right when I land, I'm greeted by a skull on skull collision with Fenrir's head. It causes me to roll to my side and I fall on my torso. I quickly recover and get back to my paws, only to see Fenrir's growling face a few feet from mine.

He shows his fangs and I show him mine. We circle each other like our rabid ancestors would. He and I, eye to eye, locked in what seems like an eternal fight. Our stare down is the personification of our family issues, sibling versus sibling until death remains.

There's no exchange of words this time, we just fight.

He lunges at me armed with his fangs. I move to the side and watch his jaws miss my body. His leg is exposed, so I sink my teeth in and watch the blood spew out. He grimaces a bit, but is too focused to howl in pain. My position leaves my neck open, and I feel him bite down on my collar. His teeth cut deeply, and I let go of his leg to shake off my wound. We back away from each other and acknowledge the stalemate.

His leg is bleeding and blood flows from the top of my neck. We observe each other cautiously as our injuries show.

I try to take advantage of this pause in action.

"Fire!" I yell.

A blue bullet comes out of my helmet toward Fenrir at point blank range. He's fast and lunges out of the way. Still, the shot clips his tail, and I see bits of it fly off into the thickness of the smoke that surrounds us.

Like a machine, he ignores it, and once again flies towards me. This time, he uses his front paws to swipe me in the face and, surprisingly, it stuns me. His paws got some contact with my eyes. I stumble backwards, shaking my head, temporarily blinded from the blow. When I recover, I only see jaws closing in on my snout.

I swiftly duck under his head, reacting like lightning. His body collides with mine, but I have my paws firmly planted to the ground. The contact causes him to become off balance and his lunge transforms into a tumble. He flips in the air, doing a complete summersault and falls to the floor with a thud. His head smacks the ground hard.

What a lucky break. He's stunned, discombobulated. I almost don't believe my eyes, I actually bested him. I was finally able to out-guile the strongest and most agile of my brothers. All my life I've been trying to top him, and now here he lies on the ground, helpless, his life at my judgment.

I don't hesitate this time.

"Fire, fire, fire, fire, fire, fire!" I yell.

The shots rip from my helmet. Some hit his body armor, but most tear into his body, causing blood to burst from his torso.

"Fire, fire, fire…" I say over and over again.

He yelps and howls as each shot splits open his skin and leaves a red mark. I must've fired at least ten of them. I attack Fenrir without mercy.

He's holding on for dear life but still alive. He uses his front paws to crawl away from my direction. I don't intend to shoot him anymore, he's done for, but I curiously follow him to see where he's going.

The cloud starts to disappear and I see he's inching back to where he began, his flimsy metal cover right near the teleporters. I didn't realize how close our battle moved us there.

"No!" I hear what sounds like a sapien woman screaming. She throws her body on top of his. "Leave him alone!"

It's not a human, it's a halfkind. She has pointed cat like ears, an orange complexion, and fur lightly sprinkled on her skin. Locks of human hair shine from her head. I know this halfkind, her look is very distinct. It's her, it's Iris Lawton.

"Out of my way," I growl.

She doesn't appear to understand me. It's because she speaks human.

"Out of my way," I say again in human.

She doesn't respond, not because she fails to comprehend my order, but because she refuses. That look in her eye, the mix of rage, despair, and passion, I recognize it. She loves Fenrir and will never let him go. She'd do anything to protect him. Her hand slides to her hip, and I see her reaching for something. A weapon, an energy gun. It's a motion I've seen thousands of times. She wants to kill me.

And thousands of times, I've stopped it.

"Fire," I say. A shot hurls directly at her hand. It gets cleanly blasted off her arm and blood erupts from it like a geyser. She screeches loudly, holding her stump while grasping onto Fenrir.

As she rattles in agony, I make contact with Fenrir's eyes. I only see a look of deep anguish.

This is how it ends.

Chapter 35 - Iris Lawton

Severed

May 7, 3043 10:02 PM

My hand is gone. Blood empties from it like water from a broken pipe. The agony is surreal. My arm is shaking, the stump that's appeared feels like it's on fire. It's almost as bad as being on Lucy's operating table.

But I don't care. The only thing I care about is putting myself between this psychotic wolf and Fenrir. My body is thrown on top of his as the enemy points her helmed weapon at both of us. She looks remorseless. There's not an ounce of sympathy from her cold gaze.

"Don't," I mutter out as the exhaustion and trauma sets in. "He can't die."

The wolf looks unmoved by my statement. She doesn't utter a response, the only thing she does is lower her head to prepare for her final shots.

Well, old friend, at least if we die, we'll die together. And I'm okay with that. At least I'll be by your side.

Suddenly, things fade out and I see images of a future without him. A figure with a black mask and hood. Animals of different kinds held captive. A withered woman, old, and empty inside. Earth on fire. It's not a vision, just flashes before my eyes, but they scare me. What do these random images mean? Is this the kind of stuff you see before you die? If this is part of the future, it's one that I don't want to be involved in. I'll gladly take my end here peacefully.

Fenrir turns his head and looks at me. He wants to say something, but is too shook up to motion out the words. The only way he can communicate is through his eyes. They look sullen as he heaves the air into his lungs. But they also look like they're up to something. I look back at him, and I feel a rush of terror. I think I know what he's trying to tell me, and it's not good news.

"Bo..omb," he whispers out. A small metal canister pops from his armor right in front of the other wolf.

I know what it is, she knows what it is. Her emotionless expression morphs into frenzied fear. She panics and looks at me. I return her glance and realize she is actually staring at the operational teleporter behind me. It's the only way out.

She hurls herself at my direction, desperately trying to reach for the pod. Yet, as she lifts her body into the air, Fenrir uses all the strength he has left to do the same. Fenrir lifts me off of him, shoving me right into the teleportation pod and intercepts the other wolf. Her last second rush is halted as their two bodies collide. I teeter backwards, falling right into the teleporter.

The two wolves slam into the ground, and with one final glance, Fenrir looks at me and forces out a weak smile.

A burst of green and blue flames erupt into the air, engulfing everything surrounding it. Yet, the view starts to fade from me, and a blinding, yellow light absorbs my body whole. Within milliseconds, the explosion is no longer in front of me, and I close my eyes from the brightness of the teleportation pod's illumination.

When the flash dims, I open my eyes. I'm still in the pod, but I see Lucy a few feet away at a control console and Bastion on the ground, still unconscious. I frantically get out to see that I'm in a completely new room. There's no smoke, no damage from a bomb, no wolves, just a large empty place that's clean and untouched. The teleportation worked.

"Where am I?" I shout to Lucy.

"Made it to other side," she says in her robotic voice. "Currently on island in Pacific Ocean. Changer's backup facility."

She looks at my arm, still dripping blood.

"You are injured," she says.

"We left Fenrir behind. Start the teleporter again, we need to go back to him," I say while ignoring her concern.

She pushes some buttons on her console.

"Appears other side not operational," she says. "Not receiving communication from source teleporter. Possibly shut down or damaged."

The bomb. It must have wiped the whole place clean.

"No, no!" I yell hysterically. "We need to go back. We need to!"

"Impossible," Lucy says. "Also, require medical attention."

I fall to my knees and start to cry. Lucy looks uncomfortable with the situation.

"Appears need time alone," she says. "Will take Bastion to backup medical station, and fetch supplies to repair hand."

She drags him out and exits the room.

I sit there, defeated, sobbing away my pain. I am alone, both my body and my soul. My life, my heart, has gone up in a storm of flames. My hand isn't the only thing that has been severed. Fenrir isn't there to comfort me, it’s simply the echoing of my cries that's left to burn my dread.

Chapter 36 - Brock West Report

May 21, 3043 11:00 AM

Winde and I wait in a reception area at central HQ in Allied City. It's been two weeks since we wrapped up our work in the Bay Area and we've completed our final report. General Rox wanted a personal meeting for our briefing to go over our findings on Operation HORUS, so here we are.

The door slides open and out he comes on four feet. He's looks like a standard Rottweiler dog, but his posture is tall and his uniform is pressed. I always see him with his trademark frown and, while he's professional, even battle-hardened soldiers like myself can get intimidated by his presence.

"Come on in, boys," he says. He looks rather excited. Perhaps he's found something in my report that's got him anxious. I see it sitting on his desk.

He goes around the table and sits on his cushion while Winde and I sit on ours.

"I read the details of your report," Rox says. "I saw that you suffered some losses."

"Yes," I say mournfully. "Waylon, Ingle, and Clipper were found dead. Looks like HORUS offered some resistance that we were not anticipating. They were good soldiers and friends, I will miss them."

"I'm sorry for that."

We all look down in a moment of silence.

"So what is the current status of HORUS?" Rox asks.

"Completely destroyed," I say. "We swept the grounds multiple times and encountered no other hostiles. Everyone is dead, the place is a ghost town. The USASD have gutted the place out and confiscated anything that might be of interest. After we cleared out their machines and resources, they demolished the place and filled it up. There's nothing but soil and stones where it used to be."

He appears pleased by the news.

"Excellent," Rox says. "I knew that you would be efficient, that's why I assigned you on the case after that fiasco with Simon Trevor and Operation Halfkinds. You passed your primary objective with flying colors."

"Thank you," I respond.

"And how did your secondary objective go?"

"Winde is our tech expert, he can handle that one."

Winde is more nervous than I. He's not used to talking to such a high ranked official, and I can see the worry on his chimp face.

"Go ahead Winde," I say.

"Uh, yes, well I can tell you we have good news," he says sheepishly. "When I hacked into Lionel Changer's security servers, I was also able to obtain access to all of his data files. I copied his research and found some incredible stuff, things that are far more advanced in the implant field than anything I've ever seen. As delusional as Changer was, no one can deny he was a genius that was ahead of the game."

"Well what did you find?" Rox asks.

"Nanotechnology based implants. I'm talking about microscopic machines implanted into your body that can help stimulate and repair things on the fly. His designs were still in the early stages, but, theoretically, they could give you strength, heal wounds, and make you smarter in ways that we never dreamed. Currently, the only kinds of implants out there are for restoration and stabilization, but this stuff, man, this stuff could change the world. I can only wonder what kind of advancements we can create with Changer's data. I mean, he created cross species beings with this research and I think that was only the start."

Rox looks downright giddy.

"Yes, that is what I've been waiting for," he says. "We've taken that kind of tech out of the hands of a madman and placed it where it belongs, among Alliance science officers. Your team has done a great service. The Alliance will create history not only in the medical field, but in the military one as well. I can't wait to see what we can do with this kind of technology."

Winde and I look at each other and smile. Hearing this kind of praise is truly gratifying after all that hard work.

"Also, we were able to capture one of the scientists there, Mark Allen. He should provide valuable knowledge as we start dissecting Lionel's work. He's an average worker, and not deluded with visions like Changer. I think it'll be quite easy to get him to cooperate with us," I say.

"Smart move, but don't let him get too cozy. Even if he wasn't a fanatic like Changer, he still worked on that illegal operation. We'll use him for as long as we need, but, eventually, this Mark Allen will have to pay for his crimes. What he did still makes him an enemy of the United Species Alliance, understood?" Rox says.

"Yes," we both say.

"Looks like you did your job well. Anything else you two want to report?"

Winde and I glance at each other to see who is going to say it. Winde balks. I guess it's me.

"Yes, in a secret compartment of the facility, we found the bodies of five wolves. All of them were burnt. It appears to the result of some kind of incendiary grenade. The damage was quite large," I say.

"Wolves?" Rox responds curiously. "You mean real wolves, not those halfkind abominations?"

"Yes, real wolves."

"What were they doing there?"

"We don't know, but some identification tests were done and it appears all five belonged to the Snow family."

Rox looks even more intrigued.

"You mean the Snow family as in Fenrir Snow?" Rox asks. "The renegade soldier from Operation Halfkinds? Last I heard, he and his whole family dropped off the map. There were rumors that the Brotherhood assassinated them and others say they went to mercenary work."

"I can confirm those five bodies belonged to them," I say. "There's more."

"What?"

"Two of those five were found alive, but barely."

"Really. That's quite amazing."

"I agree. They're currently held on life support in an Alliance facility, though their condition doesn't look like it'll improve. Both are vegetables and it seems they'll be that way for a long time. Do you want us to terminate them?"

Rox looks at some files on his desk and takes some time to think. After a few moments, he responds.

"We have Changer's research," he says. "Let's see what we can do with it."

"Sir, where are you going with this?" I ask inquisitively.

"Eventually, after we understand what Changer's work can do, we'll need to test it. Perhaps some donor vessels have landed on our lap. I'm just thinking out loud, though. Anyway, that's for another meeting. Anything else you'd like to report?"

"Yes, the tech guys were looking over Changer's files, and they found some stuff about Iris Lawton."

"Iris Lawton, you mean the halfkind that got away from Primm?"

"Yes."

"Do you think she was there at HORUS?"

"Possibly. It would make sense since we found the Snows there and there were rumors about their involvement with Iris. In the exploded part of the facility, where we found the Snows, we discovered a piece of her remains, a burnt hand. It's possible she may have been there with them and been incinerated by the explosion."

"I see. Well, than that's a good thing. HORUS is gone and Operation Halfkinds is finally wrapped up. The mission has gone beyond expectations. Excellent work. I'll look into getting your team some awards and substantial bonus creds for what you've done. Be proud, the Alliance is in debt to you."

"Thank you, sir. Is the meeting over, then?"

"Yes. I'll look over the details and meet with you again later this week, West. Enjoy your break."

"Thank you again, sir."

We stand up from our cushions and head to the exit. We go through the doors and it closes behind us as Rox continues to read our report.

Chapter 37 - Bastion

Birth

June 1, 3046 10:31 AM

Iris has been up all night and I start to worry. I can only imagine the amount of pain she's in right now considering this is her first time. I'm glad Lucy is here to help make the process smooth, she's always good with that medical stuff. We've been making a lot of improvements to the medical care facility since I knew this day was coming, and it looks like it's paying off. Lucy has everything she needs.

This place was a bit of a mess when we first arrived. I don't remember it, but Lucy tells me she barely had the equipment she needed to heal my deep cuts. I was on the brink of death, but she saved me. I owe her my life.

I touch the scars on my chest. They're still there, that bear slashed me pretty good. I can't believe that was three years ago, it seems like yesterday. I guess time flies when you have a lot to do, a lot to rebuild.

Lucy has been more distant over the years. She's so into her work, I thought we were going to leave that behind. But, I can't be surprised. She's like Lionel. The resemblance I see brings back good memories. I've taken up his name, he will not be forgotten.

Lucy has her goals and she'll work non-stop to accomplish them. She'll also do whatever it takes to get there. Hell, sometimes I wonder if the stuff she's done to Iris is just part of her master plan.

No, I can't think that. This is a happy moment. I shouldn't be suspicious.

Iris groans, she's been at it for hours now, and it looks like she's going to pass out. She's a fighter, I know she'll be able to do it. She clutches my hand tightly. I can't believe this is happening. I thought it was impossible. I hear a ringing in my ear, no, a cry. But it doesn't belong to Iris, it belongs to someone else. Someone new, someone miraculous.

Lucy holds a sloppy, bundled, half-man, half-cat phenomenon in her arms. Our child has been born, a purebred hybrid. She's small and fragile, but I can already tell that she looks like mom and dad.

"Congratulations," Lucy says. "Have produced healthy female. What name will you give?"

Iris looks at me, sweaty and exhausted.

"Ivy," she says. "Her name is Ivy."

"Very good," Lucy says. "Will record findings."

She hands the child to me, and walks over to the other side of the room and records notes on her tablet. I look at Iris, showing her our little wonder. Iris gazes at her daughter and smiles. It truly is the happiest moment of my life.

Yet, in the background, I can faintly hear Lucy talking as she makes notes.

"Birthing implants successful," she says to herself. "First stages to perfect specimen complete. Today is huge step."

That's all she murmurs. I don't know what she means by this. I don't really care, either. All I care about is being the best father I can be. I will do my best to make sure Iris and our child will grow up safe in a world that will forever want us dead. I have found my calling. Lionel's dream is dead, mine has arrived.

I look at Iris as she holds little Ivy in her hands. What a day it's been, what a day. I can only imagine what the future has in store for us next.

About The Author

Andrew Vu is a novelist who was born in San Jose, CA. He graduated from UC Berkeley in 2007 and currently resides in Oakland, CA. During his spare time, he enjoys movies, video games, and watching sports. He roots for his California Golden Bears, the Kansas City Chiefs, the Golden State Warriors, and the Oakland A's.

www.ingramcontent.com/pod-product-compliance
Lightning Source LLC
LaVergne TN
LVHW050923080826
845145LV00001B/190

9780988520615